Summer in the Land of Skin

Summer in the Land of Skin

Jody Gehrman

First edition August 2004

SUMMER IN THE LAND OF SKIN

A Red Dress Ink novel

ISBN 0-373-25066-5

www.RedDressInk.com

Printed in U.S.A.

For Kathryn

ACKNOWLEDGMENTS

One of my favorite shower fantasies while I was working on this book involved mentally composing this page. There have been so many indispensable people who have helped me, I'm afraid I'll drag on and on like the worst of Academy Award winners. To avoid such a nightmare, I'll try to be snappy. Thanks to: Ed Gehrman, Sherry Garner and Jamie Gehrman-Selby for lifelong love and support; my agent, Dorian Karchmar, for her sharp eye and spot-on instincts; Barbara Lowenstein for giving me a chance; my editor, Margaret Marbury, and her team at Red Dress for their hip sensibilities and professionalism; Tania Hannan for editing out every "throbbing clitoris" and thus saving me from infinite shame; my teachers, most notably Patti Reeves, Carolyn Moore, Carol Guess, Gina Nahai, David Scott Milton, T. C. Boyle, John Rechy and Tristine Rainer; my colleagues at Mendocino College for their ongoing support; my students, who teach me so much about writing daily; Tommy Zurhellen for years of rock-solid writerly encouragement and friendship; Ted O'Callahan, for reminding me during early drafts that fiction isn't just about wish fulfillment; Chris Herrod and Dexter Johnson for their guidance in my luthier research; Arlan Lackie, Kathryn Stevenson, M. Harvey Anderson and Colville Melody for their inspiration. Most of all I want to thank David Wolf, the only man in the world who would stay up all night reading an early draft of this aloud, keeping me well-stocked in Kleenex when the chapters were awful and seeing beauty before it was even there.

Everyone has a summer that changes them forever. Mine takes place in a dilapidated Victorian in a rainy, northwestern town, where a good day smells like blackberries turning fat and moist on the vine, and a bad day smells like the ghosts of rancid pulp drifting east from the mill. The sound track is a slide guitar, a sad harmonica and the repeated click of a Zippo. The props are cigarettes, coffee cups, gin and tonics with wedges of lime suspended amidst clouds of bubbles. The days are textured with the fine dust of cocobolo rosewood, and the silk of a Honduras mahogany neck pressed tightly against the thumb. Every year of my life, when June rushes in with girls in spaghetti straps and boys strutting shirtless, their limbs still kissed with the pale of winter, I will think of the summer that gave me back my senses.

Learning to Taste

I guess it's obvious now that my father had some secret fatal flaw—a defect eating away at him somewhere inside his heart—but in the years leading up to his death I remember him as filled with the vigor of a yogi. His body was sinewy, long and lean, his hair a wild mixture of silver and brown spilling over his shoulders. Everyone agrees he was a genius; he built some of the finest, most intricate guitars in the world. I used to spend hours in his shop, caressing the stacks of wood that felt warm and alive under my small hands, putting my cheek against the cool mother-of-pearl. I would watch him patiently bend the rosewood sides over a heated tube, then clamp them into S-shaped molds to be sure the curves came out just right—"like a beautiful woman's hips," he used to say. I replay my memories of watching him work; I search his unguarded face, looking for clues. But he always seemed too alive, too otherworldly to be headed for such a seedy death. He had strangely feral eyes, dark as polished mahogany, with a visionary zeal so startling he could only be a god or a demon.

I think of those eyes as I tighten the focus on my binoculars, getting ready to study Magdalena. I do a cursory search of the others, skimming over their windows quickly—an exhausted mother changing her baby's diaper, a young couple arguing as they gesture with shiny martini glasses. But the one I'm looking for is the slim, kimono-clad woman with raised bamboo blinds. There she is, on the third floor, watching the fog roll over the western hills. A single, flawless black braid snakes over one shoulder and her skin is so pale it makes me think of calla lilies. There is something in her eyes that always reminds me of my father—it's the look that infants get when they gaze into the air with wild, unfocused bliss. Just give her a few hours, though. By midnight, she will stare out over the city with the hollow listlessness of a concentration camp inmate, a gaze that says she's seen too much to go on looking.

I sketch her quickly in my notebook, and label it *Magdalena: Manic as Usual.* Then I spend hours jotting down notes about her childhood in Florida, her career as a flamenco dancer, and her inevitable suicide here, in San Francisco. She's the type to slit her wrists in a bathtub. She thinks it will be pretty—all that red—like liquid roses.

I know I'm supposed to be somewhere tomorrow morning at seven. Namely, decaying in a lukewarm office before a computer screen, accomplishing data entry. But somehow I haven't been able to move from this spot for days. I have a secret life here, wrapped in my beige apartment, recording the lives and deaths of my neighbors. Their bodies are real. Their histories—and their suicides—are all mine.

Maybe this is how it started with my father. Genes are very

tricky, you know, millions of random cells dividing in a state of anarchy. I could have easily inherited the fatal flaw, the firing synapses that led him to that Motel 6, left him staring blankly at the cheap, flocked ceiling, wet with his blood.

I know I will not sleep. I have insomnia. Like him.

This is how I pass the time. Watching other people trying to live.

It is early in the morning when my mother comes whipping into my apartment in her high heels and tasteful, butter-yellow pantsuit. She sees me with my head propped against the wall, binoculars cradled between my thighs. I am naked, except for the old army blanket I have draped over my shoulders. I have not slept in five days. Her expression tells me that I am a despicable sight. She stands there, her thumb hooked on the strap of her suede briefcase, and surveys me with the edges of her mouth twitching.

She tries to flip her hair away from her shoulder casually—a habit left over from when her hair was very long, though she's worn it in a pixie cut for fourteen years now and there is no longer anything left to flip. She pretends not to notice herself doing this and comes to sit on the edge of my bed.

"Christ, Anna," she whispers.

She can look very mournful in the right light, though it is her practice to wear an optimistic smear of blush on each cheek and a precise smile, not too toothy, since there's a gold cap next to her right canine. She takes a handkerchief from her pocket and reaches over to wipe a bit of sleep from my eye.

"Let's get you in the shower," she says. "Then we'll put something nice on and go get breakfast. How does that sound?"

The muted morning light is resting on her face and hands, and the graceful curve of her neck is shining. I can recognize the fragile beauty my father must have seen in her—pale and vulnerable, with a dancer's delicacy.

"You're skin and bones. Let's not talk until we've got you a nice omelette, a shot of espresso—"

"I'm not hungry," I say.

Her hand seizes my wrist. "Listen to me," she snaps, her eyes turned abruptly dangerous. "You will get in the shower *now*, do you hear me?"

"Jesus," I say, and try to pull my hand away from hers.

"NOW!" Her jaw is clenched; I can see a vein at her temple throbbing rapidly.

"Okay," I say "All *right*. My God." This is my mother: fragile and sunlit one moment, pulsing with rage the next. I stand up, a little shakily, pulling the blanket around my body. "I'm twenty-five, you know, not ten." I take a few steps in the direction of the bathroom, but everything seems unreal; I try to focus on my kitchen table, but the edges go blurry. I look up at the ceiling, the walls, the antique clock my grandmother left me. My legs become liquid, and a warm wave of nausea washes over me. I think to myself, *Okay, then, I'm dying,* and the thought registers something like relief before the room goes black.

I open my eyes and the world is filled with white tile, glass, and my mother's face hanging over me, gaunt and transparent, like a ghost. The shower is on full blast, shooting ice-cold water at my solar plexus.

"Did you take something?"

I raise my head enough to view my hands, both of which look very distant. They are lying like dead fish in the shallow water of the tub.

"Sleeping pills, Valium? What?" she demands, pushing my hair back from my forehead.

"Nothing," I say.

"You're sure?"

"God, Mom, I don't want to *die*," I say, sitting up and reaching over to turn the shower off. "I just didn't want to go to work."

I watch as she pulls herself out of her crouching position, brushes imaginary lint off her pant legs and sits on the toilet. She rummages in her pocket and produces a pack of Virginia Slims.

"After Hours fired you. Did you get that message?"

I shrug. "You've been working on me to quit since I started there."

She exhales impatiently. "I want you to use your degree."

"Yeah. Big demand for anthropology majors."

"I want you to use your *mind,* is what I mean. Data entry for a condom company is just not you, sweetheart. But this way you can't even use them as a reference—that doesn't help you move forward."

Move forward. My mother is the queen of forward movement—with her sporty silver Fiat and her Silicon Valley life, where she drinks double espressos like water and occasionally sleeps with programmers visiting from Boston or Berlin. She hurls herself forward with the streamlined perseverance of a bullet train, but in her eyes there is a panic that is pure animal.

She smiles knowingly now and tells me, "Derek called yesterday. He said he was worried about your 'stunted spiritual evolution.'"

I roll my eyes. "Derek. Jesus."

"I told him, 'It sounds like you've been dumped, buddy.'"

I've been with Derek for five years, and until recently I'd never asked myself why. He is thirty-six years old. He has an early-morning paper route to supplement the paltry cash he earns teaching meditation at a grubby little Buddhist center in Corte Madera. Now that we've broken up, I cannot even summon enough pathos to cry.

"Maybe it's good," my mother says. "A blessing in disguise."

I can tell the cigarette cheered her up some.

"Maybe *what's* good?"

"This little nervous breakdown you're having," she says. "Or whatever it is."

"That's great, Mother," I say, pulling on some jeans. "Maintain your condescension, even in crisis."

"Sometimes the only way to heaven is straight through hell."

I stare at her. "What did you say?"

She looks up at me, startled. "What? What's wrong now?"

"What did you just say?"

"About your nervous breakdown?"

"No. The other part."

I watch her as she realizes her mistake.

My mother hasn't spoken my father's name even once in the fourteen years since he died. Very rarely, though, she will slip up and use an expression of his. My father had his own idioms—quirky phrases he repeatedly tirelessly. These words are buried in us, my mother and me, like tiny scraps of shrapnel.

She looks like a frightened child, now, caught in a lie. "Isn't that funny," she says. "I really don't remember." She flashes the precise, practiced smile that does not show her gold tooth. "I'm dying for some good coffee. How about you?"

Although my mother consumes on a daily basis the most exotic, trendy foods money can buy, when we're together, she invariably insists on Josie's, where the entrées jiggle under pools of grease and the espresso tastes like battery acid.

"Why do you like this place so much?" I ask. We're standing in line to order, studying the menu, which is written in bubble letters with Day-Glo chalk on huge blackboards.

She glances around. "Some places just feel like home."

Why my mother would feel at home here is a mystery. The place is filled with pierced faces and torn clothing, magenta shocks of hair and prominently displayed tattoos. My mother, sunny and fresh in her silk pantsuit, looks like Martha Stewart in a mosh pit.

We give our order to the girl behind the counter, a sullen, ungroomed thing with lots of beads knotted into her hair. Then we take our laminated number and find a table near the windows, where we wait in awkward silence for our food. I can tell my mother is aching for a cigarette. She keeps scraping at her cuticles like a nervous insect. They bring us our shots of espresso, and after she knocks hers back her face visibly relaxes. For me, though, the bitter brown syrup is a shock to my system; my mouth explodes with sensation. Five straight days without food or sleep have left me clean and high and empty; the world has a surreal pallor. The people and shapes of Josie's move around me like an animated collage.

When our food arrives my mother orders another shot of espresso and digs into her ham-and-cheese omelette with embarrassing fervor. I raise a fork and touch the porous skin of my crepe. It gives under the blade of my knife much too easily, and something in my belly flips upside down.

"I know!" my mother says, talking out of the side of her mouth as she chews. "Suppose you took a class in computer programming?" She delivers this with a semblance of fresh energy, leaning forward like it's an idea she's just now hit upon, not the same suggestion she's been making weekly for the past three years.

"Mother," I say, my voice low with warning.

"But, no, I suppose you *like* data entry. I guess that's your *calling*?"

"That's over, now."

"Oh, you'll go groveling back there—"

"Don't tell me what I'm going to do!"

We're both surprised at how loud this comes out. A girl at a table near us glances over; she looks like a *Rocky Horror Picture Show* die-hard, and I resent her white face turning in our direction. I shoot her a dirty look and she averts her eyes. All at once I feel strangely powerful. I still haven't even nibbled at my crepe, and I am floating on that weird, food-and-sleep-deprived hollowness that tastes like enlightenment.

"All right, Anna," she says. "So you tell me. What *are* you going to do?"

"Sometimes the only way to heaven is straight through hell."

"Don't talk to me like that," she chides, as if I have just cursed.

"What's wrong with quoting my own—"

"I can't," she says, looking around helplessly. "I can't do this."

But I don't want to stop—I'm empty and reckless, empowered by the sound of my own voice. "I'm not even *living,* Mom. I haven't been *alive* for fourteen years."

She gets up so suddenly that her chair knocks against the plate-glass window and her empty espresso cup topples over. She rights the cup quickly and snatches her briefcase. "I'm going outside," she says, already moving toward the door. A muscular bike messenger inadvertently blocks her way for a moment, and she elbows past him, fumbling in her pocket for cigarettes.

Alone now with the crepes and the coffee, a calm comes over me, and the smell of food fills my head. I cut a piece of crepe with the edge of my fork and skewer a strawberry. I place the bite in my mouth carefully, like someone conducting an experiment. I chew slowly, and the flavors unfold with an intensity that shocks me; I can taste every seed inside the berry, every ounce of sweetness, the butter in the crepes, the eggs, the cream—it all sings on my tongue with a symphonic unity. For fourteen years, everything has tasted like variations on oatmeal. And now, suddenly, this wild thing is happening inside my mouth—a reminder of what it's like to be alive.

That night I find myself sitting across from Aunt Rosie in the hip little Mission District dive she favors, The Boom Boom Room, where the lights are Chinatown red and the people all wear loud, retro-print shirts.

"I want you to know, kiddo, I think it's just great you told your mother off." Rosie is compact and feisty, with a bit of the bulldog in her. She has a boxer's nose, thick, ungainly lips, and her body is built like a miniature tank, with almost no visible neck. She always wears platform shoes, and glitter on her eyelids; occasionally she is mistaken for a drag queen. "God knows she needed it. If Helen had her head stuffed any farther up her ass, she'd have to have it surgically removed." She laughs at her own joke—one quick, staccato bark—and then looks unconvincingly contrite. "I'm sorry, kitten, I'm not here to badmouth your mother." She takes a swig from her Miller Light. "She wasn't always so uptight, you know. Back in the day, she was quite the party girl." She rotates her beer bottle, a sad smile lingering on her lips. Then she sees me watching her, and looks suddenly self-conscious. "So anyway, what's next?"

Without knowing I'm going to say it, I blurt out, "I want to build guitars, like Dad."

She looks at me in surprise, then smiles. "Groovy," she says. "Do you still play?"

I shake my head. "Not since he died. Mother didn't want any music in the house."

"Good God. That woman." She takes off her pink fur coat and finishes her beer. "I don't know why she has to be like that. It's not good for you. It's not good for her, either."

"She acts like he never even existed."

"I know," she says. "It's sad. I always thought it was sad." She pushes my White Russian toward me. "Drink up, baby girl! You haven't had a sip."

I put the straw to my lips and suck a little of the sweet, creamy liquid. I'm not used to drinking, really. I'm not used to going out at all, lately.

"Well, I'm not surprised you want to learn the trade. You've got guitars in your blood. Your dad and Bender were legends."

"Who's that?"

"Elliot Bender. Old friend of your dad's. They had a business for years—shit, they made guitars for Jerry Garcia, Bob Dylan, Bo Ramsey." She looks around the bar dreamily, remembering. "They had a falling-out—everything fell apart. It was ridiculous, really." She turns to me abruptly, her eyebrows raised high. "I have an idea," she says.

It takes me one day to prepare, with Rosie's help. I break my lease and fill my dad's old leather backpack with four changes of clothes, ten pairs of underwear, a toothbrush, floss, and a notebook. I've got a thousand dollars to my name. Rosie insists on lending me her third ex-husband's pickup truck. I leave my furniture and most of my belongings in her cluttered garage, with little hope of ever finding them again, buried in that sea of ancient trunks and stereo speakers, plastic shower curtains and milk crates full of yellowed photos.

Standing outside her old Victorian in go-go boots and a red chenille robe, Rosie cuts quite a figure in the chilly morning fog. It's too early for her—seven a.m.—and it shows. Her hair is hectic with static electricity, and rings of mascara circle her puffy eyes. She yawns wide as she hands me an envelope and a carved statue of a Hindi god that fits in the palm of my hand.

"What's this?"

"Shiva was your dad's favorite—he took that thing with him everywhere. I figured you should have it." I stand there on the sidewalk, fingering the smooth, cherry-colored wood, trying to imagine it in his hand. "Open the envelope later. It's another good luck charm." She smiles sleepily, and I hug her. "Now get out of here," she says. "Before someone sees me like this."

I forget all about the envelope until I'm in Portland, late that night, surrounded by the quiet gloom of a rest stop. I've been driving so many hours, when I rest my head against the steering wheel and close my eyes, I still see the road rushing at me. I reach for my backpack and take out the envelope, hold it in my hands a moment before opening it carefully. There's a Bob Dylan quote scribbled in large, messy letters on the back of an ATM receipt. *Kitten: She's got everything she needs, she's an artist, she don't look back. XOXOXO, Rosie.* I sit there, smiling in the dim yellow cast by the dome light, reading her words over and over, lingering on the urgent X's and O's. In the envelope is a crumpled one-hundred-dollar bill. As I pull back onto the interstate, I can feel a dull stinging behind my eyes, and I know if I weren't so out of practice, I would cry.

On impulse, I get my hair cut in Seattle. I decide to let Ray, a high-strung man in a shaggy vest and leather pants, have total creative freedom with me above the neck. It takes hours, and there's a lot of paraphernalia—intricate layers of foil, multiple applications of toxic-smelling goo. When he's done, he spins the chair toward the mirror, and I barely recognize the girl staring back at me. I look like a 1920s starlet—he's fashioned me in a chin-length bob, shorter in back like the flappers used to wear, and he's highlighted my blond with streaks of bright gold.

"Girl," he says, appraising me proudly, "I've really outdone myself today."

As I'm driving the last seventy miles north to Bellingham, I tug at the rearview mirror now and then to look at myself. Each time, I'm startled by the strange woman staring back at me.

So This Is Bellingham

I arrive. My mouth is so dry, it feels like somebody replaced my tongue with a wad of cotton. I drive past old houses painted creamy whites and weather-beaten yellows, wild gardens filled with morning glories and nasturtiums tossing gently in the breeze. The blues are bluer here, the greens greener. I turn a corner and catch my breath; there's the bay, its wind-textured surface catching the gold. My heart is thumping inside me as I drive. Everything—the cars, the buildings, the people strolling about on the sidewalks—seems like moving photographs, hand-painted in tasteful colors. On the air I can smell a trace of salt, mixed with a strange, pulpy odor.

Driving along the main street that slopes gradually toward the bay I pass the old brick buildings of a small downtown. The sun is warm through my windshield. There are couples and students window-shopping and sipping from paper cups. They look sleepy and content.

I hear a loud shriek and I turn to see a girl in a dress and combat boots, one hand on her hip, the other hand pointing directly at her companion, a long-haired guy leaning against an old station wagon, covering his eyes and shaking his head. The girl begins kicking at the tires of the car, her brown hair flying. I slow to a crawl, mesmerized by the rage in her movements. She looks up at me for an instant, her hair still in her face, making her look feral and dangerous; our eyes hold, and the moment stretches on strangely. The man turns and stares at me now, too. Then all at once, the girl cries, "What are you looking at, bitch?" and the car behind me starts honking.

I shake myself from the trance and pull my foot off the brake, put it back on the gas. From my radio, Johnny Cash sings, *Drive on, don't mean nothin', drive on.*

It takes me a good two hours to find Elliot Bender. Aunt Rosie wasn't able to dig up his phone number, so he has no idea I'm coming, and all I have is a Post-it with a barely legible address scribbled on it. What I find there is a startled woman in a terry-cloth sweatsuit and a couple of astonishingly fat kids. It's a rundown cabin near the train tracks. A greasy yellow dog with brown teeth strains from the end of a chain and barks so loudly my head throbs. When I ask if she knows who lived there before, she nods and squints up at the sky.

"Weird fellow," she says. "We used to drink together, back when I lived in that little shit hole over there." She points her chin at a trailer across the way. "Heard he moved onto a boat."

"A boat?" I echo.

"Down at the marina," she says. "Out by that stinky old mill. I wouldn't live there if you paid me."

I've never known anyone who lives on a boat, but I've always been fascinated by pirates, so I'm a little titillated. After a half-hour spent asking around down by the docks, I'm finally able to locate his slip. When I see the size of it—no more than thirty-five feet, bow to stern—I realize that my half-baked assumption that this guy could put me up for a while is out of the question. No guest rooms here.

There's a locked gate separating the boat owners from the world at large, and I'm standing behind it, my fingers laced in the wire diamonds, staring at the two lines of sailboats knocking quietly against the docks. The guy at the office told me to look for slip number thirteen. I hadn't anticipated the problem of how to announce myself, when there's no real door to knock on. As I'm standing there, staring at Elliot Bender's boat, a mounting shyness nearly turns me back around. I reach into my pocket and feel for Shiva, finger the comforting lines of the wood, warmed by my body.

"You looking for somebody?"

I jump a little, then locate a very small man sanding the bow of a sailboat. He's not even four feet tall, with disproportionately long arms and a pink, bearded face.

"Elliot—um—Elliot Bender?" I stammer.

Before I know what's happening, he's hollering in an unnaturally loud voice, *"Bender!"* He looks at me, rolls his eyes, and mutters, "Lazy bastard," then resumes with even more volume, "BENDER!" We both watch the rundown old boat intently, but nothing happens. Gentle waves swish against the docks, while a seagull screeches disapprovingly. The little guy goes back to sanding. "Who are you, anyway?"

I stand there, trying to find the right answer. I grip Shiva tighter in my pocket, and I can feel the wood sliding against the wet of my palm.

Just then, a head appears from below deck. It is turned away from me, and all I can see is a wild mess of dark gray hair.

"What do you want, Stumpy?" Stumpy gestures in my direction, and the head turns abruptly toward me. As he rises from the hole, there's a flash of blue eyes, a face grown silver with stubble, and a great swell of belly beneath a grease-stained undershirt. He freezes, visible only from the waist up, and something tells me he's not decent from the waist down.

"Yeah?" he says to me, blinking in the sunlight.

"Are you Elliot Bender?" I force my voice into a deceptive evenness.

"Who wants to know?"

"I was wondering if I could talk to you for a minute. Is this a bad time?"

"Look, I paid that dentist bill, if that's what you're after—"

I smile. "No," I say. "It's nothing like that."

"What, the phone?"

I shake my head.

He sighs, starts patting at his mess of hair, stroking it into submission like it's an animal that must be tamed. "Do I know you?" he says, his tone still wary.

"Sort of," I say. "I'm Anna Medina."

He stares at me. I watch as his Adam's apple bobs once in a hard swallow.

"Just a minute," he says finally, and disappears down below.

Stumpy climbs over onto the dock and opens the gate for me. "Man doesn't know how to treat a lady," he says, winking.

I thank him, then stand there awkwardly, waiting for Elliot Bender to reappear. I am still exhausted from the hours of driving, and feel ill-equipped to deal with this unexpected turn of events. I imagined my father's partner as a quaint, pipe-smoking man, with an immaculate, spacious studio filled with the finest guitars, smelling of lacquer, spruce and rosewood. Here I am, with a midget sailor and an overweight, half-naked man who thinks I'm trying to collect on a dentist bill.

"Climb on board," he says, having reappeared in a pair of ragged corduroys and a flannel shirt whose buttons don't match up, holding a can of Budweiser.

I carefully make my way onto the boat; it is old, plagued with layers of peeling paint, and as I get a better look I see it is cluttered with beer cans, crumpled newspaper, piles of tangled rope gone black with grease.

He sees me looking around and shrugs. "Home sweet home," he says, his voice flat.

His free hand floats again to his hair, patting it down. I see he has attempted to slick it down on top, though rather unsuccessfully; it is now matted and greasy in places but springs rebelliously to life everywhere else. I look around for a place to sit, find none. He sees this, sets his beer down and scurries below deck, then emerges with a lawn chair in one hand and a bucket in the other. He flips the lawn chair open and sets it down, nodding at it in invitation, then sets the bucket upside down and sits on it, reclaiming his beer and taking a long swig.

"You take the chair," I say.

"Never," he says. "Go on, sit."

I do as I'm told, though the sight of him balancing on that bucket is dangerously comic, and I'm afraid I might laugh, I'm so giddy with nerves and lack of sleep.

"Offer the lady a drink!" Stumpy yells from across the dock.

"Hey," Bender says over his shoulder. "Mind your own damn business!"

He smiles a little, sheepishly, and for a second I catch a glimpse of the handsome young man he must have been, with the square jaw and heavy brow of a young Marlon Brando. The sunlight glints on his eyes; they are the brightest blue I've ever seen.

"You want a beer? You old enough to drink?"

"I am," I say, sounding prim in spite of myself. "But no thank you."

He lets his eyes rest on my face for an unnaturally long pause. I touch the back of my head, feeling the foreign shortness of the hair there, and start to blush.

"Yep," he says, softly. "You're Medina's kid, all right."

"What makes you say that?" I say, smiling at my shoes.

"That smile," he says. "Your mouth's got Medina all over it."

I look up and see him feeling for the button of his shirt at the place where his belly is biggest, making sure it's still fastened. I realize it must be very hard for him to find shirts that fit, and for a second I feel sorry for him. He looks back at me intently, and I find myself staring shyly at my shoes again. He drinks from his beer, a long hard swig, then he crushes the can beneath his foot and tosses it near the bow, where it settles with a tinny *clang* amidst a pile of others.

"You sure you don't want a beer?" he says, getting up and grabbing another Bud from a beat-up ice chest.

"No thanks," I repeat.

He pops open the can and tilts back his head. Then he sits on the ice chest, and I'm relieved that I don't have to watch him teetering on the tiny bucket anymore.

"I don't have guests very often these days," he says. "Don't have much to offer—you just let me know if you change your mind about the beer." I nod. "So, what brings you to Bellingham?"

"Well..." I can feel my face going hot. I take a breath and say, "I'm interested in learning a trade."

"What trade is that?"

I force myself to look him in the eye. "I want to be a luthier."

"Is that right?" he says. "Your father teach you much?" I shake my head.

"Still doesn't really explain what you're doing up here."

"I was hoping you could teach me." He's staring out over the water, that serious brow and the silver stubble making him look like an old-time sea captain. He brings the can to his lips again, fastens his mouth to the hole, and slurps loudly, then burps.

"You want to be a luthier…." He won't look at me now. He gets up abruptly and fishes in his pocket, produces a book of matches. "You smoke, Medina?"

"What?"

"Do you smoke?" he says, exaggerating his enunciation as if I might be slow.

"No. Why?"

"I quit. Ten years ago. But times like this I could really use a smoke."

He stuffs his hands in his pockets. I want to say something that will put him at ease, but I've got a feeling just my being here is the worst part. He shakes his head and stares out at the bay, shifting his weight from side to side, making the boat rock a little. I hold on to the aluminum armrests of the lawn chair.

"Do you still have a shop?" I ask.

"Oh yeah. This right here's my shop," he says. "They come from miles around for their Bender guitars!" He shakes his head again, drinks his beer.

"My aunt Rosie says you're the best."

A small grin takes over his mouth, seemingly against his will. "Rosie. I should've known. She put you up to this?"

"She told me about you."

"Your aunt is one crazy woman," he says. "Almost as crazy as your mother." He sits back down on the ice chest. "I guess your dad didn't tell you much about me, huh?"

"Not that I remember," I say.

"No," he says. "I guess he wouldn't." The grin is still there, but now it looks more like a grimace; his mouth curves up at the edges, but there's no pleasure in his eyes. "Well, I'm sorry you came all this way, but I can't teach you anything, Medina. I haven't touched my tools in a long time."

I swallow, try to make my voice sound polite. "So, what do you do now?"

He finishes his beer, leans forward so his elbows are resting on his knees and twists the empty can in his hands. "This is what I do," he says, staring at the mangled can. "You're looking at it."

I wander the streets as the sun goes down. It's moving in slow motion—a torturous slide into the water. The mill sits like a big rusty beast near the bay and belches white smoke into the air. Clouds huddle along the horizon, gradually starting to display a spread of garish pink. I pace the sidewalks, trying to concentrate on the windows. In the orange light, the neighborhood takes on a watercolor glow.

I keep walking.

The absurdity of this mission is all too clear to me. I am several states from anyone I know, homeless, jobless, sporting a haircut that only this morning was glamorous but now is a ridiculous anachronism—I'm a flapper lost in space. Bender is a hopeless drunk, and my plan to apprentice with him is a farce. Yesterday morning, Rosie was a radiant goddess in go-go boots, launching me into my destiny. Tonight, she is revealed as a bored divorcée, tinkering with my life to escape her own.

My pace increases. I can't remember where I left the truck. I walk and walk, as if the feel of the concrete under my shoes will keep me from floating away, balloonlike, into the sky.

Rounding a corner, I hear a few strains of slide guitar. It's a song I used to know. The sun is finally down, and I can feel a chill trying to seep through my T-shirt to my skin, but my legs keep moving, pumping heat into the rest of me. *Oh, sweet mama, your daddy's got those Deep Ellum blues.* I move in the direction of that voice, that guitar. I figure it must be coming from a bar somewhere, but I'm lost in a neighborhood quite a few blocks from downtown. I'm surrounded by trees and rows of old houses, some elegant, some abused and graying. The flowers that line their stone paths and white fences are bathed in a fiery light. The street sign says Walnut.

Without warning, there he is, leaning back in a weather-rotted easy chair, his feet propped up on the porch railing. His hair is long and brown and falls below his shoulders. A cigarette dangles from his lips, the orange tip glowing, and he works that guitar with his head swaying easy, his fingers gliding. His voice is a low, mournful growl, and it is so much like my father's that I stop walking and stare, the chill spreading through me. *Oh, sweet mama, your daddy's got—*

"Hey, baby?" a woman's voice cries from a window upstairs.

He stops playing, examines his fingers. "Yeah?"

"We need cigarettes!"

"Can you wait a minute?" He starts in on the chorus again.

A head pops out of the window—dark hair, naked shoulders. "The question is not, 'Can I wait?'" she says. "The question is, 'Can you get your lazy ass downtown and get me smokes, or do I have to do everything myself?'"

He chuckles, shakes his head. "I hear that," he says, and flings his cigarette onto the lawn, where it smolders in the grass. The head disappears from the window.

The man stands, gripping his guitar by the neck; he looks out at the orange smear of clouds on the horizon. His cheekbones are high and sharp, his eyes dark. He takes the metal slide from his finger and shoves it into the pocket of his jeans. As he turns to go inside, he catches me staring at him from the sidewalk.

I drop my eyes and start walking again, past their yard, across the street, and I do not look up again until I hear the door slam.

★ ★ ★

The temptation to get mystical is ever-present. This is all I'm going to say: after I hear that door bang shut, I look up, and the first thing I see is a sign in the third-story window across the street: Room For Rent. Before I know what I'm doing, my legs are marching me up the steps, and I'm ringing the bell, reading the words painted on the glass in neutral white lettering: *Dr. Andrew Gottlieb, D.D.S., Painless Dentistry Guaranteed.*

I glance at my watch and see that it's a little past eight. Too late for a dentist's office to be open. Still, something keeps me on this olive-green porch, swept to perfection. This building stands in sharp contrast to the others on the corner. There's a faded blue place across the street, once grand, no doubt, now dirty and somehow institutional; kitty-corner is an even more neglected house, with a yellow paint job that's peeled down to a white undercoat in huge patches, giving it the mottled look of a fried egg. The depressing effect is heightened by several broken windows. A couple of kids in dreadlocks are tinkering under the hood of a rusted van in the driveway. On the east corner is the house the guitar man disappeared into; it is a pale pink, three stories high, with a turret at the top. Like the others, it must have been stately once, though now it looks weather-beaten, and the porch is strewn with several rotting chairs.

Dusk is starting to settle in, and I feel a pang of longing for a dark room and my binoculars.

"Looking for me?"

I spin around. A man is standing there in the doorway, bare-chested, wearing tight cutoffs.

"I saw a sign," I blurt out.

"A sign?" He has a droopy black mustache that bobs as he speaks.

"In the window. You have a room for rent?"

"Ha! It's been up there so long, I forgot." He scratches his hairy chest. He looks like the guys that used to hang out at the roller-skating rink when I was a kid—feathered hair, desperate eyes. "You new to town?"

I nod.

"From where?"

"San Francisco."

"I have a cousin there—a vegetarian. I told him, our teeth are built for meat. He won't listen, though, crazy bastard." He tilts his head to one side, sticks a finger in his ear and wriggles it wildly for a moment. "Come on in," he tells me. "Room's upstairs."

I follow him through the lobby, where the walls are lined with strange, vaguely erotic photos of mouths. We pass a couple of rooms with dentist chairs, another with a sink and several rows of disembodied, pink-gummed dentures, their white teeth glowing in the dwindling light.

As we climb the stairs, he says, "It's a nice room. Very feminine. My ex-wife decorated it. I've got a little office downstairs with a couch and a shower—sometimes I sleep overnight, but not often. Here we are!" At the top of the stairs, he flings open a door, revealing a tiny, cramped room with an orange shag carpet and a large bed covered in a pink and green plaid bedspread. There's a sink and hot plate in the corner, a dwarf-sized refrigerator next to that. The wallpaper has a disturbing milkmaid motif: a Nordic girl in blond braids with huge breasts works cheerfully at various farmyard tasks. "You can use the toilet and shower downstairs, in my office," he offers, interrupting my moment of hypnosis before the rows of milkmaids. "Like I said, I'm hardly ever there."

"Right," I say, blinking.

"You've got nice teeth," he tells me. "Orthodontics?"

"No. Genetics."

He laughs. I look away quickly, my eyes moving automatically to a milkmaid bending over the butter churn. The room reeks of a sickly sweet air freshener—peach, I think. I'm about to murmur something polite and bolt for the door when the little window by the bed catches my eye. I cross the room and pull the frilly curtain aside. Across the street, I see the long-haired guitar man, framed in a large bay window, smoking a cigarette in a white T-shirt.

"How much?" I ask, not turning around.

By my third night in the god-awful milkmaid room, I'm thoroughly familiar with the Land of Skin. That's what I decide to call this corner—the place where Walnut and Garden cross—because every time there's a ray of sunlight, however tenuous or cloud-filtered, everyone strips down to the bare minimum, and the whole corner comes alive with half-naked natives. To a girl from California, it's a little overwhelming to see such an abundance of bone-white bodies. I am fascinated by their obscenely pale thighs, their shining, colorless chests.

I have the whole neighborhood mapped out and labeled. I've determined that the blue place is a halfway house, which I've named Purgatory Corner. Across from that is Goat Kid Hovel. The pink house where Guitar Man lives is an old Victorian that's been converted into apartments. The tenants there all smoke out the windows, and on the shared porch, so I've named this place Smoke Palace. I sketch the area in a notebook and label each house neatly.

Tonight Goat Kid Hovel is swarming with activity; every ten minutes a new pack of young, tattered white kids in dreadlocks or shaved heads pull up in beater cars. Loud, discordant music rattles the broken windows, each song crackling with the static of a stereo pushed beyond its limits. A couple of potbellied men sit out on the porch of Purgatory

Corner drinking from soda cans. Every now and then, one yells, "Turn that shit down!" But the kids only laugh, rev their engines, and shake their matted hair like gleeful little beasts.

By midnight things have quieted down, but I still linger near the window, my mind racing. Every once in a while I can hear someone laughing from inside Smoke Palace; later, a nocturnal argument erupts, but it's hard to tell where exactly it's coming from. These are the hours when my thoughts drift back to the subject of suicide: why people do it, what it feels like the moment you slice open your wrists or pull the trigger. Are there doubts, like pacing the high dive and seeing the nauseating spill of distance below you? Or is it lucid, light, with freedom so close you can taste it, like right before an orgasm?

When I was fifteen, I started filling sketchbooks with drawings and notes I secretly named my Suicide Maps. I would make up fictional characters and plot their self-imposed deaths; I documented the whole process with an investigator's eye for detail. But even more intricate were the maps of their postmortem experiences, loosely inspired by my favorite old tome, *Afterlife Mythologies.* I took perverse pleasure in rerouting my subjects to unexpected locales: Catholic priests might find themselves in Nirvana; a Mormon housewife could awake in Valhalla. Suicide was just the first step in an intricate journey toward more and more outlandish planes of existence. Their deaths were my fairy tales, my science fiction.

My mother must have found that stack of sketchbooks. One day I went to add a new entry and they were gone. I knew better than to ask. My obsession was an embarrassment to us both, something that could not be mentioned, like masturbation. Still, it didn't stop me from making new ones.

Tonight I'm working on an entry for Raggedy Ann at the Goat Kid Hovel—a tall, gawky girl of around sixteen, with a head of hair that looks like it's on fire. Sometimes I squint and imagine she is an animated matchstick. She wears striped socks and a heavy, oversized trench coat, even when everyone else is nearly naked. I think she might be deaf; she never reacts to the people around her, and nobody bothers to address her directly. She's definitely the sort to hang herself in some dirty, grease-scented garage. I sketch her dangling from rafters, her orange hair hanging limply over her face. I map out the afterworlds she'll escape to: a brief stop in Hades, followed by a journey to the core of the earth. Here she's reborn with the smooth, deeply sad voice of a blues singer. I show her singing to a pool of lava, surrounded by enormous insects; a fiery glow bathes her face and hair.

Around two a.m., Guitar Man appears on the porch wearing boxer shorts and a loose cotton tank top. He sits in one of the rotting chairs and starts to play his old Gibson. I can feel my palms sweating as I put down my notebook and train my binoculars on his neck, studying the soft brown skin where it disappears into the white of his shirt, then reappears in the round curves of his strong shoulders. Whenever I see him, I start to sweat. It's not just that he's beautiful—and he *is* beautiful, with his sinewy arms and his long, dark hair—where did he get his tan? His body is made of sandalwood, and all around him the people are birch—it's that he is so inexplicably alone. His eyes search the air, his arms and legs unnaturally still, like a Bodhisattva. Even when his girlfriend is perched in his lap like a languorous cat, his eyes say he's far away, lost in some tremendously difficult equation.

I turn to a new page in my notebook and try to sense how he would do it: .38 special in the mouth? Pills? But my attention is consumed by his hands; I watch as they move gracefully up and down the neck. Through the binoculars, I can see how tired and sad his face is, pinched with worry and concentration. I only wish he would play louder, so I could hear what his fingers are doing to those strings.

Thursday, I am startled from my afternoon observations by a knock on my door. Gottlieb is in my room before I even have time to stash my binoculars.

"What are you doing?" he asks, nodding at the binoculars and notebook.

"Zoology." I blush wildly, even though he doesn't seem accusing. "I'm a—bird-watcher."

He doesn't ask any more questions; I can see there's something else on his mind.

"I want to show you my work," he blurts out. I think of the haunting rows of pink-gummed molds downstairs, but instead he pulls a piece of paper from his pocket and sits down next to me on the bed. He's wearing tight jeans and an argyle sweater; he looks nervous, like a kid at his first piano recital. "You seem like the artistic type," he says shyly. Then he reads from the page, his hand trembling slightly; the smell of cheap cologne and soap fill my head. "'Your heart is a stone, your eyes glitter like glass shards, I wish you were dead.'" He looks at me expectantly. "It's a haiku."

"Oh. Interesting…"

"Here, let me read you this one—it's better. 'Fingernails like knives, mouth like a red bleeding wound, stay away from me.'" I sit there a moment in stunned silence, taking this in. "I'm working on a collection," he says. I stand, and lean against the opposite wall, near the door. "I've got a hundred and twenty-four of these. The working title is *Ex-Wife*."

"That's great," I say, my voice thin and insincere. "I mean, good for you."

"I'm sending them to a publisher next week," he says. "Guy I did a root canal for."

"That's great," I repeat, unsure of what else to say.

He looks up at me and licks his lips. "You think they work?"

"A hundred and twenty-four of those, huh? Wow."

He gets up from the bed and takes a step toward me. "I'm getting better," he says, clutching the poem in his hand. "I'm just starting out, but I've been reading this book about the artist within and—"

"You hayseed bastard!" A woman is screaming in a murderous voice. "Get out of my house, you goddamn redneck!"

I rush to the window, my curiosity momentarily eclipsing my urge to flee the dentist. There, flying down the pink porch steps, is Guitar Man's girlfriend. She flings a stack of CDs onto the sidewalk, and when she stomps on a couple with her boots the sound of plastic cracking is audible from here.

"That girl again," Gottlieb says bitterly, peering over my shoulder.

I watch as she marches back into Smoke Palace, taking the steps two at a time. "You know her?"

"Name's Lucy—short for Lucifer." He snorts. "She's a real live wire."

"I wonder why she's..." I begin, but I trail off, hypnotized by the sight of Lucy charging down the stairs again. She marches into the street. A truck turns the corner going too fast and swerves just in time to miss her. She appears not to notice. She's got her boyfriend's beautiful old guitar in her hands—the rosewood gleams in the afternoon sunlight, and she's holding it high above her head. I've studied this guitar through my binoculars for days. I'm pretty sure it's an antique Gibson. I could tell from the way Guitar Man touched it that this thing is as much a part of him as his own lungs. He is both familiar and reverent with it. Something in me panics at the sight of that beautiful Gibson hovering on the edge of destruction. I bolt down the stairs, through the lobby, out the front door, and stop dead on Dr. Gottlieb's porch.

Guitar Man is out there now, trying to coax the guitar from

her as she holds it to her body and screams like an enraged child: "Get away! Get AWAY!" She keeps twisting to evade his grasp, but he is at least a foot taller, and her arms are so occupied with the guitar that she can't keep his from surrounding her. This only seems to incite more rage. She raises her voice to a volume beyond screaming, beyond any comprehensible words, yanks herself out of his hold and thrusts a knee into his crotch. He doubles over in pain.

Gottlieb appears behind me and hollers, "Leave him alone—Jesus!"

"Shut the fuck up!" Lucy cries. "And don't look at me like—"

Guitar Man sweeps one arm around her waist from behind and, holding her immobile, tries to wrench the guitar from her grip. She grunts like a little ape and hugs the Gibson furiously, struggling to keep it from him. I watch in frozen fascination as a Ford Explorer turns the corner and Guitar Man's girlfriend flings the Gibson in its path. I see it as if in slow motion: two children pressing their faces against the glass in the back seat; a harried mother craning her neck as she drives, trying to see what the fuss is about; and all the while, the Gibson is crushing, splintering, making its last sounds under the weight of that mammoth front tire.

The woman in the Explorer leaves the motor running, gets out with a confused diatribe already spewing—part concern, part irritation about being late for yoga. Occasionally she turns to the children, who remain captive and staring from the back seat, and calls, "Mommy's coming. Stay put!" Gottlieb is lecturing Lucy in loud, dogmatic tones, but she herself is now remarkably quiet. She lights a cigarette and looks bored, as if none of this has anything to do with her.

Guitar Man goes to the remains of his Gibson and stares, then kneels and rubs his hands over the splintered mess of strings and wood. "I didn't even see it until—" the woman begins, but one quick look from him silences her. Lucy holds her cigarette in the air, frozen in place. I do not dare to breathe, as Guitar Man examines the irreparable damage gingerly. He runs a hand through his hair, stands and stalks into the house.

"That's all you give a shit about!" Lucy explodes as the front door slams. "You wish that was *me* under those tires!"

"*I* sure do," Gottlieb says, just loud enough to be heard.

Lucy, who is making her way toward the house, spins on her heel and screams at the dentist. "What did you say?"

"Chump needs to show you the door!" He laughs, glancing at me.

She narrows her eyes at him. "You stupid fucking rapist!" He takes a couple of steps toward her, and she stands there, ready, chin jutting out defiantly.

"Is everything all right?" the woman calls from beside her Explorer. She is patting her upper lip with a handkerchief. Nobody answers for a long moment; I can hear someone starting up a lawn mower in the distance. "Is everyone okay?" the woman says again, a little impatiently.

The front door of Smoke Palace whines open, and Guitar Man emerges in a wide-brimmed suede hat, a large duffel bag slung over one shoulder and a sleeping bag tucked under one arm. He does not look at any of us, just moves quickly down the steps, tugging the brim of his hat a bit lower as he turns the corner and heads for his station wagon.

"That's it!" Lucy yells. "Just slink away, you lowlife bastard!" The engine revs aggressively, and she raises her voice above it in a challenge. "Just drive off, you fucking hypocrite!" The station wagon yanks into reverse and arches backwards, wheels spitting up gravel, then disappears.

"Do I need to call the police?" the woman from the Explorer asks, digging in her handbag for a cell phone.

"You need to mind your own fucking business," Lucy says, her voice cold and flat.

The woman stands there, bewildered, with one hand on her vehicle. She's sweating profusely, though it's not that warm out. The armpits of her blouse are two large, dark patches, and her big pale face is glistening. She looks questioningly at me, and I nod reassurance at her. She finally gets in her car and drives off, leaving a cloud of exhaust.

Gottlieb retreats in the direction of his office, a little unsteadily.

"Who are you supposed to be, anyway?" the girlfriend says, squinting at me.

"I'm Anna." I put my hand out for her to shake, but she just stares at it.

She makes a sound, something between a scoff and a sigh. "I don't know about you, but I need a drink." She is already turning toward downtown, taking a couple of steps in that direction. "You coming?" Her eyes are dark brown, with thick lashes. She pauses and jerks her head slightly in the direction she's headed, as if convincing a dog to get moving. Her lips are curved into a small, wry smile, barely discernable. I watch as her sheer summer dress flutters in the breeze, pressing and then releasing from the curve of her breasts and the slim shape of her hips. "Come on," she says, quietly, knocking the toe of her combat boot against the pavement. "I could use some company."

"Sure," I say, fumbling in my pockets. "I'll have to get some money, though—"

"My treat," she says. A gust of wind blows a sheaf of newspapers strewn about the Goat Kids' yard, scattering them in the street. One page drifts lightly toward her, and she kicks it away.

"Oh, I couldn't let you—"

"Sure you could," she says, showing her small white teeth, miniature and flawless like a doll's. "It's no big deal."

I smile in answer, and we start off down Walnut Street, leaving the butchered guitar and the Land of Skin behind us.

"I think I've seen you around," she says, squinting at me again as she lights a cigarette. Her eyebrows are mesmerizing. They're shaped like Jackie O's—two perfect, slim lines that curve elegantly high at the outer corners—and give the impression that she is constantly amused. She is a study in smallness—a tiny, childish nose, delicate, miniature ears. She squeezes her wedge of lime and we watch as the pulpy juice drips into her gin and tonic, clouding the clear bubbles a little. "You have a habit of watching people, don't you."

I look up at her, startled. My face gets hot.

"Well, don't look like that," she says, laughing before taking the thin red straw into her mouth. She sips from her drink with her eyes on me. "I caught you staring at us once, downtown. We were making fools of ourselves, and you were rubbernecking. I wanted to kill you." She smiles. "Some people have a habit of becoming public spectacles. Other people watch. It's how the world gets divided." She nods at the package of Camels on the table. "You smoke?" I shake my head. "I didn't think so."

"Are you from here?" I ask, gripping my Heineken.

"Yeah," she says. She looks around at the sad little dive she's steered us into; it is empty except for the overweight bartender and a couple of crusty, flannel-clad locals watching a game show and eating pretzels. "I grew up right here, in this bar. Listen, I'm not into small talk, okay? It wastes my time. We're all going to die, you know—that's important to keep in mind. Why don't you tell me the real reason you're here in Bellingham?" She takes a drag from her cigarette and blows the smoke sideways. Her lips are a dark, unpainted pink. I blink and gather my thoughts. "Don't plan everything," she says. "Jesus, why is everyone so edited, so—"

"To kill my father," I blurt out.

Her cigarette hand freezes midway to her mouth. "Really?" she says, her eyebrows arching even more. "How?"

"I don't know yet," I say. "He's dead, but he needs to die a little more."

Her mouth makes that tight, wry shape again. She taps her cigarette against the edge of the plastic ashtray and says, "My name's Lucinda, by the way. You can call me Lucy sometimes, but never Lu or—God forbid—Lu-Lu. Nice to meet you."

We drink all afternoon into evening, and not a moment is wasted. She smokes and pries, drinks and searches, confesses without a trace of apology or sentiment. She talks about death like it's a bus we have to catch, or a party we're going to—a pressing engagement that requires we say everything now, without hesitation. She drinks four gin and tonics, one on top of the other; the bartender brings the new rounds without even asking, like he's a part of her meticulous war against wasted time. After my initial Heineken he starts bringing both of us gin and tonics, with matching red straws and identical wedges of lime. I keep up with her, drink for drink, and I can feel myself getting looser and sloppier, my words coming easily but without precision. The room takes on softer hues; the men at the bar become shadows, while the bottles behind them turn to a blur of blues, greens and golds, catching the light and sparkling like Christmas ornaments.

When the two windows of the bar are turning colors—from the dregs of a terra-cotta sunset to a deep, melancholy blue—Lucinda finally gets around to the pedestrian details. "Where are you staying, anyway?"

I look at my hands. "Above Dr. Gottlieb's."

"No way! That fucking sicko? You've got to be kidding me—"

"It's only temporary," I say.

Her eyes light up, a new idea hatching behind them. "Listen, it's perfect timing. Why don't you move in? You can't go back to that bastard's."

"He does give me the creeps."

"Of course he does! He's the creepiest! He seriously tried to rape me once," she says, tapping a fresh pack of Camels against the Formica.

If it weren't for all the drinks and the overall surreal hue of the day, I would react with shock and sympathy, but between my tipsiness and Lucy's nonchalance, attempted rape barely registers.

"I'm surprised he didn't try you, already. You're staying with me. Absolutely."

"Are you sure?" I ask, trying to be reasonable.

"Sure, I'm sure," she says, ripping the Camels free of their cellophane wrapping. "You've got no choice."

"But you just met me today."

"What's that got to do with anything?" she says, annoyed. She tugs a cigarette free from the others and touches the flame of her Zippo to it with practiced precision. "You want me to check references or something?"

"We've had a few, is all," I say. "I don't want you to feel weird about it later."

"Hey, what you see's what you get. I'm no different, sober or drunk. I'll still like you tomorrow. Besides," she says, pausing for a drag, then exhaling slowly, "I'm never alone."

When we get back to the Land of Skin, the CDs and the Gibson are gone. I suspect they've been scavenged by the Goat Kids. In the entryway of Smoke Palace, the carpet is peeling back from the floor, and the air reeks of damp dog and mold. We go up two flights of stairs and Lucinda throws the door open with drunken flourish. It is dark inside. I can make out only vague shapes in the moonlight.

Lucinda crosses the room, stumbling once, and gropes at the wall. There is a flicker of yellow and a buzzing sound as the ceiling light struggles to come alive. It fills the room with ghostly fluorescence, and I see Lucinda in a momentary cameo, digging in her pack for a new cigarette before the light goes out. "Fuck," she whispers. She crosses the room again. I hear a *thud* as she bangs against something.

"You okay?" I ask.

"Fuck."

I can hear her fumbling with another light switch, and then the room goes bright again. I squint against the brightness instinctively, though it is kinder this time—not fluorescent but a soft, filtered red. I see Lucinda, standing next to an old lamp with a red chiffon scarf draped over it. She is struggling with her Zippo, a cigarette hanging loosely from her lips, and then a tall flame shoots up, throwing a gold pallor across her tiny features. Her expression loosens some as she lights her cigarette and inhales, but as she exhales her face goes rigid.

There, seated on a long black leather couch, is Guitar Man. The suede hat dangles beside him on the armrest, and his hair shows the place where the brim was. A couple of strands are standing up, animated by static electricity.

"Hey, Luce," he says, watching her. It occurs to me that he is like a darker version of her, with their matching brown hair and their black, birdlike eyes. "Who'd you bring home this time?"

"What is this shit?" She tries to put her cigarette in her mouth, but her hand is shaking, so she just dangles it at her side. "What are you doing here?"

"I don't know if I'm up for guests," he says, ignoring her question.

"Anna's my new roommate," she tells him, sinking into a

chair by the window. She keeps her eyes on him as she adds, "Aren't you, Anna?"

I swallow hard.

"She can't stay," he says, his voice low and even.

"Fuck that. She's staying." They stare at each other for a long, elastic silence. I keep expecting him to rise from the couch and strangle her, that's how angry he looks. The dim light, diffused through the red chiffon, makes their faces and the lumpy, secondhand furniture look hot and molten.

I rush blindly for the bathroom, somehow sensing where it is. I hit the door frame with my shoulder, turn the corner, aim at the toilet and vomit. The sound of it splashing against the toilet water fills me with a fresh wave of nausea, and I wretch again, spilling what's left of me. Then I stand there, bent at the waist, panting, a long string of drool stretching from my lips.

A small, cool hand touches the back of my neck. "You okay?" She hands me a washcloth and flushes the toilet. "You want something?"

I wipe my mouth and shake my head. I go to the sink and splash my face with cool water. The cold feels good on my skin. I turn to see her leaning against the door frame, her head tilted slightly to the side. "Don't worry about him," she whispers. "He's all bluff."

"Lucy!" he calls.

She rolls her eyes. "What do you want?" she yells, as if he's a great distance away.

Silence.

She shakes her head at me, sighs, and disappears. I can hear their voices rising and falling in suppressed tones as I study myself in the dimly lit mirror. I look startled and young. The beige T-shirt I put on this morning is hot pink in the light spilling in from the hallway. My haircut still shocks me. "You'll like her," I hear Lucinda saying, her voice high and sharp, before their tones drop back down to murmurs. "You've got no fucking right," she says. And a little later, "This is my place as much as yours!"

I close the bathroom door softly, lower the lid on the toilet and sit there in the dark, my face in my hands, trying to focus this kaleidoscope of sensations into a plan. I consider slipping out into the street and going back to my room, but the prospect of sleeping such a distance from a toilet seems dangerous. Besides, Gottlieb might actually be there, and I'm in no mood to deal with a haiku-obsessed rapist. I might rent a motel room, but this would take so much energy. I long for a dark room, binoculars, and a safe, anonymous window to look out from.

I hear the sound of their bodies moving: a thump against a wall, feet shuffling. Then Lucinda's laughter rings out, stops short, and I hear breathing. I lift my face from my hands and sit there, perfectly still, listening hard. Nothing. I stand, wobble slightly, touch the wall for support. I go to the bathroom door and peek out carefully. The living room is still red, but now it's empty. The bedroom door is open just a crack, and through it I catch a glimpse of Lucinda's naked knee, then a flash of her dress. I stand there, holding my breath, listening to the silence of that ancient, dilapidated house. Then the bedsprings begin, barely audible and erratic at first. They get louder, faster, and finally fall into a rhythm as steady and relentless as rain.

I make my way into the living room, careful to move in silence. I lie down on the leather couch. It is hard and uninviting, like the couches in school infirmaries. The room spins around me. I close my eyes and try to make it stop. When it slows, I feel sleep pulling at me, making my body heavy. I let the creaking bedsprings lull me to sleep, until I'm dreaming of melting furniture and a hot, stinging rain.

The Sex Queen of Fanny's Barbecue Palace

Lucinda and I walk into Fanny's Barbecue Palace at eight. It is brightly lit, with pink-checkered tablecloths and families eating piles of sauce-smeared ribs, getting their fingers sticky as their jaws chomp violently. The men at the tables look up at us quickly, then back down at their plates before their wives can notice. We make our way to the door at the back of the restaurant, which leads to the bar: orange vinyl stools, pool tables, loungy chairs before a dimly lit stage where the band is pausing between songs.

"Ready for more?" a man says into the mic. He is thin and freakishly tall, with a shock of white-blond hair and a gaunt face. He looks like a cross between David Bowie and Gumby. He reaches a lanky arm out and fingers a tuning peg. "We call this one 'Fuck Sean Cassidy.'" He takes a pick from his pocket, poises it above the strings and glances at the other members; there's a bald drummer behind a gleaming gold kit, and a badgerlike guy in black leather pants on bass. But the one I notice is Guitar Man. He's wearing a thin cotton T-shirt and faded jeans. A red electric guitar hangs low on his hips, and his eyebrows furrow in concentration as he watches for his cue.

The lead singer mutters, "One two three," and then they all seize their instruments like cavalry rushing into battle; their arms flail and their faces ball up like fists. Guitar Man is the only one who doesn't look ridiculous; he stabs at the air with the neck of his instrument again and again, but somehow the aggressive gesture isn't cliché, it's plain sexy. The singer leans his long, gangly body toward the mic and screams words, but I have no idea if they mean anything; *fucking pigs,* he screams. *Now now now, bend over, bend under,* and later, when the song has gone on so long I fear I am trapped in a time warp—some ruthless hell of distorted audio-loops—he raises his voice to a feverish pitch that makes my throat feel sore, and cries, *Fuck the Queen, fuck CBS, fuck Sean Cassidy, fuck YOUUUUUUUU!* and just like that the whole thing slams to a halt.

Guitar Man looks up now, sees us and smiles. His face, beaded with sweat, glistens in the yellow lights; he pushes a strand of damp hair off his forehead. For a second, I think he's looking at me. Only when I realize that his eyes are locked on Lucy does my pulse return to normal.

Another song begins, and the cocktail waitress comes over to take our orders. Lucy tells her we want Tanqueray and tonics. We don't speak as we wait for our drinks to arrive; we just sit in the swivel chairs near the stage and let that huge wall of sound numb our senses. The lead singer is at once repulsive and compelling. He has a face that skids from pretty to ghastly so quickly, you cannot determine whether you really saw either. When the waitress puts our order down, I pay her, waving Lucy away when she tries to hand me a five. We touch the edges of our glasses together midair and drink.

On our second round, she scoots her chair over near mine and speaks directly into my ear. "That's Danny Dog." She nods at the lead singer. "He's got two different colored eyes, like an Australian shepherd." She gives me a meaningful look before adding, "He's got real problems. If you're a masochist, you'll fall for him right off—though I don't recommend it."

"What about the others?" I ask.

"You could fuck them in a pinch," she says. "But I don't recommend that, either."

I roll my eyes at her. "I mean, what are their *names!*"

"Oh. Right. Drummer's Sparky. Total zero. Bill's the rat-faced punk on bass. Ew. Don't even get me started." She lights a cigarette, waves it in the direction of Guitar Man. "Arlan, of course. But you *live* with him."

In point of fact, this is the first time I learn his name, and for a moment the strangeness of my abrupt involvement with these people stuns me. Last night is still a blur of drinks and fragments—their matching black eyes, the taste of my own vomit, the sound of bedsprings creaking as I lay spinning in that dark red room. It all seems surreal and unreliable. In the morning, when I woke in a disheveled tangle on their hard black couch, Guitar Man was gone, and there was Lucy, clutching a mug of fresh, hot coffee in one hand, holding out three aspirin in the other. I struggled to keep my head from pounding louder than her words as she urged me again to move in with them. I didn't really say yes, but I didn't say no, either. She and I spent the day together. It was hot out; we floated in the lake outside of town, napping in the sunlight and drinking bottles of water to cure ourselves of the grimy film all that gin had left inside us.

"Hey," she says. "I just got a new lipstick yesterday. Put it on for me, will you?" She takes a tube of lipstick from her pocket and hands it to me.

"What?"

"Put it on me—I can't do it without a mirror."

"But—the light's so low," I stammer. "Maybe you should do it in the bathroom."

"Don't be ridiculous," she says. "Put it on me, then I'll put it on you."

I uncap it and turn it until it rises from its canister. It's hard to tell in this light, but it looks like a deep, rich scarlet—the sort of color I would never even consider wearing. I lean over and touch it carefully to her bottom lip. Her mouth has the bee-stung look of a porn star's. I trace the upper lip now, making sure to stay within the lines. I rub my lips together, demonstrating, and she does the same. I nod my approval.

"Okay," she says. "Now I'll do you."

"No thanks," I say. "It's not my color."

"Come on," she says. She downs the rest of her drink, leaving a red crescent against the rim of the glass. "A deal's a deal."

"No, really," I say. "I don't wear makeup."

"That's exactly the point," she says. "You have to start doing the things you *don't* do." She snatches the lipstick from me and holds it close to my face, staring at my mouth.

"But—" I protest.

"Hold still, for God's sake." She scowls with concentration. "You've got to *reinvent* yourself, or there's no point."

"Playing dress-up?" I look up to see the blond singer staring down at us. He is sweaty, and his eyes are lit up from the inside, like lanterns.

Lucinda finishes painting my lips and looks over her shoulder at him. "Hey, Danny. This is Anna. Try not to scare her off."

"Lovely introduction," he says. He reaches over, takes my drink in his damp-looking palm and downs it.

"That was hers," Lucy says.

"I know," he says. "I'm about to get her a fresh one. She needed a clean slate. Gin and tonic?" I nod. "Lucy? You ready for another round?"

"I'm always ready," she says. "You know that. Be sure it's Tanqueray, though—none of that well shit."

He disappears in the direction of the bar. The place is filling up now. There are swarms of barely-legal types milling around; the girls wear short skirts, the boys wear baseball caps. The air is getting thick with cigarette smoke and a headache-inducing mélange of designer scents. I recall seeing signs in town for a university, and its evidence is here; the girls are pretty, with traces of confidence. They laugh loudly and touch their hair often. The boys drink with grim determination, avoiding eye contact. Fanny's Barbecue Palace, only minutes ago all ours, is now bristling with the chatty, neurotic electricity of kids recently released from the grip of their parents.

Danny returns with three gin and tonics, sets them down, and remains standing, surveying the room. Soon Arlan and Bill come over and join us, too, lighting cigarettes and carrying glasses of whiskey. Sparky comes over last, whacking his sticks restlessly against his thighs, an empty chair, anything within reach. Finally, Danny sits down. I'm glad; someone that tall is distracting when he's towering over you. He looks right at me, and I see that Lucy wasn't kidding about his eyes. The right one is a light hazel, the left is a gray-blue. He just sits there staring, so I start to speak out of nervousness.

"What's your band called?"

Danny doesn't answer. He just goes on staring.

Bill says, "Called Buddhist Monkeys. My name's Bill, by the way." He thrusts a hand across the drinks for me to shake, which I do. His fingers feel clammy, but his grip is fierce.

"Anna," I say.

"I'm Sparky," the drummer tells me. His voice is high-pitched and irritating. He rubs his sticks together like he plans to start a fire right in his lap.

Arlan sits there drinking his whiskey and staring around the room in silence.

"Place is really filling up," I say. "You going to play another set?" Even before I've finished my sentence, Danny's eyes narrow.

"They're done for the night," Lucy says. "There's another band starting in a few minutes."

"Really?" I say, trying to suppress my relief. "What kind of—"

"Pussy rock," Danny says.

"I'm sorry?" I say.

"You like pussy rock?"

"Danny," Lucy says. "'Pussy' is not an adjective, okay?"

At this Arlan chuckles, though he's shown no signs that he's been listening until now.

"I just asked her a civil question," Danny says. He has a faint accent—Canadian, I would guess—and he speaks so loudly, I can hear him perfectly in spite of the adolescent commotion swelling all around us.

"Define 'pussy rock,'" I say.

"Apolitical, inarticulate ass-wipe. Feel-good, cunt-worshiping cereal jingles. Answer your question?"

"Danny," Lucy says, whipping around to face him. "If you didn't bombard every woman with fucked-up pejoratives for her anatomical parts, maybe you'd actually *get* some."

"Where you from, Anna?" Bill asks. He has a nervous twitch in his cheek.

"San Francisco."

"So you're visiting Lucy?"

"She's *living* with us," Lucy announces, her eyes locked on Arlan across the table. Bill looks from her to him to me with confusion. Arlan just keeps sizing up the room, smoking his cigarette. "I've adopted her," she adds, and smiles at me. Her tiny, adorable teeth seem to glow in the dark.

"Mother Lucy," Danny says, his voice filled with sarcasm.

"Motherfucker," she spits out.

"Arlan!" Danny calls. "You want to keep your woman in line?"

Finally, Arlan ends his contemplation of the room and turns in our direction. He looks first at Danny—a quick, dismissive glance—and then at Lucy. His eyes rest on her face and fill with a tenderness so visible I could swear they actually change color. "She keeps *me* in line," he says without a trace of apology, "and she knows it."

Within an hour, Danny is asleep in his seat. His chin tucks into his throat, and his head, with its shock of white-blond hair, sways side to side every now and then, like there's a breeze nudging it. I can see the very beginnings of balding at the crown—a hairless spot no bigger than a quarter.

He awakens occasionally and disappears for several long trips to the john, and each time he gets up, the other guys shoot each other glances. I wonder if he has severe digestive problems or narcolepsy or something.

"Danny's a junkie," Lucy whispers, as we cross the bar toward the bathroom. "In case you haven't noticed."

"I wondered what was wrong with him."

"Pisses Arlan off," she says. "Sometimes he's so fucked up he can barely play."

"How'd Arlan end up in this band, anyway?"

"He's not a self-promoter. He's an artist—way more than these shitheads—but Danny's the one with enough ego to get gigs." She closes herself into a stall. "You should hear Arlan play alone. He's a genius."

"Yeah," I say, studying my deep red mouth in the mirror.

She flushes the toilet and reappears. "What do you mean, 'yeah'?"

"I mean, yeah, I bet he is."

She looks at me for a moment before washing her hands.

Later, when we've had too much to drink again, and the pussy rock band plays a song with a beat that echoes through your chest, a song that makes you feel foolish and alive, Lucy drags me out on the dance floor. The place is now packed with sweaty students, wriggling and rubbing up against each other like frenzied fish. At first I just sort of wobble from one foot to the other, painfully self-conscious. But then I close my eyes, forget about the room and find the rhythm with my hips. I move without thinking to a night one summer when my parents threw a party; I can taste the air, heavy with the smell of grass, and I can hear their instruments coming together magically. My little-girl body flings itself from side to side, caught up in the waves of their frantic laughter, their strumming and banging and singing.

"You dance like you're on Ecstasy," Lucy says into my ear.

My eyes open, and the room is back, with its pool players leaning against the walls, coolly appraising. I see Arlan sitting at the table, smoking, watching.

"What does that mean?" I ask.

"It makes people want to have sex with you," she says, not smiling.

"Oh," I say. "Wow."

"Don't act so naive, Anna," she tells me, and now her face softens to a teasing smirk. "It's not convincing."

I keep moving, the frenetic beat of my parents' music still pulsating in the back of my mind. I tell myself, as an experiment, *Everyone here wants to have sex with you.* It makes me smile and rotate my hips with more insistence. I tell myself, *Even Arlan wants to have sex with you,* but that makes me feel guilty, so I push it out of my mind. I tell myself, *You're the*

Sex Queen of Fanny's Barbecue Palace, and this makes me laugh softly as I spin, gazing up at the dark, grease-stained ceiling.

I wake on the black leather couch, an old quilt tossed over me, and my mouth tastes like it's been stuffed with sand. Out the window, lit by a streetlight, a huge maple lets its branches be tossed by the night wind. I lift my head and peer into the kitchen: the digital clock on the microwave reads 3:12. A leaf releases from the maple and flies recklessly against the windowpane—a kamikaze mission—one sharp tap against the glass before it disappears. I close my eyes and envision it plummeting the two stories down, careening with breakneck speed into the sea of dewy grass below.

I can feel my psyche winding itself. It is the familiar beginnings of insomnia: brain blossoms at the wrong hour, in the dark, like a transplanted jungle flower.

I get up and cross the room, wrapping the quilt around my shoulders. The air is chilly, suffused with the yellowed scent of the old house. A gust of wind rattles the walls; more leaves tap themselves to death against the window. I study the guitar cases leaning against the wall. There are two there—one is the electric Arlan played tonight. I wonder if the case next to it is for the crushed Gibson. I look over my shoulder, across the hall to their bedroom. I can just make out the faint wheezing sound of someone snoring. Very carefully, I lay the guitar case on the floor, undo the brass latches and lift the lid. It's a Martin D-28—the exact model my father had. I run my hands over its polished surface, thick with lacquer, and I imagine I can smell its long, patchwork history—all those years spent in bars and living rooms and bus stations, pressed against laboring bodies, stroked by so many fingers. My hands are shaking as I lift it very carefully out of its case and carry it back to the couch.

I haven't held a guitar in my arms since I was eleven. The

cool feel of the body curving against my thigh is at once familiar and strange. I stretch my fingers into a G-chord and touch the strings tentatively, strumming just loud enough to bring back a rush of memories. I play the first couple of lines of "Folsom Prison Blues," humming softly. I think of Danny's heroin, and I wonder if this is how it feels—warm, dark relief spreading through your veins.

"You play?"

I jerk my head up to see Arlan in the doorway, little more than a shadow. I can actually feel the thumping beneath my breast against the rosewood.

"I'm sorry," I mutter, getting up to put it back. The guitar knocks against the coffee table and I curse under my breath.

"Sit down," he says. I do. "Don't worry about it." He crosses the room, yanks the window open, and props it up with what looks like a towel rack that's been ripped from the wall. I'm wearing only a big T-shirt Lucy lent me, probably Arlan's. The wind comes through the open window and I pull the quilt around my legs. He sits and lights a cigarette.

"So, you play?" he asks again.

"I used to, when I was little."

"Lessons?"

"My dad taught me," I say, trying to make my voice sound casual.

"He plays?"

"Played." I'm glad it's dark enough that he can't see my face. "He's dead."

I wait for a response, but there is none, just the orange glow from his cigarette, and the faint sound of breath as he produces a ghostlike puff of smoke. After a while, I play a couple of chords very quietly. My fingers seem to remember. "Where'd you get this guitar? It's gorgeous."

"Some old guy sold it to me," he says. "It's probably worth

three times what I gave him, but he was in a hurry to unload it."

"Play something?" I ask.

He hesitates. "Lucy might wake up."

"Just softly?"

He listens a moment to the silence. "I guess she's out." I cross the room to hand it to him, being careful not to bang it against anything this time. I am aware of my bare legs, my naked breasts under the soft, thin T-shirt. Our fingers touch as he takes the neck from me. I go back and sit on the couch again, shivering, and fold my legs under the quilt.

"Cold?" he asks.

"A little."

He stubs his cigarette out in a coffee cup and closes the window, taking great care not to let it slam shut. "You want another blanket?"

"I'm okay."

He glances across the hall to their bedroom door before he eases the old Martin onto his knee and checks the tuning. He takes a pick from the case. Then he sighs once in the dark, and very quietly, with fingers so precise and nimble I long to see them in full light, he begins to play. He starts quietly, and I have to lean forward to hear the notes, but as he gets going, the melody hits the air loud and clear. It's a sad, old-sounding song. He doesn't sing, but his hands pull stories from that guitar: blue, tattered tales set in some humid place, full of whiskey and moonlight, black stockings, trains and smoke. I close my eyes and lean back against the cool leather of the couch. There is nothing like this. I want to sit here forever.

"What was that, anyway?" I ask when the song is over.

"Oh, I was just messing around," he says. He puts the guitar down, gets up and takes a bottle from the freezer. He pours himself a drink. I think he's embarrassed. "You want a drink?"

"No thanks."

He sits back down and stares out the window. He doesn't look at me when he says, "Trouble sleeping?"

"Yeah. You?"

He nods, still looking out the window. There's a long pause. "Sometimes," he says, "I'd give anything to sleep all the way through to morning." We listen as the wind rattles the house, and more leaves tap against the window. He tilts his head in the direction of the bedroom. "Lucy sleeps like a baby, every night. She sucks her thumb." I giggle softly. "I don't understand people who can sleep like that." He stares at the bedroom door.

"What do you do?"

"What?" He looks startled, as if he'd forgotten I was there.

"When you can't sleep. What do you do?"

"I don't know. Smoke. Play guitar. Drink. You?"

I pause. "Look out the window, mostly," I say. "Soothes me. Watching, I mean."

He considers this in silence. "Well, then," he says, after a while. "I'll get out of your way."

"Don't be silly," I say. "This is your house."

"No, I'm taking up the window seat. Go on. It's all yours." He puts the guitar away and carries his drink toward the bedroom. I'm tempted to ask for another song, but somehow I know better. "'Night," he says, pausing in the doorway for a moment.

"Good night," I whisper.

When he's gone, I lie back down on the hard couch and pull the quilt up to my neck. I reach between my legs as I listen to his body moving quietly in the bedroom. I imagine him taking off his sweats, sliding into bed next to Lucy. I envision his hands carefully moving to her breasts, see his dark fingers against her white skin, and I breathe in time to the memory of those same fingers plucking songs out of the darkness. When I come, I bite down on the edge of the quilt to keep from making noise. Then I lie there, sleepless but not restless, staring at the branches swaying and rocking, throwing shadows on the walls. I listen to the cryptic Morse code of the maple leaves against the window. The message behind their urgent tapping is anybody's guess.

Caliban

It's strange, I know, but I don't really think about what I'm doing until Tuesday. Thursday the Gibson got smashed, Friday I became Queen of Fanny's Barbecue Palace, Saturday I retrieved my things from Gottlieb's and left a note: *Have made new arrangements—Anna.* Tuesday morning I awaken sitting straight up on the couch, afraid.

The weekend is lost in a haze of gin and secondhand smoke—I've never consumed so many drinks in my life, nor spent so many hours in smoky bars. There was the smack of pool balls, the rattle of ice cubes against glass, the torturous seduction of Arlan's guitar late at night. Lucy and I went to the lake again, we shopped for bras one day, we went to coffee shops. We are suddenly enmeshed in a baffling intimacy, a rhythm of lives interwound, as if my nightly return to their couch were a state as natural and inevitable as the movement of stars.

Still, there are more secrets here than understandings. Where they get their money, for example. Arlan paints houses—that much I've figured out. On Monday morning he pulled away in his station wagon, wearing paint-splattered clothes and a baseball cap. Lucy mentioned having recently lost her job at a Texaco station when she refused to provide her boss with the lurid details of her sex life. She's now stubbornly, willfully unemployed, and I get the feeling this is her status more often than not. Her main interest is the 'zine she puts out every month, a low-budget one-woman operation she calls *Pulp*. In it she blends feminist parody with *National Enquirer*–type headlines: "Serial Killer Claims He Saved the Planet from Blood-Sucking Sluts," or "Confessions of a Mutant Abortion Survivor." I'd pored over the back issues Sunday night when I couldn't sleep. The writing was good, the humor morbid and clever. I find it hard to believe this girl barely graduated from high school.

There have been allusions to Arlan's wealthy grandmother, but other than that, I'm left to assume that they live off Arlan's occasional painting jobs, and Lucy's even more occasional month-long stints at gas stations, head shops, ice-cream parlors—whatever takes the least energy. The 'zine, though widely distributed, is nothing but a financial drain, and Arlan's band gets paid mostly in drinks. Lucy and Arlan don't live in gluttonous luxury, but I know the expenses must add up: there are the cartons upon cartons of cigarettes to buy and the endless nights spent in bars, drinking heavily, feeding the pool tables with quarters and tipping the bartenders lavishly in moments of giddy, drunken humanitarianism.

But it's not until Tuesday morning, the fifth of June, that I wake up startled by my own couch-inhabiting role in the Land of Skin. The money from Rosie and my own savings won't last long in this environment; in fact, after gas, Gottlieb's room, and all the drinks this weekend, I discover I've spent five hundred dollars already—almost half of the paltry stash between me and selling my body on the corner of Garden and Walnut. The air of mystery around my hosts' financial situation only adds to my general queasiness. I've got to figure out what I'm doing here.

In this state of semi-panic, still befuddled with the aftermath of last night's gin, I eject myself from the terminally firm couch, throw on jeans and toss down a cup of coffee. Lucy and Arlan are giggling in the bedroom. The sky is filling with low, billowy rain clouds. I decide it's time to face Elliot Bender again.

I had hoped I might find him in plain view, but when I arrive, there's nothing except the late-morning sunlight breaking through the clouds, washing over the peeling paint of the old boats and the gleaming white fiberglass of the newer ones. I listen to the sound of waves lapping and ropes stretching tight, metal bits clanking against masts, the sides of boats knocking softly against the docks; it makes me a little sleepy. A pelican hovers over the bay, its wings balanced perfectly on the light breeze, then free-falls recklessly into the water. I giggle as it splashes—there's something so slapstick about pelicans.

"What are you laughing at?"

I turn to see Elliot Bender heading in my direction. He's got a grocery bag in each arm and a Mickey Mouse ski cap on his head.

"There you are," I say. "I was looking for you."

"It's your lucky day—here I am. Could you—?" He hands me one of the grocery bags and unlocks the gate. "You hungry? I've got pork chops in here somewhere. I myself was planning on a Slim-Fast shake, but I always provide solid meals for guests—the four basic food groups all in attendance. You look skinny. Do you eat?"

I realize with a pang of guilt that I haven't eaten a solid meal in ages. By the time I get ready to answer, though, he's already forgotten the question.

"Well hey, look at that—it's my friend, Caliban the Pelican. You can tell it's him because he's got that crazed, half-monster look. Hey, Cal! How's the fishing? Ah well, that's the trouble with pelicans, they're always so awkward when you try to engage them in conversation." He disappears below deck. Something crashes to the floor and I hear him cursing. "Will you hold on a minute?" he calls. "I can't even walk and chew gum at the same time. I'll be out in two seconds."

I unfold his lawn chair and sit facing the bay. He's certainly in better spirits than I found him in last; maybe that was just a fluke. Caliban lands on a nearby boat and eyes me suspiciously. He does seem to have a crazed gleam in his eye. I wave to him, but he continues to watch me with a look of distaste.

"I don't think Cal likes me," I yell to Bender.

"What's that?"

"Cal. He's looking at me like I'm regurgitated slime."

"That's a good sign. He loves regurgitated slime."

In a moment, Bender emerges with a can of tomato juice in one hand and a can of Budweiser in the other. "What did you say about the pork chop? You want one?"

"No thanks."

"You want something to drink?" I nod, and he tosses me the juice.

"My father used to drink tomato beer," I say. He looks at me for a moment, then nods, but says nothing. "You ever have that?"

"Fantastic," he says, "A can of Bud, a little Snappy Tom."

"Did my dad turn you on to those?"

"I taught him the damn recipe!" We both drink from our cans and look out at the water. "Summer's moody around here," he says. "Like San Francisco, only more rain."

"I kind of like it," I say.

"Gets old." A mosquito lands on his forearm. He smacks it dead with his big, leathery palm and smears it on his pants. A faint, feathery line of blood appears there. "Not much work in Bellingham," he says. "College kids snatch up most of it."

"Yeah?" I say, feeling the panic I woke with swelling anew in my belly. There's an awkward pause.

"Surprised you're still here," he says finally. "Thought you'd be back in San Francisco by now."

"No. I'm not going back there."

"Really?" He raises an eyebrow. "Why not?"

A big, gray-bloated cloud slides in front of the sun. "Because." My voice is plain and quiet. "I was dying there."

"Oh yeah?" he says. A small, mean twist creeps into the corner of his mouth. He dents his beer can slightly with his thumb. "What was it? Rush hour? Cost of living?"

"No," I say.

He chuckles, but any warmth or humor is now obscured by the dark glint in his eyes. I think of an obese wolf. "Listen, Medina," he says. "You're young, okay? You're healthy. You got nothing to worry about. You don't know shit about dying."

"When you're in the sixth grade and your father blows his brains out, you learn something about dying pretty quick."

To this he burps softly.

I shake my head and stand up. "Obviously, this is a waste of time. I was hoping you could take a momentary break from guzzling Budweiser to show me a few things." I'm confused. The tomato juice tastes acrid in my mouth, and the tiny, nagging headache I've been fighting all morning starts to invade the better part of my brain. It feels like there are bees rattling around in my skull. "I guess you never gave a shit about my father, or you wouldn't be treating me like—"

"Cut the pathos, okay?"

"—like a four-fingered leper!"

Silence. Caliban crashes into the water somewhere to my right, but I don't look. I keep my gaze leveled on Bender.

Slowly at first, and then with more speed and rising volume, Bender begins to chuckle. Within seconds, he is laughing openly and hysterically, wiping his hand over his face and shaking his head.

"What's so funny?"

"A four-fingered—" His face convulses, and his voice is choked with laughter, making it impossible for him to speak. When he catches his breath, he tries again: "Leper—" But he's racked with giggles, holding his gut with one hand, jiggling his beer with the other. "Oh, man! You got that from Chet, didn't you. I haven't heard that in twenty-five years!"

He's right. I hadn't realized it until now, but that was one of my father's expressions. "I—guess so," I say. I sit again, trying to regain composure, but his laughter is infectious. I find myself fighting a sheepish grin, and once that's taken over, giggles start rising up out of me like air bubbles.

"Chet," Bender says. His face is as pink as boiled ham. "He had the godamndest way with words!" He yanks a handkerchief from his back pocket and runs it over his face twice in rapid succession. His fingers wander to the buttons on his shirt, making sure they're still fastened. "What are you looking at?" he mumbles, patting at his wild, half-greased hair.

In that moment, I like him with such force, I can hardly keep myself from blurting out something stupid.

He saves us from any maudlin show of emotion by gripping his beer a little harder (I can see the fresh dents taking shape under his fingers) and getting businesslike. His voice goes gruff and vaguely paternal. "Listen, I'd like to help you. I would. I can see you're in a spot. The thing is, I don't have a pot to piss in. I unload more stuff every day. I'm even thinking about selling this old rowboat and getting a motorcycle. I got some bills and...you know, things stack up. I might need to be mobile." Here he pauses, licks his lips. "I'm in no position, is what I'm saying..."

"When did you stop?" I ask.

"Stop what?"

"Being a luthier?"

He smiles sadly and fishes a toothpick from his pocket. He uses it to poke at his gums somewhere deep in the recesses of his mouth, then lets it dangle from his lips. "I never stopped being a luthier," he says.

"So you still make guitars?"

He takes the toothpick from his mouth and runs the tip of it under his thumbnail. "Need a shop for that. I mean it's in me, is all. Certain things you can't shake," he says, wiping his mouth.

Caliban is hovering again, suspended above the water with his enormous wings splayed out, feathers trembling in the light breeze. We watch him, his beak poised like a spear, his beady eyes fixed on something below. "What would it take," I say cautiously, "to get you back in business?"

He snorts, snaps the toothpick in half. "A lot," he says. "More than you can—" He stops, midsentence.

I turn and he's staring at me with his mouth clamped shut, his eyes burning. "What? Did I say something wrong?"

"Is your mother involved in this?" he asks, slowly and deliberately.

"My mother? No, I told you, Rosie's—"

"Is Helen in any way, shape or form behind this? I want to know."

"Sh-she doesn't even know I'm—" I stammer, but he's

tossing his can down and stomping on it. The boat rocks violently.

"I'm not a goddamn charity case, and you can tell her I said that."

"Tell who?"

"Don't give me that! I see it, now. Helen sends her spawn to—"

"But my mother doesn't even know I'm—"

"I hear she's doing pretty good now. She can afford a wind-up derelict. I see she hasn't lost her bleeding heart!"

"I don't know what you're talking about," I say, but it's like he can't hear me—the wheels in his brain are turning too fast. "My mother never even mentioned your name!" I say, raising my voice.

I've stumbled upon the password; his rage dissolves.

He makes a futile attempt to smooth his hair down again, turning away from me. "No," he says, softly. "Of course she didn't. How stupid of me."

"Rosie's the one who told me about you," I add cautiously.

"Right," he mumbles, sitting down on the ice chest. "You said that…"

"I did."

"Listen." He scowls out at the water. "Why don't you just tell me why you're still here?"

I take a deep breath. "I was hoping you'd change your mind," I say softly. "About teaching me."

"It's got nothing to do with my mind," he says. "I've got no shop, no money. I don't know how else to say it. Go back to San Francisco, find someone there—"

"I'm not going back." My tone is icy.

He hesitates. "Well, what do I know?" he says to the bay.

"You want me to leave you alone?" I ask, when the silence has gone on too long.

He takes his handkerchief out and blows his nose with tremendous volume. Caliban flaps away across the water. He watches, his face expressionless, and shoves the handkerchief back into his pocket.

"I'm not much company," he says.

"I'm sorry," I mumble, standing.

"Don't be."

I step from his boat onto the dock carefully, feeling my headache again. The clouds have moved in full force, though there are still a few stray beams of sunlight leaking through here and there. Bender stays seated on the ice chest, his back to me. His hair matches the color of the clouds. I want to say something so the moment won't seem so amputated, but nothing comes to me.

I have my hand on the gate when I hear him say, "Medina." I turn around. He gets up from the ice chest and heads toward the cabin. "Hold on a minute," he says. "I'll be right back."

I walk back to his boat, and in a little while he reappears with a paper towel in his hand. He hands it to me. There's red ink scribbled across it, barely legible. *Dr. Riley Evans,* it says, and beneath that is a local phone number.

"Guy I used to know," he says. "Teacher up at Western. Musicology or something. He knows everyone around here—see if he can hook you up. You got a degree?" I nod. "Maybe he's got some research you could do. No guarantees, but you could give it a shot." I try to look grateful. "Tell him your name. It means something to guys like him."

"Because of Dad?"

He picks up a scrap of toast lying on the floor of the boat and tosses it to a seagull, who catches it midair. "You just tell him who you are. You'll see what I mean."

We're playing pool at the Station Pub with Arlan and Bill that night when Lucy mentions Grady Berlin for the first time. "Grady called today," she tells Arlan. "He's coming home in a couple weeks."

"No shit," Arlan says, sounding happy as a kid. "Is he really?"

I take my shot—a difficult one I'm sure I won't make—and miraculously the 4-ball sinks gently into the corner pocket. I try not to look overly proud of myself and move around the table slowly, assessing my next move.

"Nice," Lucy tells me. "You're getting better."

"Grady the tree hugger?" Bill says.

"He's an arborist, asshole."

Bill takes a long drink of beer, burps quietly and says, "Lucinda, what have I done to make you so hateful?"

"Don't flatter yourself. I wouldn't waste hatefulness on you."

I take another shot, an easy one this time, perfectly lined up, and miss.

Arlan steps up to the table and sinks five balls in a row. His face is tight with concentration as he moves about, but his body is loose, leaning over and lining up his cue with the ease of a practiced shark.

"Who's Grady Berlin?" I ask.

Bill looks at me in surprise. "You don't know Grady?"

I drink my beer and shake my head.

"No," Lucy says. "Of course not. He left for Argentina way before she showed up." She turns to me. "Grady's the guy you'll fall in love with," she tells me. Then she looks over my shoulder and adds, "Oh. Arlan fucked up. Your shot."

Almost a full week passes before I get a chance to meet with Dr. Riley Evans. It's summer, so the university is in slow motion, which makes it frustrating tracking him down. I reach him by phone Friday afternoon.

"Anna, you say? Fine, well, let's see—not that god-awful mandolin again! Good Christ, what have you done to—" and here he drops the phone a moment, before returning, a little out of breath, and laughing. "Who's this? Right, Anna—Monday, then? Say noon?"

I show up at his office five minutes early, and he appears twenty minutes later, carrying a fake leather briefcase and trailing a long piece of string from his shoe. He's a slim, lip-licking type with flaky dry skin around his mouth and eyes. His hair is a brown bowl atop his head. He lets us into his office, settles himself behind an enormous desk piled high with books, and points to a chair in the corner for me. I move it slightly so I can see around the chaos of his desk to his enormous, fishlike eyes.

"Well then, what seems to be the problem, Amy? Worried about the midterm?"

"My name's Anna," I say. "And actually, I'm not a student."

He pauses, a little thrown by this—I've veered from the script on my first line. He leans back in his leather chair, brings his hands up close to his face and taps the tips of his fingers together rapidly. "Not a student?"

"Elliot Bender gave me your number. I've come here to work with him, only..." I pause, looking around the room. "I want to make guitars, but..."

"Yes?" he says expectantly, licking his chapped lips.

"I thought Mr. Bender could teach me, only he can't—well, he won't."

"He's fallen on hard times," Dr. Evans says, nodding soberly. "I heard about that. He's a legend, though—he's to luthiers what Christ is to Christians—the Les Paul of the acoustic cult, the—"

"Yes," I say. "He's quite good, then, I guess?"

He snorts. "Let's face it, there's not a soul in the civilized world who knows a thing about guitars and doesn't positively worship the Bender construction—the signature inlays, the priceless tone. In my *History of Stringed Instruments* course I spend at least two weeks on Bender and Medina, their collaborative and solo years—of course, Medina was nearly his equal until he went off the deep end in 1988."

"1987," I say.

"I'm sorry?" A milky-white string of saliva has been gradually thickening between his bottom and top lips. I watch it quiver as he pauses with his mouth slightly ajar.

"Chet Medina killed himself in 1987," I say.

"1988," he snaps, tapping his fingers again quickly.

"1987," I repeat.

"What is your interest, here?" he asks, after studying me.

"I told you. I want to make guitars."

"We don't offer hands-on classes. We study the history, musicology, theory—not the craft. Now I'd like to help you, but I've got an appointment across campus in—" he paws through the papers on his desk "—five minutes. Have you got the time?"

"It's twelve thirty-five," I say, reading the clock above his head.

"Right," he says. "Are you looking for information? Is there something in particular I can help you with?"

I stand, shoving my hands into my pockets. "I don't think so."

Déjà Vu

Lucy and I are eating lunch in the filthy little room next to the taco stand we love. I watch as red liquid drips from the tilted curve of her folded corn tortilla; it is difficult to tell if it is blood from the carne asada or just salsa. It lands in dark drops on the paper lining her plastic basket. Flies buzz impatiently in the air.

Tacos Jesus hovers between two poles: earthy hedonism and food poisoning. The tacos are amazing, the meat so tender and perfectly spiced, you have to close your eyes as you chew, thinking of Mayan hunters closing in for the kill. Your immediate surroundings are more mundane; the only place to sit is this weird, dirty room sandwiched between the taco trailer and a butcher shop. The tables are always sticky, the floor is covered in green, peeling linoleum. There's nothing to drink but Mexican sodas that come in lurid colors or fake sangria that's really just sugary grape juice. Still, Tacos Jesus is strangely addictive; after you've had it once, it is impossible to go more than a couple of days without craving the firm texture of the carne asada between your teeth and the soothing warmth of the tortillas in your hands.

"So," I say. "Tell me more about this Grady guy."

"What's there to tell?" she says. "The important thing is that you're curious."

"Come on," I say. "Of course I'm going to be curious. You told me I'm going to fall in love with him."

"Or not," she says. "I mean, he's definitely not good enough for you, but I doubt you'll let that stop you."

"What's not good enough about him?"

"He's smart, but he's not as smart as he wants to be. Like most men, he doesn't listen—he's good at pretending, but he won't hear you. He's incredibly cute, but don't tell him that—he'll assume you're shallow. He climbs trees for a living and he's supposedly an anarchist or a communist or something, but if you've ever seen him fold a shirt you'd know the anarchist bit is bullshit, and he went to Yale, so I have a hard time imagining him a communist. Those are the most important things to know about Grady." She wipes a little drip of salsa from the corner of her mouth with a napkin. "Now, let's stop talking about him—Grady's boring, especially since you're not even fucking him yet."

I have to concentrate on swallowing so I won't choke on my tamarind soda. "I haven't even met him!"

"Right. My point exactly." She spreads her lips into a grimace and exposes her gleaming little teeth. "Do I have food in my teeth?"

I look. "No. Do I?" She examines mine and points to a spot. I dig with my fingernail until I dislodge the leaf of cilantro.

"Forget about Grady for now," she says. "If you say too much you ruin everything."

On the way home, I let Lucy drive, and I find myself gripping my own arm so hard, there are fingernail punctures for hours afterward. She handles the wheel with nonchalance—it's merely an accessory she can fling around, while her cigarette is the main event.

A cop passes us on the left. Lucy is digging down into the seat-belt hole, trying to find her lighter. The truck veers dangerously in his direction, and I can no longer resist—I grab the wheel and tug the vehicle back to the center of the road, as gently and firmly as I can. I can see the cop car gliding slowly in the lane next to us; he hovers there for a long moment, assessing us in his rearview mirror. Lucy, unhindered by her seat belt, digs deeper into the recesses of the hole, oblivious to the road. By the time she returns to the wheel with the lighter, an "Aha!" of triumph on her lips, the cop is slowing to a crawl beside us. "What's your problem?" she asks me, and when I nod toward the cop in answer, she says, "Ha! I eat them for breakfast." After a couple of seconds, the cop moves on. I reluctantly surrender the wheel to her again, leaving traces of sweat behind.

"Lucinda," I say, letting out my breath.

"What? I've got it!"

The car in front of us flashes two bright-red brake lights, and I hold my breath again as she concentrates on lighting her cigarette. At the last minute, she slams on the brakes. She laughs and takes a drag, looking at me sideways.

"You've got an interesting driving style," I say.

"This is nothing," she tells me, adjusting the rearview mirror so she can examine her eyebrows. "You should see me when I'm drunk."

Lucy and Arlan are out tonight, and for the first time since I came here, I'm home alone. Buddhist Monkeys has a regular gig on Friday nights at Fanny's Barbecue Palace. Of course, I'm always invited, but tonight I'm not in the mood to watch Arlan's talent being eclipsed by Danny's absurd theatrics. It's painful watching the handful of alcoholics who constitute Buddhist Monkeys' fan base being replaced with a full-on crowd when the lame headliners, Honkey Dory, show up. Still, I don't blame the kids around here for preferring Honkey Dory's saccharine, top-forty tunes to Danny's clumsy attempts at social commentary set to the assault-on-the-senses he calls music.

Since I met him a couple of weeks ago, my distaste for Danny has increased exponentially. His concept of the cosmos revolves around three reference points: Mad Max, Black Flag, and shooting up. If you try to steer the conversation away from these three topics, he inevitably stares with glassy-eyed vacancy at a point in space just above and beyond your left shoulder.

As for the other band members, Bill is more likable than Sparky, though by a thin margin. Sparky is enamored with Danny, and because he has no discernable personality of his own, his willingness to laugh at everything Danny says makes him guilty by association, in my eyes. Bill is more a devotee of Arlan, which gives us something in common, at least. He's also more civilized than the others, but his rodentlike eagerness is a turnoff. Once, I saw him make the moves on a disgustingly drunk college girl who'd just been publicly dumped. Her mascara was still wet and the front of her shirt was slightly vomit-stained; Bill went right up and handed her another drink.

Tonight, I'm determined to take advantage of the only privacy I've had in weeks. Soon after I watch Lucy and Arlan drive off in his station wagon, I fix myself a cup of tea and snuggle into the window seat. I breathe into the cup and feel the steam rise against my face in a thin vapor. Outside, the evening sky is deepening its melancholy blue by several shades, and the college kids are beginning their Friday night by clomping downtown in their heavy-soled hipster shoes. The stillness of the house is startling. I can't remember the last time I was alone.

In my old life, I'd grown used to days on end of virtual solitude. Even when I worked at After Hours, I was isolated inside my cubicle, with nothing but the low, compulsive hum of office life between me and silence. On weekends, I sometimes went out with Derek; we'd dine on lentil soup and organic juice at his favorite restaurant in Mill Valley, where the faint smell of ginger and dirt always clung to the air. Or my mother and I would spend the obligatory meal in one another's company. As soon as we'd finished eating, though, we'd flee, both of us taxed by the accumulated weight of things we were too tired or frightened to say.

This summer my loner facade has been under siege. Since I've started living with Lucy and Arlan, every day begins and ends with the sounds of other people—the toilet flushes, coffee beans are ground, a tray of ice cubes is being twisted until it cracks, someone is yelling at someone else to bring them cigarettes. Sometimes I sleep by myself in the living room, listening to Lucy and Arlan have sex; more often, Bill or Danny or Sparky or all three are snoring somewhere nearby, collapsed on the floor in various shapes. I live in a hive of human sounds, filled with the buzz of other peoples' needs and impulses.

The Land of Skin is active tonight. As it gets dark, I unwrap my binoculars from the wool sweater stashed deep in my backpack. I feel a little dirty as I crouch closer to the window and begin to focus. The hairy fixture of Purgatory Corner appears in life-size detail, his baseball cap perched backwards on his head, his stringy brown hair parting to reveal large, fleshy ears. He's yelling something at the Goat Kid Hovel, and I open the window to hear better. "Get a life!" he bellows. "Goddamn disturbance of the peace!"

Across the street, the Goat Kids are attempting a barbecue of sorts. A cacophony of distorted guitars is pulsing from their windows. Out on the lawn, there's a group of seven or eight of them clustered around a trash can half filled with debris. One of them douses it with lighter fluid and tosses a match in. A cluster of flames emerges suddenly, like a devil they've conjured. The flames increase in intensity, turning the Goat Kids' faces gold. I hear the guy on the porch scream a half scolding, half admiring obscenity from across the street, but they're too enraptured to notice. Someone carrying a package of hot dogs emerges from the house, and several of them dangle the dogs close to the flames. By the time they've managed to impale one or two on sticks, the flames have died down to embers.

I watch for a long time, lost in the familiar pleasure of it. I fold my legs under me and press my binoculars to the glass. I look for Raggedy Ann, but she's not there. I feel half guilty, as if her absence is a direct result of my failure to look for her lately. I think of Magdalena and all those I watched with such vigilance back in San Francisco. Something in me longs for the beige of my apartment, the uninterrupted hours spent in anonymous bliss, soaking up the details of other peoples' lives.

Some time later, I hear the scratch of a lighter behind me, and I turn so quickly that I feel a pain shoot down my neck. Lucy's lighting her cigarette, standing there in her little red T-shirt and a barely-there skirt, with one boot tapping against the carpet. "So," she says, and little puffs of smoke emerge from her lips as she speaks. "You're one of those."

I stand up and try to force my binoculars into my backpack.

"Don't," she says simply, but I've spilled the contents of my bag now, and am busying myself stuffing shirts and underwear and packages of gum back where they came from. "Anna," she says. I meet her gaze, and she smiles. "You're blushing," she tells me. "You're so lovely when you blush."

"Don't make fun of me," I say.

"I'm not." She comes closer, and I can smell the smoke on her, the sweet, fruity smell of her shampoo, and her breath laced with gin. "I would never do that." For a moment, we just stand there, very close. Her face is tilted upward slightly toward mine. I can see the dark red lipstick, and the place where she went just slightly outside the lip line, to make her lips look even fuller. There are tiny marks where she plucked her eyebrows. Her eyes are so dark, and she's watching me so intently, that the tiny hairs on the back of my neck stand erect. I look down.

She takes a step back and falls onto the couch, her limbs spreading in a way that tells me she's drunk. "I don't humiliate people I like," she says. "But I don't mind telling you—watching is a form of rape."

I sit, and concentrate on cinching my backpack closed.

"By the way," she says, and she takes an extralong drag off her cigarette. "How can you go through life without smoking? Don't you feel impovish—" She pauses and wraps her mouth around the syllables more carefully. "Impoverished?"

"How so?" I ask, glad that she's changed the subject.

"You've been robbed of your prime smoking years!" She takes a cigarette from the pack and hands it to me. "Go on. Try one."

"No thanks," I say.

"You like to watch? I'll take you someplace. Tomorrow. Saturday."

"How come you're back so early?" I ask.

"I got tired of their shit," she says, running her fingers through her hair. Her legs are parted and I can see the red of her underwear. "I live in a jungle of perverts." She pauses, gives me an eerie, knowing look. "You're as bad as them, aren't you."

I can feel my cheeks growing hot again.

"Don't blush. It's only cute the first couple times." I stare at my hands. "Oh, don't listen to me." Her voice softens and she slips from the couch to her knees, crawling across the floor until she's sitting at my feet. "Don't let me hurt you—I always hurt people, dammit." She looks up at me, and her eyes go so liquid I think she might cry. Instead, she sneezes. Then she rests her face against my leg and takes a long, pensive drag from her cigarette. "I should be more like you," she says, sighing smoke.

"Like me?"

"More…Shirley Temple. All those little-girl curls." She looks up at me quizzically. "How old are you, anyway?"

"Twenty-five."

"Same as Arlan," she says. I blush again, and I look out the window, hoping she won't notice. "Good God," she says. "You're blushing at *that?*" She pauses, and I can feel her watching me. "You like him, don't you."

"Who?" I say, still staring out the window.

"There's my answer," she says, chuckling. "Don't worry, everybody worships him. Except me. That's why I get to have him." She lays her head down in my lap again, like a sleepy child. Her cigarette has burned down to the butt. She flings it at the window; it hits the sill and lands in the carpet. I watch it for any signs of smoke, but it's dead. "He's all mine," she murmurs. "Because I don't give a shit."

She starts snoring softly. I can feel her breath in hot little gusts against my thigh. It takes a while, but eventually I fade to a thin, tentative state of unconsciousness. I dream I've got a warm animal sleeping in my lap. At first it's a cat, but when I pet it, the thing raises its head and I find myself staring into the face of a bat with dark, leathery ears and black, black eyes.

Saturday night, Lucy directs me to a depressing section of Seattle; it's got much of the tawdry, faded-carnival feel of Fisherman's Wharf, only it looks less successful at separating visitors from their money. We park the truck and she pulls me into a concrete building with a sign, *Déjà Vu: Hundreds of beautiful women and three ugly ones,* printed in bubble letters across the front. We walk in the door and find ourselves in a very disorienting corridor, lit with blue and ending in a burst of raucous color. There's a guy behind a counter sipping a Slurpee through a straw and touching his stiff, gelled hair with one hand.

"Hi," Lucinda says, lighting a cigarette.

"Twelve-dollar cover, ladies," he tells us, releasing the straw from his pouty lips just long enough to get this out.

I expect him to be surprised or curious about two young women walking into Déjà Vu on a Saturday night, but he is clearly much more enthralled with his Slurpee than with us or the logic that brings us here.

"Is Lorna working tonight?"

"She is later. You a friend?"

"You could say that." Lucy smirks. "Do we really have to pay?"

"Wednesday's amateur night," he informs us. "No cover then. Tonight's twelve dollars."

"Look, we're not going to stay long. Just…come on. Please?"

He chews the inside of his cheek and examines us with glassy eyes. His expression reminds me of someone watching late-night television. "If you stay past eleven, I'll have to come collect." He shrugs and goes back to his Slurpee, which is evidently our cue to go in.

The explosion at the end of the corridor opens and swallows us: streaks of pulsating, colored light, music impossibly loud with a bass beat that makes your stomach wobble, white teeth turned neon in pools of black light, red booths shiny as patent leather. We wander through this storm of stimulation. No doubt our faces show we're confused, like nocturnal animals stumbling into excessive sunlight. We make our way to a couple of chairs near the corner.

The bass beat shifts: vintage Madonna blasts from the speakers and a male voice pumped from within a smoke-colored Plexiglas booth urges us to give it up for Sasha, this year's statewide winner of the Hardbodies of America contest. Sasha leaps onto the stage. She wears a bright white nurse's uniform, starched, seductively tailored, a stethoscope dangling between her enormous breasts. She is rather short, in spite of the un-nursey spiked heels, and she dances with the aggressive, crisp athleticism of the more gymnastics-inclined cheerleaders, the ones that do flips from the top of human pyramids. Before long, her nurse's uniform comes off with an efficient flick of the wrist. Velcro, I think to myself. Ingenious.

The more naked she gets, the more fascinated I become. I am authentically perplexed by the sheer spectacle of her body: thighs ropy and taut as suspension cables, concave belly, breasts so large they should be ponderous, yet they are firm—rigid, even. Not real, I tell myself, which I find stupidly reassuring.

"You like to watch? This place is made for watchers," Lucy whispers into my ear.

The waitress comes around to take our orders, but they don't serve anything except soda, so we pass. Lucy chain-smokes, and I sit there, half fascinated, half fuming. She wouldn't tell me much on the hour-long drive down, and I'm sick at the thought of being marched through a moral drill. If she intends to show me the error of my ways, she's got it all wrong; this place has nothing to do with me. I'm an anthropologist. These people are perverts.

But as I survey the crowd, I have to admit, they don't look much like perverts. They look bored. Sasha, the number-one hardbody in the state, is now doing things with the pole center stage that imply her limbs are made of rubber. She twists and turns round that thing with the agility of an ape and the grace of an acrobat. Yet the crowd stares at her with the same listless, numb eyes the boy at the counter showed us. She's up there practically removing her own bones from their sockets, and what does this crowd offer her? Apathy. They might as well be cows, gazing at the same pasture they've seen every day of their lives.

An hour passes, measured by the transformation of one pop song into another, and the continual stream of cigarettes passing from Lucinda's lips to the ashtray. The dancers replace one another seamlessly, each with her own icon: the businesswoman, the Catholic schoolgirl, the Parisian vamp. They all have huge, gravity-defying breasts; they're all leggy and lean from the rib cage down. I can feel my face slipping into the passionless shape that matches that of all the other faces in the audience—the vacant eyes that seem to broadcast *you've seen one, you've seen them all.*

Right around eleven, Lucinda turns to me and mouths over the riotous wails of Mick Jagger, *Let's go.* She jerks her head toward the exit for punctuation. Just the thought of fresh air tugs me from my stupor. *Yes, let's.* I nod back at her. She pockets her pack of Camels and her Zippo. We make our way through the maze of zombies and head back down the eerie, blue-lit corridor, past the Slurpee guy, toward the black, scuffed-up door with its metal bar that need only be pushed to obtain freedom. I fixate on that metal bar, and the night air that circulates beyond it. But just as Lucy places her hand on it and starts to lean her shoulder against the door, it swings open more suddenly than it should, and she nearly collides with a girl who was on her way in. I'm shocked to see a tall, tanned version of Lucy in a tiny spandex dress. Her hair is dyed a garish red and her makeup is thick and exaggerated, but her eyes and mouth match Lucy's so precisely, they might be clones.

"Holy shit," the girl says, her eyes going wide. "What are *you* doing here?"

"Hey, Lorna," Lucinda says, forcing a casual tone. "We just stopped by."

"Mom send you?" Her eyes dart toward the Slurpee guy, slide past me, before resting again on Lucinda. "Come out here," she says, stepping back into the parking lot.

We start to follow her out, when a pack of five or six overdressed, fortyish men intercept us on their way in. They reek of cologne and cigar smoke. "Hey now," the one in the lead says, enunciating sloppily. "This is what *I'm* talking about! Are you the beautiful ones, or the three ugly ones?" The men behind him explode into gales of laughter. I watch Lucy and the redhead give them identical withering looks. We move past them, out the door, and though it takes me a couple of breaths to clear my head of the smoke and the stink of cologne, the air outside is delicious.

Lucy and Lorna both light up cigarettes immediately.

"Mom needs money? Is that it?" Lorna's voice is raspy, harsh.

"Jesus, Lorna, we just stopped by, okay? I haven't even talked to Mom." Lucy glances at me, then, as if suddenly remembering I'm there. "This is Anna," she says, nodding at me. Then she turns back and faces the girl, and with her cigarette clenched in the side of her mouth, she mumbles, "My sister, Lorna."

"Nice to meet you, Lorna."

She gives me a look. "Whatever," she says, running her long pink nails through her hair and turning back to Lucy. "Just—why are you here?"

"Why are you being such a bitch?"

"I don't hear from you for months and now you pop in for a—"

"Anna wanted to see where you work," Lucy says. "No big deal."

Lorna glances at me with more disdain than ever. Her mouth is so twisted with anger, I can hardly see the prettiness there anymore. "Slumming it?"

"Get off it, Lorna."

"No, *you* get off it, Lucy!" They're both smoking furiously, now, puffing at one another with their eyes squeezed into tight little slits.

Lucy shakes her head in disbelief. "Forget it, okay? Just—"

"Get out of here, then!"

"We're on our way!" And Lucy stomps off toward the truck.

I trail behind, feeling ridiculous. I glance over my shoulder and see Lorna there, watching us. Her fierce red hair glows in the neon light from the Déjà Vu sign, and her face looks old, withered, though she couldn't be more than twenty-five. She glares at me and crushes her cigarette under her platform shoe, twisting her ankle back and forth again and again.

It's half-past eleven when we pull into a shopping center parking lot and ease up to the window of the espresso shack. There is a teenage girl with acne working there; her hair is cut very short and dyed blue. She has that pasty, gloomy look that so many people in the Pacific Northwest cultivate. It's at least an hour's drive back to Bellingham. We've agreed to get doubles and stay up all night.

"Two double mochas," I say to the girl. She has the eyes of someone who will come to a bad end. "One with whip, one without."

"Tell her I want cinnamon on mine," Lucinda says, and lights a cigarette.

"The one with no whip—can you put cinnamon on

that?" The girl nods, but I can see that we've crossed the line of reasonable requests, from the way she bangs around inside her little shack and takes her time about getting us our drinks.

She hands us our order at last, and Lucinda sighs with something like relief when she takes her first sip. I take a tentative taste, sipping through the hole in the plastic lid—the whipped cream is cool and it tames the heat of the sweet, chocolaty coffee. I cradle the paper cup between my thighs as I drive. We get a little lost, but eventually we find I-5 North and accelerate to eighty on the nearly deserted freeway. I can feel the race of the caffeine hitting my system. Suddenly, for no apparent reason, I feel happy.

"My sister used to work at Wal-Mart," Lucinda says, staring out the window so I can't see her face.

"Yeah?"

"I don't know which is worse, really." She takes off her shoes and presses her bare feet against the dash, contemplating her toes. "My mom lost her house at the casinos. She's there almost every night." I try to read her voice, but it is monotone, a simple recitation of facts.

"Huh," I say.

"She lives in a trailer."

"Who, your mom or your sister?"

"My mom," she says. "My sister lives with this disgusting guy who's fifty years old and thinks he's Don Johnson. God. He wears pink shirts unbuttoned down to his navel and a stack of gold chains. He tried to touch my boobs once. I kneed him in the balls." I chuckle at this, but she just keeps staring out the window at the darkness whirling past. "I didn't really," she says, after a long pause.

"You didn't really what?"

"I didn't knee him in the balls," she says impatiently. "I can't do that to people. When I see how much they need something, I end up feeling sorry for them—even if I hate them. It's an involuntary reaction."

"Yeah," I say. "I see what you mean." I'm not sure I really do see, but the moment is too fragile to withstand debate.

We pass exits to various suburbs. We pass shopping malls and fields of vegetables and the lights of a reservation casino—gaudy, pink, blinking promises of luxury and riches to the sad, desolate freeway. There is nothing to say the rest of the ride home, so I drive in silence through the trees and past lakes, until the Bellingham exits begin, and we take ours, then make the left turn toward home.

Lemon Cookies

Lucy and I get up on Sunday morning around eleven. We stayed up until four watching old movies the night before, so we're both groggy. We go to The Horseshoe and we hang out there for a while, trying to wake up. Lucy works on an article for *Pulp* while I try over and over to compose a simple postcard to my mom: *Hi, Mom, just wanted you to know I'm fine.* I put my pen down and sit there for twenty minutes, studying the haircuts and summer fashions all around me. I erase what I've written and start again: *Dear Mother: I know you're worried, but don't be.* After three hours, I've erased so many times, the postcard starts to disintegrate. I turn it around and see that the photo of Puget Sound is now sporting a tiny but conspicuous hole near Orcas Island. I throw it away.

Everything here is so far from my mother; even the cigarettes at Smoke Palace smell different from her familiar Virginia Slims. I can't believe how good it feels to get away from her. Even if she does want the best for me, escaping her grasp is like a cool blast of bracing wind on a hot, humid day. I've tiptoed around her neurotic silence for as long as I can remember, and it's tainted everything between us. I'm not ready to let her know where I am.

When we drive up to the house, Arlan is out on the porch with somebody I've never seen before. The day is turning cloudy and the air suddenly smells like rain. Driving by, I can only make out their basic shapes—the stranger is sitting on the wide, flat railing. Arlan is slouching in one of the gutted chairs.

"Who's with Arlan?" I ask, as we turn the corner to park in the back.

"Don't know," Lucinda says. "I thought he was painting today."

We get out and walk down the gravel path toward the front porch. The stranger leans back over the railing and turns toward us. When I see his face—green eyes, dark blond hair, a couple of days' stubble on his cheeks—I somehow know who it is.

"Grady!" Lucy screams. She runs directly to him and almost knocks him over with her hug. I climb the porch steps slowly. "When did you get back?" she asks.

"An hour ago. Earlier than I'd expected." He looks up at me. "Hi," he says.

"Hello."

"Grady, Anna. Anna, Grady," Lucinda says in a rush; this formality clearly annoys her.

He reaches out his hand. His fingers are cold.

"Grady just got back from Argentina," Lucy says, putting an arm around him. "He's trying to be the Brad Pitt of South America."

"You're wicked as ever," he says, messing up her hair. I

notice his shirt has a huge anarchy symbol splashed across the chest. "She's a compulsive liar," he tells me, nodding at Lucy. "Keep that in mind." Lucy elbows him. "Arlan was just telling me about you." His eyes sparkle at me, teasing. He has the skin and the bone structure of a Calvin Klein model.

"Really?" Lucy says, her smile going stiff. "What was he saying?"

Grady pulls Lucy to him and squeezes her affectionately. "Nothing important, little vixen. God, you're nosey, aren't you."

Arlan picks up his cigarettes from the arm of the dilapidated chair and says, "Come on. Let's go get drunk."

We go to the Ranch Room, a rundown little bar tucked inside a diner where they sell chocolate bars, lottery tickets and cigarettes near the door. The walls are covered with fake wood paneling and the bartenders pour the well drinks with such heavy hands, you can get stumbling drunk for six dollars, tip included. After we order the second round, I excuse myself to the bathroom, and Lucy follows. I wait until she ducks into one of the stalls, and then I look myself over; there is something vaguely humiliating about primping in front of Lucy, who is incapable of looking less than stunning and therefore requires no adjustments.

"Remember," she says, talking over the sound of her pee hitting water. "Whatever you do, don't tell him how cute he is. Your best shot is ignoring him."

"Why do you assume I'm—?"

"Look," she says, emerging from the stall and washing her hands. "Grady's just like every other guy. If he thinks you've got a thing for him, he'll bolt. If you look like you've got better things to do, he'll be banging down your door."

"Interesting theory."

"Reality," Lucy says. "Not theory. Sex is always an act of hostility."

"You need your own talk show," I say.

Lucinda takes out her lipstick and applies it. After a moment's consideration, I say, "Can I borrow that?"

"Grady hates makeup. The only girl I ever saw him fall for was this plain Jane hippie chick with hairy armpits."

"I see," I say, taking her lipstick from her. "So I'm supposed to go ungroomed because this guy you've picked out for me has a filth fetish?"

"Don't be so hostile. I'm only trying to help. When was the last time you got laid?"

"None of your business." I apply a coat of lipstick and hand the tube back to her.

"There's my answer," she says.

Watching Grady Berlin, I try to imagine that he likes his women dirty. He is almost eerily polished, himself. In spite of his slightly messy, crookedly cut hair and his stubble-shadowed cheeks, there's something too poised about him to pass for grubby. He and Arlan are sitting side by side, and I'm struck by their contrast. Arlan is somehow weatherworn; he reminds me of driftwood. He sips from his whiskey and Coke with a face that is sometimes bright-eyed, juvenile, and then suddenly goes ancient without any transition. Grady is cosmetically perfect—but he's not sexy, somehow. He doesn't have Arlan's complexity. He smells like soap and tells stories like he's rehearsed them in front of a mirror.

"Anna's from San Francisco," Lucy says to Grady. He and Arlan were talking about Felonious Monk, and the announcement is weirdly timed, but we've all had enough drinks to overlook the non sequitur.

"Really?" he says, and turns to me. I nod and sip my drink. "Which part?"

"I grew up near the Haight," I say.

"Wow!" he gushes. "That must have been wild. Are your parents total hippies?"

"Sort of. I don't know. Not anymore."

"How'd you end up in Bellingham?"

"I wanted to learn a trade," I say. "Or something. It's hard to explain."

"She's here to kill her Dad," Lucy says, giggling.

"Lucy!"

"What? Grady's cool. He'll understand."

"I had personal reasons for coming here," I say.

"Murder?" Grady suggests. He and Lucy laugh.

"So, did you get any more acting gigs in Argentina?" Arlan changes the subject and I look at him gratefully. Lucy and Grady laugh harder.

"Grady's going to be a Bolivian porn star," Lucy says, and rattles the ice in her glass. "They're going to make him fry doughnuts naked."

"You guys are never going to let me live that down." He leans back in his chair and addresses me with his eyes; I can see he is happy for a new audience member. "These two have heard this story—I regret the day I let it slip—but it's rude not to tell you, so I will. A couple years ago, I was visiting Bolivia, and some guy approached me in a market, talking up a storm. My Spanish wasn't very good, but I could get the gist of it—he wanted me at some audition." He takes a drag off Lucy's cigarette. "I did some acting in college," he says. "Nothing much. But I thought, 'Hey, here's my lucky break!' So I go to the 'audition.' God. It's in the back room of this absurd little pastry shop, and the first thing I see is this naked woman shaving her—you know, not her legs—"

"Cunt, pussy, beaver," Lucy chimes in. "You have to practice, Grady, just say it—"

"Anyway," he says, giving her a look, "needless to say, it wasn't exactly high art they were engaged in."

"So did you do it?" I ask.

"Jesus, no—talk about performance anxiety! They waved big bills around, and I considered it for about two seconds—I was flat broke—but I couldn't go through with it."

"Oh, come on," Lucy says. "It's so exotic! Arlan gets hard just hearing about it."

Arlan just flicks his cigarette at this.

Grady turns to me with a prim mouth, folding his hands in front of him like a schoolgirl. "They think I'm an exhibitionist, but I'm really very shy," he says unconvincingly.

"Yeah, right," Lucy says. "You're shy and I'm a virgin. You want to see shy, check out Anna. She blushes if you say her *name*, even." They all turn and look at me, and just like that, I feel myself going red. "See?" Lucy laughs, triumphant.

"God," Grady says, in a soft, mocking voice. "That's amazing. You could join the circus with that trick."

"Stop," I say, covering my face with my hands.

"Beet Woman," Lucy says.

"From female to vegetable in seconds!" Grady and Lucy join in mutually hysterical laughter. They tip their heads together drunkenly.

Arlan looks a little bit bored; his eyes move around the room slowly. I follow his gaze, trying to see what he sees. There's a jukebox flipping selections mechanically for a girl in a checkered halter top as she slips quarters into its slot. I study the fake wood paneling on the walls and the moose head watching us with dusty glass eyes. The aging waitress races from table to table, her face worn and angry. In the corner is a bent twig of a man, maybe sixty or so, drinking shots with soda chasers. Arlan's eyes catch on mine for a moment.

"We could use another round," he says, twisting in his seat to flag down the waitress as she flies past us.

★ ★ ★

It's two a.m., and everyone is looped. We're walking back toward the house, making slow progress. Lucy and Grady are singing a Patsy Cline song at the top of their lungs. Arlan's a couple of paces ahead of them, while I stay behind, watching their hair reflect the yellowish glow of the streetlights. The buoyancy of the gin I've consumed turned to gravity an hour ago. The bubbles of the tonic were lovely and sparkling when they were in my glass; now they just make me burp.

For some reason, I'm thinking of Roddy McNair, the quarterback I dated in high school for two weeks. He was physically flawless. He had that rare sort of skin that only got more enticing when he overheated; his cheeks turned ruddy in patches along his Slavic cheekbones, and sweat dripping from his hairline only made you want to press your palm flat against his forehead to feel the heat and moisture gathering there. He had a habit of sticking his fists under his T-shirt and rolling them against the fabric—it was a jock thing, and it made my pulse race every time he did it. I gave him my first blow job. I was awkward and timid, afraid I would hurt him or slobber too much. The penis amazed me, seen at such close range; the surface was nearly translucent, and the veins beneath were so blue. It seemed to me that nothing so naked should be allowed outside the body—it was an internal organ that had escaped, sheathed with only the flimsiest membrane of baby-soft skin.

"What are you thinking about?" Arlan is suddenly beside me.

"Nothing," I say. "Just—nothing."

Grady and Lucinda are still singing. *"I see a weeping willow, crying on his pillow, maybe he's crying for meeee..."* Lucinda stops walking and screams, "Wake up, you assholes!" She has her face turned to the dark windows of the brick apartment buildings lining the street. "We're all going to die!"

A man leans out from a pocket of light on the third story and yells, "Shut up, bitch!"

"Who're you telling to shut up, you cocksuck—"

Grady cups his hand over Lucinda's mouth and yanks her forward along the sidewalk. "Lucinda," Arlan says softly, shaking his head. He shoots me a sideways glance. "This isn't really your scene, is it?"

"What do you mean?"

"You drink slowly. You don't smoke. You don't blurt out every little thing that comes into your head."

"Anna!" Lucy screams as soon as Grady has removed his hand from her mouth. "This man is silencing me! I'm being oppressed!"

"Shut up, wench," Grady says. Lucy punches his arm, and he punches her back. She howls.

"I'm used to not fitting in," I say.

Lucy jumps on Grady's back and he falls over. They lie sprawled near the sidewalk, laughing up at the stars.

"That can be a good thing," Arlan says.

"It's mostly lonely."

"Yeah," he says. "I know."

When we get back to the house, I discover that Grady lives upstairs, in the apartment with the turret. Lucy tries to talk him into staying the night, but he says he's had enough of sleeping on floors and couches after three months on the road. One minute the four of us are out on the porch, and then suddenly Arlan and Lucy have disappeared, leaving me standing there with Grady in awkward silence.

"Well, good night," he says, backing away from me, and I see the steps behind him, but it's too late, he's already falling back, his face alive with surprise in the moonlight. He stumbles but somehow rights himself, landing on his feet on the third step, agile as a cat. "That's right," he says. "I meant to do that."

After he's gone, I collapse into one of the ugly porch chairs. I stare at the upstairs window of Gottlieb's; I was there, I think, and now I'm here. I remember the milkmaid wallpaper and the orange shag carpet. What a different world I live in now. I think of my beige apartment in San Francisco, my beige towels, the wool army blanket on my bed. I sit there, picking at the exposed foam on the arm of the chair, watching the moon. It's almost full, surrounded by a soft halo.

I realize now what made me think of Rodney McNair. Grady has that same look, with the same maddening quarterback confidence. He's the kind of boy I wanted in high school—someone I could go to the prom with and keep a photo of in my wallet. My mother would fawn over Grady; he's funny and slick, the human equivalent of her silver Fiat. If I dated him I'm sure she'd view it as a miraculous evolutionary leap—Derek is a one-celled organism compared to him. But when I try to think of Grady in a sexual way, my mind drifts stubbornly back to Arlan: his eyes catching mine in the Ranch Room; our conversation on the way home; the song he played when we couldn't sleep, so plaintive and lonely.

Lucy and I are lying side by side on the bed and she is smoking out the window. Arlan and Grady are out on the porch, playing guitar. Through the window, we can hear Arlan toning himself down for Grady's benefit, since Grady can do little more than strum a few chords. They finally find an old Elvis Presley tune they can both play, and now their voices are finding each other, Arlan's warm and confident, Grady's tentative and searching for the notes as he goes, pausing occasionally to laugh at himself: *"Don't be cruel to a heart that's true."*

"Grady likes you," Lucinda whispers.

"Oh, come on."

"We've been hanging out with Grady Berlin for years, okay? If he doesn't like you, he won't even sniff in your direction, *especially* if you're a woman." Before I can ask what this means, she goes on. "You're too good for him. If you want him, don't forget that. He has to think you have a secret brain tucked inside yourself somewhere—something he can never get to. When he touches you—"

"Whoa," I say. "I just met this—"

"Okay, forget about touching. When he fucks you, he has to believe there's a secret cunt hiding just behind the real one." I imagine multiple vaginas crowded together like a clump of sea anemones.

"That's the weirdest advice I've ever gotten."

"You've got to play your cards right."

"Lucinda. I'm not looking for any kind of—"

"Everyone needs a good fuck," she says. "Don't pretend you're any different. I'm just looking out for your best interest. Grady's obviously the only candidate. Sparky's got a dick the size of a peanut, Bill looks like a retarded rat, and Danny..." Her eyes narrow and she lowers her voice slightly. "Danny's the scum of the earth. I seriously suggest you consider him only as an act of complete desperation."

"You really hate him, don't you."

She exhales impatiently and squints at me. "Did I ever tell you how Arlan and I got together?" I shake my head. "I was with Danny. He's the one who introduced us. I can't believe I ever fucked that guy. Really. Turns my stomach." Her eyes dart to mine and then back out the window. "When he asked Arlan to be in this band, I did everything I could to stop him. But Arlan wanted to play. You can't stop him when he really wants something." She pauses and twists the silver ring on her pinky. "Pretty fucked-up situation, huh?"

"You seem to handle it all right."

"Yeah, well, I'm sick of handling it. I wish he'd just go

ahead and die." She runs her fingers through her hair, and the hard set of her jaw makes me think of her sister.

Later, the four of us go downtown and spend an hour or so wandering through a big used book store. I run into Arlan in the music section. He's looking at a Grateful Dead songbook. I tell him that my father built a couple of guitars for Jerry. Then I'm afraid he'll think I'm bragging, so I pull a book off the shelves—the first thing I see, a Simon and Garfunkel songbook, and say, "I really like these guys." I chatter on. "Did you know Art Garfunkel was an actor? He was in that movie—what was it called again? Based on a novel…"

"Catch 22?"

"Exactly!"

"That's one of my favorite flicks." We're speaking softly, hushed by the towering shelves of books. He smiles curiously and says, "Why are we whispering?"

There are certain moments you immobilize with memory, like an insect trapped midstruggle in a droplet of sap. With time, the image will harden and age into amber, movement turned forever motionless, entombed in hues of light. This is one of those moments; later, I will turn the picture over in my mind—the amusement in his eyes, the long dark strands of his hair, the column of sunlight streaming through the skylight above him, illuminating a cosmos of dust particles circulating slowly just above his head.

That night, back at the Land of Skin, we get stoned and try to figure out a recipe for lemon cookies, because Lucy has a craving. She, Grady and I are crowded into the small open kitchen, while Arlan sits on the couch with his guitar, accompanying our efforts.

"Let's see, we need lemons—Jesus, I've only got two—Grady, go outside and find us some more."

"Two's enough," Grady tells her authoritatively.

"Leemooons," Arlan sings. *"Got to have lemons, 'cause the sour in my heart just ain't enough."* He strums a couple more chords and then downs the shot of tequila balancing precariously on the arm of the couch.

Lucinda lights a cigarette and starts rummaging through the cupboards. "We need sugar!" she yells to no one in particular.

"Babe," Arlan says. "Don't smoke in the kitchen."

"I'll smoke where I want to smoke! Who are you, my mother?"

"I ain't your mother," Arlan sings, *"I ain't your brother. I'm just your man, sweet thing, your good-time lover."*

I'm about to slice one of the lemons with a big butcher knife when Grady cries, "Wait!" Everyone watches in stoned silence as he reaches over and carefully removes it from the cutting board. "You don't *slice* lemons. You *undress* them. Slowly." God. Grady's too much. He talks like he's auditioning for a porn flick twenty-four hours a day.

"What kind of fruity talk is that?" Arlan demands; he gets up to pour himself another shot.

We're all reasonably smashed when the first batch finally comes out of the oven. The near-empty bottle of tequila and the two joints may explain the runny, gelatinous mess jiggling on the cookie sheet. It is difficult, in such a state, to recall the importance of tiny, teaspoon-sized elements, like baking soda and baking powder. These are not the ingredients your tongue recalls, and so they're lost.

Grady bends over and sniffs at the steamy yellow ooze. Lucy does the same, then sticks her tongue out, catlike, and laps up a tiny bit.

"Ouch!" She recoils and covers her mouth with the back of her hand. "Fuck!"

Arlan puts his guitar down and joins the three of us. We all hover there, gazing at the liquefied mess with crispy edges.

We're transfixed. Lucy snaps out of it first. She orders Arlan to put ice on her tongue.

"I want ice on my tongue, too," I say.

"Arlan, give Anna some."

"No can do," Arlan says, not looking at me. "Only for the injured."

Lucy shows me the ice cube Arlan has just deposited tenderly into her mouth and says, "Come get it, baby!" She opens her mouth and sticks out her tongue, winks at me, says something incomprehensible, and gestures with her hands.

"You can't just go giving that shit away," Arlan scolds. "That there's medicine, child."

"That's right," Lucy tells me. Her eyes light up; she digs her lighter from the front pocket of her jeans and she takes a step toward me. "Come here, Anna," she says. "Earn your ice!" I laugh and take two steps in her direction, and suddenly we're standing so close to each other that I can smell the vanilla lotion she uses. She flips open the Zippo and rubs it alive with her thumb. She holds it up between our faces; I can see the flame glowing orange on the reflective surface of her eyes. "Come on," she whispers. "What are you afraid of? Open up."

"Did you guys ever read that William Carlos Williams story? About the doctor and the little girl—he has to force her mouth open?" Grady's voice sounds distant. "What was that called?"

"'The Use of Force,'" Lucy says, without moving her eyes from mine.

"Yeah!" Grady says. "Exactly. Huh. What a story."

I open my mouth and stick out my tongue. I can taste the heat of the flame, sharp and metallic, against the very tip.

"Hold it now, girls," Arlan says, employing a paternal tone. "Somebody's going to put a tongue out, if you're not careful."

I move my tongue even closer, my eyes locked on Lucy's. We're mesmerized by the flame. We're moths, I'm thinking. We'll do anything for light and heat.

Just as I am about to sizzle my tastebuds, the flame disappears.

"Good enough," Lucy says, snapping the Zippo closed. Then she stands on her toes and, never touching her lips to mine, deftly spits the ice cube into my mouth.

Mama—Mama, Please

I've been in Bellingham three weeks, and I have three hundred and eighty-five dollars left, with no prospects of making more. Tuesday afternoon I tell myself I'm just going for a walk, just getting out to breathe the scent of blackberries and trees, so I can clear my lungs of all that smoke. Underneath this pretense I know I'm headed straight for Bender's.

He doesn't look surprised to see me. He's sitting on his ice chest, carving a piece of driftwood with a pocketknife, and when I lace my fingers through the mesh of the gate, he just gets up without a word and lets me in, as if we've been meeting like this all our lives.

"What's shaking, Medina?"

"Nothing much," I say, following him back to his boat and accepting the chair he unfolds for me. The day is hot and a little humid; the air is filled with the scent of seaweed.

"You go see that prof, like I told you to?" he asks. I scoff. "What's that supposed to mean?"

"I did," I say. "But he wasn't too helpful."

"Why not?"

"All he did was name-drop and he practically pissed his pants when I corrected him on something—"

"He knows his shit—"

"He was talking about my *father*," I say, indignant.

"Did you tell him who you are?" I gaze at my lap. "You didn't, did you?"

"I didn't want to stoop to his level," I say.

"My, my," Bender says. "A bit righteous, aren't we?"

"Well, he was so insipid—I'm not a stool sample of my father's he can examine—" At this Bender throws back his head and roars with laughter. "I'm not," I repeat, sulking.

"No," he says, trying to be serious. "You're no stool sample, Medina. But you sure as hell remind me of Chet. That's just the sort of attitude he'd cop, I guarantee it." He goes back to his driftwood, carving slowly. There's a small pile of shavings at his feet.

"What are you making?"

"It's a portrait," he says.

"Oh yeah? Of who?"

He holds it up in the air, and I see that half a pelican is emerging from the pale, knotted fist of wood. It's so minutely crafted, I can even see individual feathers at the tip of its one finished wing. "Caliban!"

He nods and pulls it back, tucking his chin and letting his face return to the scowl of concentration. We sit there in silence for a few moments, with the sun beating down on us and the waves lapping at the sides of the boat listlessly.

"Am I really like my father?" I ask after a while.

He pauses in his carving but does not look up. He scowls at his pocketknife, poised above the beak, and says, "DNA doesn't lie." I watch as he uses tiny, meticulous movements to get the tip of the beak sharper. The knife slips, and abruptly a half-inch of scarlet blooms on his thumb. "Goddammit!" he snarls. He examines it briefly before sticking it in his mouth; the lines between his eyebrows deepen into sharp, hard grooves.

"You should be careful," I say.

"I'm careful," he growls. He takes the thumb from his mouth, shakes it twice and goes back to carving, ignoring the blood.

"You're getting blood on Cal," I say. He looks at me, and the force of his glare is enough to make me tuck my hands under my thighs nervously. "Well, you are."

"Thanks for the commentary, Medina."

We sit in silence for another few minutes. As I watch him carve, I try to find something familiar about him, some memory of his face from my childhood, but nothing comes to me.

"Do you remember me, from when I was little?"

"Sure." I wait for more, but he's silent.

"You hung out with my parents a lot?"

"All the time."

"Do you think my mom and dad were good together?"

He holds Caliban up close to his face and squints at him from different angles. "Good? Hell, I don't know, Medina. How should I know?"

"You were friends."

"People tend to drive each other crazy. Your mom and dad were no exception."

"Did you ever get married?" I ask, aware that I'm pushing my luck.

"Sure," he says. "Lady named Sheila."

"Where's she now?"

"Arizona."

"Alone?"

He looks at me and grins like someone posing reluctantly for a photo. "No. She left me years ago. Ran off with a real estate agent."

"You got any kids?"

He stops carving all of a sudden and flicks the knife closed. I can see where the blood has turned Caliban's head the color of rust. "What do you say we quit the inquisition, huh?" He gets up from the ice chest, rummages around inside it and fishes out a can of beer. He offers me one and I accept, though I despise Budweiser. The sun is hot and I'm thirsty and besides, I could use something to take the edge off this conversation.

"Listen," I say, after I've choked down half my beer and Bender's tipping back his second. "I don't want to keep bothering you. I just...I can't get it out of my head—about making guitars, I mean. Just tell me, seriously, what would it take to get you back in business?"

He studies me; his eyes are as glossy and blue as the bay. "I've got my tools in storage," he says. "But I'd need a shop. Materials. None of that comes cheap."

"Like, how much?"

"I don't know, Medina. Lots. Why, you loaded?"

I bite my lip. "No," I say.

"Well then, let's stop with the pipe dreams, okay?"

I don't answer. My chest feels heavy as I contemplate my three hundred and eighty-five dollars. The silence stretches on. The air has grown dense with the weird, dirty smell from the mill. I feel paralyzed, doomed. Bender must sense my mood. He does what he knows how to do: offers me another beer.

"No thanks," I say.

"Listen, Medina," he says, putting his beer down. "I'd like to give you a few things. I'd just as soon get them off my hands."

"What's that?"

"Hold on," he says, and disappears down the stairs. When he comes back, he's holding a rectangular brown bundle. He hands it to me. Looking at it more closely, I see that it's a stack of envelopes wrapped in a square of leather and tied with a length of twine. "Chet sent me these," he says. His hands drift to his hair. "I thought you might want them."

"What are they?" I ask, tracing the twine with one finger.

"Letters."

The word hangs on the air, and I feel my throat tighten. I touch the leather. It's old and scarred in places but still soft. The twine forms an intricate shape—some sort of sailor's knot, I guess. "Maybe he wouldn't want me to read them."

"Maybe not," Bender agrees.

I wait for him to say something else, but he just stands there, looking out at the water. "Then maybe I shouldn't," I say, my voice so quiet I can barely hear it myself.

"Up to you."

"If he wrote them to you—" I hold the bundle out toward him "—maybe you should keep—"

"Please," he says, closing his eyes. "Will you take them?"

I leave with the letters tucked under my arm, the worn leather touching the soft skin there. I read somewhere that's the softest skin on the body, that stretch between the armpit and the elbow. I walk slowly back to Smoke Palace as the heat of the day eases to a soft, humid sigh. The first breezes of evening press against my face, and the swallows, revived by the lengthening shadows, dart about in a frenzy, calling to each other in shrill, irritable chirps. I stop once and hold the letters up to my face, inhaling the rich scent of leather.

I used to have an incredible sense of smell before my father died. I remember as a child walking around our neighborhood convinced that I could smell the insides of houses—not just what they were cooking, but their carpets, the drapes, the people, even. The world became real to me through my nose. I was also an enthusiastic but intensely opinionated eater. My father used to joke that I was the only culinary snob in the world who hadn't yet graduated from junior high.

After he died, my sense of smell, and with it my sense of taste, went into hibernation. Throughout high school and most of college, well-meaning teachers and nervous relatives were perpetually hinting that I might be anorexic. It's true, I didn't eat much, but it wasn't out of vanity or compulsiveness so much as a sincere lack of interest. Everything tasted like dishwater—repugnant in its sameness. My mother, who once loved to spend hours cooking lavish, sensual meals, must have lost her culinary urges, too. I don't remember her preparing even one of her famous dinners after his funeral. We lived on what could be microwaved or warmed in a toaster.

I had a roommate my junior year in college, Natalie. She was obsessed with food. She was portly and homegrown, a girl who knew how to bake her own bread by the time she was seven. She used to fill our little apartment with the most luscious scents—fresh basil, crisp and green, paired with tomatoes that reeked of summer; oxtail soup; sizzling bacon; chocolate chip cookies so fragrant they made you dizzy with longing as soon as you walked in the door. I remember the year I lived with Natalie more clearly than the rest of my teens and early twenties combined. It wasn't that we were close, or having fabulous times together or anything. It was just that her cooking revived all the senses that had been dormant in my body for so long—the connection between the nose and the tongue that says, here it is—life—come and get it.

Colors seemed brighter that year, my clothing felt fluid or

itchy, tight or loose; I noticed the difference between when I was hot and when I was cold. All the sharp edges of life that had been lost on me for more than a decade started to announce themselves again. It was as if the smells Natalie exposed me to opened a floodgate, and all the rest of my senses came rushing out of their tomb.

But then Natalie was raped at a party in Pacific Heights, and she went home to Ohio. I never heard from her again. I went back to Top Ramen, mac and cheese, an occasional listless apple. And my senses, informed of the false alarm, went to sleep again.

As soon as I enter Smoke Palace, I know something is very wrong. There is chaos in the air—I catch the faint scent of vomit as I pass the bathroom. I can hear Lucy before I turn the corner into the living room.

"He's not— Danny—is he even breathing?" Her words tumble over one another like dominoes. I enter the living room in time to see her take a small mirror from her bag and prop it up in front of Danny's face, which is lying on the floor, looking more than a little gray. "I saw this in a movie," she announces, her eyes glowing. She watches intently. "It's not—he's not breathing!"

Arlan sees me and nods. He's in the kitchen, pouring himself a Jack and Coke. As I find my backpack and stuff the letters into it, Arlan crosses the room and sits in the chair by the window, where he can study Danny's face better. "Looks a little weird, doesn't he?"

"Anna!" Lucy says, crawling over to me. "He's not breathing! He's not!"

"What's going on?" I ask. The smell of vomit hits me again and I feel a little dizzy. "Something wrong with Danny?"

Lucy holds onto my legs and whimpers, "It's happening, Anna! I said he should die, now look! He's dead!"

I move into the room, closer to Danny. As I approach him, my head feels light and my shoes touching the popcorn-strewn carpet seem unreal. Across the street, one of the Goat Kids screams at the top of his lungs, then dissolves into laughter.

"Goddammit!" Lucy cries. "We got to get him to a hospital." She's drunk; her face is splotchy and red. "Jesus, Arlan! Get him out of here!"

"You're joking, right?" Bill says. "You're totally joking."

I move to touch Danny. He's wearing a tank top, and as I make contact with his bare shoulder, I shiver involuntarily. One arm flops to the carpet, and I see the track marks there—sickly bruises tracing the web of veins. I feel a faint tickling at the back of my throat, as if I might get sick, but I swallow hard and look at Arlan. "How long has he been—?"

"He's not breathing! I'm serious!" Lucy's huddled down close to Danny's head, holding the mirror up to his mouth again.

Arlan comes over and looks at the little mirror. "Fuck," he says. "Okay. God." He dashes into the bedroom. "Where are my keys? Luce? Where are my—?"

"I can drive," I say.

"We have to take him now!" Lucy yells. She slaps Danny's face desperately. "Wake up, stupid! Jesus!"

Arlan and Bill pick up Danny by his legs and arms awkwardly. They're both wasted. On the way to the truck, Bill leans over and pukes into the grass. Lucy keeps screaming, "Hurry up! Jesus! He's not breathing!" She keeps putting the mirror in front of his mouth frantically. I get into the truck and start it up. The cab only has room for three at the most.

"Arlan, you come," I say.

"No," Lucy says. "He's drunk. I'll go."

"I need someone to help me carry him in, though."

"I'll go," Arlan tells her.

"You assholes," she says. Her red, mottled face goes tight with anger and she kicks the front tire. "Go on, then!"

We drive to the hospital in a grim, sickly silence, broken only by Arlan's occasional "left here," or "right at that light." It feels like it takes forever to get there. Arlan props Danny up, but whenever I make a right turn, his arm slides toward me and the cool clamminess of Danny's skin makes me feel like I'm going to wretch. The sun is setting as we drag his long, limp body into the hospital, where nurses put him on a stretcher and wheel him off to a corner of the room shrouded in green curtains.

Later, a doctor with tiny spectacles and a smooth, moon-like face tells us if we'd waited any longer he'd have died, but I cannot tell if he's congratulating or scolding us. There's a grown man crying out, "Mama—mama, please!" from behind one of the curtains in a way that sets my teeth on edge. All I want is to get out of here, away from the smells of piss and disinfectant, away from the clinical faces and their matching, efficient hands—the overweight nurses with sad, dour faces, and the doctors, some of them jocular, some silent and corpselike themselves, moving around with clipboards, putting on and taking off their latex gloves.

As Arlan and I walk back to the truck in silence, one of the lights in the parking lot flickers and then goes out. We climb into the cab and sit there a moment, staring out the windshield.

"Jesus," he says finally, leaning his head against the window. "What a night."

"Yeah," I say. "You want to stop somewhere for a drink?"

"Better not. Lucinda was pretty worked up."

"Right," I say, feeling stupid. "Forget I asked."

There's a weathered pack of Camels on the old bamboo table between Grady and me. He picks it up, turns it over, and a single cigarette falls into his lap, slightly bent.

We're sitting on the porch back at Smoke Palace, watching the night grow black. Stars appear one by one. Occasionally, a bat swoops into our line of vision, a small wad of darkness jetting past. Upstairs, Lucy and Arlan are fighting. Their voices float through the open window now and then.

Grady fishes a book of matches from the pocket of his shorts and lights the salvaged cigarette. He exhales, and I watch the smoke as it twirls into thin, abstract shapes before us. "Smoke bother you?" he asks. I shake my head. He draws in his breath in a contemplative way before continuing with a thought he initiated five minutes ago. "Kerouac's good—so raw, such an anarchist, in his own way…." He taps the ashes from his cigarette off the arm of the chair.

"You just left me here!" Lucy screams. "You don't give a shit about—"

"He was going to die!"

"But you weren't thinking about—"

"You told me to go!" The window slams shut, and I'm glad not to hear the rest of it.

After a silence, Grady tries again. "You ever been to India?"

"Never," I say. I wonder silently if this is connected to Kerouac's anarchy. He's been doing this for a good forty minutes, now—moving in an irregular rhythm from one random thought to the next, like someone searching for a good song on the radio.

"Amazing place," he says. "Changed my life. Tremendous poverty, of course."

I can't forget the emergency room, the moon-faced doctor, Danny's arms lying limp and blackened like rotting fruit. I can still hear the man's voice from behind the curtain: *Mama—mama, please!*

Grady looks at me quizzically. "You okay?"

"Me? Yeah, why?"

"You seem a little out of it."

I shake my head. "Just tired."

"You want to rest in my apartment?" I shake my head. I'm too tired to determine if he's coming on to me. His lips close around the cigarette; he holds it European-style, between his index finger and his thumb. I imagine him practicing this for years before perfecting it. A bat darts into the trees. Somewhere above us, a TV is droning on at top volume.

The smell of the emergency room comes back to me, a ghost of an odor, and I feel queasy. "You sure you're okay?" he asks, when I touch my fingers to my forehead.

"Maybe I will lie down," I say. "It's been a long day."

"Sure. You should rest." But neither of us move.

After a while, he sighs, and an image of him at fifty flashes before me—he's wearing a tweed jacket and a wool beret. His face is lined with age but his eyes have the same alarming emptiness.

"I like Kerouac," he says quietly to the stars, almost to himself. "But he's got nothing on Marquez. Talk about *imagination*. That's anarchy, too—a world where anything can happen."

What the average citizen doesn't realize, the TV above us warns, *is that 72 percent of lethal*—but somebody changes the channel before the warning is complete, and a laugh track explodes into the night.

Boulevard Park

In the days that follow, Lucy is icy around me. She's cold to Arlan, too—in fact, the only person she likes is Grady. She's very chummy with him, insisting he take her out for ice cream or tacos and making it clear that we're not invited. Grady indulges her, but he rolls his eyes at us when she's not looking.

Thursday evening we get word that Danny has been released to his parents, who opt to store him in a rehab center in Victoria until he can regain composure. After Arlan tells us the news, Lucinda goes off on one of her classic tirades about people being addicted to drama and fostering hideous notions about victims and heroes and other "patriarchal asswipes." In the middle of her speech, she stops midsentence and stares at us accusingly. "You people wouldn't get it if I carved it into your foreheads." Then she disappears into the bedroom and sits in front of the computer, chain-smoking and pecking away at the keyboard all night.

A couple days later, the new issue of *Pulp* appears on the back of the toilet. I flip through it and a particular headline catches my eye: "Shirley Temple Alien Invades Bellingham." There's a blurry, black-and-white photo of Shirley Temple doctored with huge alien eyes and a UFO taking off behind her. The article that follows is short and to the point:

> Bellingham, WA — Experts now agree; the truck-driving, too-cute-for-words stranger that rolled into town last month is indeed a dangerous extraterrestrial. Don't be fooled by her innocent blond locks or her rosy cheeks. In a top-secret investigation, law enforcement officers revealed that she developed her alias after years of watching Shirley Temple reruns beamed via satellite to her homeland of Io, one of Jupiter's moons.
>
> In a recent interview following her arrest, the spacewoman confessed to her crimes: fraud, impersonation and entering the planet without a visa. She also revealed, after extensive torture, her mission. She was sent by Io's secret police to thrust Earth back into the patriarchal Stone Age in which Miss Temple thrived—to overthrow any feminist gains made in the last fifty years and return us to a black-and-white world where women are women, men are men, and little girls looking for Daddy are the ultimate seduction.

The writing isn't as good as her usual stuff—it's not very funny, and I can't see her audience being amused by such a stupid little jab. I wish I could leave it at that, dismiss it as just another of her antics, like Arlan and Grady always do. What little peace there is in Smoke Palace is maintained through the guys' ability to ignore Lucy's habitual tantrums.

Instead of laughing it off, though, I start to obsess. The whole Shirley Temple thing just gets under my skin. And that shit about "little girls looking for Daddy"—what is that supposed to mean? The more I think about it, the more it gets to me.

I knew from the beginning that Lucy wasn't exactly loyal, but I didn't expect her to turn on me over nothing. What did I do? I gave Danny a ride to the hospital when he was half-dead. Is that an act deserving of all this?

One morning I awake to find the house empty. I had another bout of insomnia last night, and when I finally fell asleep I spent those precious hours dreaming about Lucy tricking me into getting naked and then leaving me in all kinds of humiliating situations. As I survey the room from the couch, I decide I can't stand this dirty apartment another second. I get out the vacuum and go to work. I discover that cleaning only feeds my bad mood; I start slamming the old Hoover against chair legs and baseboards like it's a battering ram, tossing stray shirts and pillows out of my way with fervor. Outside, a thick fog is rolling inland from the bay, and there's a chill in the apartment, but by the time I'm finished with the living room I've broken out in a sweat. I move on to the bedroom. I'm so engrossed in my task, I don't even notice when Lucy comes home, and I jump when I see her in the doorway, watching me with an amused expression.

"What is this?" she says, as the vacuum whines into silence. "TaeBo housekeeping?"

I look at her there, so smug and in control. I'm overcome with an urge to slap her. "Why don't you just tell me to leave?"

"What?" Her expression loses its teasing easiness and looks suddenly defensive.

"You've obviously finished with my services. I was just here for your amusement, wasn't I."

"Jesus, Anna—what are you talking about?"

I wrap the cord of the Hoover in place with quick, violent movements. When I'm finished I brush past her and go to the living room, where I grab my pack and start stuffing my things inside. I had no idea I was going to do this, but now that I've started, I can't stop. She's still in the bedroom, which gives me a good excuse to yell. "You got me to move in because you didn't want to be alone. Now I bore you, so you're trying to get rid of me. What is all this shit about Shirley Temple, huh? You think I take pleasure in being humiliated?"

She appears in the living room doorway. "It was just a joke, Anna."

"It's not even funny! It's just a childish little outburst—it's not even well written! I can't believe you'd sink low enough to drag 'Daddy' into it. You don't know shit about my dad, okay?"

She folds her arms across her chest. "Look, I was only—"

"You don't know anything about me, because you never even asked!"

"Will you just—"

"You don't give a flying fuck about anyone except yourself. Arlan and Grady might humor you—they let you have your little queen bee routine—but everyone knows you're a self-absorbed little monster!"

"I am *not* a monster!"

She looks so enraged I half imagine she's going to charge. We stand there, eyes locked. Everything hangs in the balance for a good three seconds.

"Oh Jesus," she says finally, and she starts to laugh. "I can't believe I just said that." She walks to the freezer and pulls out a bottle of gin. "Okay, so I'm a monster. You want a drink or what?" When I don't answer, she gets me a glass anyway, sighing impatiently. "What? Don't look at me like that! Yes,

I'm a little spoiled. You want me to get down on my knees and beg forgiveness?"

"That might help." She looks at me, and I gesture toward the floor in front of me. "Go ahead. I'd love to see it."

"Don't push," she says, filling the glasses with ice, but her voice is gentle, almost pleading.

I sense the graceful thing to do is to let it lie, but I'm not quite ready. I'm still worked up. "What provoked this whole ice queen thing, anyway? What did I do?"

She contemplates the gin she's just poured, and for a second I think she's going to cry. She looks at me, tucks a strand of hair behind her ear, and says, very quietly, "Nothing. You didn't do anything."

"Then why have you been—?"

"Look," she says. "I spend most of my time around guys. I guess I just..." She shrugs and looks embarrassed. "I don't know how to act, sometimes."

I put my pack down, and the adrenaline starts to leave me slowly, like water slipping down a drain. "You seemed really pissed off at me...."

"I get like that sometimes. I don't mean to."

I sit on the couch. She finishes making our drinks and brings me mine. We sip them in silence. After a while, I say, "I've never really had a girlfriend, either."

She rattles the ice in her drink, not looking at me. "I guess we're a couple of freaks, huh?"

"I guess we are."

I'm terrified of my father's letters. They sit there in my backpack all the time, and whenever I think of them I get all agitated. I have to avoid sitting still for too long. Sometimes I want to devour every word ruthlessly like a starving dog, but more often I'm tempted to burn them. It's what I've been craving my whole life—something to shatter the numbing silence he left behind—but the thought of actually sitting down to read his thoughts in his own handwriting makes my throat tighten with alarm.

I go for long drives at all hours of the day and night. I sit on high cliffs and stare out over the water. I watch the mountains in the east and wonder what it is I expected to find in this green, rainy town that smells of pulp and ocean. Sometimes, at night, I walk around the neighborhoods and peer into windows as I pass by slowly, trying to catch glimpses of other people's lives. It's always been easy and soothing, fabricating strangers' troubles, making up their torrid affairs, their irrevocable mistakes, their suicides. But now I've got a chance to unravel the big myth—the legend of my own father—and I haven't got the nerve. Funny, how that works. I guess I'm big on imagining; the facts, sketchy as they are, have caused me nothing but pain.

I've been avoiding Bender for a few days. I just can't bring myself to visit him until I've read at least a few pages of the letters. I wouldn't know how to explain my paralysis before that soft little pouch of leather. What if I discover that my father and I think exactly alike? Or, and this might be worse, what if we're perfect strangers—what if it's like finding a filthy little piss-scented notepad on the bus and struggling through the ramblings of an incoherent derelict? Either way, it can't be good. If we're too much the same, then I'll know I've got that little seed of self-destruction in my genes, and it's only a matter of time before I come to a bad end. But if we're nothing alike, then I'm just as fatherless as ever.

Soon after Danny's overdose, Sparky moves back to Tacoma. I think he's lost without Danny to give him his cues. No one is too sad to see Sparky go—it sounds cruel, but it's true. He's the sort of person you barely notice. Even on stage, he was just the bald head sealed within his semicircle of shining gold drums, and in social situations he just continued to slap at things with his hands or utensils, hammering out irritating, machine-gun rhythms instead of engaging in conversation. He leaves town with minimal fanfare—stops by for a quick, awkward goodbye, pays Arlan the forty bucks he owed him, then drives off in his VW bug with a couple of drums strapped to the roof, glinting in the morning sunlight. We watch until he heads left for the freeway and out of sight, then return to the task of drinking more coffee.

The same day, we go to Boulevard Park for a summer solstice festival. The manicured lawn stretches north and south along the bay, and there's a big, yellow banner hanging from the two largest elms that reads, Bellingham Sol-Fest: May the Sun Be with You. The world has suddenly peopled itself with the hippies of the new millennium, all of them twenty years old, pink-cheeked, sprouting hair in profusion and wearing corduroys under their sundresses, long johns under their shorts.

Even I have gone a little bit native today. I've replaced my usual off-white-T-shirt-and-jeans uniform with one of Lucy's dresses, a sleeveless red shift made of fabric so thin and fluid it feels like liquid against my skin. She shoved it at me this morning, insisting that my addiction to off-white is getting nauseating. Then she smiled her sly grin at me, the one I've come to recognize as a plea for forgiveness and a challenge wrapped into one.

It's the hottest day we've had since I got here, and it produces a kind of delirium in the town. The blue skies force people out of their houses in bewildered hordes, and the trees glow a hundred shades of green. The flowers are so bright they look like they belong in those grainy 3-D postcards, and the earth itself seems to hum.

The sun is on me like a huge, gentle hand, pressing me deeper into the grass. I'm lying on my back, eyes closed; pinwheels of orange and blue ignite against my eyelids. I hike up Lucy's red dress a little above my knees, and let the sun press there, too, against the very beginnings of my thighs. I doze off for a little while, dreaming of tropical-colored insects.

When I awake, Lucy's saying something excitedly to Grady, Arlan and Bill; she's crouching in the grass like a cat about to pounce. "What are you, cowards? Of course you can do it! Who's going to stop you?"

"It's not that easy," Bill's saying, his voice reaching into the nasal registers. Lucy's description of him as a retarded rat is mean but not inaccurate—he really does look a bit damaged and rodentlike. "We'd have to write new songs, for one thing."

"Arlan has enough songs to keep you busy for years!" Everyone looks at Arlan, who is lying back on the old quilt we brought, propped up on one elbow, gazing out at the water. He's got on the suede cowboy hat he was wearing the day the Gibson got smashed. "Tell them," Lucy urges. "You do, don't you?"

He nods. "I've got some songs."

"And they're *good,* you guys—they're, like, really fucking good."

Arlan chuckles. "Who are you?" he says, still addressing the water. "My agent?"

"Arlan, you know what I'm talking about! It's not this bullshit how-fast-can-we-go adolescent angst, like Danny—your music's got soul. You'd blow Honkey Dory out of the water! The only reason people around here put up with that crap's because it's better than listening to self-absorbed dicks like Danny whack off with their guitars."

"Even so," Bill says, "we can't do it with just me and Arlan. We'd need a drummer, at least."

"Exactly," Lucy says. "That's where Grady comes in."

"Oh, now, wait a minute!" Grady says, holding up one hand. "I'm not a drummer."

"You are too!" she says. "You played in college!"

Arlan's smiling at him. "Berlin! I didn't know that."

"In a really, really, really bad band, okay? For, like, one summer. It was more a joke than anything. Jesus, Lucy, when did I tell you that?"

"Anyone can play the drums," Lucy tells him. "If you won't do it, *I* will!"

"The drummer's crucial—if he's off, the whole band's—" Grady protests, but Lucy won't hear of it.

"Yeah, whatever," she snaps. "I know you want to do it, okay, so cut it out. I'm on your side, for once."

A toddler tears wildly across the lawn, her legs wobbling like a colt's, her mouth stretching wide to release a scream as loud and piercing as a siren. She's headed straight for Arlan, and before he can stop her, she's tumbled directly into his lap, her chubby legs going limp upon impact. Her round blue eyes look up at him in surprise. Arlan says, "Hey there, wild thing." Her face contorts and she starts to cry; her father appears, scoops her up and carries her off on his shoulders. Arlan follows the girl with his eyes.

Lucy, who considers babies to be the blight of the earth, shakes her head in disgust and lights a cigarette. "So you'll do it, right?" she says, looking at each one of them in turn. Nobody says a thing. There's a guy playing REM songs on a makeshift stage near the bathrooms, competing with a boom box that a pack of junior-high kids are gathered around, bobbing their heads to the two and four of rap. "How could you not? It's the chance of a lifetime."

Arlan and Bill look at each other. Bill shrugs. Arlan turns to Grady. "Would you want to give it a try, man?"

Grady gives him a shy smile. "Shit, I don't know," he says. "Maybe."

Bill says, doubtfully, "What about Danny?"

Lucy blows through her lips like this is the most ludicrous

question she's ever heard. Still, it lingers there, unanswered, until at last Arlan leans back on his elbows again and says, "What about him?"

Grady, it seems, is most at home several stories above the ground. He makes his living trimming trees—selecting which branches have to go, which have to stay. He says his customers are mostly rich people who like to hear him go on about the various plagues and virtues of local flora. He admits it is the perfect profession for someone who refuses to grow up.

At the moment, he is making his way higher in a towering fir, and he is no larger than my thumb. Arlan and Bill have just volunteered to go get food—I can see the tail end of Arlan's station wagon pulling out of the parking lot. Lucy and I are alone for the first time in days, lounging on the quilt as the sun pulls higher in the sky. I can see the white shoulders of the festival-goers starting to roast into painful pinks. A group of skinny-legged, squealing girls are waging all-out war against each other with water balloons. Their supply must be endless, because it's been going on for hours, and they just keep producing the ponderous shapes, heaving the blobs at their friends' screaming faces. They swear revenge, make and break alliances, laugh so hard that their twiggy, flat-chested bodies contort violently.

"Do you have money?" Lucy asks. She's hugging her knees, looking at me. Her skin glows along the ridge of her shins.

"On me?"

"No, what are you living on? Inheritance?"

"Oh," I say. "No. I—I have a few hundred dollars left. That's it."

She considers this for a moment, then starts rubbing coconut oil onto her legs, making them even shinier. "Me and

Arlan are about to be broke," she says. "His trust fund's drying up. Did you know he had one?" I shake my head. "Anyway, it's almost gone. He doesn't make that much painting...." She sniffs at the bottle of oil and makes a face. "This shit reeks of junior high. Oh well. I need to fry—I'm way too white." She finishes applying the oil and looks at me again. "I think I can get us some money. All of us, I mean." She pauses.

"Yeah? How?"

"I've still got to work out the details," she says, looking off into the distance. "I'll tell you soon, though." She slides a strand of hair behind her ear. Her ears are tiny and delicate, like translucent seashells. She takes out her lipstick and applies it carelessly. "It's crazy, the way things turn out. Grady's got a degree from Yale. What does he do? Yard work! Arlan's got a B.A., and he paints houses. Everyone I know went to college, and nobody uses it. Man, if I went to college, I sure as hell wouldn't do manual labor."

"How come you don't?" I ask.

"Go to college?" She shrugs. "No money, I guess."

"There are scholarships."

She looks at me sideways. "I'm not good at kissing ass."

"Do you want to go?"

She hugs her legs tighter and turns her face toward me again, resting her cheek on one knee. For a moment, she just looks at me, blinking. "Yeah," she says, finally.

"Then you should!" I say, sitting up.

"I don't know." Two tiny lines appear between her eyebrows. "I'm not good at paperwork. Aren't there, like...applications?"

"Sure," I say. "But it's not that hard. You put out your own magazine—you can handle a couple forms!"

She lifts her face from her knees and the very beginnings of hope are visible in her eyes. "You really think I'd get in?"

"Sure I do. Of course! If you wanted to, you could start

at a community college and—" Her head flops back down. "What's wrong?"

"So I'm smart enough for a stupid people's school, you mean...."

"Stupid people's school?" I echo.

"My sister's been going to Seattle City College for five years—where's it gotten her? She's more stupid than when she started."

"But a lot of people start at community—"

"No way," she says. "I'd rather slit my wrists."

"Okay," I say, changing tack. "You wouldn't have to start there. You could apply directly to a university. It's more expensive that way, but you'd probably get scholarships and you could definitely get loans." She looks skeptical, but I press on. "Well, why not? Where would you want to go?"

"Yale, Harvard or Stanford."

She's obviously given it plenty of thought. I smile. "Only the best, huh?" Her dark eyes are fastened on me now, not even blinking, and I choose my words carefully. "You might want to have a couple backups," I say. "Those are pretty competitive."

"See?" she says. "I can't do it."

"Don't get like that. All I'm saying is, you'd have your first choice and a couple second choices. Everyone does it like that." She keeps looking at me with that serious gaze, devouring my face with the unblinking intensity of a child, and then she releases her legs and flops out flat on her back.

"I don't know," she says. "It'd kill me if I didn't get in."

"You could always re-apply, if you didn't."

She stares up at the sky, her eyes wary. "I don't like to fuck up," she says, more to herself than to me.

"You could do it," I say, and it seems suddenly urgent that she apply—urgent, too, that I help her. "What about Arlan?" I say. "Would he like the idea?"

Her brow furrows. "I don't know if he'd want to leave Bellingham. Who knows? I might not even want him anymore." She shoots me a sly look. "You could have him, maybe."

"Stop," I say, staring at my lap.

"Yo yo yo!" I look up to see Bill lumbering toward us with a bag of groceries in one hand, announcing his arrival loudly. Arlan's right behind him, balancing the cooler on his shoulder.

Lucy sits up quickly, sees them coming and warns, "Don't tell *anyone*."

I nod, and she goes back to her limp pose on the blanket, arms and legs stretched out carelessly. I watch her there, lying with her eyes closed, her hair splayed out against the quilt, dark and hectic. I think of all the mysterious tensions at work behind those delicate eyelids. Is she flipping through images of her red-haired sister, now, or is it herself she sees, striding through plush green lawns, surrounded by ivy-covered buildings? I feel a curious surge of maternal warmth—an urge to guide her.

Arlan hands me a bottle of water; it catches the light against its curve of plastic. I look at it a moment before I touch it. I follow the line of the bottle to his hand, his arm, his face—the smooth, dark cheeks, those eyes—and I want him so much I feel sick. "Thanks," I murmur, and press the bottle against my cheek, needing the cold of it.

That night, I call Rosie. I don't plan on it, I just find myself picking up the phone and dialing. As soon as I've punched in the final digit, it's too late to hang up, so I sit there and wait for her husky voice to materialize.

Outside, Lucy, Arlan and Grady are playing guitar and singing on the porch. I can hear them through the open window, can smell the smoke from their cigarettes mixing with the perfume of freshly mowed grass and the dew collecting in the trees.

Rosie answers on the fourth ring: "Mmm?"

The clock on the microwave reads 11:23. "Rosie? It's me, Anna."

There's a pause, then there's the clunking sound of the phone hitting furniture before she picks up again and says, "Yes?"

"Should I call back tomorrow?"

"Kitten?"

"Yeah—sorry I woke—"

"Kitten, my love. Listen to you. You're alive." I picture her snuggling back into her zebra-striped sheets, adjusting her sleeping mask to reclaim pure darkness. "Is everything okay?"

"Pretty okay."

"The truck's still running?"

"Yeah. Thanks again for—"

"Did you find Elliot?"

"Um, yeah," I say, twisting the curly phone cord around my finger until the tip turns red and then blue.

"And…?"

"Well, he's doing okay," I say. I haven't planned an answer for this. I pull the phone cord tighter around my finger.

"So you're having a good time?" Her voice, perked up momentarily by surprise, shifts back into a dull sleepiness now. "Bellingham's not too boring?" She yawns.

"It's interesting," I say. "It rains a lot."

"Listen, kitten," she says. "There's something I need to tell you."

I unwrap my blue finger from the cord carefully, like a doctor undressing a wound. Her voice, my heart speeding up, the smell of summer out the window, reminds me of the day she told me about Dad. I used to walk to his shop after gymnastics on Tuesdays. It was late July, oppressively hot, and my sweater was knotted around my waist. I remember I had a leotard on that bothered me—the armholes were tight and scratchy. When I got to the shop, the sign in the window said, Sorry, We're Closed. Then there was Rosie's big-haired head instead of my dad's lean yogi face, peering through the glass. *"Listen, kitten,"* she said, once she'd opened the door and squatted down to hug me—more a grip, really, than a hug. She was clutching at me, as if she were losing her balance. *"There's something I need to tell you...."*

I blink myself back to the kitchen of Smoke Palace. I'm surprised to discover there are tears stinging at my eyes.

"You still there?" Rosie asks. I make a noise of assent. "It's your mom—she's totally strung out with worry—you know how she gets. I've told her you're all right, but she keeps digging at me for particulars. Do you want to talk to her?"

"Is she *there?*" I ask, panicky.

"No, of course not! I mean, do you want to call her? Let her know you're okay?" I'm silent. "She's smoking two packs a day, and she won't eat a thing."

"You think I should call?"

She sighs. "Oh, kitten, I don't know. Helen can just snap out of it, but—Muumuu, Mommy will *beat* you if you get up here again!" Muumuu is Aunt Rosie's Great Dane, and they're engaged in a ten-year war over who gets the bed. "On the other hand, she just keeps getting worse. She's missing work, and you know how she loves that silly job." During my mother's thirteen years in computers, she's only called in sick four times. She'll proudly repeat this to anyone with ears. Given her fanatical attendance record, the idea of her screwing that up is more alarming than the two packs a day.

"That does sound serious."

"I know she's a pain in the ass, baby doll, but she sure loves you. Sometimes I think that's the problem."

"What do you mean?" I hold the phone tighter, pressing it to my ear. I'm surprised by how much I need to hear this.

"She loves you so much, she can't let go."

I try to picture myself calling Mom from this kitchen, looking out these windows at the Goat Kid Hovel, smelling this damp-fog, old-smoke smell. But my life here is so far from her; it's so fantastically different from the decade I spent alone with her, pretending that my father never was.

Rosie yawns again, loudly, into the phone.

"I'll let you go back to sleep," I say.

"No, no, I'm just…" she protests, but trails off.

"You're falling asleep on me," I say.

"Are you going to call her?"

"Soon," I say vaguely. "Tell her I'm fine."

"Okay," she says. "Take care, kitten."

I place the phone back in its cradle. The sight of it there, with its mustard-yellow plastic faintly glowing in the light of the kitchen, makes me feel hollow inside. *Ain't no use, calling out my name now,* they're singing on the porch, *like you never did before.* My father used to love Bob Dylan; I wonder if he can hear them now. Maybe there's some part of him gathering in the dew, nestling into the freshly mowed grass, or maybe he's stretched across the wings of a bat, sweeping across the stars.

I think of my mother, her mouth haloed with tiny, intricate lines as she tightens her lips around a fresh cigarette. She must wonder where we've all gone—the people who used to consume her days. I can see her there, sitting in her kitchen, and the image is startling in its clarity, as if I'm viewing it through binoculars. She's just laid a pen down on a half-finished crossword puzzle, and now she's using her thumb to scratch a flame from her pink plastic lighter, touching it lightly to her Virginia Slim. The TV babbles on, preaching, seducing and threatening. Her hair is slightly squashed on one side. She's wearing her pale yellow bath-robe—the one I gave her—and her eyes look hollow, unlived in, as she flicks a few tiny tobacco leaves from her sleeve. She leans her head to one side, pulling a little at her hair, not primping, just feeling, absently, and then she exhales one long, snaking plume of smoke into the sad bluish light. The ashtray's erupting with butts, sprouting white stalks, a garden of tiny, pale bones.

The Skins

January 3rd, 1968
Einstein,

Went to see flamenco last night. Whoa, man. You would have tripped on this scene, I'm telling you. Lady moved like an animal—all color and blur—like some wild, tropical bird showing off her feathers. Can you see it? Moon rising over the courtyard, everyone just stuck to their seats, eyes glued to the magnificent flying skirts of this woman. It's trite but true: wish you were here.

After, I talked to the cat playing guitar, a real virtuoso, I mean REALLY. Those fingers were moving so fast, my head was spinning. Found out he was playing an Enrique Garcia. Pretty fine piece of work. He said something about Segovia, but his English wasn't too hot, so I never did quite catch his drift. I wanted to run my hands all over that guitar, but the guy looked a little scary (picture a Spanish Boris Karloff with a limp) so I maintained my cool and stuffed my hands in my pockets. You know I always get too excited.

España—España!

I don't mind telling you I might never come back. The women here look a lot like Aida. They dress up all the time, like she did, wear perfume and jewelry even when they're just going to the market. I love their gleaming hair and their sealed-up faces. I'd like to write a song for every one of them. In the afternoons everything closes and everyone has a big meal, drinks some wine and falls asleep. It's my fantasy! I love to dream through the afternoon, wake up with excitement in my chest, and go out into the world as evening is just dimming the sky. They call the natives in Madrid *los gatos* because they sleep in the day and go out all night. It's my city.

I met a girl in Paris named Virgo. I don't have to tell you, writing that sentence gives me a thrill. Virgo—can you believe it? She's from Greenwich Village, and she's got legs up to here (try to imagine—I know, I know!). She says she's a model and I half believe it, though she doesn't have a dime. We took the train to Italy and things got a little—how do you say?—out of control. The Village must be pretty kinky, because this chick wasn't pulling any punches. Man. I spent more than I should and I smoked enough hash to do me in, but she smoked twice as much, I swear. If everyone from the Big Apple's like Virgo, I want a bite.

Say hello to your folks, man. Did you get the new Dylan album? I can't find it here.

I'm telling you now: beg, borrow or steal to get over here and we'll have a party to remember.

Keep it real,

Chet

March 31st, 1968

Einstein,

Blackest day. I've got a headache so treacherous I want to die. No, I'm not hungover from wild nights of Stolies and sex with Danish blondes (is that all you ever think about?). Just a regular old mundane head cold.

Don't worry about Rot Gut. He'll be fine. I've never written that name before. Maybe it's Rott Gutt? Looks more like him that way. He'll never stop making guitars. I don't care if his liver shrinks to the size of a pea, that old bastard's never going to lay down the tools, so stop worrying. Just tell him to lay off the hard stuff for a while. He won't listen—he never does. Tell him anyway.

Virgo Banfield. Oh my God. If only you could see the way she walks into a room, with her amazing breasts caught in a tight, teasing bodice, her legs so long you think they'll never end. She's so regal and wanton all at once. She makes my cock ache, just looking at her. I swear I could eat her for breakfast, lunch and dinner.

I know I'm supposed to be playing the field, sewing my wild oats in this vast, fertile continent, but what can I say, brother? I'm in love with a girl from New York City—do wop do wop ad nauseam, etc. Her parents play bridge with Paul from Peter, Paul and Mary—did I tell you that already? She grew up on a steady diet of Chuck Berry and Chet Atkins. That's how I convinced her to go out with me—my name. Thank you, Mother, may you rest in peace, for your wonderful, wonderful taste. I know I must be boring you by now, but this girl, man. Mmm. She's like no other.

I'm going to ask her to marry me. I'm taking her to this little Danish village and I'm going to weave flowers in her hair, get her good and stoned, then pop the question. I'm terrified, so wish me luck. Oh man. Oh man oh man oh man.

Think of me next weekend. She's supposed to arrive here in Copenhagen on Friday. If all goes well, I'll marry her Sunday morning at a little country church. So we don't speak the language. Who cares? I do is I do, no matter what country you say it in.

My head is pounding like it's wedged between an iron block and a sledgehammer, and I've never felt so alive.

What a bastard I am. I haven't even mentioned your cousin. That's a G.D. pity, Einstein. I mean, even though you weren't that close, it's got to mess you up a little. What a ridiculous situation we've got ourselves into over there in Vietnam. Stay in school, man. As far as Uncle Sam's concerned, I'm still in, otherwise my number would be up by now. Those sorry bastards—what do the pols think they're up to this time? So glad I'm away from our mad, reckless country right now. But the point is, I'm sorry about John and I hope you won't take it the wrong way when I say it's a wasted life and a shame. I'm afraid the red, white and blue is barking up the wrong tree this time.

Keep it as close to yourself as you can,
Chet

"Here. Take them back," I say, thrusting the bundle of letters at Bender. It is eight o'clock in the morning and he is barely awake, but I am bristling with rage. The boat still rocks slightly from my furious entrance.

"I can't do that." He isn't looking at me.

"Who do you think you are?"

"All right," he says. "Come on, Medina, calm down."

"As if I'd want this schlock! Why in the world would I—"

"I can make tea," Bender says, quietly.

"What?"

"Tea," he says. "Would you like some?"

"Don't patronize," I say, my voice dangerous.

"Or coffee," he says. "But you seem like the tea type."

"Okay. Fine. Make tea."

He comes back with the folding chair and a steaming tin cup. He hands me the cup and struggles a moment with the chair. I can see by the particularly insane state of his hair, the crushed-pillow pattern etched into one check, and the inefficiency of his movements that he is still half dreaming. Possibly he is already drunk, too, or still drunk from last night. He sits on the ice chest, leans his elbows against his knees, and gazes at his hands.

"Go on," he mumbles. "You were saying...?"

His half-bored tone enrages me. "When's the last time you read these?"

"I don't know," he says, shrugging. "I take them out now and then."

"Who is this Virgo person?" I hadn't meant to ask, don't want to know, but there it is, a question already formed.

"Look," he says. "Chet was just a man."

"Just a man! Fine! But if you think I want to read his pornographic descriptions of some hippie chick named after an astrological—"

"What's the big deal? He met her in his twenties, when he was traveling. He wanted to marry her, but she died. I don't see what you're getting so upset about."

This stops me. "She died?"

"You didn't get very far in those letters, did you." I can feel my face heating up with embarrassment. "He knew her long before he even met your mom, if that's what you're so worked up about." He sighs, finally looks at me, and I am startled again by the blue of his eyes. "Lots of men have them, you know. Fantasy women. Your dad was like that with Virgo—he made her up, in a way."

I think of all the hours I've spent caressing Arlan's perfect shoulders, kissing his neck in my mind. I wonder if that's how my father was with Virgo. "I thought—I don't know. I just never pictured him with anyone but my mom."

"Chet was with Helen, after Virgo. He was with her, and he wasn't always happy, but that wasn't their fault, you know—things just happen—" his voice goes on, searching, lost "—like things you don't plan on or want or know you need until they're right there in front of you." He seems confused.

"What's your point?"

He stands up and shoves both hands into his pockets. "Lots of men have problems," he says, "with sex, and family, things like that. Men aren't like women. It's hard to explain."

"Look," I say. "I'm twenty-five. I don't need the birds and bees talk."

He opens the ice chest, looks for a beer, finds none, curses, spits, sits back down. "There's things in those letters you won't like, Medina. I can't help that."

"Like what?" My throat feels tight, and the words come out small and dry.

"A man wrote them, not God—just a regular guy trying to make sense of things. Maybe you're not ready for that."

"Then why'd you give them to me?"

"I figured they were yours."

"It's not like I'm some little girl who figures her daddy's perf—"

"You didn't get past the first couple letters, did you?"

"So? I had a couple questions! I mean you gave them to me without even a word of explanation!"

"Chet should speak for himself." There's a brief silence, and then Bender takes the letters from me. "Or maybe you're right," he says casually. "Maybe I should just keep them."

"What do you mean?"

"You're not ready for them." He runs his rough, hairy hand over the smooth leather, picks at the twine absently. "Are you?"

"I don't know," I say, petulant.

He gets up, letters in hand, and walks away from me. He's messing with something near the stern, but his back is to me, so I can't see much. "If you were ready, you wouldn't have come storming in here at the crack of dawn."

"I told you," I say. "I had some questions."

"What's wrong? Can't old men be young, once?"

This I don't answer. Something is getting away from me, here.

"You're not ready for these, and I'm tired of reading them at three o'clock in the morning. They're not doing anyone any good." There's a splash, and Bender brushes his hands together a couple of times.

It takes me a moment to understand—the letters. Gone. Heart pounding in my ears, I envision the ink bleeding into salt water, pages turning rapidly bloated, swollen, like a drowned corpse.

Before I can stop myself, I'm diving overboard. The cold swallows me with numbing force. I find myself fighting buoyancy, kicking hard for the murky, dark shape that floats easily down, twisting as it goes. I'm right behind it, arms outstretched, fingers straining, but it's sinking faster than I can, and in a moment it's dropped out of sight. I feel my lungs tightening. Air—need air—a glance at the surface tells me I'll have to kick hard to get there. My lips purse against the urge to open and gasp; I keep my eyes on the shimmer of light above, the pale blue sky gone wavy and distorted. I break the surface just in time to suck at the air madly.

Bender's smile is so big, it takes up half his face. "Guess you *are* ready," he says, and laughs so hard he has to lean on his knees for a moment.

"What the hell!" I sputter. "They're gone!"

Magically, he produces the bundle of letters and holds it aloft, his eyes bright with amusement. I stare, uncomprehending, blinking the salty water from my eyes. "That was a bottle of motor oil," he says. Then he laughs some more.

"You actually enjoy this," I say, as he helps me back on board.

"Enjoy what?"

"Humiliating me."

He hands me a towel; it's a greasy, suspicious-looking thing, stained in rust-colored stripes. "Not at all," he says, still looking like he's having the time of his life. "Hurts me more than it hurts you."

When I leave Bender's I'm still damp and shivery, too pensive to go back to Smoke Palace. I get in the truck and drive south, through Fairhaven, onto Chukanut Drive, down the coast, watching as the islands appear for brief moments through the thick lining of trees. The air coming through the window smells like morning and water, sunlight and distant fog. I think of Bender and my father as they must have been: young, handsome, a little unkempt, with intense eyes and messy hair, trading insights on Dylan LPs and carving techniques.

I remember, without meaning to, the day of my father's funeral. It was a small service, attended by a ragtag group of hippies who quoted Kahlil Gibran and Leonard Cohen in their speeches. When we came home, my mother went into her room without a word and shut the door. I wandered into the kitchen, and I saw my father's favorite coffee cup sitting on the counter. I picked it up. There were a couple inches of cold black coffee in it. I couldn't decide whether to dump it down the sink or not. For a split second, I considered throwing it against the wall with all my might, watching the black inside splatter into an inky pattern on the white wall. But I didn't; I knew it was too precious to waste. Two days ago he had been drinking from this cup, and if this coffee disappeared down the drain, then that much more of him was gone.

I took the cup to my room, coffee and all, and hid it under my bed until the inside grew so moldy it repulsed me just to look at it. On the day my mother took all his things to the Goodwill, I buried that mug in the backyard, memorizing the exact spot. I knew that to keep such a precious artifact above ground was to risk losing it entirely.

The bundle of letters are sitting on the seat beside me, and I vow to read at least a couple more before the morning is through. Instead, I drive and drive, turning from one strand of country road to the next. I pass a rotting barn being devoured by morning glories. The world spreads out before my windshield: green fields, rolling hills, snow-tipped mountains in the distance. The sun crawls higher, and the air warms so much that by ten, I've rolled down my windows all the way, letting the gusty breezes toss my hair. It seems I can smell the snow on the mountains, and the espresso beans roasting in town; I can smell the islands out in the Sound overflowing with pine and cypress and wildflowers. Under it all is one constant, though: the smell of leather, as persistent and familiar now as the smell of my own skin.

It doesn't take long for Arlan's band to take shape. When I get back from my hours of driving that afternoon, they've just finished practicing for the fifth time this week, and are cracking open beers, looking smug and sweaty. Grady, it turns out, scored a secondhand drum kit right away. Lucy tells me he's not exactly good, but he's not miserable, either. According to her, Arlan's songs are so filled with genius they're impossible to screw up. I haven't heard them yet. Most of their rehearsals have been out at Bill's mom's, since she's been out of town; today's the first time they've played Smoke Palace.

Arlan looks up from latching his guitar case; he's got a pinkish tinge to his cheeks. Sometimes he reminds me of those old sepia-toned photos of Indians—dark and brooding. But today he looks satisfied and radiant.

"Aaaanna!" Bill, who is still wearing his bass, serenades me to the tune of *Roxanne*, plucking out the bass line and wailing plaintively. *"You don't have to turn on the red light!"*

"Anna?" Lucy calls from the bedroom. I back down the hall and poke my head in.

"Yeah?" She's seated before their ancient computer, stabbing at the keyboard in a furious rhythm. "Would you get me more smokes? Arlan's got them." Beside her, an empty Chinese food carton is bursting with butts.

"Sure, princess." I take the disgusting carton-turned-ashtray from her and head for the kitchen.

"Oh—and maybe a gin tonic?" she adds, still transfixed by the screen. "I need some inspiration." She's wearing Arlan's old boxers, hopelessly large and droopy on her, the elastic sagging around her waist. An ancient white tank top, also several sizes too big for her, keeps falling off one shoulder as she types.

"Coming right up."

In the kitchen I take the bottle of Seagram's from the freezer and fill the better part of a mason jar with ice, then gin, noting the viscosity as it snakes its way around the glistening cubes. Liquor just wasn't a part of my world until this summer, and I still regard it with a wary respect. "Arlan. Lucy needs more smokes." He fishes a pack from his shirt pocket and tosses it to me. I lay the Camels on the counter as I slice a lime and watch with pleasure as it fizzes among the ice cubes and tonic.

I move past the boys and carry the mason jar back to Lucy.

"Cigarettes?" she says, when I hand her the glass.

"Shit. I forgot." I go back to the kitchen and retrieve the pack I left on the counter. Grady is messing with Arlan's harmonica, sliding up and down the scale randomly. Bill stands at the window, trying to strike up something with a couple of girls down on the sidewalk by leaning halfway out the window and hollering, "You girls want some candy?" Arlan's gathering bottles, and when we have to scoot past one another in the kitchen, his arm brushes lightly against mine.

The printer is grunting and groaning while Lucy hovers near it, sipping her drink. Without turning toward me, she holds her hand out and takes the cigarettes. When the printer falls silent again, she pulls the paper from the tray, lays down on the bed and motions for me to do the same.

"New issue of *Pulp?*" I ask, flopping down near her.

She shakes her head, props open the window and lights her cigarette simultaneously. "No." She lays the sheet of paper on the pillow in front of me and grins. "Our meal ticket."

Smoke Palace Productions Presents:
The Skins

Experience this hot new country-soul-blues band LIVE for the first time.

Barbecue
Beer

Sexy Party Favors

"The Skins got soul like a dog's got fleas."
Charlie Parker

"If you haven't heard these guys, you're missing out. Arlan Green's the Crown Prince of rockin' country blues."
Seattle Weekly

6:00 July 4th @ 453 Railroad, the second warehouse from the tracks. Follow the music!

"Don't just sit there," she says, furrowing her brow before the grin has disappeared. "Say something! What do you think?"

"You got a quote from Charlie Parker? Isn't he dead?"

"Is he?" She looks stricken. "Arlan," she yells over her shoulder. "Did Charlie Parker *die?*"

"Yeah," comes the answer. "Nineteen fifty-something."

Lucy pulls a pen from behind her ear, draws a line through Charlie Parker and scribbles Ringo Starr. "He's not dead, is he?"

"I don't think so."

"Jesus, I hope not," she mumbles.

I raise my eyebrows at her and point to the first line of the flyer. "Smoke Palace Productions?"

"Okay," she says. "So I borrowed it. Ideas long to be free, you know."

"How did you even—?"

"Your notebook. It was lying around. It's good. I like the map."

"I never leave that out."

"So maybe it was lying around in your bag." She presses her lips together to keep from giggling.

"Lucinda!"

"Well, what? Nobody ever tells me anything. I'm not above a little investigation."

"But that's my private—"

"Come on," she says. "Let's not get sidetracked. What do you think? Isn't it brilliant?"

I can't decide if I'm furious or what; I just stare at her, opening and closing my mouth as I consider and discard a series of possible responses. No one ever pried into my private thoughts before—who would have bothered? I've been so invisible most my life. To be sought out like this is disturbing and exhilarating. I have no idea how to reconcile all this, so I just study the flyer again, trying to concentrate.

"Are you renting a warehouse?"

"No, it's free."

"How'd you swing that?"

"Blake Charles—guy that owns the head shop downtown? It's his. He wants to get in my pants, so he's letting us use it."

"I see." I stare at the paper some more, and she squirms, exhaling smoke impatiently. "It's good," I say. "It is."

"Good? Come on, it's pure genius! We're going to be richer than God!"

"How do you figure?"

"Just like the movies. You think they make money off your seven-dollar ticket? No, they lure you in and then they gouge you for popcorn and soda—that's where the real money is. We'll do the same thing, only we'll have something more powerful than popcorn—we'll have *meat!*" There's a visionary zeal to her, an evangelical glint in her eye. "We'll undo them with the smell of searing flesh."

"And the 'sexy party favors'?"

"We'll think of something. Homemade butt plugs, maybe. I just think it sounds good—mysterious."

"You ever think about going into marketing?"

She grins. "You like it, don't you?"

"I do," I say. "I might not even sue for plagiarism."

"This is our gig," she says. "You and me. We'll run the show. You in?"

I nod. "I'm in." There's a brief pause as we watch each other. I get uncomfortable after three seconds of this, so I reach for my backpack and pull out a manila folder. "I got you something."

"Oh! You shouldn't..." Her voice trails off as she flips it open and sees the application for Stanford staring back at her. Under that are the forms for Yale, Harvard and UC Santa Cruz. She turns the pages with a look of sudden exhaustion. "Jesus. These would take me ten years."

"We'll do them together," I say. "It's just data entry, really—my specialty."

She closes the folder and sucks at her cigarette, squinting suspiciously at me through the smoke. "Why do you want me to go so badly, anyway?"

"You help me out. I want to help you."

"That's it?"

"I like you. You're smart. You should have what you want."

She smiles with one side of her mouth—a crooked, still-not-convinced look. I'm about to tell her again how brilliant and original she is, college material and all that, but just then someone bangs in through the front door and a booming voice rings down the hallway: "The Big Dog's back!"

Lucy and I both freeze, she with her cigarette halfway to her mouth, me lying in a fetal curl, watching her. Our eyes lock, and I can tell she's thinking what I'm thinking, *Holy shit. Danny.*

We don't move, we just listen to the silence that descends like snow. I can envision him standing in the living room doorway, his bony elbows locked into forty-five-degree angles, his big, pink hands gripping his hips. And there they are: newly christened The Skins, caught off guard, sucking at beer bottles innocently, their hair still damp with sweat.

Danny blurts out, "What the fuck?" His voice cracks on the word "fuck" like that of a thirteen-year-old kid.

"Hey, Danny," Bill says. "Good to see you."

"Where's Sparky?" he asks.

"Moved back to Tacoma," Bill tells him.

"No shit?" There's a silence. "So, we need a new drummer, eh?" More silence. "Berlin, you play?"

"Listen, Danny…" Arlan's voice is low and forcibly calm. "We decided to try something new."

"Is that right?"

Bill slips into his nasally, nervous chatter. "It's not that we wanted to…well, we didn't know what your plans were—we figured you'd be a while, but we didn't want to—"

"What? Fuck me over?"

My eyes are still locked with Lucy's, and now she cringes slightly; we stay motionless on the bed, except for Lucy's cigarette hand drifting now and then to her mouth for another drag.

"It's time to try something else," Arlan says.

"Fuckin' Green. You've always been a punk-assed traitor. First the shit with Lucy, now this."

Lucy sits up and stabs her cigarette out.

"You'll never get a gig without me. You're just redneck trash—you can have that ugly bitch, but this is my band."

"If you want a beer," Arlan tells him, "then have a seat. Otherwise, please get the fuck out."

"You're trying to get back at me—I got the good end of the deal, dumping that skanky whore off on you."

Lucy springs from the bed and shoots into the living room like a wind-up toy just released. "Say that to my face, Dog—I'd like to hear it!"

I go into the living room and there's Danny standing in the middle of things, looking thin, pink and surrounded.

"We don't need you here," Lucy tells him, flatly. "We should have let you die."

"Go back to your mommy's trailer where I found you,

sucking off your stepdad and—" But whatever he intends to add never emerges. Lucy, roughly half his height, takes two steps and punches him in the stomach so hard he doubles over in pain.

From here, all is pandemonium—threats and grappling, shoving, distorted faces. A beer spills onto the carpet in a foamy puddle, Bill trips over the Martin case and falls to his knees. Everyone tries to contain Danny, who is a blur of arms and legs, throwing punches at anything, cursing in that huge, booming voice of his. The two-toned eyes flash around the room. I feel sort of sorry for him, until one of his enormous feet catches me square in the shin. Grady finally gets him in an awkward half nelson and shoves him out the door.

I watch him out the window as he walks shakily back to his car. He glances over his shoulder; his face is splotchy, his white-blond hair looks like lint haphazardly glued to his bony head. He sees me in the window and turns away, then folds himself into his beat-up old Mustang and drives off.

The collective adrenaline level in the room ebbs some. A trickle of blood is seeping from Grady's forehead, where some part of Danny broke the skin. I go to the kitchen and get him a wet paper towel, which he uses to dab at the wound cautiously, studying the blood that collects in damp smears. Lucy picks up a half-empty bottle of beer and sucks some down.

"You've got a mean right hook," Arlan tells her, wrapping an arm around her shoulder. "Never even saw that coming."

Though it's not terribly funny, we all laugh and then can't seem to stop, until Lucy's choking on her beer and Arlan's whacking her between the shoulder blades in a quick, giddy beat.

★ ★ ★

Grady's walking easily on the branch of an old pine. "Come on," he cries. "Nothing to it."

He reminds me of Peter Pan up there, with his disdain for gravity and his impish face. It is twilight, the deep blue hour, after sunset but before darkness seeps in. A single star—the North Star, I guess—is glowing above Canada and the neighborhood is scented with the rich smell of barbecue coming from the halfway house. It's nearly July, and true night comes so late now that it seems we can stay up forever. Grady is half obscured in pine needles and branches; I'm trying to imagine myself up there beside him.

"I'm afraid of heights," I tell him.

"What?"

"Afraid!" I yell. "Of heights!"

"No," he calls. "Not at all."

I sigh, and contemplate the painted dragon on the old church building that's used as a *dojo*. I can hear the screech and holler of the Goat Kids' music a couple of blocks away, and under that, the guttural cries of the martial arts students warming up inside the church. I feel strangely light, a little exhilarated by the blue all around me, and I want very much just to float up to where Grady is—avoid the humiliation of climbing and sweating altogether.

"If you come up," Grady calls, "I'll tell you a secret."

He's hanging from the branch now, letting his legs dangle like they have nothing to do with the rest of his body, and I envy his fearlessness, his ease. I've never climbed a tree in my life. I inch toward the trunk and grab hold of the lowest branch, my heart picking up tempo as I leap up, grab it, kick fitfully in the air for a moment, and drop again.

"Hopeless," I pronounce under my breath.

"Other side," Grady tells me. "There's a better one to start on over there."

It takes me twenty minutes, creeping painfully from branch to branch with long, dizzy pauses, as Grady coaches, but eventually I arrive, sweaty-palmed and terrified, to perch beside him, twenty feet above the ground. He nods at me. I think it's a sign of approval, but who can tell with Grady?

"So what's your secret?" I ask.

"Secret?"

"You promised!"

"Did we pinky shake?"

"Pinky shake?"

He grins and holds out his pinky finger. "Unless you shake pinkies, the deal's void."

"I never heard of that—"

"Historical ruling—1913, Pinky versus Hand."

"Yeah, right," I say, laughing. He offers me his pinky again, and I curl mine with his. It occurs to me that I haven't had sex in several months, and even then it was with Derek, which was about as erotic as dry toast. We stay there, pinkies interlocked, and I watch the shadows from the branches above sweep back and forth across his face. His eyes are a bright sea-green; he's recently shaved, so his cheeks are as smooth as a girl's. He licks his lips; I notice they've got a shine to them—lip balm, I guess. He looks at me intently, and for a split second, I think he's going to kiss me.

Instead, he pulls his hand away from mine and his face contorts with horror as he drops backwards without warning—just falls like a dead man. I gasp and reach for him, but he's already gone. I'm stunned until I get the joke, see that he is hanging upside down with the branch nestled securely in the crook of his knees.

"Very funny," I say, as he pulls himself back up.

When he's stopped laughing, he says, quite seriously, "Okay, secret number one…"

"So there's more than one?"

"I have countless secrets," he says. "But you only get one right now."

"Okay. I'm ready."

He waits a good long beat, opens his mouth to speak, closes it again. "I can't."

"Come on!" I say. "Who am I going to tell?"

"Lucy. Arlan. Anyone."

"Never," I say. "I promise."

"Pinky shake?"

"Sure." We do.

"I just think you should know," he says, finally. "Lucy fucks around."

I watch his face for any signs of deception. "You're being serious?"

"Swear to God. She does anyone, any chance she gets. Male or female. Don't get me wrong—I love the little scamp—but she's out of control." He laughs at my shocked face. "I figured you should know a little more about the den of sin you've wandered into...." He says this with an air of amusement, like he's retelling the plot of some bodice-ripper he's half-ashamed he read. "Well, don't look at me like that! You don't have to believe me!"

"No, I mean—" I'm not sure I do believe him, but it seems silly to argue over. "If you say so." After a pause, I force my voice to sound casual as I ask, "What about Arlan?"

"What about him?" he says with a sly grin.

"Does he?"

"Hell, no. Lucy likes to accuse him of it every now and then, mostly to ease her guilt. But Arlan's pathetically faithful. He hasn't even looked at another girl since he met her."

The evening breeze sends the pine needles all around us into fragrant, whispery convulsions. Grady reaches toward me and wipes something from my cheek. "Pine sap," he says. And then, as if we've really been talking about this all along, he tells me, "I loved your map."

I stare at him. "What map?"

"Of Smoke Palace and all that. The Land of Skin."

"I really wish she hadn't shown that around," I say. A wave of anger threatens to break inside me. I picture Lucy handing my notebook out drunkenly, cackling in her maddening way, and suddenly I want to kick her.

"But it's great," he says. "You've got a vivid imagination." His praise makes me shy and angry all at once; in my confusion, I make the mistake of looking at the ground, and a brief but intense spell of vertigo seizes me. I tighten my grip on the branch. "A strong imagination," he says, "is very sexy."

We sit there for a moment with nothing to say. I keep my eyes locked on a branch a few feet away. The tension in the air tells me that if I turn toward him he'll definitely kiss me, and I try to want that, I really do, but all I can see is Arlan, shirtless and glazed with sweat, smoking a cigarette in the sunshine, and this keeps me frozen in place.

"Well," I mumble, when I'm beginning to feel awkward and dizzy again, like I might throw up. "Is it hard getting down?"

"Not at all," he says. "Just don't fall."

That night I'm sleepless as usual. My whole body is still buzzed off the events of the day—my cold-water plunge, the brawl with Danny, soaking up Grady's attention while balancing too many feet above the earth. I can't seem to work up much desire for Grady, but I'm not above savoring the rush from his flirtation; it's rare for someone with his bone structure to pay attention to me, and I can't deny that it's a little delicious.

I think of Lucy's blatant invasion of what little privacy I've got left. I know I should be mad, but somehow I keep landing on the side of flattered, instead. It's just so strange for me, being whisked inside this little hive of human activity, where there are eyes everywhere. Before this, no one but my mother had ever seen my Suicide Maps. I always assumed they were too bizarre for the light of day. I'm surprised Lucy didn't freak about my morbid habit and kick me out. Knowing that people have witnessed my dirty secrets fills me with a strange mixture of alarm and relief. There's something painfully awkward about being so suddenly and unexpectedly exposed, but there's also something almost pleasurable about it, like being discovered. I hardly know what to do with myself now that people are actually paying attention to me.

It's after midnight, and it's obvious that sleep is not within my grasp—it's nowhere close. My body and brain refuse to slip into the slow, unwound rhythm that brings dreams. I take out the bundle of letters and once again unwind the twine until the leather unfolds, exposing the age-softened envelopes, some of them bearing exotic stamps. I put the first two aside and pick up the third. I study its postmark; the ink has faded to a barely there pink, but I'm pretty sure it's from Amsterdam. On the three identical stamps there are beautiful, long-necked birds swimming over a gray-green sea.

I faintly remember my father telling me about the years he traveled on a Swedish barge, making just enough to keep going. He was in Europe for a couple of years, then spent a little time in Asia. Before that he'd gone to college for a brief stint—Stanford—but dropped out quickly when he realized all he'd learn there was attitude. Sometimes when we were hanging out in his shop he would mention those years of traveling and his eyes would become glittery, his face flushed with the vitality adults seemed to stumble upon during their second round of martinis.

August 6th, 1969
Dear Einstein,

I know it's been a long time, friend. Too long. I'm sorry. I don't know if you've tried to write…I've been drifting in a stupor for so long, I've lost track. Sorry if my thoughts are jumbled. Man. I haven't tried to make sense in a long, long time.

I think (who am I kidding? I know) the last time I wrote you I was high as a kite about Virgo. I can barely scribble her name, even now, without losing control. She was, at risk of sounding trite, the love of my life (remember Nabokov in Caldwell's English class? "Light of my life, fire of my loins"? Like that.) She was everything. Hold on.

Farther down on the same page, a new date appears.

August 20th, 1969

Sorry. Here's the thing, Ein, and I can only write this once so please God don't ask me about it ever, okay? She never showed up in Copenhagen that weekend. Later, when I went to Paris looking for her, I learned from her friends that she OD'd. I never knew she was so hooked into downers; her friend Claire said she did them morning, noon and night when she could get her hands on them.

She told me once that dying was no big deal. She said she did it once as a kid when she almost drowned in her neighbor's swimming pool. She claimed it was just like a very pleasant acid trip. She wasn't afraid of it at all.

I have to believe it was an accident, though either way it's unbearable. To think that God is fucked-up enough to let a girl like that drift out of the world—

just get lost in a Seconol maze, without meaning to—is just as terrifying as the possibility that she, knowing how I loved her, knowing that my seed was tucked inside her, taking root, inching its way closer to birth every moment—

I can't write about this.

I know you must have so much to say about Dylan's accident and all that. I heard he finally played again at the Woodie Guthrie shindig. Write me, will you? Jot down anything in that chicken scratch of yours, the more mundane the better. Tell me what you had for lunch. The last five records you bought, anything. Tell me about Rot Gut and what he's building these days.

I wish that we were sitting right now in your backyard, with your mother's soap operas droning on in the living room, and that we were taking sips from longnecks and sharing a covert joint.

Until next time, yeah?

Keep it real,

Chet

I put the page down. His pain flickers through me tentatively, like a match lit somewhere inside my rib cage. The desolation and loneliness in his smeared black ink still comes through, after all these years. She was pregnant, this girl. If she hadn't died, I would never have been born. The thought makes me a little light-headed. The implications are a frightening, tangled web. Did he settle for Mom and me, but secretly long for this dead girl and her unborn child? I fold the leather back up, tie the twine around it, wishing I could put away the swarm of questions and doubts as easily.

What more is hiding in these envelopes? I resolve to read them slowly, one or two at a time, so I won't get overwhelmed. My father's letters are like dangerous, potent medicine; if I ration carefully, I might be able to handle them, but taken all at once they could be poisonous.

I feel completely stupid about my tantrum at Bender's this morning; what was I thinking? It seems my father has the power to thrust me into adolescent mode without the slightest warning, rendering me irrational and combative with the faintest, feathery touch of his airmail letters. I guess I shouldn't be surprised. My whole life has been wrapped around his finger. Is there anyone who has shaped me more irrevocably and decisively than this man, someone who's been dead for more than half my existence?

Independence Day

"Testing, one two. Testing one two three." Bill speaks into the mic and squints across the shadows at his cousin, who is standing before a great, hulking slab of knobs and levers—the mixing board. The cousin furrows his brow in concentration and spins more dials, plays with the levers. "My dog has fleas," Bill says, before a piercing wail of feedback shoots across the room, making me duck and hold my ears. When it passes, a few titters rise up from the seven or eight college kids gathered in one corner—several girls sporting hair bright as Sno-Cones, and a bunch of short, pimply-faced boys who look like they're still waiting for their voices to change.

"Don't worry," Lucy says, appearing abruptly at my side. "This place will be packed in a couple hours."

I'm not worried, really, but I can feel the tension rising from her like heat. Her face is a shade whiter than usual, and her eyes are outlined in dark circles of exhaustion as she studies her watch. We've been working frantically for a week, sending out flyers to all the subscribers of *Pulp* and anyone else we can scrounge up. We even took to handing out flyers in bars—after a few drinks we'd make the rounds like cigarette girls, plastering on smiles and enduring tipsy flirtations for as long as we could stand it. Now Lucy looks like a Goth girl, with her little black dress, her combat boots and her bone-white complexion.

"The barbecue's ready," she says. "We've got enough hot dogs and hamburgers to feed Whatcom County—I hate meat en masse." She wrinkles her nose and makes a sound of disgust in her throat. "Do my boobs look weird in this?" She takes a step back and tucks her chin down to examine her own breasts.

"Weird?"

"Why do you insist on answering questions with questions? Never mind, it's too late to change now." She looks at me, and apparently realizes she's being snappish. Her arms curl around my waist and she nestles her face against my neck. "You look great, that's all. I hate to be upstaged."

I'm wearing her little blue sundress, the one she had on the day we met. I do feel good in it. I spent my last thirty dollars foolishly, impulsively, on a pair of vintage sandals with rhinestones at the toes. They are exquisite. Now the only thing between me and poverty is a pair of shoes.

"Why do you look so smug?" Lucy demands, having ceased the hug and slipped out of apologetic mode already.

I just shrug and grin. I really can't explain it; I just feel good tonight. Sure, it's five forty-five and there's only a handful of people here. And yes, The Skins' big debut is scheduled fifteen minutes from now, coordinated with the dinner hour to ensure that people will gorge themselves—mad throngs feeding like sharks. Instead of mad throngs, we've got the Mickey Mouse Club, and if this thing flops, we're all dead broke. But I feel good, in my dainty shoes from a bygone era, I feel really good, and even Lucy's chain-smoking snappishness cannot dissuade me from grinning foolishly at everything and everyone.

"Finished a new draft of the essay last night," she says, tugging at her dress and looking again at her own chest. "I would have shown you, but you were asleep."

"Cool! I can't wait to see it." That's the other thing we've been busy with—Lucy's application for UC Santa Cruz. It's the only school she's going to apply to, since the others only took applications in the winter. It's just as well; I doubt Harvard, Yale or Stanford would understand her particular brand of genius, or overlook the mediocre grades she got in high school. UC Santa Cruz, on the other hand, might be offbeat enough to appreciate what Lucy has to offer. Now all she has left is to take the SATs, and she's done with it. I'll admit, I'm a little nervous about the outcome, though we won't know for a while. We've gone over her essay so many times I've memorized it.

I watch her now, still tugging at her dress, like a little girl in church. She puts a Camel in her mouth, searches for her lighter, curses when she can't find it, uses a match instead. Lucy and I have spent so much time together lately, we're practically breathing in sync. I've always admired sisters from a distance—I envied that mix of pettiness and tenderness, an intimacy so casual they don't even notice it. Until now, I've only imagined what that's like.

"What are you looking at?" she asks. Her eyebrows are scowling, but the corner of her mouth is twisting into a crooked hint of a grin that says she's not as hostile as she wants to be.

"Relax," I say. "I've got my lucky shoes on. Everything's going to be fine."

"Relax yourself," she says. "If this thing flops, I'm blaming it all on you."

* * *

I've never seen Arlan nervous before. When he comes out on stage, his face is a washed-out gray. He's got on faded blue jeans and a new shirt Lucy got him—a pale, vintage Western thing with silver buttons. Bill's wearing the same eager, panting expression he always wears. Grady is leaning against the back wall, looking around casually through dark glasses. He's got on his favorite T-shirt, the one with a red anarchy symbol, and he's stroking the little goatee he's been cultivating all week.

The crowd that greets them is not exactly the roaring mass of fans we'd envisioned. I count twenty-three including me, Lucy and the sound guy. We've got the barbecue all fired up, waiting for the first slab of meat, but nobody's even wandered near our lovely food station, which consists of several coolers, three kegs, two grills and an old wooden picnic table that Grady has painted in red, white and blue anarchy symbols.

"Why does Arlan look like that?" Lucy says, chewing on a cuticle.

"Like what?"

"He's green! Look at him."

He does, in fact, look like he might be sick at any moment, but I feel obligated not to agree. "He looks fine," I say. "Just maybe a little jittery."

"I'm telling you, he's been on stage plenty, and he never looked like that before." We study him together for a moment in silence. He's tapping on his mic, tuning the antique Martin with trembling fingers. He makes eye contact with her and she gives him an uncharacteristically sweet little wave. He smiles, but barely, and with visible effort. "He's definitely going to puke," she says.

"They're going to blow everyone away," I say.

"Yeah, 'everyone'—all five of us!" Lucy grumbles. "Maybe

we should put some meat on the grill, just to get people interested," she says. She whips out a hamburger patty and tosses it on the barbecue; instantly, it starts hissing and spitting grease. "Motherfucker!" Lucy cries, clutching at her eye.

"What? What happened?"

"Grease in my eye!"

"Let me see," I say, hovering near her.

"Godfuckingdammit!" she says. "What do you want to *see* for?" She presses the heel of her hand harder into her eye socket and groans dramatically; when she finally lets go, the eye is slightly bloodshot but otherwise seems fine. She blinks twice, then waves me away. The hamburger has calmed down now; it hisses gently on the grill, looking pink and innocuous, though not exactly appetizing.

Blake Charles comes in, the head shop guy who owns this warehouse. I've met him once, talked to him for maybe three minutes about getting the keys to this place, and now he comes up and wraps his arms around me like we've been exchanging bodily fluids for years. Instinctively, I curl my arms up against my body, wedge my elbows between us, and push gently out of his embrace. He seems not to notice and moves on to Lucy, who lets him hug her but looks at me over his shoulder with a pained expression.

"Look at you, look at you!" he says, shaking his dark ringlets so they slip around on his shoulders, turning his face from Lucy to me and back again. He's a very short man of indeterminable age; he wears Buddy Holly glasses, a tie-dyed T-shirt, Guatemalan print shorts and high-top sneakers. His arms and legs are so hairy they're black. "The belles of the ball!" He lets his gaze settle on me, and he does not blink. I decide he is the kind of person who uses relentless eye contact to force people into false intimacy. I clear my throat. "Been over at Sadie's," he says, finally tearing his eyes from my face. "You guys know Sadie Tyler?"

"Yeah," Lucy says. "Real tall, right? Lots of hair?"

"Right. She's having a party out at the lake—huge! Must be two hundred people over there. Lots of love going 'round, if you know what I mean." He wiggles his moppish eyebrows, like Groucho Marx.

"Shit." Lucy looks at me. "Is that where everybody is?"

"Hello," Arlan says into the mic, but the sound level's set way too high and the whole room ducks, cups their ears as a piercing squeal of feedback eclipses whatever it is he says next.

"Can you take me out there?" Lucy says to Blake.

"Where? To Sadie's?"

"Yeah. Just to check it out."

Blake grins. I notice now that underneath those Buddy Holly glasses, his pupils are so dilated they look like black marbles. "Sure—anything for you, Lucy-girl." He ruffles her hair with one hand in a way that I know she detests, but she just gives him a tight little grin. "Let me just catch up with my bro over here, and we'll be on our way," he says, and then struts off to the sound guy, swinging his arms.

As soon as he's turned around, I shoot a look at Lucinda, but she just shakes her head at me coolly. "Don't even, Anna. It's not what you think. Just trust me on this one."

"You're leaving me?"

"Just for a minute. I promise. I'll be right back."

I'm suddenly unsure about what to do with my hands, so I pick up a spatula and smash the hamburger meat against the grill until it's thin as a pancake. "You're going to some chick's party? Are you kidding me? We've been working our asses off for this—"

"And I'm still working my ass off."

"I fail to see how you leaving is going to help—how do you think Arlan's going to feel?" I look up at the stage, where Arlan and Bill are struggling with the mic, tangling themselves in various wires and looking more terrified than ever. "He'll be crushed."

Her face goes steely. "Let me worry about Arlan, okay?"

I concentrate on flipping the sad, thin hamburger. It's sticking to the grill, and I only succeed in mutilating it. I toss the spatula down. Lucy giggles. "Fine," I say. "Laugh!"

She puts an arm around me. "Anna! It'll be okay! I'm just going to see if I can round up a few customers. If it works, you'll thank me. I promise."

"Ladies? Ready to go?" Blake reappears, stroking his ringlets away from his face. I notice he has a bouquet of black nose hairs protruding from his nostrils.

Lucy leans into me and whispers, "Be right back," before turning to Blake. "She's staying, but I'm ready."

"Oh, come on, Anna," Blake coos, and an image of black grease gurgling from his lips hits me so strongly I think I might wretch. "This is more like a funeral than a concert."

"Somebody's got to watch over the dead," I tell him.

As they're leaving, I retrieve the spatula and turn back to the hamburger; I attack it with renewed fervor, scraping its pulpy, charred remains from the grill.

Once they've got the sound levels under control, Arlan hooks his guitar strap over his shoulder and looks from me to the far corners of the room in a vague, bewildered way that makes me feel sad for all of us.

"Okay, I guess you can all hear me now," he says into the mic, staring at his feet. He glances up quickly at the room with solemn brown eyes, then looks back down at his feet. I never guessed he could be so uncomfortable. He's always at ease with his guitar; it seems to grow naturally out of his body, like an appendage. "We're going to play a little number...." He studies his fingernails with a blank look. Three of the people who wandered in wander back out, and the door slams hard behind them, followed by the sounds of their laughter, trailing off in the distance. Arlan's eyes dart to the door, and I can see him going paler still. He licks his lips, puts the metal slide on his shaking finger, and mumbles, "It goes something like this."

He starts to play, and for a moment I just close my eyes, take it in—the beauty of Arlan's fingers bringing that Martin to life, plucking and sliding. I'm seven years old again, and the sunset is filling our living room with orange light. My father's face is blissful as he cradles his guitar, his fingers moving rapidly, one foot keeping time. The sun goes down and the fog rolls in from the west like waves in slow motion. My mother brings me a plate of crackers, but I do not eat. I'm mesmerized by my father's face and the intricate tapestry of music summoned by his hands.

My eyes fly open as feedback once again paralyzes the room; Arlan has dropped his guitar. I watch in horror as he bolts out the side door. A girl with purple, spiky hair starts to boo. Instinctively, I dash for the exit.

Outside, I find myself in a damp alley. Arlan is leaning against a brick wall a couple of yards from the door, wedged between two large Dumpsters, his hands on his knees. I approach him cautiously. "Arlan?" I say softly. He does not look up; his chest is heaving, like he just sprinted a mile. As I inch closer, I see there are beads of sweat at his hairline. I feel suddenly afraid. "What is it? Are you sick?"

As if on cue, he spins away from me, his shoulders rise and his head juts out; a stream of pink vomit hits the pavement with a sickening splash. I feel my guts tighten in revulsion—even more so a second later when the smell assaults me, mixing with the scent of wet garbage—but I keep moving closer, until I find myself standing right behind him. His body heaves again, and I reach forward, pull his long hair back and hold it away from his face. Another wave of stench washes over me and I have to swallow hard or I'll gag. When he's still again, I lay my hand on his shoulder. His muscles seem to relax a little under my fingers.

"You okay?"

He wipes his mouth with the back of his hand and straightens, keeping his eyes closed. I guide him cautiously away from the Dumpsters and help him to lean against the corrugated metal of the warehouse. He tilts his head back and grimaces at the sky.

"Fuck," he says softly. "What was *that?*"

"I don't know," I say. "You trying to get out of this gig?" We both laugh. He won't look at me.

"I've never been this nervous," he says, holding his stomach. "Jesus, you got any smokes?"

"Sorry. Want me to go in and find you—"

"Never mind," he says as he finds a pack in his chest pocket. "Stupid of me." He tries to light it but his hand is quivering, so I take the lighter from him gently and apply the flame. He pretends not to notice that my hand is trembling slightly, too. "Man," Arlan groans, when he's got his first pull of smoke inside him. "I'm never going to live this down."

"Public's fickle," I say. "They'll forget."

"Public," he snorts. "Thank God nobody showed. But Bill won't forget." He exhales, squinting at the sky, then covers his eyes with one hand. "Fuckin' Grady will send me to my grave with this." He shakes his head and starts to laugh. I laugh a little, too. But now Arlan's shoulders are shaking to a different rhythm, and though his eyes are still hidden behind his fingers, it slowly dawns on me that he is crying.

"What is it?" I say, edging closer.

He leans his head back and bangs it softly against the metal twice. Pretty soon he's really crying hard, his face contorting with sorrow. I'm so thrown off I just stand there with my arms hanging at my sides. When he doesn't stop, I put my hands on his shoulders a little awkwardly and pull him toward me, wrapping my arms around him and stroking his long hair with one hand. He lets his cigarette fall and leans against me; soon the curve of my neck is damp with his tears. The feel of him in my arms—his face nestled against my neck, his body shaking—is suddenly, overwhelmingly erotic. His skin is moist against mine; his hands grip my shoulders, his chin presses against my clavicle.

"Hey, Arlan?"

Our bodies separate instantly. My veins are throbbing with adrenaline; I feel swollen, hungry, absurd. I turn to see Grady leaning out the door, sunglasses propped atop his head.

"I'm coming," Arlan says. He kicks at the ground, his eyes cast down. There is a nauseating, elastic pause. Then Grady lets the door slam shut. Arlan and I look at each other. I want only to feel him again—the heat of his body, the silk of his hair under my hands. "Sorry," he mumbles. He tucks his shirt in, pushes some hair away from his dark, tear-streaked face. "Don't know what the fuck's wrong with me."

"A lot of pressure, I guess."

He coughs, wipes at his face in a hurried, embarrassed way. "Nobody knows how much I want this."

"You're a natural. You've got no worries."

"It was different with Danny—I knew we were shitty, so it didn't matter. But this is all my stuff, and if it sucks—" he searches the air with his eyes "—then I suck."

I smile. "You don't suck. You're brilliant."

"You've never heard what I write."

"You played for me that one night." I rub the back of my neck, just to keep my hands from reaching out for him. "Only one song, but it was amazing."

"Music's the only good thing in my life," he says, staring at his shoes.

"The only good thing?" I raise an eyebrow. We both know what I'm asking. *Do you love her? Do you?*

"Okay…you're right. There's Wild Turkey and cigarettes." The corners of his mouth turn up in the faintest of smiles, but his eyes are still melancholy.

The combination of cynicism and vulnerability in his face makes me totally sick with desire. He's still leaning against the side of the building. Before I know what I'm doing, I've got my palm flattened against his chest, pressing against him. I want more than anything to lean my whole body into his, feel his hipbones, his torso, his lips melting into mine. Instead we stand there at arm's distance, staring, electricity passing between us until my whole body is pulsing. I watch him for some kind of cue, but neither of us moves an inch.

The sound of a woman's laughter, high-pitched and irritating, comes out of nowhere, startling me. I jerk toward the source instinctively, and see a redhead in jeans passing the entrance to the alley, her arm wrapped around a young girl. The moment slips away. He lights a new cigarette.

"Where's Lucy?" he whispers.

"She left."

"Where'd she go?"

"Took off with Blake. I guess they went to some party."

He nods, and a tiny muscle in his jaw quivers slightly. I want to ask him how he does it—what keeps him entangled with her no matter how she hurts him, but even in this state, sweating with the effort it takes not to kiss him, I know better. "I guess I should get back," he says. I nod. "Anna?"

"Yes?" I hate how eager-sounding it comes out.

He opens his mouth just barely, closes it again. "You're a good friend to her," he says. And then, softly, conspiring, "She probably doesn't deserve you."

"I could say the same to you."

He shrugs. Looks at the door. I'm pleased to hear the reluctance in his voice as he mumbles, "I've got to go back in."

"Yeah," I say, unable to meet his eyes. "You better."

As the door bangs behind him, I slump against the metal siding of the warehouse and sink to the ground. I am still so charged up, my blood is racing, but I'm also depleted and dizzy. I put my face in my hands and there's Arlan staring from the dark of my closed lids. I try to breathe steadily. A few drops of rain fall, tentative at first, and then the sky opens up like a faucet. I just sit there, watching the clouds, letting the rain form a tiny pool at the base of my throat and run in rivulets over my skin.

When Lucy comes in, The Skins still haven't returned to the stage. The pathetic crowd has long since dispersed, and I've started communing with the keg. I'm working on my third pint, and that sweet, bubbly absence of pain has spread all the way to my fingertips when Lucy materializes at my side, bright-eyed and triumphant.

"I did it," she says. I nod pleasantly and burp. "I mean it! You don't believe me, do you?"

"All depends," I say. "What are you taking credit for this time?"

"I saved the day. Just watch—you'll see." She smirks and tries to take my beer from me, but I grip it tighter and pull away. "What's wrong with you, anyway?" she demands. "Where is everyone?"

"Arlan got sick."

"Sick?"

"Sick," I repeat, and smile for no reason.

"Are you drunk?"

"Maybe."

Without warning, a group of eleven or twelve people come pouring in, followed soon after by more. I spot Blake at the door, collecting their money as fast as he can. Before long, there are fifty people swarming into the warehouse, and still more keep appearing: heroin-chic, artsy types in black; ex-ravers in fake fur vests and ponytails; neo-hippies in ragged cords and flouncy dresses. The place is crawling with twenty-somethings. Tattoos flash, pierced body parts are on display—there's even one girl dressed head to toe in patent leather.

"Where are they all coming from?"

"I told you I was working my ass off," Lucy says. "And look." She glances around quickly, then tugs a bag from the inside of her boot. It's full of little white pills with dolphins on them.

"Hey," I say. "What's that?"

"This—" Lucy smiles at me, her eyes full of wonder, "—is *love*."

"Drugs?" I whisper.

She bursts out into peals of laughter. Her teeth are shining white, her pupils are huge and black. She's not afraid of anything, I think. "What are you going to do with all those?" I ask.

"What do you think?"

"You're going to sell—what is it? Speed?"

"Ecstasy," she says, and her lips open to the word with voluptuous pleasure. "Best thing since cunnilingus."

"Who'd you get them from?"

"Never mind," she says. "Here's the thing—we're going to get all the cash we need, tonight. So just tell me—are you in?"

"What if we get caught?"

She rolls her eyes. "Oh, Anna… come on, are you in or out?"

I hesitate. The smells of vomit and smoke, the thick silk of Arlan's hair flash through me, and I understand with startling clarity what a terrible friend I am. All I want now is to be what Lucy is: vivid, fierce, unafraid.

"In," I say. "On one condition."

"What's that?"

"Let me have one of those."

She grins, takes one from the baggie, and slips it between my lips.

The room is pulsing. A girl with a red lollipop has just paid me thirty dollars for one of my lovely little pills, and we are smiling now at one another, flushed with mutual affection. It occurs to me that money is pure and beautiful—erotic, even—fluid energy flowing from one pair of hands to the next, pouring like a waterfall, splashing negative ions into our ready lungs. I am a goddess, exchanging pure love for pure money, and it's all the same thing. I offer the girl with the lollipop another pill, and her eyes question me a moment—liquid hazel eyes outlined with glitter—before she willingly produces more cash. I slip the pill into her open mouth, goddess that I am. She swallows, and nods to the pulse of the room, her platinum-blond head bobbing, and I move on.

By the time The Skins come back on stage, I've forgotten all about them. So has everyone else. The room is packed, the grill is smoking, and people are buying hamburgers like they haven't eaten in years. It's such a pleasant surprise when Arlan steps up to the mic and says, "Well, better late than never," and a riff pours out like honey from his fingers, slow and thick, each note clinging to the last. For a moment, the crowd seems stunned. Then a roar rises from the teeming bodies, like some prehistoric god moaning with pleasure. I turn in time to see Arlan smile. It's a small, beautiful smile, full of childish pride, and it makes me ache for him. Then Grady comes in with the drums and Bill starts in with the bass and Arlan's fingers start to fly up and down the neck of that Martin like he's possessed. The whole room starts to writhe.

Behind the picnic table, Lucy flips a burger and smiles across the room at me. This is it, I think. The summer everyone waits for. If I make it through this alive, there's no turning back.

The Penny Guy

After the Fourth, I know just how treacherous I am for staying at Smoke Palace. As soon as I felt the weight of Arlan's body and smelled the smoke in his hair, I knew how desperately I wanted him. How can I look Lucy in the eye without feeling vaguely criminal? She's taken me in, confided in me, shared her coffee, booze and secrets like we're sisters. How do I repay her? By lying on her couch and dreaming of her boyfriend's body every night.

I don't know what other people mean when they say love. I have my own definition, though it's not very precise. The only person I'm sure I loved was my father, mostly because when he died it felt like something was being ripped from my intestines. All other bonds, in contrast, seem illusory and tenuous by comparison. I know I never loved Derek; his eyes were too close together, his hands too indecisive. I'd like to say I love my mother, but how can I when the thought of her voice makes my stomach cramp painfully? Sometimes I think I do love Arlan, especially when he plays the slide; what Arlan has is sadness, and that's what I've learned to equate with love.

And Lucy—sometimes I think I love her too. Except I don't want her the way I want Arlan. I can't imagine our bodies together, molding to one another, or when I try to imagine it, I only get so far. It's not simply that we're both women—girls—whatever. It's that Lucy has a cruelty I'm afraid of. She's too scary to think of having sex with, whereas Arlan's so magnetic that most nights I can think of nothing else.

A few days after the big bash, I make up my mind to approach Bender with some news. While our foray into drug dealing didn't, as Lucy had hoped, make us "richer than God," it did give us enough to pay rent through the end of August and still have enough left over to live on for about as long. It also provided me with the opportunity to forge a little deal with Blake Charles. In the throes of his high, with his pupils so huge I thought they'd never contract again, I convinced him easily to rent Bender and me the workshop next door to the warehouse.

It's a perfect little space—I'd wandered into it by accident while searching for a bathroom, and immediately the vision washed over me: Bender and me, hunched over a nearly finished guitar, with the scent of lacquer filling our heads and sunlight leaking in through the high, filthy windows. Blake let me have it through September for a ridiculously paltry sum of forty dollars. I was pretty sure my share of the Fourth money would more than cover the cost of materials, at least for one guitar, and Bender had already admitted he still had his tools. After we finished one, I figured we could sell it and reinvest. I hadn't planned too far ahead, but I knew we had a start. We did if Bender could be convinced to give it a try, that is.

I find him sitting on his boat, with the late-morning sunlight rendering his silver hair almost white. He is, to my surprise, smoking a large, rather soggy-looking cigar. When he sees me, he pulls the cigar from his lips so rapidly it seems he will actually try to hide it; just as quickly, though, he puts it back in his mouth and puffs defiantly. "What's cookin', Medina?" he says, as he gets up to unlock the gate.

"I thought you quit."

"I'm not a quitter," he says.

"So I see."

"Can I get you anything?" He offers me the lawn chair—by now, I've come to think of it as mine—and takes his usual seat atop the ice chest. "Beer?" He gestures with his Budweiser. "Tomato juice?"

"No thanks," I say. "I can't stay long. I'm going to the lake later with a friend."

"Ah. So you're just stopping by?"

"I've got news," I say.

"Sounds ominous," he says.

"I found us a shop."

"A shop?"

"A place to make guitars. And I've got a little money now—for materials." He stares at me blankly and takes a swig from his can. I prattle on. "You said you still have your tools—I figured that's the biggest expense, so we're lucky you kept those. The shop is perfect. It's got lots of natural light, plenty of space. I already paid for it—we've got it through September. I figured we could—"

"Whoa, now. Slow down."

"We could just build one guitar, you know, for starters, see how it goes—"

"Medina." He looks at me with those searing blue eyes, and I bite my lip. "You don't give up, do you?"

"What could be the harm? I'm not asking for any big commitment—just do one guitar, let me help out.... Would it kill you?"

"Listen," he says. "I haven't done shit for seven years, okay? You think I can just start again because you want me to?"

"It would be good for you—"

"Good for *you*, you mean!"

"Good for both of us," I say, my voice dropping to barely above a whisper. He looks out at the water and stuffs the cigar between his lips, puffs a few wads of smoke into the air. The smell is sweet and dirty at once. Without knowing quite why, I pull Shiva from my pocket and hold him in my lap, speaking without looking up. "My mom sold her sax and her harp and all of Dad's guitars a couple weeks after he died—she listens to light rock stations now. She's never even talked about him all these years. I came here because—I don't know—it wasn't right. And you do the thing he loved most...."

"I used to—"

"You've got to miss it!"

"There's a lot you don't get, Medina."

"Like what? Tell me."

"Sometimes things happen, and you just—" He works his lips without sound for a second. "The things you once loved become...unbearable."

"But why? Rosie told me you were the best—better than Dad, even. She said you loved guitars."

"But I'm done, now."

"How can you be? Don't you crave it?"

He crushes the beer can between his fingers. "Sometimes, you just lose the—"

"What?"

"The desire. That's all." His hair, standing at unruly attention, makes me want to cry, suddenly.

There's a long silence. A flock of seagulls circles above us, cawing into the bright blue sky, screeching and flapping, riding the air currents, oblivious to our misery.

"What happened to you?"

He looks at me for a moment, then flings the cigar overboard impulsively, as if it suddenly disgusts him. "Life," he says.

"Did you miss my dad?"

"I do miss him," he says. "But your dad and I parted ways long before he—well—"

"Killed himself," I say firmly.

"Right. Before that." He twists the empty beer can with both hands. "There was other stuff, too."

"Like what?"

"My wife. I told you about that."

"She left."

"Right. Took off with some Realtor. Johnson or Jarvey or something."

"So that was it? Your wife leaving?"

"No," he says, his eyes distant, almost dreamy. "That wasn't all of it."

"Just tell me," I say quietly.

He scoffs, tears the beer can clean in half. "Frankly, I don't see the point. We've all got problems—no use crying about it."

"Look, I came all the way up here, I live on someone's couch, I compromised myself in any number of ways to get us a workshop, which I've already paid for." I'm surprised at the sudden hostility in my voice. "If you're going to sit around drinking Budweiser instead of teaching me to build one lousy guitar, I deserve to know why."

"I don't owe you anything, Medina."

"All I'm asking for is—"

"I didn't invite you up here—why would I?"

"So you want me to leave?"

"You expect me to be grateful to you? I'm supposed to jump up and down because some little shit wants to waltz down memory lane?"

"Fine! You want me to go? I'll go!" I stand up.

"You're acting just like your mother, you know that? She couldn't take no for an answer!"

"Better than you—you sit around and drink yourself to fucking death!"

"That's my prerogative."

"Good! Kill yourself—see what I—" But the last word is drowned by a torrent of tears. I can barely catch my breath as I hug myself, sobbing.

"Okay," Bender says, hovering near me. He puts his hand on my back, removes it, puts it on my shoulder. This only makes me cry harder. I feel foolish but I can't stop. I sit back down and he puts his hand on my head. The warm force of his palm makes me feel like a kid. I cover my face with my hands and let go.

I find myself adrift in a scene I didn't know was inside me; my father is staring out the window, and I am crying. I'm young—maybe five or six years old, I don't know for sure, but I can feel the smallness of my own body; the grown-up world is all-powerful and beyond comprehension, a league of giants who speak another tongue. We're on the couch, and his huge hand, fragrant with the essence of wood, is on my head. This is supposed to comfort me, I know, but as I watch his eyes on the window, my bones ache for him. I want him to hold me, to pull me tight against him and make a home for me with his arms, his stained T-shirt, shelter me with his great sculpted jaw. But his eyes are so far away. I'm only a child, my world is made of crayons and apple juice, graham crackers and paste, but even I recognize the glazed look of restlessness in his face—the dizzy hunger for freedom. In his mind, he is outside, flying down a freeway, the wind making streamers of his hair. His tank is full of gas, and the ocean spreads out before him like a bright liquid dream. Even as his fingers rest heavily on my head, I can feel the world pulling him out that window. I know better than to ask him to hold me. It's bad enough that I'm keeping him here.

In my peripheral vision, a splotch of red appears. I peek through my fingers and see that it is a handkerchief. I take it, and try to clean my face as the tears keep coming. I blow my nose. Bender lingers near me, and for a split second I think he might wrap his arms around me. I wish he would. But he waits too long; his hands find their way to his mess of hair instead. He sits back down on the ice chest.

"You feel any better?" he asks, when my tears have subsided.

I consider this. "Sort of."

There's the sound of wings in the air nearby, and I look up to see a huge, fat pelican hovering ten feet from the water, eyeing us. "There he is." Bender smiles. "Old Cal, king of the sea." Caliban nosedives, showing off. He emerges with a fish; it wriggles in his beak, its silver scales catching the light like tiny mirrors. Bender chuckles. Caliban flies away, his prehistoric shape moving off into the blue.

"It was my son," Bender says.

"What did you say?"

"My son," he repeats. "He was in an accident. Killed. On a motorcycle." He gets up, retrieves a fresh beer from the cooler. "Sixteen years old." He yanks at the tab, releasing a thin froth of bubbles that rise and then settle into a circle of liquid around the rim. "Scottie." He doesn't look at me. "Couple years after, Sheila left me. Things just fell apart. I didn't build any guitars after that."

"How long ago did he die?"

"Been seven years, this summer."

We sit through another long silence. The water slaps against the docks, sways the boats gently side to side. Somewhere in the distance, a car starts; its fan belt whines, the engine revs several times, then dies. I try to picture his son: a lanky, cocksure version of Bender, with long, skinny arms and a random smattering of freckles across his nose and cheeks. I bet I would have liked him.

"Did he play guitar?" I ask.

"Who?" Bender looks startled.

"Scottie." The name sits in the air, and for a moment I fear I've gone too far.

"No. He was a drummer." His voice shakes a little as he speaks. "He liked heavy metal. And opera. He was a funny kid."

"I'm really sorry," I say, but as soon as it's out of my mouth I remember how much I grew to hate that phrase after my dad died. "I wish I could have met him."

He looks at me with a small, barely-there smile for a moment. Then he stands, walks to the bow and stares out at the water with his back to me. "Well, shit," he says. "I guess I'll never get rid of you till I say yes."

"I guess you won't," I say.

He turns to me with a rueful expression. "Jesus, Medina. You're so goddamn stubborn, I could slap you sometimes."

"So you'll do it?"

"I'll look at this 'workshop' of yours, anyway. See if it's decent."

"It is! Oh, you're going to love it!"

"Meet me here tomorrow around noon?"

"Absolutely!"

"And, Medina?"

"Yeah?"

"I want Indian rosewood, okay? Sitka spruce, ebony... If we're going to do this, we might as well do it right."

"Understood."

We both stand, and suddenly we're awkward. I stuff Shiva back in my pocket. He holds his beer in one hand, reaches the other palm out to shake. I take a step toward him, grab his hand, and pump it up and down with such enthusiasm I embarrass myself.

May 5th, 1970

Einstein,

Passing through a village near the Sea of Japan. Children watch me like I'm a god or maybe a drooling lunatic. Is this what it's like to be a rock star? Only the middle-aged squares pretend they don't see me. What a trip this country is. My ship leaves in a couple weeks. I'll barely have time to try all the different colors of raw fish and seaweed before I go.

And where am I headed next?

Home, brother.

For the last few months San Francisco's been calling my name relentlessly. Is it a siren's song? Will I be smashed to pieces on the rocks of Big Sur before I reach the Golden Gate? California, that whole anarchic state, seemed for a while like a dream I could barely remember. But now it calls to me with such a muscular, breathtaking force, I can't resist any longer. Old Rot Gut's shop on Cherry Street and the cool of the fog creeping in from the bay. The head shops on the Haight and the girls in their faded jeans, their tight turtlenecks, their acid-rich eyes. I hope you're diggin' it, man, because even though I love this little country with its rice paddies and it's swaying bamboo, cherry blossoms and sake, right now I would give my left nut just to walk with you into Rot Gut's shop and waste all afternoon watching him sneak sips from the flask he keeps behind the radio while he strings his new archtop.

You're always mindful, though. You're always diggin' where you're at. Not like me. I've always got one eye on the next exit. Well, I'll try to be more like you, huh? I'll study you when I get home.

Don't disappoint me, man. I want a little Panama Red when I step foot on San Francisco soil. Keep a stash in reserve.

Later on,
Chet

Lucy and I lie on our stomachs, stretched out on too-small terry-cloth towels we found in the back of Arlan's station wagon, while the sun burns through the clouds and lays its warm rays on our shoulder blades. The guys dropped us off an hour ago and are supposed to meet us here later. Our faces are turned toward each other, pressed sideways against the terry cloth. Something about the mossy-wet smell of the lake and the intimate quiet mixing with the sight of Lucy's childish features makes me feel like we're little girls. Every now and then, the wake of a distant boat reaches the shore and we can hear the waves lapping up on the crumbly sand.

I'm thinking about my father's letters, how human and fragile he seems at times on his see-through airmail stationery. It still makes my heart pound every time I see his cramped cursive there; I read them with wary slowness, and always in absolute privacy. I can't stand the thought of anyone else seeing his letters. Knowing Lucy's history of investigations, I've taken to wrapping the little leather bundle in several layers of T-shirts and stuffing it all into a paper bag, then stashing it behind the seat of the truck, which I keep locked. It's one thing for her to read my notebooks—my Suicide Maps are now highly edited, anyway. But if she ever read my father's letters, I think I might kill her.

I can't explain why it's so essential that I keep him all to myself. Maybe it's just habit, after all the years I spent hoarding my memories of him in the private storage unit of my heart, where no one could ship them off to the Goodwill. Or maybe I fear other people's eyes will render him mundane—just someone's dead father, writing letters. How could I reconcile that with the god I've turned him into?

He was human, of course. That's what Bender keeps reminding me. And still, when I think of him with those zealous eyes, it's hard to imagine he was of this world.

I remember the exact moment I realized that my mother was human. I was twelve—it wasn't long after my father died. My nanna was visiting, and my mother tried to cook an eclectic, international meal—Brazilian stuffed peppers with risotto and shitake mushrooms—only she was out of practice, and it turned out badly. The risotto was soupy, the mushrooms were scorched black, the peppers were limp and too salty. It was impossible to fake our way through it. We pushed our food around for a few minutes in silence, and then my nanna pushed her plate away and smiled sadly at my mother. That's when my mother did something I'd never seen her do: she folded her hands around her face and she moaned. It was a soft sound, hardly even audible, but it made my hair stand up. I remember thinking it was a childlike sound, almost infantile. That's when it hit me, a huge, blinding lightbulb snapping on in my brain: my mother was afraid of Nanna. And when I saw that, the rest came with it, a string of epiphanies about the tenuous, tinny nature of the adult world, understandings colliding like dominoes. They were just little kids who got bigger. They couldn't keep me safe; they were terrified themselves.

And yet somehow my father had remained untouched by

this realization. His death and all the weakness it exposed should have been the ultimate proof of his vulnerability. Yet I think of him still as beyond human, instilled with divine power and elusiveness. In my mind his body is a long curl of smoke, and only his eyes are real.

"What if I don't get into college, Anna?" Lucy's voice tugs me back to this: the lake, the sunlight, my friend.

"Then you'll apply again."

"Never." She has big, tortoiseshell sunglasses on, but now she takes them off and I can see the anxiety in her eyes. "If they don't want me, fuck them."

"You'll get in," I say. I think, *What if she doesn't?* but I try to push the thought from my mind.

"You didn't tell anyone I applied, did you?"

"Of course not."

"You sure? I'd die if Arlan or Grady found out."

"You're not going to tell Arlan, even?"

She adjusts her bathing suit top and squints at me. "No, and if you do I'll kill you."

"Relax," I say. "I'm not telling anyone."

"Arlan doesn't know everything," she says. "He's not my keeper." She watches the opposite shore.

"How long have you two been together?"

"Four years."

I hesitate, remembering the gossip Grady divulged to me that night in the tree. "Did you ever mess around?"

She laughs. "You, Anna, are the queen of euphemisms. I never 'mess around.' Period. Doesn't mean I never fucked other people. I mean, come on, I was eighteen when we got together."

"So you have?"

"I'm not one to pass up an opportunity." She puts her sunglasses back on. "Arlan is like good furniture, you know? He's like your favorite pair of socks. When you come home, you want those things. But they never keep you from getting bored."

I roll over onto my side and try to see if she's being serious. "Arlan is like *socks?*"

"Oh, sure," she says. "He seems glamorous to you. But that's because you're infatuated with him. Spend four years with him, see what he looks like then."

I'm not at all eager to discuss my infatuation with Arlan. "He's madly in love with you," I say. "He doesn't think of you as socks."

"He's just more sentimental. Or he doesn't get bored. I don't know." She flips over onto her back and stares up at the sky. "He does love me, though. Last week he went all the way to Canada just to get me these little chocolates I was craving. Or one night I was on the rag and out of tampons, so he ripped up one of his T-shirts for me. He's good, don't get me wrong. He's great." She raises herself on her elbows abruptly and shakes her hair back from her face. "But then again, he threatened to kill me twice, too, so let's not romanticize."

"Are you serious?"

"Of course," she says. "He's no saint."

I roll over onto my back and watch as she lights a cigarette. "Why? What did you do?"

"Now that's a fucked-up question, don't you think?"

"No, I mean, not that you would deserve it—I just meant, what made him that mad that he would—"

"There's two things Arlan and I are really good at. Fighting and fucking. Our worldviews are not exactly aligned—I mean, he has a lot to learn from me, if he would just shut up and listen—but these are two things we have in common. Sometimes, when yelling our heads off and throwing things isn't satisfying enough, he threatens to kill me. It's like an aphrodisiac."

"Sort of a dangerous way to get off, don't you think?"

"Getting off is always dangerous," she says.

Before I can think of more questions, she throws off her glasses, leaps up and charges into the water. When she comes up for air she screams and shakes her dark hair, sending tiny shards of water flying in every direction, refracting light. "It's fucking *cold!*" she squeals, and the pleasure in her voice makes me get up and follow. I ease in slowly, feeling the surface as it grips higher and higher up my legs, then around my hips, and at last encircles my waist. By the time the waterline is even with my nipples, I have given in to its cold; I catch my breath and float under. The world underneath is olive green. The sunlight filters past the surface in angelic beams. I can hear the distant, high-pitched buzz of a motorboat.

I float in the water for a long time. When I run out of breath, I stay above the surface just long enough to gather more, and then I propel myself under again.

I feel something grab ahold of my calf. I'm whipping around to see what it is, even as I'm clawing for the surface. Dead body, I'm thinking. Corpse grip. I can imagine the blue-green skin, the decaying flesh, sunken eyes and the crone claws holding tight to my leg. Whatever it is lets go, then grabs again, at my thigh this time. I catch my breath, heart pounding, and turn again, kicking madly, trying to see what it is and get away from it all at once.

Arlan surfaces, laughing, and then he looks surprised. "I'm sorry! I thought—"

"What's going on over there?" Lucy's balancing on a huge floating log, riding it sidesaddle, about five yards off. "You guys—" Suddenly, the other end of the log rises out of the water and Lucy goes screaming overboard in one swift, unstoppable movement. Grady and Bill appear on either side of the disrupted log and high-five each other with wet palms.

"I can't believe it!" Bill laughs. "We finally found a way to shut Lucy up!"

Lucy comes sputtering out of the water and kicks toward shore, indignant. Bill climbs up on the log and tries to ride it like a surfboard, but it's too round, and after a brief, hard-earned moment of balance, he goes flying off with a cowboy "yee-haw!" that tears across the lake. I hear Arlan laugh and am surprised to see that he's still treading water near me.

"Sorry about scaring you," he says. "I thought you were Lucy."

"Yeah," I say. "I figured."

I look at his face, dewy with lake water, his hair slicked back and shining in the sunlight. He looks happy and childish. Arlan always looks either heartbreakingly innocent or brooding and scary; there is no in-between.

Grady's head pops out of the water. "Let's swim out to the dock," he says, looking first at me and then at Arlan.

"Not me, man," Arlan says. "Smokers don't swim."

"Anna?"

"Yeah," I say, squinting at the dock about two hundred yards off. "Let's go."

When we get back to the beach about twenty minutes later, Arlan has disappeared, and Lucy's looking at Bill like she wants to bash his head in. "Bill, you can shut up about that—" she says, her voice just a notch above normal volume.

"Don't tell me to shut up—"

"You don't know anything about it!"

"All I know is, I saw what I saw." Bill crosses his skinny, naked arms across his chest. With his hair wet he looks more like a rat than ever. "I saw you, and I saw Zukerman. What am I supposed to do? Three o'clock in the morning, you know? Why would I lie about that?"

"You know, that's very interesting," Lucy says, with a tight little smile. "Because *I* never said you were lying. Why would you even mention lying? All I said is, you don't know anything about it."

"And that's why I'm asking."

Grady and I sit awkwardly a little distance from Lucy and Bill.

"Anna," Lucy says. "Pay attention, here. This is exactly the brand of misogyny I'm always talking about. A man sees a woman coming out of a motel with an old friend of hers—what does he *immediately* assume?"

"Look," Bill says, his tone softening. "I just asked a question, is all—"

"And does he approach the *man* about it?"

"Zukerman's not my best friend's girlfriend—"

"Arlan's your best friend now, is he?" I can see there is hatred in her face. "I don't expect you of all people to understand this, but I am *nobody's* girlfriend, all right? Don't you *ever* fuck with my privacy—"

"I just thought I should ask, instead of wondering—"

"We were visiting the girl who works the desk, you idiot—but that's beside the point."

"Well, then, I misunderstood, Lucy. I thought—"

"I know exactly what you thought—Jesus! You think I don't get this shit all the time? If you have tits you're automatically suspect. The point is, I don't have to explain *anything* to you. I could fuck the entire town of Bellingham—you excluded, of course—and I wouldn't have to explain a single goddamn thing to you, understand?"

Silence. A motorboat passes us. A little kid waves. Bill is the only one who waves back. After a pause, the wake sloshes against the shore in heavy, rhythmic spills.

"Lucy," Grady says softly, turning in her direction. "Where's Arlan?"

"Fuck if I know," she says.

"He took the car," Bill says. "I guess I pissed him off."

"Fuck Arlan," Lucy says, getting up. "Fuck all of you."

We watch as she throws on her T-shirt and jeans, then walks to the edge of the road and sticks out her thumb.

The first car passing picks her up.

The three of us remaining have lost our enthusiasm for frolicking at the lake. We gather our towels and trudge across the beach to the road. It's early afternoon, and it's getting downright hot all of a sudden. The cool of the morning cloud cover has dissipated entirely, and the sun is glaring. A fly buzzes near my ear and I swat at it. I am thirsty and I feel a headache coming on.

We stand at the edge of the hot black asphalt, holding our thumbs out in silence. I've never hitchhiked before, and I feel a little nervous; visions of my face staring back from a milk carton swim through my mind. Still, I don't have any better ideas, so I keep my thumb out and try to look casual.

"I just asked her a question," Bill says, after half a dozen cars have passed us. "I didn't accuse her of anything." Grady and I just nod. "After the Nick Ferrari thing, we all know what she's capable of."

"Who's Nick Ferrari?" I ask.

Bill looks at me quizzically. "When did you move in?"

"June."

"It happened before she met them," Grady says, looking out into the empty street.

"*What* happened?"

Just then Arlan pulls up in the station wagon. "Where's Lucy?" he says, leaning across the seat to the passenger window.

"She hitched a ride," Grady says.

"Goddammit." Arlan shakes his head. "I hate it when she does that."

We climb in and Arlan heads back to the house. Nobody

says a thing. Arlan turns on the radio; there's nothing but Christian music and static coming in. He swears softly and shuts it off. Grady and I are in the back seat. I struggle with the ancient, rusty handle, trying to roll the window down. When I look up, I see Arlan's eyes in the rearview mirror. All the innocence I witnessed earlier has drained away completely, and he stares at the road with a menacing concentration. I reach up to stick my fingers out the window, into the cool of the breeze, and when I look at the mirror again, he catches me staring at him. The black of his eyes makes me feel suddenly cold; I shiver and roll the window up.

Midnight. Lucy's still not back. The four of us maintain an increasingly medicated vigil. We've worked our way through two six-packs of Coronas and are now well into our third. Bill polishes off some leftover pizza, but the rest of us don't eat. Twice, now, Arlan has gotten in his car and driven the streets, insisting on going alone. Three or four times he has gone into the bedroom and made short, terse phone calls. I consider going for a walk, but I can't bring myself to abandon the tight little wad of misery we've formed. We let the room grow dark, keep the radio loud, and say little.

At one point, Arlan and I find ourselves in the kitchen. Bill and Grady are out on the porch, smoking. This is the first time we've been alone since the Fourth. I am standing at the sink and he lunges unsteadily past me for the door of the fridge. His wrist grazes my hip as I turn. His fingers grab the handle of the fridge; he steadies himself with it instead of opening it. We look at each other, and I think of his mouth on his harp—the way his lips tighten around it, his eyes closed. The refrigerator hums loudly. We don't move. I wish he would kiss me and I hate myself for it. Instead, he yanks open the fridge and frees another Corona from the cardboard container.

"This isn't the first time she's disappeared," he says. I just watch him, hoping my face looks purely concerned, as if I have been thinking of Lucy all along, and not of his mouth. "She took off for a month, once." He leans against the fridge, takes a swig of beer. "No note or anything." His eyes hold mine, and he says very softly, "I almost killed myself." All the air seems to go out of the room. A surge of hatred rises behind my eyes; how could she do this to him? But then I think, he loves her cruelty. He laughs, as if he's heard my thoughts, and says, "We deserve each other, I guess. I'm no walk in the park." I think, Oh, Arlan, I want to be so close to you that the smell of your body fills me up.

"She won't stay away long," I say. And I know she won't, because I'm here. I'm just enough of a threat to keep her tethered to Smoke Palace for now; she's reckless, but not stupid. He just nods, drinks his beer and stares out the window.

I wake to the sound of voices. I try to seize a pillow—something to drown out the noise—but all I feel is hard vinyl.

"Don't tell me what to do! Arlan— Get your fucking hands—"

"You're gone all night long—and you come in here like—"

"Tell Bill to get off my goddamn floor—I want him out of my house."

"I'm driving around like a maniac…I called your mom, your sister—"

"Why? Jesus, I had some drinks, so what—"

"What is this shit about Zuckerman?"

Something crashes to the floor. I stare into the darkness. Out the window, the sky looks close to dawn. I wait, holding my breath.

Silence. More silence.

Lucy giggles. Arlan laughs quietly. "You little moron," I

hear him say, but all the anger has left his voice. There is another long pause. Soon, I can decipher the sound of breathing, a soft, stifled moan, and, "Shh! Arlan..." and then, "Jesus, babe." Then nothing.

I look around the room. In the half light, I can see the silhouette of Bill collapsed on the floor, his elbow cocked at a weird angle under him. Someone has thrown a blanket over me—a scratchy, grandmotherly thing made of pale yarn. As I am studying it curiously, I feel the eerie presence of eyes on me. I look up and there is Grady Berlin, slumped in the chair by the window, with the dark gray, dimly illumined sky filling the glass panes behind him. He is leaning all the way back, his legs splayed out in a wide V. I can barely make out half of his face in the dim light from the window. I can see that his eyes are open, though.

We stare at each other, listening to the sound of Arlan and Lucy making love across the hall.

In the morning, Arlan, Grady and Bill go out for breakfast, but Lucy refuses to go, and I decide to stay behind with her. We lie on the bed, drinking coffee and staring out the window. We don't say anything until she's finished her first cigarette. Then she drains her coffee and says flatly, "I'm pregnant."

I look at her. "Oh my God. How do you know?"

"I just know," she says. "I've never been wrong before."

"So it's not the first time?"

She shakes her head and glances at me, then stares out the window again.

"What are you going to do?"

"Come on," she says. "What do you think I'm going to do?"

We both stare out the window now. The Penny Guy—this weird little man with orange, wiry tufts of hair—appears from the alley behind Smoke Palace and stops below the window. He shields his eyes with his hand to peer up at us. His left eye is sealed shut, and the other roams a little toward the street. He carries a ragged burlap sack that sags at the bottom. "Hello!" he cries, seeming happy to see us. "Any pennies today?"

"Hold on," Lucy says. She goes to the desk and opens a drawer. It's full of little plastic baggies filled with pennies. She takes one and returns to the window. "Here you go," she says, and tosses it down to him. He catches it and flashes her a grin so enormous and gleeful, I half wish she would toss him more.

"Thank you!" he calls, ripping open the plastic and letting the pennies clatter noisily into his burlap sack. "You have a good day, pretty ladies!" He disappears back into the alley.

"That guy," she says, shaking her head with a little smile.

"You have a stash especially for him?"

"I like him," she says. "I can't help it."

I study the side of her face—her perfect, miniature nose, the long dark lashes, the pale, creamy cheeks just slightly kissed with sun. I wonder if I'll ever really know her.

"What are you looking at?" she asks, throwing me a bashful, sideways glance.

"Nothing." I make a fist on the windowsill and rest my chin on it. "Will you let me go with you?" I ask, after a while. "To the clinic, or wherever?"

"If you promise not to turn it into a drama," she says.

"Since when am *I* the drama queen?" I say.

"Sure," she says, quietly. "Come." And she puts one hand in my hair for a brief, unexpected moment, before she comes to her senses and reaches for another cigarette.

There's a postcard of a Waikiki sunset, and on the back my father has written Bender a note in such miniaturized script, it's barely legible.

June 16th, 1974
Hey Einstein,

I'm so sunburned. We drink mai tais for breakfast. This is the life. For lunch we eat fruit and fresh coconut flesh. For dinner we file into fancy restaurants filled with loud, obnoxious families and other honeymooners, all of them looking tired and furious. I'm no exception. Something about marriage makes a man irritated. Never mind—too many mai tais for me today.

Just wanted to thank you for your speech at the wedding. Never knew a man could be so drunk and articulate at once.

They play these really wild little ukuleles here. Maybe we should try making one. I know they seem sort of dwarfish and generally inferior, but I've seen some here that really turn me on. The abalone inlay would blow your mind.

Later,
Chet

The next letter is written on the blank side of a yellow flyer advertising a free summer jazz festival in Golden Gate Park.

March 23rd, 1975
Bender,

Okay, I know you and Sheila are only honeymooning for another ten days, so I guess it's pretty ridiculous, me writing you like this, but I am SO GODDAMN EXCITED I CANNOT HELP MYSELF, brother, so HOLD ON, I'VE JUST GOT TO TELL YOU.

Tuesday morning, ten o'clock, you'll never guess who walked through our doors. I'm working on that twelve-string for the old fart, Edelman, and I'm concentrating so hard I barely even notice when the bell jingles on the door. When I finally realize we've got a customer, I yell from the back, "Be right there!" Couple minutes later I wander out and who's standing in OUR FUCKING SHOP? BOB DYLAN AND JOAN BAEZ.

You think I'm shitting you. Would I shit you about this? You know I would not.

Dylan ordered a guitar from us, man. He likes our shit. No, I would have to say, given the amount of dough he's willing to spend and the look of restrained giddiness he wore as he looked around, I would have to say he LOVES WHAT WE DO.

Joan is twenty thousand times more beautiful than you ever could have thought possible. Her eyes are as wise as a crone, but she has the playfulness of a little girl.

God, I wish Rot Gut were around to see this.

We're in the big time now,

Chet

"So?" I can barely conceal my impatience. "What do you think?" Bender looks around the workshop with an unreadable face. Sometimes I could swear he means to torture me. He takes his time, circling the room slowly, searching for electrical outlets and checking for leaks in the roof as he gnaws on a toothpick. This is the first time I've seen him without a Budweiser clamped between his fingers. He looks oddly naked.

"All right," he announces at last. "Might take some work, but it'll do." Not exactly the enthusiasm I was hoping for, but I remind myself not to take offense. It's a big deal for Bender even to leave his boat, so I'm trying to keep my expectations reasonable.

For an hour, we lose ourselves in plans; Bender does all the talking, since I know almost nothing. He muses about where to put the table saw, joiner and planer, how to keep the moisture controlled with a hydrometer. A soft rain begins to tap against the windows that line the upper part of the southern wall. The glass is beige with years of dust, and the rain makes muddy streaks. We've got the doors open, and the fragrance of wet pavement fills the room. I listen to Bender rattle on about exotic woods whose names evoke whole worlds: cocobolo rosewood, Hawaiian koa, Sitka spruce. Faint memories of my father's shop come back to me in pieces: the high-pitched whine of his saw, the dust motes in the air, the strange smell bone emits when it's sanded.

After a while, Bender stops talking. We slip into a companionable silence as we linger near the doorway, watching the rain come down. Without giving it much thought, I ask, "Who was Rot Gut?" Immediately, his mood shifts, and I half regret having mentioned it.

"Chet had pet names for everyone," he says. "What did he used to call you?"

"All kinds of things," I say. "Mostly Gripper Girl, though. Sometimes GG for short."

"Gripper Girl," he repeats, nodding. "Where did he get that, again?"

"When I was a baby, I used to clamp onto things like a maniac. He claimed you could stick me to the wall—said my hands were like little suction cups."

"I remember that, now." He takes the toothpick from his mouth and examines it. "You did have quite a grip...."

"Why did he call you Einstein?"

"Hell, I can hardly even remember. I guess I used to do a lot of homemade experiments—they always went south, of course. He called me Einstein once when we were kids and it just stuck." He starts picking at his gums methodically with the toothpick.

"So who was Rot Gut?"

"That's what your dad used to call my uncle. He was a luthier—had a shop in Palo Alto when we were kids. We used to hang out there whenever we could. He taught us the trade, when he wasn't too drunk to see straight."

"He drank a lot?"

He chuckles, but it's a sad sound. "You think *I'm* bad…Uncle Dave drank Jack Daniel's for every meal."

"Is he still alive?"

"No. Liver gave out on him." He takes out his handkerchief and blows his nose twice. "So you've been reading those letters, I guess."

"Uh-huh. One by one. I never knew he was so obsessed with Bob Dylan."

He sits down on the stoop, and I do the same. The rain is falling harder now. A playful breeze tosses damp candy bar wrappers and cigarette butts this way and that in the alley. "Did he ever tell you he jammed a couple times with Dylan?"

"No."

"I guess Dylan even suggested he might open for one of his shows. Your dad really wanted to be a star, you know. That was never my trip—I just wanted to make good guitars. But for Chet, fame was this mirage he couldn't shake."

"So did he do it?"

"Do what?"

"Open for Dylan?"

"No. He was rehearsing like crazy for a year after this comment Dylan made in passing. When Chet finally called him up and told him he was ready to tour, I guess the guy barely remembered who he was. Crushed him. He was depressed for months after that. It was a chore just to get him out of bed."

Suddenly I remember something I haven't thought of in years: my mother and me whispering so we won't disturb Dad. It's the middle of the afternoon, and it's hot, and we've got to keep all the windows closed so none of the noise from the street will seep in. I remember the oppressive, stuffy quiet and the closed bedroom door.

"When did that happen?" I ask.

"Oh hell, I don't know. Must have been twenty-seven, twenty-eight years ago, I guess."

"He got depressed a lot, didn't he?"

He nods. Then he stands and forces a little grin. "How's about we get my tools over here Monday?"

I'm getting used to Bender unceremoniously changing the subject. I shrug. "What's wrong with tomorrow?"

He chuckles, and a wild, silver curl rises from the mess of stiff, gelled ones, drifting upward on a breeze from the doorway. "You sure are a slave driver."

"What? You need Sunday off, already?"

"Hell, no—I just thought you might have a date or something."

"Right," I laugh. "Fat chance."

"Swing by the docks around eleven?"

"Sounds good." I look at him, and try to envision the young man my father wrote to so many years ago. His tragedies have etched themselves into the lines around his eyes and the deep, pensive grooves at the corners of his mouth. His body has given way to excess and gravity, but maybe years ago he was lean, before the beers added up.

"Think I'll just walk back," Bender says, pulling the hood of his windbreaker over his head. I notice now that the elbow's been patched with duct tape.

"No," I say. "I'll drive you."

"It's good for me," he says, stepping out into the rain. He looks pleasantly Hemmingwayesque, there, with his hood on and the rain falling all around him. He nods goodbye at me, tosses his toothpick into a puddle and heads off in the direction of the marina.

"See you tomorrow!" I call to his back. Without turning around, he raises one hand in the air, turns a corner and disappears.

Stains

Almost a week later, Lucy still hasn't informed me of any appointment, and it's making me nervous. She's been drinking more heavily than usual, smoking more, eating less. Her beauty persists, but her face is more severe than it used to be—her cheekbones are more extreme, and her eyes are a little crazy.

Thursday afternoon, after working with Bender on the shop, I come home to find her sitting outside, gazing listlessly into space. She's leaning back in one of the increasingly disgusting porch chairs. I install myself next to her, in the even more decayed one, shifting to avoid the two or three exposed springs in the seat cushion. She reaches out and brushes a bit of sawdust from my arm. Across the street, the Goat Kids turn their music up so loud, it sounds like chainsaws. Their stereo is obviously unable to handle their volume expectations.

"Goddammit," Lucy says, rolling her eyes. "Those people need to kill themselves."

At Purgatory Corner, there's a new guy on the porch wearing overalls and looking like a cadaver propped up on the steps; he screams at the Goat Kid house, "Turn that shit *down!*" You'd never expect that much sound from him, just looking at his sickly frame. He must have disproportionately large lungs.

Lucy shakes her head and says, "This corner is nuts, man. White trash everywhere you look."

I go upstairs and pour us both some coffee. When I join her again, I ask casually, "Where's Arlan?"

"Painting."

"That's right." I pause before asking, "What's the latest on the baby front?"

She scoffs. "Fuck, I don't know. We have to decide soon, though."

"I thought you'd already decided."

"Arlan thinks he wants it."

The coffee is bitter and lukewarm. I put it down. "Do you?"

She curls her legs up close to her and wraps one arm around her knees. "I don't think so. But the clinic has to be the creepiest place on earth."

"How many times have you been?"

She looks at me. "Three. This will be the fourth."

"Oh," I say, trying not to sound shocked.

"Don't look at me like that," she says, bristling.

"Like what?"

"Like you're looking at me."

I pick up my coffee again and choke down another sip. "I'm not looking at you like anything."

"I don't believe in their guilty fucking stupid Catholic rhetoric, okay?"

"Whose?"

"The whole world's," she says. "I have no guilt about taking care of what needs to be taken care of. It's their attitudes that get to me. I don't need to be exposed to that. I don't like doctors sticking shit up inside me and then giving me a lecture about birth control, and I hate those insipid nurses with their sanitary outfits and their caked-on makeup—the whole thing just gives me the fucking creeps."

"Yeah," I say. "Okay."

"Don't 'Yeah, okay' me," she says, raising her voice. "I'm serious. I don't know if I can go back there."

"Aren't there other clinics—like in Seattle?"

"Sure," she says. "They're all the same. Creepy, creepy, creepy."

The Goat Kids turn their music up even louder, and the cadaver on the porch screams, "Hey! HEY!" He gets no response.

"Call me crazy," I say, "but I don't think dreading a trip to the clinic is a good enough reason to commit yourself to a lifetime of parenting."

She covers her face with her hands. "Oh God," she says. "I need a drink."

"Not to mention nine months without alcohol—or smokes."

"Forget that," she says. "No way."

"What—do you want to pickle the little thing inside you? Have it come out reeking of gin and bumming a smoke, first thing?"

She stares off at the distance, and I wonder if she even heard me. After a while, she says, "Sometimes I think about it. Imagine a baby that's half Arlan, half me. What a weird, fucked-up creature that would be!"

"A beautiful little monster," I say.

"I've got to tell him no way. I'll make an appointment tomorrow. I mean, come on, what are we thinking? It's too crazy."

I reach out and remove a strand of hair from her eyes. "Just tell me when the appointment is. We'll smuggle in a bottle of vodka or something."

She laughs without opening her mouth. There are tears in her eyes. "Sometimes I'm really, really tired," she whispers. She blinks, and her lashes knock a pair of tears over the pinkish rims of her eyes. "This morning, I could barely get out of bed."

"Hormones," I say, wiping one of the tears away with my thumb.

"Just *tired*," she says. "Tired of everything."

We sit there, staring out over the yard, watching the fog, until the Goat Kids' music gets so unbearable, and the cadaver's protests so belligerent, we have to take our coffee cups and head inside.

I'm trying to sketch a timeline of my father's life, and I see now how many pieces are missing. It's frustrating and a little eerie, like trying to spell your own name and suddenly realizing you've forgotten most of the letters. I know the basics: born and raised in Palo Alto. Tried Stanford, dropped out to travel. Pretty soon after he got back to the States he started taking classes at the music conservatory in San Francisco. He didn't last long there, though, before dropping out again—I remember he told me once it was too stuffy, that the professors wouldn't know funky if it bit them in the ass. He married my mother, the harp and sax player with soft gray eyes. She was a little older than he was, and had just graduated from the conservatory with honors. In the wedding pictures they both look stunned and confused—very fresh and alive but also startled, like they just said something they wished they could take back, only it was too late.

He had money, and she didn't. It was a big issue. Both his parents were dead by the time he graduated high school, but they left plenty behind. I never heard much about them—in fact, I hardly remember him reminiscing about his childhood at all. Mom would occasionally bring up his inheritance with bitterness, implying that he was spoiled and pampered. She grew up dirt poor in some little town near Fresno, a place she never wanted to visit and rarely mentioned, except in her blackest moods.

Sometimes I liked to imagine a romantic wrong-side-of-the-tracks sort of courtship between my parents. My father in crisp, expensive slacks and a bloated bank account enchanted with my mother, who could barely make rent in her little studio above the Chinese takeout joint. Unfortunately, I know it didn't turn out to be much of a fairy tale. I remember the arguments; my mother was obsessed with home furnishings, good wines and shoes. She was always pining for a vintage pinot noir, or some sleek, strappy sandals down at Nordstrom, even in the early days when her hair was long and she smoked pot and cooked tofu. My father, on the other hand, hated to talk about expenses. He seemed to think that money was dirty, and that the best way to deal with it was to deny its existence entirely; that was the only way to be sure it didn't own you. Sometimes, when she got on him about the new leather couch she had to have, he would chant at her, quietly but relentlessly, "Make money your god and it will plague you like the devil," until she stormed out of the room.

Early in my parents' marriage, Bender and my father opened the shop. I've pieced together the basics on that, too, though it's taken a little prying on my part. Bender seems reluctant to talk about their friendship in too much detail, as if he's worried I might ask the wrong questions. They started the business when they were in their early twenties; they'd been friends since high school, and it seemed natural to make a living doing what they loved. They'd been messing around with building and repairing stringed instruments for years, hanging out in Rot Gut's studio every chance they got since they were fifteen. It started out as a small business, mostly doing repairs and fixing up antiques they got for cheap at flea markets or estate sales. Slowly, they started building their own guitars from scratch. They named their shop The Mermaid Garden, based on some shared LSD trip Bender was hopelessly vague about—he claimed he'd forgotten the details, but the shine in his eyes told me otherwise.

Sometimes he'll start a story and then he'll trail off or change the subject with an awkward non sequitur, looking embarrassed. He seems okay when I ask about the early years; it's the later ones that make him jumpy and uncomfortable. Instinctively, I sense his hesitance hinges on the mysterious falling-out they had, just before he sold Dad the business and moved to Santa Fe. I was only about three when that happened, and I can't remember any of it. I get the feeling there was some event that tipped their friendship over a cliff, leaving only broken pieces behind.

The Skins are off and running, with the help of a slick, pierced, very pretty bunch of groupies who apparently saw God at the debut on the Fourth and haven't stopped talking about it since. The band has had half a dozen gigs now, and each time the crowd size swells. Already, people are yelling out titles and singing with the choruses, as if they were raised on these songs.

The secret, of course, is Arlan. Women peer over their dates' shoulders at him, hang around after and try in vain to strike up conversations. His first moments of terror on the Fourth seem like a distant memory. Now he stands on stage with unshakable confidence, gripping his guitar with nonchalance. He wears a metal harness to hold his harmonica; the harness is vaguely reminiscent of headgear, the kind geeky boys wore in junior high. But when you see his mouth sliding up and down the slender, silver shape, eliciting noises that are part train, part animal moans, you forget all about headgear. In fact, you forget all about everything when you see Arlan like that.

Arlan's songs are almost always built around a woman's name—something outdated and not terribly pretty like Virginia or Alice. He makes you want to be these women, and you know if you were you'd reinvent the name; you'd be wearing some thin, shapeless cotton slip in Tennessee and maybe you'd have braids and definitely you'd smoke; you'd hang laundry out to dry on hot summer evenings and Arlan would come driving up in a rusted-out Cadillac or an ancient Ford truck with a thin cloud of dust rising under his wheels, the sky turning a melancholy blue in the wake of a violent sunset, and you'd watch him get out and squint at you, his face sweaty and dark, his hunting knife glistening on the dashboard, and you really wouldn't care if he planned to slit your throat or brush your hair back tenderly—the difference would be minimal, because you'd be ready for anything with him.

Every woman in the audience knows these things, when we watch Arlan's fingers caressing the frets, stroking the mic as he leans in a little closer, his lips nearly touching the metal mesh. We can't take our eyes off him. But Arlan never really looks at us when he plays. His ecstasy is always moving past us, over us; his eyes might rest on a face for a moment, but there is nothing more than a fleeting trace of recognition before he moves on to another world, someplace hot as whiskey in your chest, someplace beautiful and dark. It is precisely the private nature of this ecstasy that makes every woman watching him think of sex—not foreplay or flattery, but the moment when a man comes inside you, the moment that is never really yours.

One of the pages in my bundle of letters is undated, and it seems more like a journal entry than a letter. He hasn't even written Bender's nickname at the top of the page, like he usually does. It's scribbled in particularly difficult-to-read lettering on a piece of heavy paper torn from a notebook. One edge is ragged and uneven, obscuring a few letters at the margin, as if he ripped it out carelessly.

> Oh God. Going up is so easy. One minute the walls are just walls, the next they're multidimensional tapestries dripping with the history of the universe. On the way up there's a surge of wonder and delight, like discovering it's the first day of summer vacation, and here you were thinking it was the dead of winter. It's down that creates the problem. Gravity is the enemy. Now that I'm back between the walls, the fit is tighter than ever.
>
> Helen and I went for a walk in the afternoon. It was just us for the first time in forever. We walked to the Mission; she smoked a little pot, but she didn't want to shroom because last time she felt the top of her head disintegrate and run all over her face and it scared her so badly she hasn't tried it since.
>
> We walked to that Nicaraguan place we love, and on the way I told her about the time Aida taught me to samba. It was wonderful. She smelled of peppers and musk and her hips were like an intricate, well-oiled machine, shifting and reversing with incredible precision and grace. I was right at eye-level with her breasts; they were moving in time with her hips, and her low-cut blouse showed the clean, dark line of her cleavage.

I remember staring at that crevice with such simple, pure awe, wondering how one line could hold such mystery.

This was before everything happened, of course. I was maybe twelve, and the world was just opening up, and a woman's body was still the strangest, darkest fruit of all. I didn't feel shame, that afternoon, learning the quick, mincing steps and the oiled hips of samba. What I felt was alive.

I wanted to tell Helen all of this; I wanted to re-create for her the light on Aida's hair and the luminous cinnamon of her skin. I guess it was just that the world seemed open again, as we walked. The mothers were calling to their children in Spanish and the bananas were piled high outside the corner market and the air smelled of meats turning tender in baths of salsa. I thought if I could connect this moment to that one, this beautiful day to that beautiful day, with Helen as my witness, maybe the world would become whole again.

The optimism of the magical plant kingdom.

I was just getting to the part about Aida's breasts when Helen looked at me and said, "That woman practically destroyed you. How can you love her still?" And I thought, don't we all destroy each other? Isn't that what we're doing right now? Killing each other with good intentions? I wanted to tell her about the nature of forgiveness—but more than that, I wanted her to see what a beautiful day it was, when I was twelve, when a woman's body contained absolute mystery, nothing more, nothing less.

Instead we walked the rest of the way in silence.

Tuesday, as we're building a counter along the south wall, I take the nails out of my mouth and say, "You knew Dad a long time, right?"

"Met in the fifth grade," he says.

"Do you know who Aida was?"

He pounds a nail in with two quick strokes, lines the next one up, does the same. "Sort of."

"What do you mean, sort of?"

"She disappeared when we were pretty young."

"Who was she?"

"His stepmother."

I struggle to recall anything my father might have mentioned about a stepmother, but there's nothing. All I can see now is him dancing with a dark-haired woman, her breasts swaying in time to their movements, and then I hear my mother: *"That woman practically destroyed you."*

"She was kind of wild, I guess. There was twenty years at least between her and old man Medina." I imagine the wedding photo: an old man, silver-haired and bent slightly at the waist, his tux immaculately tailored and yet somehow too large. He drapes an arm possessively around the young, tan bride with the mischievous smile.

"Did Dad like her?"

Bender shrugs, takes a tape measure out and measures the width. "I guess he did," he says, when I don't stop staring at him.

"Why would my mother say Aida destroyed him?"

"She said that to you?"

"No, to my father. I read it in one of his letters."

He takes a handkerchief from his pocket, wipes the sweat from his brow. "You want to take a quick break?"

"Okay," I say, a little surprised.

"Let's go get an iced tea or something."

"Sure."

We walk downtown, and I see that the warmth of the day has brought the half-naked throngs out of doors again. We go to the Little Cheerful, a popular college hangout, and we order large iced teas, then sit outside in the shade of the awning, at a table that seems too small for Bender. He squeezes a wedge of lemon into his tea and pours from the sugar dispenser until the bottom of the glass shows a thick layer of white. "Old Southern recipe," he says, when he notices me staring.

We sit a couple of minutes in silence, sipping our tea and watching the girls in tiny halter tops and hippie skirts, boys in nothing but shorts, their bodies gleaming white.

"You remember when I gave you those letters? I said you weren't going to like everything."

"Yeah." I feel a little nervous, suddenly. I decide I want my tea sweet, too, so I pour as much sugar as Bender did, and he smiles.

"You're also not going to understand everything," he says, his face going serious again. "There were things he maybe didn't want to remember."

"Like what?"

"Oh, you know. Unpleasant shit."

"No, I don't know." Suddenly, I realize the power Bender has over me. He knows who my father was, and I don't. "Tell me."

"I don't know if it's my place."

"Why is everyone so secretive about him? He's dead. He forfeited his right to privacy, as far as I'm concerned."

Bender sighs, and when his eyes meet mine I see the sadness there. "Aida was a very unstable woman. She was lonely in the States, I think—her English wasn't great. She was from Brazil—did you know that?" I shake my head. I think about adding that I didn't even know she existed, before today, but I don't. "She married your grandpa, and then he got pretty sick right away. She was only in her thirties, and everyone knew she was restless. Well…" He stares at his iced tea, his mouth tight. "Shit, Medina. I really don't know how to say this. She, uh, and your dad. Were lovers, I guess you could say."

I feel suddenly sick to my stomach, but also riveted, like I'm straining to see a grisly car wreck. "Lovers?"

He nods, not looking at me. "When your grandpa died, she took her share of his money and moved back to Brazil. Your dad was almost eighteen. He moved in with us for the last semester of high school."

It takes a second for all this to sink in. The closed door of my father's adolescence opens a crack and allows me a sliver of a view. I'm not sure I like what I'm seeing. "Did he hate her?"

"He was pretty hurt. But I think he always loved Aida—even after she left. She was a little crazy, you know. I'm not saying what she did was right, but she had a good heart, in a way. She was very musical; she got your dad into guitar when he was young. She did a lot of things wrong, but she got some things right." He gulps down half his tea. "At least, that's how I saw it.

"Your mom saw it different. She never met Aida, but she hated her. Everything that was wrong with your dad, she blamed on her."

"What do you mean, 'wrong' with him?"

He considers me for a moment, seeming to weigh out how much to tell me. "He was pretty up and down. One minute he'd be on top of the world, ready for anything, the next he'd be in his room with all the shades drawn. He wanted to be enlightened and he wanted to be a star—those were his trips. Sometimes he was a helium balloon, and then suddenly he was dead weight. Your mom had her hands full, you know, just keeping up with him. We all did." He takes another swig of tea, squeezes more lemon into it, stirs the coating of sugar that's settled at the bottom.

I sit there, gripping my glass, feeling it sweat against my

palm. I can see the past trying to rearrange itself again, shifting to make room for this new information, like a kaleidoscope twisting into a new design. I think of the words *incest* and *molestation*, such ugly, contaminated syllables. Somehow I sense they don't apply, but then, what words do? Was Aida like a generous whore? I wish so much that he was here to answer my questions—to unravel his past for me with his own interpretations, instead of leaving me to navigate the shadowy forest of his life, with only Bender and the bread crumbs of his letters to guide me.

The past is so slippery. It can redesign itself in seconds. And what about the people who hand it to us? They, too, can disappear on any ordinary afternoon. You can go to gymnastics on a Tuesday in July, and when you're done, the whole universe can be rearranged, because one person decided to leave it. When they leave, they take all their stories with them.

I look at Bender and a sense of urgency comes over me. He knew my father better than anyone. I can't waste my time with him; he could die at any moment, and then all of his stories would vanish, too. I lick my lips and try to make my voice sound easy, not at all desperate and needy like I feel.

"Bender, what happened with you and Dad?"

"What do you mean?" His voice gets a defensive edge to it. I lean forward onto my elbows and speak quietly, trying not to scare him off.

"Why did you sell him the business and move to Santa Fe?"

He sits back in his chair and stares out at the street. In profile his face looks utterly defeated. "A lot of reasons."

"Name a few, then."

"It's a long story," he says. "We should get back to work. You almost done with your tea?" I look at my glass, three-quarters full, then at him. "I'll get you a to-go cup," he says, standing.

"You promise you'll tell me sometime?"

He avoids my eyes, mumbles, "I guess so."

"Bender." I wait until he looks at me. "Promise?"

He laughs. "Medina—you're such a hard-ass. Okay, okay, I promise."

Friday the thirteenth, The Skins are playing at Fanny's. Lucy drinks too much, gets sick in the bathroom, and leaves while I'm dancing with a funny French exchange student. It's a little past eleven when I realize she's gone. I drive the streets looking for her, until it occurs to me that maybe she hitchhiked home.

As I walk into Smoke Palace, the stairway emits a strong stench of urine, and I feel some kind of dread creeping into my bones. Inside the apartment, the bedroom door is closed. I knock softly, and press my ear to the door. Nothing. "Lucy?" I call. "Can I come in?" No answer. I can feel my heart pounding against the wood; it's beating so violently, I could swear it's audible. I think of that suite at the Motel 6, covered in blood. I never saw it, but I've imagined it so many times, it's more real to me than most places. I can hear someone laughing in the apartment directly below us. "Lucy?" I call again. "I'm coming in, okay?" Still no answer. I push the door open. The first thing I see is a towel on the floor, smudged with dark red blood. It's still wet; the blood glistens on the crumpled white terry cloth and my heart starts flopping around inside my chest crazily. "Lucy?"

Downstairs, the laughter becomes hysterical. "You—you were so—" the woman gasps. "Your face!"

"Luce, it's me, Anna. Are you okay?" I come around the bed and find her curled into a fetal position on the floor, with her forehead pressed against one leg of the nightstand. Her face is hidden by the matted, sweat-damp mess of her hair. "Oh God," I whisper. "Lucy. Jesus. What happened?" She's wearing underwear and a huge flannel shirt, unbuttoned. Her bare breasts are exposed; I see now that her underwear, once a pale pink, are soaked in blood. I kneel beside her, and as I touch her shoulder, she starts, stares at me wild-eyed, her nostrils flaring like a horse about to bolt. "What happened?" I ask her.

She sits up and looks around; her eyebrows furrow into a bewildered V. She searches my face, repeats my question back to me. "What happened?"

"Come on. Let's get you off the floor."

"I was peeing." She rubs her forehead. "I was thinking about my sister."

I wrap one of her arms around my neck and help her onto the bed. "You're bleeding," I say.

She looks down between her legs and frowns. "Uh-huh," she says. She looks at me imploringly. "I need a cigarette." I search the bedroom, but all I find are three empty packs. I go into the living room and discover an almost full pack in Arlan's jacket. I return with it and hand her one. She finds some matches in the pocket of the flannel shirt. She takes a long, hungry drag and exhales with her eyes closed, then flops over onto her stomach and leans out the window. I lie down beside her. Her hair is tangled and disheveled, her eyelids puffy.

"Bizarre," she says, and her breath reeks of gin.

"Did you take anything?" I ask her.

"'Did you take anything?'" she mimics.

"Did you?"

"Not nearly enough," she says.

"Luce, this is scaring me. There's a towel all bloody on the floor, you're all bloody, this is not normal." My voice is shaking. "What happened? Do you remember?"

"I told you. I was peeing. I was remembering this time when my sister cut my hair. It looked like shit, and I called her a miserable cunt." She giggles. "I was only twelve. Pretty good for twelve, huh?"

"Did you get your period?" I ask.

She looks at me like this is the most asinine question ever, and continues with her story. "I wanted her to cut it like Erica on *Days of Our Lives*, but she made me look like Davy Jones. I tried to cut hers—chased her around the yard with the scissors." She coughs, quietly at first, and then in great, hacking spasms. She has to sit up for a second to catch her breath. When she's recovered, she lays down again and ashes her cigarette calmly. "I almost got her," she says, her voice distant. "She was too fast, though."

"Did you miscarry?"

She continues to stare out the window. "No drama, Anna," she says. "You promised."

"Look," I say, trying to steady my voice. "I'm not the one who was moaning and bleeding on the floor two minutes ago. I just want to know what's going on."

"I wasn't moaning!" she says.

"You were, too."

She smiles faintly, still not looking at me. "What would you do without me? I'm a constant scandal."

"Are you sure you're okay?"

She turns to me and gestures with her cigarette. "I'm lucid enough to smoke, right? That's good enough for me."

"You want some water or something?"

"How about something a little stronger?"

"Lucy, you didn't do anything, did you?"

"Like what?"

"Like take anything or—I don't know."

"Drama, drama, drama," she sighs. I look at her skeptically, and she widens her eyes at me. "You want to search the place for coat hangers, or what?"

"I didn't mean that."

"Then what *do* you mean?" She grinds her cigarette into a coffee cup impatiently.

"Just, are you sure you're okay?"

"I could use a shower," she says, rolling onto her back and surveying her body. Her thighs are smudged here and there with rust-colored patches. "I'm pretty disgusting."

I get up and turn the shower on without a word. When I come back into the bedroom, Lucy has tears streaming down her face. "What?" I say.

"You're so great, Anna," she says. Her lower lip trembles. She tries to light another cigarette, but her hand is shaking too hard. I take the matches from her and strike one, hold the flame up, and she starts crying harder now, so hard that she can barely get the cigarette to stay put between her quivering lips. My match goes out. She gets a tobacco leaf stuck on her upper lip and she picks it off carefully. "You're my favorite woman," she says. "Ever. In my whole life."

"You going to smoke in the shower?" I ask her.

"Smart-ass." She manages to hold her cigarette somewhat steadily between her lips. I light a new match and touch the flame to the tip; we both watch as the paper catches and the orange glow begins.

I stroke Lucy's wet hair until she falls asleep. Now that the bloody towel is in the dirty clothes basket and she's got a tampon in, things seem more manageable. It's two in the morning. I stare out the window with my hand moving automatically along the slick, damp slope from her forehead to the pillow and back again. It's soothing, like petting a cat. She smiles dimly in her sleep—just the ghost of a smile, bending the edges of her mouth subtly. I've got her tucked under the old quilt. One bare foot sticks out and dangles over the edge of the bed, hanging at an odd angle, like it's not attached quite right at the ankle. I see that she's painted her toenails a silvery white, then scraped most of the polish off.

I think about the blood, and beginnings, and how some

things can't cling long enough to reach fruition. Then I think about that word, *fruition*, how it has *fruit* inside it. I think of a line in one of my father's letters, *a woman's body was still the strangest, darkest fruit of all,* and then I start to fall asleep, lulled by the sound of Lucy's soft breathing.

When I awake, Arlan is standing in the doorway, his guitar in one hand. His eyes are moist and his jaw is tense. He looks at once angry and tender—it's a strange combination. For one startled moment I believe this look is directed at me; then I see that he is transfixed by Lucy, who is dead asleep with her mouth wide open and one arm thrust out over the windowsill.

When he notices that I am awake, he composes his face, setting his guitar gently against the wall. "I saw her hand dangling out the window when I drove up," he says.

"Oh yeah?" I say, not sure what this means.

"It just looked weird," he says. "She okay?"

I sit up and hug my knees. It's gotten foggy out, and the open window has turned the room very cold. "She is now."

He turns from where he's setting his keys and a pile of change on the desk, being careful to make little noise. He looks at me with questions.

"When I came in there was a lot of blood—" I hesitate. "Anyway, she's fine." I pause long enough to wonder if there's a better way to do this. "She's not pregnant anymore."

He looks away from me and scratches the back of his neck. He goes into the kitchen and I can hear him pouring himself a drink. He reappears briefly in the doorway long enough to whisper, "You want anything? Whiskey? Gin and tonic?"

"Gin and tonic," I say, getting up and following him into the living room. I sit on the couch and whisper, "Thanks," as he hands me my drink. He's garnished it with a slice of lime. He sits by the window and stares out at the street. I hate myself for wanting him, even now.

There is a long silence, during which I manage to get half my drink down. He's poured it with a generous hand. When I start to feel the very beginnings of pleasure taking root, I say, "How was the second set?"

He looks at me blankly.

"I don't know," he says, shaking his head. "It was a blur." He tugs a pack of cigarettes from his shirt pocket, fishes one out, lights it, and as an afterthought, gestures to me with the pack. For some crazy reason, I nod and he tosses it to me, then reaches over and hands me his lighter. Our fingers don't touch, but even coming this close to touching—the distance of his lighter—makes me feel light-headed. I put the cigarette between my lips and try to light it, but nothing happens.

After several more tries, Arlan laughs and says, "It's child-proof." Then he crosses the distance between us, kneels next to me and flicks the lighter with his thumb. He brings with him the perfume of barbecued meat, cigarette smoke and whiskey, plus something all his own under that—something sweaty and powerful. The flame appears, perfect, sharp. Our eyes find each other as he touches the fire to the tip; I breathe in, feel the sudden rush of smoke inside me, and panic. I cough uncontrollably in his face. He holds up his hand to shield himself, laughing.

"I've never smoked," I say, when I can speak.

"No kidding." He's still kneeling beside me.

"I don't know why I'm trying," I say. He's still very close. I stare at him idiotically, trying not to cough. From the bedroom, Lucy moans quietly in her sleep. His face becomes instantly expressionless, and he goes back to his seat by the window. We sit there, him smoking, me holding my lit cigarette limply, afraid to put it to my lips. The room begins to fill with smoke. We haven't turned on any lights, but the street lamps are bright enough to illuminate the languorous shapes it makes, drifting in slow motion toward the ceiling.

He finishes his drink and gets up to pour himself another. He offers to refill mine, but I'm nursing the last of mine slowly, letting the knot of ice cubes melt some, weakening its bite. Once he's settled into his chair again, he downs half of his whiskey and looks at me. His long hair hangs about his face. "So she lost it?" he whispers.

I nod.

He nods.

I concentrate on the tiny shreds of lime that find their way to my tongue as the smoke continues to wrap itself around us.

I do not sleep that night. After several hours of watching the empty streets, I creep outside to the truck, retrieve my father's letters, and return to the couch to read. I huddle under the blankets with a flashlight, like a kid after bedtime.

October 23rd, 1976

Dear Einstein,

I'm writing from the hospital cafeteria. God, I wish you were here this fall. The air is delicious this week…it tastes like fog and morning dew, but the sky is Easter-egg blue day after day. I've never seen the city so beautiful. October is a gift from the gods, laid out in all of its crisp, lucid, Indian summer wonder.

Anna Marie Medina was born at 5:45 this morning. After twenty hours of labor, Helen looks like she's been run over repeatedly by a fleet of semis, but Anna is fresh as a flower. I'm trying to choke down this ghastly, shit-colored concoction they call coffee so I can stay awake another hour and stare at her some more.

Did anyone ever warn us about the mystery, the sheer power of a day like this one? I guess it was implied in books and movies, songs—especially Segovia, or Beethoven's Fifth—but nothing came close to preparing me. How can I describe the weight of her in my arms, so real, or the complexity of her face, torn between terror and peace? She is indescribably miniature. Her toes make me want to get down on my knees and kiss this old, crusty earth. I've never seen anything so new.

About seventeen hours into her labor, during the excruciating, messy time the nurses refer to euphemistically as "the transition," Helen screamed at me to make it stop. "Baby," I whispered in her ear between contractions. "Everything's okay. Sometimes the only way to heaven is straight through hell." I thought she was going to rip my head off right there. "You go to hell!" She screamed. "Fuck heaven!" Thankfully, another contraction came and swept her rage up with it. Amazing how pain can take everything away but itself—it's almost like meditation, though I'm sure Helen would laugh and then shoot me for that analogy, when for her it was brutal beginning to end. Well, now she's fast asleep, and I hope her dreams are soft as Anna's skin. God knows she deserves her rest, after that.

I won't bore you with more parental drivel. I hope your dad is better soon, or at least finds his peace where he can. Tell him I'm thinking of him, will you? He was like a dad to me, too. I hope he knows that.

Everything's cool at the shop. I'll fill you in when you get back. Any idea when that'll be? We can talk soon. I just needed to write everything down, after this surreal day.

Peace, brother,

Chet

I read this letter again and again, clinging to each word with something like gratitude. Or maybe it's just surprise. I never imagined a piece of paper like this existed in the world. Eight by eleven, blue ink, a faint coffee stain in the upper right corner. I want to memorize every inch of it.

When I finally do dream it's in fits—brief scenarios featuring me trying to get blood out of everything: towels, shag carpets, underwear, ceilings.

Arlan gets up at seven, showers and slips out the door. He's working, though it's Saturday—there's a big job out on Lummi Island. Soon after, Lucy gets up, makes coffee and brings me a cup, looking well rested and a little devious. Her hair is tied back in a ponytail, and her eyes have a glint of determination. I lay on my side and pin the letters between my rib cage and the couch, trying to keep them out of view.

"We're going to Sequim," she says.

"Where's that?"

"The edge of the world. You look like shit, girl. What happened to you?"

"Couldn't sleep," I mumble. I take a sip of coffee, rub the sleep from my eyes.

"I'll drive, then. But we have to go."

"Where?"

She sighs impatiently. "Sequim! Come *on!* I have to get out of here today or I'm going to die."

"Why Sequim?"

"I have to see my mom. She's been begging me to come. And I need to get away from this—Arlan—the whole scene. Please, Anna, you have no idea what this means to me." She stares at me with that face she shows so rarely—begging—and already, against my better judgment, I can feel myself giving in.

"I'm supposed to meet Bender at the shop."

"Tell him you can't make it," she suggests.

"He'll be disappointed," I say. "I hate to let him down."

"We'll only be gone a couple days."

"But the Hawaiian koa's supposed to arrive tomorrow."

She squints at me. "Are you fucking that guy?"

I nearly choke on my coffee. "Gross! No way!"

"Then there's no excuse. We have to go. He'll just have to understand."

By my second cup of coffee, I surrender, though something about this day makes me very uneasy. We made it through Friday the thirteenth, but barely, and today feels bleaker, more ominous. Though Lucy chatters happily as we burn toast, pack, brush our teeth and shave our legs, there's an edginess to her that verges on manic. It reminds me of my mother after a triple espresso; a switch flips, and the world goes explosively bright. She'll prattle on gaily about computers, cars, the news, all the while flashing that stiff, practiced grin. I've learned from experience that these bursts of cheer can get scary; what goes up in flames must eventually fall in ash. Lucy has that fragility this morning. She radiates the artificial glow of someone who's fooling herself.

The Edge of the World

On the road to Sequim, I feel very briefly that today is in fact a good day, not a bad one, and the ominous pressure in my head dissipates, leaving me almost giddy. The sun is shining, I've learned there's a ferry on our journey, and we're passing onto an island now, via a great expansive bridge. People huddle on its edges, snapping photos, their hair whipping wildly in a wind that is so strong I can feel it banging against the truck, tempting the wheel this way and that.

"Deception Pass," Lucinda says, gazing out the window, raising her voice to be heard over the wind. I nod. We drive on. It seems we are very young right now. I concentrate on the smell of wet, green fields and of ocean air, of burning tires on the semi in front of us, and the cigarette smoke trailing as always from Lucy's fingers.

By the time we're in line for the ferry, though, optimism

has leaked out of me for no particular reason, except that the man two cars ahead who gets out to stretch reminds me of Bender. This yanks me out of the moment I was accidentally floating in. I think of his face when I stopped by to tell him I had to leave town. His eyes went instantly distant. "Just for a couple days," I'd insisted, but he was already turning his back on me, misting a blade with WD-40. I gushed an apologetic little monologue, but he was unmoved. He just kept bending over the blade, studying it as if it held some secret in its greasy teeth.

"I don't believe in monogamy," Lucy says, as I turn off the engine. "Coupling is evil."

"Then why are you doing it?"

"What?"

"Coupling."

"I'm not, really. Arlan and I live together, but so do you and I."

"It's not the same thing," I say, feeling very tired.

"I'm all about the community," she says, lighting a fresh cigarette. "We're not meant to go off in pairs. The Noah's Arc story is fascist propaganda." She examines her teeth in the flip-down mirror. "I don't care if you fuck Arlan. Go ahead."

I massage my forehead. "Lucy, stop talking like that."

"Honesty really rubs you the wrong way, huh?"

"Did you drag me out here to tell me this?"

She laughs. "Anna! Don't be so afraid of me! I'm not conspiring! I'm only saying, you can have what you want. Why shouldn't you? I take what I want, don't I?"

"I'm not in the mood for this," I say. And then, because it seems like something to do, I add, "Let me have a drag off that."

"You want one? I'll give you one of your own."

"Okay," I say, but with a hint of repulsion, remembering the taste in my mouth last night, the violent coughing. She fishes one from the pack and lights it for me. I cough the first couple of drags, but after that it goes down easier, and seems almost pleasant. Lucy watches me, looking rather satisfied.

"You're not really inhaling," she says.

"Leave me alone!" I scream, laughing. Before long I've got a serious buzz going; I feel dizzy and clear-headed at once.

"Grady never really did it for you, did he?"

"He's nice," I say evasively.

"But you two never did anything, huh?"

"No. Not much chemistry, I guess."

"You think he's gay?" She's back to the mirror again, this time trying to get her eyelashes in order.

"Never occurred to me."

"Anyway," she says, flicking the butt out the window, "Arlan's the only one worth having." Then the line starts moving toward the ferry, and I hurriedly snuff out my first real cigarette.

The ferry drops us off in Port Townsend, where Lucy insists we get a tripmocha.

"A what?"

"Tripmocha. Come on, we're on the road, the sun is shining, the wind is crazy, we need a mocha."

"Oh—a *mocha*."

"Tripmocha."

The town itself is adorable, in that tourist-infested, desperately quaint sort of way. Its main street is lined with old brick buildings. On one side, cliffs reach straight up to the sky, and on the other, the Sound churns quietly, dotted with sailboats and kayaks. We find an old-fashioned ice-cream shop packed with middle-aged people wearing fanny-packs and baggy shorts, yelling at their children. We buy mochas there, though it takes forever. When at last we're back on the road, I'm glad to leave Port Townsend.

I don't know what comes over me. Maybe I'm just a little bored. As we turn onto Highway 101, I ask, "Who's Nick Ferrari?"

She looks at me. Looks back at the road. Looks at me again. "Why would you ask that?"

"Just wondering."

She shakes her head. "Goddamn Bellingham," she says. "I need a city. I need to be a whore in a sprawling, anonymous place where I can do whatever I want, get paid for it, and expose all their stupid fucking Christian, virgin-worshiping mythologies. Jesus!" She lights a cigarette. "You want to know what disgusts me? Hypocrisy! I would rather eat a pile of human feces than deal with their double-talking bullshit—"

"Whose?"

"Arlan, Bill, Grady, all their stupid groupies! The whole town! The whole world!" She shakes her head sadly. "Arlan's proposed to me—okay? More than once. But I don't say yes because I don't believe in that shit! I have no interest in ownership. It makes me want to hurl, seriously." She exhales smoke out the window, reties her ponytail tighter.

"Nick Ferrari, if you must know, is a boy. Okay? He's fifteen. Younger brother of this guy we know, Colin. Anyways, I fucked him last winter, because he begged me to, and it was fun. But then Colin walked in on us and suddenly we've got the whole town talking. I mean, who gives a shit? Everyone was high and it was a good time and then later it becomes this horrifying secret or something. Scarlet Letter city. I don't give a flying fuck who knows. I really don't. They can drown in their own dogma, for all I care." She stares straight ahead in silence, as if daring me to speak.

"Okay. I was just wondering."

She turns toward me now, her voice shifting to a soft plea. "You understand, don't you, Anna? You know we have a right to do what we want?"

I consider this for a moment; I'm all for liberation, and

Lucy's open rebellion fascinates me, but is she being fair to Arlan? "I just don't understand why you hold on to a boyfriend."

"I told you—fuck him if you want to!"

"That's not the point."

She takes a big swig of mocha and cries out, "Ow! I burned my tongue." She examines it in the mirror before continuing. "I'm not possessive! Don't you get it? I play by *my* rules, not theirs. Arlan's good for me, but we don't own each other."

"And do you tell Arlan when you're with someone else?"

She hesitates. "Arlan knows everything. He's fluent in my language."

We ride in silence the rest of the way to Sequim. Even when we see a bald eagle hovering near the water, wings spread wide like he knows he's beautiful, she points him out in silence. I guess we've said all we need to, for now.

Lucy's stepfather is terrifying. One look at him and instantly the prophetic lump I've been carrying in my gut since this morning makes sense. He smells of motor oil and cheap cologne. His face looks like half-cooked dough—raw, pale, lumpy. His eyes, set close together, are small and glassy.

"Hi, Dad," Lucy says, as we enter the cramped trailer. It is furnished with endless knickknacks sprawled across every surface: ceramic dolls, music boxes, tiny vases, statues of little boys peeing carelessly here and there. Living amidst these decorative items are bits and pieces of functional (or once functional) objects: corroded batteries, filthy car parts, spools of thread, severely abused kitchen utensils. I feel right away that I am suffocating.

"Dad" doesn't respond immediately. He is carefully attaching two pieces of wire with a bit of duct tape, which apparently takes all his attention. When he does finally look up, he laughs. His cheeks vibrate slightly. "What are you doing here?"

"Came for a visit," Lucy says, yanking open the refrigerator. "Where's Mom?"

"No hug for your old dad?"

"Nope," Lucy says flatly, biting into an apple. Then she goes to him and wraps her arms around him fast, lets go. She looks at me over her shoulder, and announces, her mouth full of apple, "This is Anna."

"Anna," he says, nodding slowly. I try to smile, but I don't get very far. I feel a little sick. "Your sister's supposed to be here," he says in an unnaturally loud voice.

"Shit. Are you serious?"

"She said so. Looking for cash, sounds like. Her old man dumped her."

"Good." Lucy spits out a bite of apple in the trash. "Ew! That was gross."

"Mind your manners," he says, going back to his wires.

"Why'd he dump her?"

"You think anyone tells me? All I know is, she's sniffing around here for handouts." He attaches the pair of wires to a battery and suddenly there's the flash of a bright white spark, along with a loud popping sound; it makes me jump, and my elbow hits a small pewter castle, which knocks over a glass of lumpy milk. It spills onto the plywood dresser in misshapen, grayish blobs.

"I'm sorry," I say. "Do you have a paper towel?"

"Leave it," the dad says.

"I should at least wipe the—"

"Leave it!" he repeats in a weird, hollow tone.

In the gloom of the trailer, it is easy to imagine he has no chin at all. I pull my cardigan closed against the chill.

"Where's Mom?" Lucy asks. He shrugs. "We're going downtown. See you later." He doesn't respond.

As soon as we leave the trailer, I feel relief flooding my body like a cool drink of water.

In downtown Sequim, there are a few bars to choose from; Lucy picks what has to be the darkest, the most depressing, the one that reeks the strongest of stale beer and decades worth of cigarette smoke. It's been here forever, you can tell. I try to picture what it was like in the 1950s, when girls like us would be at home in curlers, painting our toenails, and men could tell their jokes without us, indulging in their melancholy fraternity. I rest my hands on the old wooden bar and think of all it's seen—all the sadness and celebrations it's witnessed, all the lost souls that have leaned against this very spot.

"Get me a Tanqueray and tonic," Lucy says. "I'm going to go pee," and she disappears down a shadowy hallway. There's a TV mounted above the bar. I watch as a slim, toothy game show hostess raises one hand gracefully to indicate the categories lighting up near her fingertips. The host drones on in a soothing, oily voice; the bartender squeezes the remote control and the room erupts with the sound of a bright, irritating polka as a dancing couple glides across the screen.

I order our drinks and take them to a table in the far corner. There's more people here than I'd expect—maybe ten or twelve, all men—but I don't really look at their faces. I just sit down and study the ice in our glasses, watching the bubbles swim rapidly for the surface. I try not to be afraid of this town—the doughy stepdad, the ominous sister, this bar. I think of Arlan and a pang of homesickness assails me. I want to be in Smoke Palace, drifting on one of his long, elegant riffs. I can see Bill accosting teenage girls out the window and hear Grady talking excitedly about something exotic clipped from his Argentinean newspaper. The thought of that house and the smell of Arlan's body—sweat, paint, smoke—makes me want to cry.

When Lucy comes back, she downs half her drink and says, "You hate it here, I can tell."

"What makes you say—"

"You're so painfully obvious, Anna. Don't ever play poker."

"I'm fine. Don't worry about me."

"We'll leave first thing tomorrow," she says.

"We just got here."

"Let me get drunk enough to go home and face my mother. Then we'll pass out and drive back in the morning."

"Didn't you want to come?"

"I don't know what I want half the time." She puts her face in her hands briefly, then downs the rest of her drink. "Anna, if I don't go to college I'll kill myself. I need to get as far away from this rat's asshole as I can." She chomps on her ice. "Only sometimes—I can't explain it—I have to come back. Like needing to see your blood when you cut yourself, you know? Some kind of morbid trip like that."

"You need another?"

"Yeah. And smoke a cigarette with me, will you please? I love you, Anna, I swear to God."

Lucy quickly accomplishes her goal; by the time we're ready to leave this dank place, she's on fire with Tanqueray. Her eyes are not focusing properly, and her walk is so lopsided I have to slip an arm around her waist to get her out to the car. I prop her up with one hand as I unlock the truck. "Why do you always lock everything?" she complains. "Like an old lady."

"It's not mine," I say. "I'm trying to take care of—"

"Whose uz it?" She tries again. "Whose is it?"

"My aunt's. I told you that. Can you get us back to your mom's? I'm not sure I remember." She gets in on the driver's side and sits there, staring blankly at the windshield. "Scoot over." I giggle. "I've got to get in, too." She slides over just enough for me to wedge myself into the driver's seat. As I slam the door and turn to her, she kisses me sloppily on the mouth. "Okay," I say, pulling away. "Now I know you're drunk."

"Don't you want to kiss me back?"

"Maybe some other time." I've never kissed a woman before, and the feel of her lips on mine is at once familiar and foreign. Bewildering. She starts kissing my neck very softly. "Um," I say. "Lucy? I don't know if this is—"

"Shh," she says, and kisses me on the lips again. This time she pushes her tongue against my teeth and I can taste the gin on her mouth. I give in a little more—I'm still stiff and awkward but I turn toward her slightly, mostly because I don't want to offend her. I feel oddly removed, like I'm outside myself, watching two girls kissing, thinking, "How odd—look at that." She puts her hand on my breast, and that startles me out of my trance. "Listen, Lucy, you've had too much to drink, is all—"

"Check this out!"

I jerk around and see a man's face practically pressed against my window—a small, pinched, hairy face with hateful eyes. Behind him are the muted colors of other people—a green baseball cap, a brown leather jacket—and the sound of men laughing; a beer bottle clatters to the pavement. I push Lucy away from me and, panicky, terror-stricken, I slam down the lock on the door. One of the men yells, "Lesbos!"

Lucy starts yelling in a rough, drunk voice, "Fuck your mothers, motherfuckers!" This gets me giggling. She starts giggling too, and repeats the battle cry several more times. The man with his face pressed to my window clambers toward the passenger side door. The fear that flushes through me makes my laughter catch in my throat; I lunge for the lock. I get it down just as the man tries the door. He pounds like an orangutan on Lucy's window with small, furry fists. I stab at the ignition with my keys, somehow make the right one fit, and pull away as Lucy starts up with her chant again: "Fuck your mothers, motherfuckers!"

This is not turning out to be a restful getaway. We spend the night curled up in the cab of the truck, freezing. We park near the trailer but we never go inside. When Lucy sees that her mother still isn't home, she refuses to leave the truck. I'm not thrilled about sleeping in the cab, but I'm not anxious to go in, either. Her stepdad's lumpy profile is visible through the tiny trailer window, illuminated by the eerie blue flicker of late-night TV.

Not surprisingly, I have a hard time sleeping sitting up. I spend hours replaying the fuzzy home-movie of the evening over and over again in my mind. I wonder why Lucy kissed me. I'm not quite naive enough to imagine that she's been carrying a torch; I suspect she came on to me because she was bored and drunk. The thought irks me so much I'm tempted to wake her up and tell her what a jerk she is. Sometimes I feel like I'm just second-rate entertainment for a restless, cruel little queen. I thought I was outside the realm of her sexual playthings, and more intimate with her precisely because I'm not someone she can kiss when she's sloppy drunk and there's nothing better to do. I suppose I might be flattered, under different circumstances, but tonight, slumped before the steering wheel in a ridiculous parody of rest, I'm mostly just pissed off.

In the morning, my body feels like one big bruise. Lucy leans against the passenger door, scowling in her sleep. I think of the kiss and the pack of jeering men, feel briefly irritated, then try to push it from my mind and get out of the truck to stretch. The trailer is parked in a large field of lushly unkempt grass dotted with yellow and purple flowers. There's a Volkswagen Bug, a gleaming motorcycle, a few gnarled apple trees, and a metal post with a deflated yellow ball hanging at the end of a rope. The scent of bacon is in the air, which fills me with a tentative optimism.

I really have to pee, but I can't bring myself to go inside the trailer. I'm not accustomed to squatting outdoors, but my bladder's so full, I can't think of what else to do, so I find a small bush—a large clump of grass, really—and get it over with. Soon, Lucy stirs, and she lights a cigarette before she's even rubbed the sleep from her eyes. There's something sad about the smell of smoke mixing with the foggy clean of the grass and air. I want to stretch out somewhere and sleep for real, but this is what I get today: a scowling girl, smoke, and my body curled in on itself like a pretzel. The inside of my mouth feels dirty. I spit.

"What?" she demands.

"Nothing—why?"

"You're staring at me," she says, her voice a challenge.

"Look, I'm not in the mood, Lucy."

She looks away. "My mom's finally home," she says, pressing a finger against each eyelid. "Fuck. I hate this place. Why did you let me come here?"

"You begged me."

"I tell you, it's some kind of chip she implanted in me at birth. Remote control." Through the window of the trailer, I can hear the sound of a man snoring. This, too, seems sad. "Maybe we should just go," she says. I look at her.

"Without saying hi to your mom, even?"

"Jesus." She flicks some ash into the grass. "I really hate it here. Did I mention that?"

"Do you think she's up?"

"Yeah. No. Probably." After a moment, she walks over to the trailer, tosses her cigarette into a dilapidated flower box, and goes in. I wait by the truck, trying to stretch the kinks out of my joints. I listen as high-pitched sounds of greeting come from the trailer. They talk for a while, then the door bursts open and a tiny woman with Lucy's eyes and a helmet of reddish hair says, "Come on *in,* honey—don't be scared!" She's got a thick Southern accent and a huge, frightening smile. I smile back and go on into the trailer.

The smell of bacon is thick, and as soon as I'm seated, Lucy's mom starts clearing away the figurines and car parts from the table, and shoves a plate of white toast, bacon and an unidentified gray mush in front of me. "You like grits and bacon?"

"Sure," I say.

"Mom! Grits?"

"Nothin' wrong with grits." She lights a cigarette, and so does Lucy. They stand there, watching me eat. On the bed, the stepdad snores on, facing the wall. I nibble at the bacon.

"Try the gray shit," Lucy says.

Her mom swats her on the butt. "Watch your mouth!"

I take a small forkful of the grits and taste. "Mmm," I say, nodding politely.

"You're so full of it!" Lucy laughs. Her mom laughs, too, a shrill, whinnying sound.

Things seem better with Lucy's mom here, though she's a little over the top with her Southern hospitality and her aggressive grinning. We pass the morning sitting outside on lawn chairs, drinking coffee. Lucy and her mom smoke cigarette after cigarette and talk about people I don't know, the volume of their voices rising and falling according to the topic. I'm content just watching the fog burn off, listening now and then to their conversation, but mostly letting my mind drift randomly from memory to memory, dozing in between. I think of Arlan getting sick on the Fourth of July, and of my father's habitual silence in the mornings. I think of how long my mother's hair was, once—how silky and shiny it would get, like some exotic fabric, after she washed it.

I start wondering how I ever got to be friends with Lucy. We're so different. Look at how she grew up; this whole scene is the opposite of the places I spent my childhood, with their gleaming hardwood floors and billowing linen curtains. I guess we never had loads of money, but my parents both had artistic, bohemian taste, and our apartments were always beautiful in a spare, European sort of way. Even my father, with his disdain for shopping, had a good eye for nice things, and he wasn't above indulging once in a while.

For the first time, I try to imagine Lucy's childhood, and I have to say it makes me a little sick. I know there have been at least three stepdads in her past, and her real father never bothered to make an appearance. It's one thing to lose your father, but what's it like to live with a series of bizarre, predatory dads—men like this lumpy, volatile guy in the trailer now? And even though she's never said it straight out, it doesn't take a genius to intuit that Lucy's been fucked with big time. Maybe not by this one—maybe not since she was little—but one of the dads, at least, messed with her. I feel suddenly guilty for having judged her so harshly last night. What could I possibly know about the nightmares she's survived? So what if she tried to kiss me? Yes, half the time she's possessed by the spirit of reckless boredom. Is that a crime? I think of something she said that night at the Ranch Room: *"Sex is always an act of hostility."* Maybe the first time for her was hostile, and so she kept on thinking of sex as a battlefield, a bloodthirsty game between animals.

I'm yanked out of my drowsy half dreams by the growl of a black Camaro speeding toward us. As it careens closer, I can see it's Lucy's sister behind the wheel, and when she stops and before she's even slammed the car door, I know this can't be good. She looks even more hostile than when I met her in Seattle, and not nearly as pretty. Her face is slightly swollen. Her eyes have a distant, stoned appearance; she's outlined them with gobs of black eyeliner, making her look absurd and ghoulish in the afternoon sunlight. She's got on a pair of tight Guess jeans and a pink sweatshirt with the neckline cut out of it. Across her chest, in sparkly letters, is the word *Princess* with a little crown on the *P*. Her left cheek is sporting a yellowish bruise, and above her left eye is a dark blue one the size of a silver dollar.

She greets Lucy the same way she did in Seattle: "What are you doing here?"

"Nice to see you, too, Lorna."

"Mom, what's she doing here?"

"She came to visit, sweetheart. Look at this! I've got both my girls at once. Anna, have you met Lucy's sister, Lorna?" I nod, and Lorna looks at me without a trace of recognition.

"What happened to you?" Lucy asks, taking a step closer and squinting at Lorna's injuries.

"Fuck off."

"Lorna," her mother chides. "We have guests."

"Fuck her, too. Do you have any Diet Pepsi?" She slams into the trailer without waiting for an answer. Lucy and her mother exchange a knowing look.

"Tim?" Lucy asks.

"Who else?" her mother says.

It takes only a minute or two for an argument to erupt inside the trailer. Their voices are low at first, but as they grow in volume I can make out his rant: "Soon as you pay the bills around here, you can talk shit! But as long as you're—look at me when I'm talking to you—as long as you're sniffing for handouts, you better just shut up, missy!"

Lorna explodes out the door, clutching a can of generic diet cola. "Since when did you stop buying Pepsi?" she says to her mom. "This shit's nasty."

"Tastes the same to me." Her mother pats her helmet of hair and turns to me. "Sweetheart, would you like a soda? I've been so neglectful, haven't I."

"No thank you," I say.

"Lucy, go get us a couple of sodas, would you?"

"Mom, we're going to take off," she says.

"Oh, no! Not so soon! Stay another night!"

"Huh!" Lorna scoffs. "You never say that to me!"

"Of course I do, sweetie. I want you both here—please? Anna, you can stay one more night, can't you?"

"I, um—"

"No, Mom. She has to work. She's got a life, all right?" Lucy wraps her arms around her mother and squeezes her.

I can see her mother's face over her shoulder; the skin at the corners of her eyes gives way to an intricate burst of wrinkles. For a brief second, the pain in her face is unmistakable. As soon as Lucy releases her, she goes back to beaming.

"I'll call you in a couple days," Lucy says.

"No, she won't," Lorna says.

"Shut up, Lorna," Lucy tells her.

"You think you're such hot shit."

"Come on, Anna," Lucy says, touching my arm.

Lorna takes a step toward her. "You just prance in here and act like—"

"See you later, Mom." Lucy starts to move in the direction of the truck. I nod at her mom, then follow Lucy.

"Don't walk away when I'm talking to you!" Lorna shouts at her back.

"Fuck off, Lorna," Lucy says, still not turning around.

"I said, don't walk away from me!"

We're almost to the truck when I hear the sound of someone running up behind us; Lucy's head yanks back and she yelps in pain. I turn to see Lorna with about half of Lucy's hair gripped in her fist. Lucy twists to escape, but then screams louder, as this only intensifies the pain.

"Bitch!" Lorna sneers. Her face is pink and her black-rimmed eyes have narrowed to slits. "You little cunt! Don't walk away from me!"

"Let *go*!" Lucy screams.

I lunge forward and push Lorna as hard as I can. She loses her grip on Lucy and falls backwards into the weeds. Lucy sees her chance and jumps into the truck, starts it up. I run around to the passenger side and get in. We drive off, but we're not on the road—that's behind us; we're bouncing through the open field, over huge clumps of mud, small boulders and weeds. We narrowly miss an apple tree.

"Lucy! Turn around!"

"I'm not going back!"

"But the *road's* back there!"

"So?"

"We can't just drive through this—look, it's all wet up there—go left!"

"I can't go—"

"Hard left!" She swings the wheel to the left, but it's too late. Our front tires are already sinking deep into a swampy field. She keeps her foot pressed hard on the gas, but the wheels only spin wildly, splattering the windows with plumes of mud. The motor dies; the truck makes a soft, groaning sound and falls silent.

Lucy turns the key in the ignition again and again, but nothing happens. She starts hitting the steering wheel as hard as she can with her fists, yelling, "Goddammit, you stupid motherfucker! Go!" She turns the key one last time, but again, nothing happens.

Finally, she gives up and lights a cigarette. I take a drag off hers and we stare through the windshield, dazed, letting the smoke fill the cab.

A couple hours later, after Lucy has smoked most of a pack, we see the black Camero driving off at top speed. Lucy walks back to the trailer then, and convinces her stepfather to take a look at the marooned truck. He comes over wearing a filthy yellow bathrobe and knee-high rubber boots. He wades out into the swamp, takes a couple of pulls from a bottle of malt liquor he keeps in one pocket, pops the hood and squints at the motor, whispering instructions to himself. After about fifteen minutes, he slams it shut and nods at us, his huge, fleshy face shimmering with sweat.

"Got your distributor all wet," he announces.

"Oh," I say. "Is that serious?"

"Depends. You in a hurry?"

I look at Lucy uncertainly.

"Can you fix it?" she asks.

"No. No fixing it. You've just got to wait."

"Wait?" we say in unison.

"Sure," he says. "You got it all wet! What do you usually do when something gets wet, huh? Think, girls, think!" I can see he's enjoying this immensely.

"Dad. Jesus. Cut it out. You're saying it's, like, too wet to work?"

"Bingo!"

"And it's got to dry out?"

"Ding-ding-ding-ding!" he cries.

"How long do you think that will take?" I ask.

He looks at the storm clouds gathering in the east and says, "Around here? Fuck if I know. Now, if we were back in Texas—"

"But we're not," Lucy says. "Thank God we're not in Texas. How long will it take *out here?*"

"Let me say it again—fuck if I know."

Lucy wants to hitchhike. "Let's just *go,*" she keeps saying.

"How?" I keep asking.

"You've got a thumb, don't you?"

"What—and leave the truck here?"

She doesn't ever answer; she just sulks, eyeing the trailer warily.

But I'm not hitchhiking all that distance through these backwards towns, and I'm not leaving Rosie's truck here in this sad little swampy field. We spend the night in Sequim, stretched out in the truck bed, wrapped in the blankets Lucy's mom brings out to us. Luckily, the storm clouds bypass the peninsula, and it's not too cold with all the layers of wool above and below us. When the stars are all out, I can't stop watching them; the sky is vast and thick with specks of light. It's a relief to feel so small.

Trying to fall asleep, I can't stop thinking about Lucy's family and this claustrophobic world they inhabit, filled with glass trinkets and auto parts packed together in an airtight trailer. It's pretty amazing that Lucy turned out as sane as she did. It occurs to me that ever since I was a kid, I assumed other people had it better than me. I imagined their families huddled in warm communion on couches, munching popcorn from one big bowl and planning rapturous seaside vacations. It never even crossed my mind that some families were more tragic than mine.

Lucy is murmuring softly in her sleep—something about teeth and Pepsi. She's curled semi-fetal on her side and her jaw slopes slightly, dangling open. "I hope you get into Santa Cruz," I whisper, glad that she can't hear me. I tuck a strand of hair behind her ear. "You deserve it. Even if you are a bitch, sometimes." Right now she's like someone behind glass; she's at once vulnerable and far away, unaware of my eyes on her. I've watched very few people sleep, in my life. It's weirdly intimate and lonely.

In the morning, before Lucy wakes, I try the truck. When it still won't start, I go inside the trailer and use the phone to call Bender. Lucy's mom is cooking breakfast—bacon and frozen hash browns. She's still beaming and smoking, smoking and beaming. I wonder if all that smiling is hard on her facial muscles. I can see the DNA at work in her small hands—so like Lucy's—and in the Jackie O eyebrows.

I have a short talk with Bender, explaining as little as possible. It's not exactly comfortable, pleading with him under my breath to tell me what to do, but I don't have enough money on me for a tow truck, and I'm not staying stranded in Sequim. I thought about calling Arlan or Grady, but Lucy insisted she would kill herself if I did. I guess she hates to be saved, but we really need saving this time, one way or another. So Bender agrees to borrow the Jeep of a guy who owes him and drive the three hours out here.

After I hang up with Bender, I decide to call Arlan, just to let him know we're okay. I give him an estimated time of arrival and tell him not to worry. He tries to ask more questions, but I whisper that I've got to go. His voice is so warm and familiar, it makes me want to tell him everything, but I force the phone back onto its cradle; I've betrayed Lucy enough already.

When Bender arrives with his hair shooting out in all directions, a pair of big, bug-eyed sunglasses on, I want to wrap my arms around him. Instead I just smile shyly and mumble my thanks. Ever since I called him this morning I've been a little worried about introducing him to Lucy; I know it's irrational, but I'm afraid that if my two Bellingham worlds touch, some sort of nuclear reaction will ensue. Much to my relief, Lucy's too exhausted to say more than a sullen hello, and Bender doesn't seem interested in pursuing the conversation beyond that, either.

On the ride home, with the truck trailing behind us and Lucy asleep in the back seat, I sneak glances at his face, illuminated by the dashboard light. I'm pretty exhausted, too, and at times the soft rocking motion of the Jeep almost puts me to sleep, but some bright little sensation in my chest keeps me awake. Unlike Lucy, who hates to admit defeat, I'm oddly exhilarated by this rescue. I guess being saved is a luxury I've gone without for too long.

"Bender?" I say, when we've been driving for a long time in silence.

"Hmm?"

"Do you think two people who are completely different can be friends?"

He thinks about this a minute. "Yeah," he says. "Sure. Your dad and I were nothing alike."

"Was it hard being friends with him?"

"Sure. Very hard." He puts his blinker on, and eases around a Greyhound bus that's creeping up the hill. He's a good driver. He makes me feel safe. "I guess I never pick people who are easy. Seems to be a habit. I always like the difficult ones."

"Yeah," I sigh. "Me, too."

Bombay Sapphire Gin

We arrive in the Land of Skin just after dark. We're exhausted, our hair is irrevocably tangled from the long ride in the Jeep, and we haven't showered in a couple of days, so we're both pretty ripe. As we make our way through the yard to the front door, a loud, two-fingered whistle sounds from the upstairs bedroom. There's Grady with his elbows on the windowsill. "Hold on," he calls out. "Stay right there!"

"Go away," Lucy snaps. "We're tired."

"You absolutely positively must not move!" And with this he disappears. Just as we reach the front door, he pops out from behind it and puts a hand on each of our heads. He closes his eyes and, in a thick, poorly executed French accent, says, "I sense you are returning from a very long journey…."

"We both have to pee, okay, so get out of our—"

"Yes, yes…I feel your bladders—very full. But you must

not venture into this abode just yet, or evil will befall your every step."

"Come on!" Lucy whines. "Jesus!"

"Ladies, ladies, come with me. I will show you to my priceless toilette, where you will empty your bladders with great comfort and ease."

"I don't want *your* fucking toilet," she says. "I want *my* toilet."

"No, no, I assure you. My toilette will please you beyond compare."

Lucy tries to squeeze past him, but he grabs her arm and guides her toward the stairs to his place, linking his other arm in mine.

"What's going on?" She eyes him suspiciously. "You're stalling or something, aren't you."

"I assure you, the toilette to which I lead you is vastly superior to any toilette you have known. You will urinate in golden waterfalls; your bodily functions are my command."

"What is this? Arlan has a chick over, huh?"

"Chick? I know not what you mean—what is this 'chick'?"

By now we're both laughing as Grady goes on and on in his terrible accent. We arrive at his apartment, where I wait patiently for my turn to pee.

"But wait," he says, as I come out of the bathroom. "I am sensing...yes! I sense a sign will soon be clear." He stomps on the kitchen floor three times. We wait a moment, and three little taps become audible through the floor—it sounds like a broom handle against the ceiling. "Gracious God, there it is! A sign from below." He crosses himself and nods soberly. "Yes, and now we go. Come, come!" He gathers us up again, and leads us arm in arm back to Lucy and Arlan's, jabbering nonsensically the whole time.

As we open the door, the smell of roasted chicken is overwhelming. The apartment is toasty; I'm peeling off my sweater as we walk down the hallway. I hear Lucy gasp, and as I free myself from my sweater I see why. The whole apartment is shimmering with candles—hundreds of them—on the tables, the speakers, the stereo, the windowsills.

Persisting with his accent, Grady spreads his arms out, palms up. "You like, no?"

"Holy shit," Lucy says.

"Oh my God," I say, touching her fingers.

"And now," Grady tells us, "I sense there is a—how do you say?—a big bird on its way to you." Arlan, who looks a little embarrassed, pulls the chicken out of the oven. It is a perfect, golden brown; it glistens in the candlelight, moist and steamy. "And gin—" Grady produces from the freezer a huge bottle of Bombay Sapphire gin with such arm-waving theatrics I suspect he's already had his share. "Let the night begin!"

Of course, we all drink too much. We stuff ourselves with roasted chicken, baby potatoes and Greek salad until we can hardly move, and then we lie around with John Hammond on the stereo, drinking some more. By midnight we're downright sloppy drunk. Arlan looks so good in his white T-shirt, his skin an even deeper tan from working all weekend out on Lummi Island. He and Lucinda kiss every five minutes, it seems, and I can't take my eyes off them. His dark hand on her white-white cheek makes me reach for my gin and tonic every time.

Whether it's out of drunkenness, exhibitionism or bliss, they don't even bother to close the bedroom door tonight. Grady and I find ourselves alone in the living room, surrounded by the debris of our hedonism: chicken bones, greasy napkins, empty bottles of tonic, plates strewn with bits of potato and flecks of rosemary swimming in butter. He clears his throat and reaches for the hulking bottle of gin. I'm sitting on the floor by the doorway, and as he kneels near me I can smell a trace of aftershave, something tasteful and expensive. He pours at least three fingers into my glass, and though I protest meekly, I drink it down anyway, without tonic this time. I stand up—I'm not sure why, it just seems like the thing to do—but as soon as I'm on my feet I want to sit down again, since the room is flashing by me with alarming speed.

Grady stands, and the next thing I'm aware of is his body pressed up against me, pinning my hips to the wall. His hands grope at my breasts and his mouth fastens on mine. When I turn my head away, confused, I'm looking through the bedroom doorway at Lucy's naked back rising from a disheveled quilt. Her hair is blue-black in the flickering candlelight. Arlan lies beneath her. He pulls her to him, gripping her just below the rib cage; his fingers look so enormous on her tiny waist, it seems he could break her.

Now Grady has one hand down my jeans, groping between my legs. I start to breathe heavily as his fingers find their way inside me. I keep my eyes the whole time on Arlan's hands and Lucy's back swaying like a reed caught in a current. Grady is watching them, too. Dimly, I'm aware of how pathetic we are, feeding off the sight of them, but I'm too excited to look away.

When Grady tugs me toward the front door, I only resist for a moment. I don't want to go anywhere; I want to hear them call out, watch their bodies shudder. I can hear Lucy's words ringing in my mind, *"Watching is a form of rape,"* but I wonder—isn't watching also love? Still, somewhere in the distant corners of my brain I know that I can't stay here, so I let Grady lead me out the door, down the steps, across the dewy lawn toward his place.

* * *

Grady's kitchen is egg-yolk yellow. On one wall there's a rack with twenty different kinds of spices, alphabetized. In his bedroom there's a woodblock print of Fidel Castro, a poster of some obscure jazz trio, another advertising an Italian movie from the Cannes Film Festival. In the corner is a fish tank where he has allegedly hatched several generations of sea monkeys; now it's dry and contains a collection of tiny, meticulously trimmed bonsai trees. There's an old-fashioned secretary's desk near the window, and he's got track lighting, which he dims so low that the room is bathed in a warm gold.

As soon as I walk through the door I'm strangely calm and sober. His apartment is so precise and tasteful, the messy scene we just left seems like nothing more than a drunken fantasy. We sit on his bed and start to giggle. He takes off my shirt and kisses my breasts. I wait for something to happen. Nothing. I try kissing him softly and running my hands through his hair, but it's all in vain—there's no heat between us. We struggle another five minutes or so, faking it halfheartedly, and then we just give up. He lends me a pair of flannel pajamas, strips down to his boxers and turns off the mood lighting. We lie side by side in his bed, staring at the ceiling.

"What's wrong with us, Anna?"

"We're obsessed with other people."

"Never stopped me before."

I laugh at this. He flips over onto his side, looks down at me intently. "You dig Arlan, don't you." His face is lined with the shadows from the venetian blinds.

"I guess it's obvious," I say.

He nods. "Everyone wants Arlan."

"I'm such a cliché…."

"Yep. Get used to it."

"What about you?" I whisper. "You like Lucy?"

"Lucinda?" He laughs. "She's cute as a button, but not my type. No, I'd take Arlan over her any day."

I sit up. "What? Really?"

"Don't look so surprised."

"You mean you're— I didn't know you were—"

"I'm not," he says. "Not really. But every once in a while, someone comes along who's—" he searches the dark for the right word "—inspiring. Arlan's like that."

I lie back down and stare at the ceiling again.

"I wouldn't lose any sleep over it," he says. "Believe me. They're never breaking up."

"You think they're good together?"

He considers this. "Not really. I think they're just equally fucked-up and scared. That goes a long way these days."

Later, when Grady's fallen asleep, I get up and go to the window. From this high up, you can see all the way down to the bay, and the trees between here and there all seem to be waving their leaves in the moonlight. There's a woman leaning against a truck parked on Purgatory Corner; she's staring at the front door of the halfway house, not moving. I wish suddenly and urgently that I had my binoculars on me. I can almost feel the grooved dial under my fingers, turning a blurry mess of light and shadow into a sharp, clear moment: a woman's face. Her hands. Her body tense, waiting for a door to open.

Quietly, I slip out of Grady's pajamas and put my clothes back on. I try to ignore how thirsty I am as I creep out his door, down the stairs, down the gravel path and back into Smoke Palace, concentrating as I slip into Arlan and Lucy's apartment, trying not to make any noise. As I'm passing their bedroom, I pause and look in. One candle is still burning in a jar on the dresser, though it's melted down to little more than a disfigured lump. Their bodies are curled against one another, with one of Arlan's hands resting limply on Lucy's hip. His face is serene and looks somehow noble, even with his lips parted slightly in sleep. Her expression is obscured by her hair, which has spilled down onto the pillowcase in a dark, chaotic mess.

My backpack is wedged between the wall and the couch; I dig in it until I find my binoculars, and hook them around my neck with the thin black cord. Then I slip back outside, across the lawn and, taking a deep breath, begin to climb the long, rusty fire escape ladder that leads up to the roof. Twice, I almost turn back around, as the yard and the Land of Skin grow smaller and smaller beneath me; instead I fix my eyes on the misshapen moon above me and keep pulling myself skyward, one rung at a time.

When I reach the sloping, shingled plane of the roof, I pull myself up onto it, heart racing, and sit hugging my knees near the rain gutter, looking out over Bellingham. As my breathing steadies, I inch my way slowly toward the crest of the roof, until I am perched near the very top. I stare at the world that spills out in all directions below: the decrepit mill still hissing clouds of smoke into the navy-blue sky; the inky Sound, glimmering below the moon with pools of silver light; the proud, weathered houses dotting the hills, announcing their victory against all those years of rain.

I raise the binoculars and peer through them; there's the woman, still leaning motionless against the truck, her eyes fixed on the front door of the halfway house. She is lit up by the streetlight, caught in a yellowish wash that makes her face look slightly sallow and ill. I fine-tune the focus until I can see every detail of her profile. She is young, somewhere in her early twenties, and it's clear that she's been crying. I think she's probably pretty, though her face looks sunken with exhaustion, almost skeletal. I wonder who or what she's waiting for, watching that door with such intense scrutiny. Occasionally her hair moves gently in the breeze, but other than that she's perfectly still.

Suddenly she turns her head and, tilting her face upward, fixes her eyes on mine. I catch my breath and nearly lose my balance, pulling the binoculars away jerkily. There she is, in miniature now, watching me from the sidewalk with one hand on her hip, having abandoned the statue-like pose of her vigil. She raises her other hand into the air in a gesture I can't quite decipher. I look through the binoculars just in time to catch a glimpse of her, eyes squinting angrily; she's giving me the finger.

As she drives off in her truck, I sit there, my binoculars hanging heavily around my neck, and it seems a great weight is pressing me down into the roof, crushing me with the force of all those stars and all that sky. I can hear Lucy saying, *"Oh, so you're one of those,"* and before I know what I'm doing, I've yanked the binoculars off and thrust them in a high, arcing trajectory that sends them sailing out over the street and down the three stories until they crash against the pavement in a final, surprisingly audible explosion of parts.

The Garden of Earthly Delights

A couple of weeks after our chicken feast, we've turned the corner into August, and the light is changing from the harsh glare of July to the more liquid tones of almost autumn. The summer moves into a slower, more sluggish rhythm, like a dancer going through the motions halfheartedly. Bender and I meet at the shop just about every day around ten and work until evening. I savor the sweet exhaustion that washes over me at night. Life at Smoke Palace is a lot less frenetic than usual. Bill's got some hot little sixteen-year-old he's been taking to the movies a lot, so he's hardly ever around. Grady's been trimming trees six days a week, and he mostly keeps to himself in his off hours. He plays with the band for their usual gigs, but doesn't hang around so much after, like he used to. Lucy and Arlan are as they always are: she's loud, he's gentle. They drink and smoke and sex themselves to sleep at night, while I pray that the hard work of the day will sweep me into unconsciousness before their soft moaning starts in the bedroom.

One morning I wake at dawn and go to the truck to retrieve my father's letters. Then I walk through the neighborhood until I discover a path that winds its way above the university, through a gorgeous, whispering arboretum. It's a steep climb, but before long I find myself at the top of a lookout tower, alone with the sun rising at my back and the Sound before me, glossy and still. I carefully unwrap the leather bundle and take the next letter from its envelope. The postmark says it's from Death Valley, California. I feel a little shiver along my spine.

August 30th, 1977

Look, man, I'm going to make this as brief and uncomplicated as possible. You don't need to know where I am. I'm fine. I just had to get away. I'll be back to finish that job for Kleinzahler. Even if I have to work twenty-hour stretches I'll get it done, you know I will. I couldn't share a bed with Helen even one more night, so I've gone someplace where I can be alone, listen to the sound of my own breathing and try to piece together the thoughts littering the floor of my brain.

What do you take me for—a drooling idiot? I know the signs of love. When she looks at you with her cherry lips laughing, parted wide, inviting, her eyes spitting light at you, how could anyone miss it? You both willfully refuse to acknowledge plain fact. You deny the undeniable; no one can look at you together and miss it. Sheila pretends not to notice, but I don't have her gift for oblivion. You love Helen the way I loved V—with a furious need, the kind of longing that scorches the throat, sends tendrils of smoke into the eyes.

There's nothing to be done, but I do wish to God I'd never touched her in the first place, so you could be together and our lives could make themselves whole. As it is now, even I'm realistic enough to know it's too late for that. Maybe if Anna didn't exist, we could try to go back in time, but her life is too delicate and important for such radical experiments. Years ago, when everything seemed more like a game, we could play at anything—it was all the same to us. Hell, with Nam going on and half the guys we grew up with six feet under or (worse) watching their own brains rotting slowly inside their skulls, who could take anything seriously? We were lucky just to be alive, so who's going to cling to the rules when your number might be up any second and you could find yourself at the business end of an M16? But I've lost some of my wild abandon post-Anna. Suddenly, the world's fucked-up death wish isn't just an excuse to get high and get laid, it's a real time bomb, and the ticking is always audible in my heart. Even worse is my own ability to fuck up, which is a constant, gnawing danger that keeps me awake at night, sweating under the sheets.

But I digress. I guess brief and uncomplicated was never my style.

If you want to know the truth, I've listed our choices and they're all equally fucked-up. In fact, they're so repugnant I had to puke twice before I finished jotting them down. Finally, I threw the I-Ching. All things being equal, I've let a few pennies determine my course.

I'll go back to Helen. I'll be a father to Anna. I will never mention any of this again. What I want from you is respect for my family. I know you can't stop wanting her, but I ask that you stop displaying it. We will live a charade, carefully choreographed, and we will be polite about it. No one knows better than me the price for such pretending, but as I said, I've reviewed our options until I'm sick and empty; this is no more or less evil than the others.

Of course, you can refuse. I might even be relieved at such a refusal. At times I've fantasized that you two would escape, run off to some tropical locale and never resurface. But if you accept, you've got to keep your word. Don't show the slightest twitch of affection. Keep your hands in your pockets and your eyes on the floor. What can I say? It goes against everything we ever believed in, but it's possible, and it's necessary. Living by what we believed has only gotten us here.

Give me a sign,

Chet

I read it three times and then fold it up carefully, place it back in its envelope. I stand there for a long while, staring out over the treetops. I feel like I've been dipped in ice-cold water, and any second my teeth will start to chatter, but for now I have the brief blessing of no feeling whatsoever.

I walk slowly to the shop. As I near downtown, an image jumps out at me every block or so: my mother, young and radiant, her hair in two flirtatious braids, laughing playfully with Bender, who stands just an inch or two closer than expected. His wife, Sheila, looking the other way. My father in some lonely Death Valley diner, making a list.

When I get to the shop, I let myself in. It's still early; Bender won't be in for at least an hour or two. I study our guitar, still just pieces getting ready to make themselves whole. We're working on setting the braces just right so the soundboard will be strong but resonant. Bender keeps harping on how important that is. The braces remind me of a woman's corset, pulling the curves into some kind of order.

They gather close together at the waist and fan out along the hips. I trace them with my fingers lightly, barely touching them, trying not to think about anything except the shape they make.

I want this guitar to be beautiful; I wonder if this anxious need and worry is how a bride feels about her wedding dress. I've imbued the materials with mystical potential. If these planks of wood, these bits of abalone and ivory can come together in just the right way, something alchemical will happen, and I will be someone new. And yet right now I'm tempted to break everything with my bare hands, listen to the wood we've labored over splintering and cracking like frail bones.

When Bender gets there, he doesn't see me at first. He gives a little yelp and spills his coffee when he catches me standing perfectly still in the corner, staring at him. "Jesus Christ, Medina! Why didn't you say something?"

"I don't know."

"I didn't expect you yet," he says.

"I got up early."

He dabs at the spilled coffee on his jeans with the sleeve of his jacket and squints at me. "What's up with you? You look…"

"I look what?"

"Different," he says. "Is something wrong?"

"How come you never told me you were in love with my mother?"

There's a long, precarious pause. He sips from his coffee carefully. "It was a little more complicated than that."

"I'm listening," I whisper.

He chuckles nervously, looks away. "Your dad thought I was. But he had it all wrong."

"Did he?" I don't like how he's avoiding my eyes.

"Of course," he says. And then, when I don't stop looking at him, "Medina! Think about it! Would I have given you those letters if your mom and I were sneaking around?"

"I don't know. You might."

"Why would I? That would be crazy."

I shrug. "Maybe you needed to confess."

"I'm not Catholic," he grumbles. "And besides, that's not my style."

"So he was completely off base? You must have liked each other, at least."

He stuffs his hands in his pockets. His hair is unusually tame today, slicked, almost successfully, with what must be copious amounts of gel. "We liked each other, sure. I mean we *loved* each other, but like friends, you know—family. Before Chet flipped out—" he looks at me sideways "—we were all very close. Chet, Helen, Sheila, Rosie—all of us. In those days, people weren't so uptight—we did everything together."

"Everything?" I raise my eyebrows.

"Come on! You know what I mean. We were close, that's all."

"What did your wife think about all this?"

"Sheila?" I nod. "She wasn't the jealous type. Things were different back then. Besides, her mind was on other things...." I don't know what he means by this, but he looks so nervous and out of place, suddenly, so short and fat and tired, that I'm hesitant to press him further. He sees his chance to change the subject, and seizes it.

"You ready to put some hours in? We've still got a long ways to go on this thing."

I just shrug.

He puts his coffee down and goes to the soundboard, starts examining it with a businesslike air. "We've got to make some decisions soon about the inlay," he says. "These braces look pretty good, huh?" When I don't say anything, he glances at me expectantly, and I can see how anxious I'm making him, so I mumble my agreement and go over to him. As he rattles off a list of instructions, I listen silently, keeping my expression as blank as possible.

Ever since I read the letter from Death Valley, things have been strained between Bender and me. We don't joke around as much, and he doesn't offer any anecdotes from the past—funny luthier stories featuring my father or Rot Gut. We work mostly in silence, with just the whine of saws and sanders as our music. I miss our easy rapport, but I can feel my own discomfort and confusion wedging a thin layer of ice between us. I sense there's so much more to know about what happened between him and my mom. As with all the other questions unleashed by my father's letters, I want the answers almost as much as I dread them.

Sunday night, I come back to Smoke Palace with fine rosewood sawdust coating my skin and clothes. The house is empty, and the phone is ringing, on and on, relentlessly; I can hear it all the way up the stairs. When I answer it, I'm surprised that the person on the other end knows my name.

"Yeah, this is Anna."

"Oh, kitten," Rosie says. "I had nothing to do with it, I swear."

"With what?"

"You mean she's not up there?" I can hear her clomping around in heavy shoes. "Damn! Sorry—stupid teakettle. Burned myself."

"Who's not up here?"

"Your mother."

"Why would she be?"

"She's insane." There's a sudden burst of static on the line, but then her voice comes back loud as ever, midsentence. "...determined to come find you."

I can feel my breath coming faster. I sit down on the couch and hug my knees to my chest. "Wait a minute. My mother? She's coming here?"

"She's probably there already, the way she drives—she left yesterday morning. She grilled me for hours, trying to pry your address from me. I didn't know what to do!"

"Okay," I say. I get up and pull the leftover Sapphire gin from the freezer, pour myself a little, down it fast. "You think she's up here somewhere?"

"I guess by now—"

"Rosie!"

"I know, but what could I do? She was on fire—I couldn't stop her!"

"Okay. Okay, stay calm," I say, more to myself than to her. "She left yesterday?"

"Muumuu, get down! Yeah, in the morning."

"Oh God. She's probably here somewhere."

"You know how she gets, kitten. Go easy on her."

"Go easy? On *her?* Are you—"

"I know, I know. But she's been so worried. She only gets this way because she loves you so much!"

"Did you give her this number?" Silence. "Rosie? You did, didn't you!"

"What could I do? She wouldn't take no for an answer!"

"But not the address?" I close my eyes.

"No. Just the number. I figured you could take it from there."

"Okay. Fine. I'll just deal with it." I'm about to hang up, when something occurs to me. "Rosie, I want to ask you something. What was the deal with Bender and Mom? Did they have an affair, or something?"

There's a pause. "Is that what Bender said?"

"No, he denies it. But did they?"

"Look, kitten…maybe you should ask your mom. Your

dad and Bender had a falling-out. I guess it had something to do with Helen. Other than that, I just don't know...."

"Yeah," I say. "Or you just won't tell."

"Your mom knows better than I do—that's all I'm saying. Maybe when she gets there, you could ask her."

"Maybe."

We say our goodbyes, mine a little sulky, and hang up.

My mother. Here.

There's unusually raw and violent music coming from the direction of the Goat Kid Hovel. I look out the window, gripping my drink, trying to pinpoint the exact day I learned to pour gin on a racing heart. In the Goat Kids' yard, five or six of them are taking turns trying to smash open what appears to be a parking meter, severed from its pole. One wields an ax, but the others have less conventional weapons: a couple of feet of rebar, a cast-iron skillet, an old burlap sack of something heavy that attacks with dull thuds. Raggedy Ann stands a little distance away, mesmerized. I try to lose myself in the weirdly brutal little scene. I watch them until the gray metal of the parking meter is dented and pockmarked with their blows—but all I can see is my mother gulping espresso from a paper cup and racing along in her silver Fiat, hurling herself closer and closer to the Land of Skin.

December 30th, 1982
Einstein,

Three years ago, when you left San Francisco, I promised myself I would erase you from my consciousness, like footprints in sand washed smooth by the rising tide. But I'm the worse kind of fool, Einstein. I can't even successfully deceive myself. I should have known you would never disappear so easily—you were always a stubborn son of a bitch. I may have succeeded in obliterating your face from my days, but at night you amble right into my dreams with your hair all fucked-up and your eyes blank and friendly, just as if nothing's the matter.

Lately my insomnia has gotten so bad that I might be granted a reprieve, but instead you haunt me even when I'm not sleeping. You show up at the foot of my bed with a stack of Mose Allison LPs, looking for the stereo, or you materialize while I'm making a sandwich, excitedly explaining how to bookmatch koa so it lines up seamlessly. I'm sick of it, man. I'm starting to feel like a goddamn drooling loony. I'm not saying that writing you will be my cure, but it beats doing nothing.

Can you believe we're thirty-three this year? Remember when we used to think everyone over thirty might as well just cash in their chips, seeing as you either had to bend over for the system or go completely mad? Obviously, I've chosen the latter. No regrets. But the face that appears over the bathroom sink every morning invariably shocks me. Who is this old fart with his long shanks of gray hair and vacant eyes?

Vanity, vanity, all is vanity.

It's all the same fucking day.

I didn't know what I was doing when I sat down to write you this morning. Like so many things in my life, it seemed like one of many possible poisons, and at last writing you was less repugnant than not writing you. When did the landscape I live in become riddled with nothing but rocks and hard places? A hundred years ago I was a different man.

Now that I've spent three hours eking out this paltry sum of words, I can safely say that I'm writing you to find out what I'm thinking. You were always my reluctant confessor. Remember senior year talking me down from that fucking ghastly orange sunshine trip?

I told you every passing thought I'd ever entertained from the time I was five or six. It's amazing you didn't keel over with the stupefying boredom of it.

But I'm almost done with this limp little letter and I still don't know shit about what I'm thinking. All I can see is an ungodly whitewash of loneliness. Food tastes like ash. Colors no longer pulse or bring pleasure. I dwell in the past compulsively with a mix of nostalgia and nausea. It's good you'll never see me like this. I would make you sick.

I heard from Rosie that you and Sheila tried for another baby but lost it. I'm sorry, man. I know that doesn't do shit, but it's what we say when these things happen, knowing it's no better or worse than any other trite syllables we might offer. I also hear Scottie's doing well. I hope he's some comfort.

Write if you want. If you don't I can't blame you.

Chet

The next day, Bender and I work hard all morning, but I'm too distracted to get much done. I spill a bottle of lacquer, nearly slice my finger off with the saw, and am generally useless. By noon, I'm a nervous wreck. Bender's been trying for hours to instruct me on the proper way to sand the neck, but it's delicate work, and if you mess up even a little the whole thing is ruined. The mahogany's not as expensive as the koa or ebony, but it's still not exactly expendable. I apologize profusely, but my hands just won't cooperate.

I can't stop thinking it, over and over, like a compulsive mantra: *My mother. Here.* Twice, I almost tell Bender about it, but I can't bring myself to form the actual sentence out loud. I'm afraid his face will light up, and I'll see what my father saw that terrible August—the betrayal that sent him out into the desert, searching for options.

Suddenly Bender looks at me and says, apropos of nothing, "Medina, let's go to the mall."

"The mall? Are you kidding?"

"No. Come on. You need a break. Don't look at me like that! I need some things," he laughs.

I look around at the shop. We spent a good two weeks ensuring it was perfect—we cleaned all his saws, routers and planers, set up comfortable, well-lit work spaces, bought a stereo with a turntable and a stack of old Motown LPs at a yard sale. "What do you need?" I ask.

"Just some stuff. Socks. A tie, maybe."

"A *tie?*" He's wearing his usual uniform: a pair of grease-stained Levi's and a threadbare, flesh-colored T-shirt. "What do you need a tie for?"

"Who says I *don't* need a tie?" He stands up straighter, looking indignant. There are stray flakes of sawdust in his tangled nest of hair.

"Guess I can't argue with that," I say.

"Let's go. We can grab a bite on the way back." He tosses the sandpaper aside and brushes the sawdust from his clothes. "I look okay?"

"Get the sawdust out of your hair," I say. "What's going on, anyway? Hot date on the horizon?"

He swats at his hair a couple of times, then fishes a toothpick from his pocket and grips it between his teeth. "Look," he says, "I'm out of socks, okay? Big deal."

We go outside and get in the truck. Arlan finally fixed it for me; now it's running even better than it did before the doomed excursion to Sequim. The morning is overcast, but patches of blue are appearing here and there in the sky. As I drive, Bender stares out the window. Halfway there, he says quietly, "Haven't been to a mall since Scottie died."

"Why not?"

"No reason." After a long pause, he adds, "Just overwhelms me, I guess. Smell of new clothes, waffle cones. Families getting all worked up. Depresses me."

"So why go today?"

He shrugs, still staring out the window. "Need some socks."

As I park the truck, he gazes at Sears with a vague look of apprehension. "I guess after Sheila left, I forgot about shopping." His stare becomes distant and melancholy. "They say hardly any marriages survive, after your kid dies."

"I've heard that," I say softly.

"Yeah. Well," he says, taking off his seat belt and opening the door, "might as well get it over with."

Bender purchases four pairs of cotton socks, two pairs of wool ones, and a package of navy-blue T-shirts. We look at some ties but they're all either too hokey or too boring. I get the giggles trying to imagine him in the one he likes best: a yellow one with dark zebra stripes. He opts to forget about the tie. On our way out, he dashes impulsively into a candy store and buys a pound of cotton-candy-flavored jelly beans. "I used to love these," he says, stuffing a few in his mouth and holding the bag out to me.

"Mmm," I say, trying one. "These *are* good."

"If you can't have cigarettes, these are the next best thing."

As we're wandering through the parking lot, trying to remember where we left the truck, Bender says, "Your dad and I had a game we played, back in Palo Alto, when we were kids."

"Oh yeah?"

"Well, not exactly a game, I guess—just a way to pass the time. We used to make up stories about the people we saw. Give them names, occupations, exotic diseases..." A man gets out of his shiny black Alfa Romeo near us. "Like this guy." Bender drops his voice to barely above a whisper. "Mickey Daniels. Top chef at a chichi little place called Sarah's in Seattle. Came up here because he's got the hots for a little number selling lingerie."

"Only he's also got two ex-wives," I say. "And they're both suing him because he won't pay child support. They've become best friends and they're starting an organization in Minneapolis called Ex-wives United."

Bender chuckles. "Otherwise known as EU. You're a natural, Medina."

"It's easy to figure people out," I say. "As long as you never actually meet them." For a moment I almost tell him about my Suicide Maps, but I decide not to. I don't want to deflate the sweet airiness of this moment.

"Your dad liked to play that for hours. He never got tired of it."

I think of my father's eyes, eagerly watching the world. They could absorb every cell of color and light; I can see him reading people's clothing, decoding the creases around their mouths. Nothing could get past him.

Before we go back to the shop, we have lunch at a Thai place next to a sex shop. We order Drunk Noodles and Spicy Whole Fish. We laugh at the phrase printed at the top of the menu: *We serve to bring you long happiness.* "Looks like they've got some long happiness next door," he says, referring to the window display of multicolored dildos we passed on the way in. I get a Thai iced tea and when Bender takes a sip of it he likes it so much he orders his own, drinks it down in three long gulps.

"You don't drink beer when you work, do you?" I ask.

"Nope. Guitars and booze don't mix—making them, anyway. Playing's another story. Good to stay sober when working with power tools. I like to keep all my limbs intact."

I'm surprised when a memory assails me: my father was missing part of one finger. I can't believe I'd forgotten this.

"I just remembered," I say. "One of Dad's fingers was messed up, wasn't it?"

"Yeah. I was there when he did that." He chuckles. "Poor guy. Your dad could handle a lot, but the sight of blood made him sick. He sliced it open on the table saw. I had to wrap the whole thing up and hide it from him all the way to the hospital, or he'd faint. I'm driving with one hand, holding his finger on with the other, and telling every joke I'd ever heard about a mile a minute, to keep him calm. He was the color of split-pea soup for hours!" He laughs.

"You two were good together, weren't you."

"Sure," he says, still smiling. "I guess so."

"So what happened?"

His smile dissipates. "This again?"

I'm fully aware that I'm spoiling the light mood of the day. The mall, the jelly beans, making up stories in the parking lot, joking about dildos—I'm risking it all as I steer the conversation toward something that happened over twenty years ago, when The Mermaid Garden became Medina Designs. But the further I get into my father's letters, the more I'm frustrated by how little I know. His own words are so ambiguous; they're poetic, thoughtful, raw at times, but they only stir more questions in me, and I'm getting more impatient to find the answers.

"You promised you'd tell me," I say. "Remember?"

The food arrives; we spoon the fish and noodles onto our plates. Finally, Bender says, "I don't think your mom would like it if I told you everything."

"She shouldn't have any say in it."

"Well, that may be true, Medina, but what gives me the right to spill what's been unspilled all these years?"

"You haven't even talked to her in a couple decades," I say. "Why should you care what she thinks?"

He sighs, looks up at the ceiling. "We might as well start there, if you insist on forcing confessions. I have talked to your mom. Fairly recently."

My stomach drops. "You didn't tell her where I'm staying, did you?"

"No—not that recently. I mean, you know, a year or two back. We met in Seattle."

"On purpose?" I toy with my food, suddenly not interested but trying to look casual. He nods. "What for?"

"Well, when people know each other for such a long time, and care about each other, and, you know, have certain tragedies in common, it's natural." I've never heard him speak like this—like someone going out of his way to find euphemisms.

"What's natural, exactly?"

"Please don't look at me like that. You wanted to know, I'm trying to tell you. If you get all pouty, I'm not even going to try."

I force a small grin. "I'm not pouting. Go on."

"So, yeah, your mom and I have been in touch, here and there." I want to ask him why he never told me this before, but I know it will sound accusatory, so I keep quiet. "And we—well, we were always fond of each other." He says this so stiffly, I almost laugh, but I force my face into a neutral expression. "She's a very particular woman, you know—um, unique and—"

The waitress comes by and asks if we'd like more water. I turn abruptly toward her, startled, and as I see her small face framed in blunt bangs, her meticulous eye makeup, her manicured nails wrapped around the glimmering pitcher of ice water, it hits me with all the force of a dream forgotten and then, all at once, recalled in totality: they were lovers. My father wasn't crazy; my mother and Bender were in love. They might be still.

"Medina," Bender says, "you want water?"

"Um—sure. Sorry." I hold out my glass and the waitress fills it to the top, hurries off to the next table. I take a sip and swallow with effort. I suddenly feel like everything I put in my mouth has the potential to choke me.

"So we stayed in touch, after your dad died. We sort of needed each other, I think. But years before—well, you know how your father felt, from his letters. He was jealous. He thought we were sneaking around. He thought…a lot of things."

"And he was right," I say quietly, barely above a whisper. "Wasn't he? You were in love."

"Oh, hell, I try not to use that word." I've never seen Bender blush before. "A word like that can turn on you, can't it? Who knows what it means?"

"Is that why you sold him the business? Because you loved Mom?"

"Things got very tense."

"Did you sleep together?"

"Look," he says. "Try to keep an open mind, okay? This isn't easy."

"I'm listening."

"Back before you were even born, when me and Sheila were just starting out, we did something kind of…dumb. It was Chet's idea, actually. He was reading all this Margaret Mead and he got the idea that monogamy was just a middle-class construct; he thought it was something we had to 'transcend.' You know your dad—he'd get an idea in his head and that was that. Anyway, one night we had too much to drink, too much to smoke, and we…" He pauses, wipes his mouth with his napkin, though he hasn't eaten a bite. "Chet went home with Sheila, and I stayed with your mom. It was an experiment—just one night. But it ended up haunting us."

"You *swapped?*"

He nods, and his face is bright red. The food grows cold in our silence. The Drunk Noodles are slowly congealing, but we don't lift a fork, we don't move at all. "I would have told you sooner, except I didn't think it was all that relevant."

"Not *relevant?*" I say, incredulous.

"Well, is it?"

"Come on—it explains everything!"

"What do you mean?" he asks, looking profoundly uneasy.

"It's why you sold him the business, it's why they weren't happy—it's probably why he killed himself, even."

"Oh come on, Medina."

"Don't 'come on, Medina' me! If your wife and your best friend were in love, wouldn't you go a little crazy?"

"There are worse things," he says. I know from his tone he's thinking of his son, but I'm mad now, and I don't want to slow down to think about his loss.

"You don't want to feel guilty…" I say. "Or Mom, either. That's why nobody ever told me."

He leans forward a little, and there's an edge to his voice. "You think it never occurred to me? To both of us? If only we hadn't—felt how we felt—maybe he'd still be alive?" There are tears in his eyes. "But there's no point in thinking like that. It just makes you crazy."

"I can't believe you saw her a year ago and you never said anything!"

"I knew she wouldn't want me to tell you, Anna—"

"Did you sleep with her then?" An older woman at a nearby table glances at me with a furrowed brow; I lower my voice slightly. "Did you?"

"We never did. After that time, I mean—back before you were born. We did feel guilty, okay? But after your dad died, we only saw each other because—I don't know—we needed to talk, I guess. About the old days…"

"Great. How come she never wanted to talk to *me* about the old days? I'm his daughter—don't I deserve to know?"

"Yes. You do, Anna. You do. That's why I gave you those letters." He takes a sip of water; he looks tired and sad. I feel my anger draining away, seeing how sad he is. "Well, it was partly that. Mostly I was sick of trying to figure them out by myself. I've spent a lot of time—hours and hours—trying to make sense of them. But I'm never going to know why he did it. Neither are you."

"I—I just thought—" I stammer, feeling very young. "I thought if I had some idea about who he was, you know? I thought then I'd be…"

"Be what?"

I look at the ceiling. "Real," I whisper, more to myself than to him.

He reaches around our plates to hold my hand. "Look, I've spent years imagining who Scott would have been, if he'd made it. Every day I think about how old he'd be, what he'd be like. Hell, he could even have kids of his own by now. And where does that get me? Seven years of sitting on my ass, drinking beer, making up a life that's never going to be."

"But that's different," I say.

"Oh yeah?"

"I'm looking for what happened, not what *might* have happened."

He shakes his head sadly. "It's all the same thing. Past, future—none of it's right now. 'It's all the same fucking day.'" He squeezes my fingers in his. "I wish I could change a lot of things—so what? Right now, I'm working on making one good guitar. That's what matters—doing something you give a shit about, with people who are alive and listening. Isn't that what you've been trying to tell *me?*"

I smile a little. "Yeah, I guess so."

"I've got nothing against history, but you can't get lost in it."

We sit there for a few seconds, just looking at each other. Then he lets go of my hand and clears his throat, waves at my plate with his fork. "We've barely touched this food, huh? The noodles are getting soggy."

I pick up my fork and try a little fish. He digs in.

Halfway through the meal, I get up the courage to speak. "Bender?"

"Yeah, Medina."

"Thanks. For telling me."

He's chewing, but there's a tiny smile there, too. "No problem," he mumbles, careful to barely open his mouth.

That night, as I'm lying on my back in the living room, thinking about everything Bender said, my mother calls. Lucy brings me the phone with her hand over the mouthpiece. She looks sympathetic as she mouths, *Your mom.*

"Hello?"

"Is this how you wanted it?"

"Mom. Rosie told me you were—"

"You want me tracking you down? Huh? Is this what you had in mind?"

Lucy brings me a stiff gin and tonic. I smile at her, take a sip. "Okay, let's try that again," I say. "Hello, Mother. How are you?"

"Don't toy with me!" I can hear her exhaling smoke. "I'm in Seattle. Are you going to tell me where you are, or do I have to call the police?"

"Mom, you're not going to call the—"

"Do you have any idea what I've been through?"

"I have a feeling you're going to fill me in."

"I haven't slept in weeks! You never even bothered to send me a note, Anna, Jesus! Of all the inconsiderate—" She stops herself, aware perhaps that she's shrieking. "I'd like to see you," she says, her voice softening a notch. "I want to make sure you're all right."

"I'm fine, Mother, really." Lucy stifles a giggle. "There's no need for you to come here." She bites her wrist to keep from laughing and disappears into the bedroom.

"You will see me," she says. "Whether you like it or not."

I sigh. "Why are you being like this?"

"I'm your mother! Don't you remember me? I'm your goddamn mo—"

"Look, maybe I should come there," I suggest. "It's not that far to Seattle."

"That's not the point," she says. "I want to see what you're doing. I want to know who you're with."

"Mother, I can explain what I'm doing when I come down—"

"I want to see," she says. "With my own eyes."

"Well, I'm sorry, Mom, but I'm not going to put myself on display. You can't always get what you want, you know?"

There's a brief, terse silence. I wonder if she actually heard me, for once. Finally, she takes a deep breath and exhales a breathy "Goodbye, Anna." Then the line goes dead.

I sit there, staring at the phone in my hand, mystified.

"Sounds like a basketcase," Lucy's voice comes through the dial tone. It takes me a second to realize she's on the other phone.

"Lucy!" I yell, running into the bedroom in time to see her putting the receiver back in its cradle. "You little sneak!"

"Don't get mad," she giggles. "You needed a witness."

I shake my head in disbelief. "She's worse than ever."

"Well, at least she's not coming here."

"Yeah," I say. "That would be a nightmare." But somehow I can't quite believe I've gotten off that easily.

June 2nd, 1986
Einstein,

The moon has a stone-cold face; she is unmoved by my terror. She watches like that old woman behind the counter at the minimart tonight—the one who wore orange lipstick and stared at me like I wasn't human, wasn't even there. Her eyelashes were fake and the name tag pinned to her smock read, "Hi, I'm Stella." The moon tonight is just like her—cynical, cold, unmoved.

There is nothing but dark and ash.

When I met Helen, it was her hands that drew me in. I watched her fingers on that harp, stroking the notes. Her hair, that's what everyone remembered her by. "What gorgeous hair," they said. But for me, it was her hands—the delicate, birdlike bones and the pale skin and the movement of them, so rapid, light, like wings. She kissed each string with her fingers.

I don't know what I'm going to do. I don't know what I'm doing.

Chet

The next day, Bender and I work on the guitar from dawn until sunset. We've been applying coat after coat of lacquer; yesterday we glued the bone on, and in the afternoon Bender removes the clamp carefully. We install the tuners, put on the strings, and adjust the truss rod. By the time the shadows lengthen and a chill begins to seep into the room, our work is done. We sit there looking at it for a long time. Its curves are sensual, smooth, like ripples in water. Every inch of it, from the abalone inlay around the soundhole to the gold Grover tuners, is undeniably beautiful. It's built of only the best materials—ebony fingerboard, Hawaiian koa back and sides, Sitka spruce top. The koa back is bookmatched, with a tiny black seam down the center. Bender calls the sides "flamed" because the grain looks like fire. He holds it in his hands for a long time, turning it this way and that, squinting at it with a scientific air. He hands it to me and I touch it reverently, afraid I'll drop it.

"Why don't you play something?" I ask, handing it back.

"That's the real test," he says, eyeing it nervously. He rests it on his knee and I marvel at the fit of it there; I never realized before what an ingenious instrument the guitar is. The spruce top has such a glossy sheen I can see my reflection in it. The pick guard is tortoiseshell with blond flecks—Bender let me pick that out. He tunes it, scowling and pursing his lips in concentration. He increases the tension on the strings, and my skin starts to feel clammy. "Haven't played in years," he says. He looks at me; his blue eyes are a little bloodshot from the long hours of work, but his face looks young, too—eager and scared. He strums a few chords to make sure it's in tune. As he begins to play, the whole shop is suddenly filled with the miraculous sound of the thing. Every time he strums a new chord, another memory comes back—fragments of summer nights spent with my parents, lulled by the smell of star jasmine and the sound of my father's guitar. I can hear his deep, raspy voice and my mother's angelic harmonies. The tune Bender's playing goes bright to dark and back again from one bar to the next; I know before he's through it's a song my father wrote.

"What's that one called?"

"'The Garden of Earthly Delights.' Like the painting—you know—by Hieronymus Bosch?"

"Oh yeah," I say. "He loved that guy. Those pictures used to give me bad dreams."

"Your dad was a trip," Bender says, smiling sadly. He hands the guitar to me again. "You want to try it?"

"I don't remember how to play, really."

"Just strum it," he says. "See how it feels." I press my fingers against the strings in a D-chord and strum. I can feel the body vibrating subtly against me. I find the A and strum again. "There you go!" Bender says, leaning forward. "You didn't forget."

"I'd like to learn again."

"Well, now you've got something to practice on," he says.

I look at him in surprise. "Wait a minute," I say. "I thought we were going to sell this one."

"No," he says, shaking his head solemnly. "This one's yours."

Night. I'm alone on the black leather couch, reading the last of my father's letters, whispering each word softly as the refrigerator hums and shudders in the kitchen. Lucy and Arlan have been gone all evening.

For days, the sunlight has poured down on Bellingham with wild abandon. Everyone in the Land of Skin walks around scantily clad, their naked limbs gleaming in the sun like those of alabaster statues. Even the nights are hot, and as I read my father's last letter, warm air perfumed with freshly cut grass pushes through the open window.

April 24th, 1987
Einstein,

We cannot know how many years it will take before the earth has ears. Now the moon loops around us night after night, trying to get our attention, but we spin on, oblivious, deaf to her cries.

I am tired. The taste of ash is thick in my mouth. I want only silence.

I heard Dylan is jamming with the Dead in San Rafael. I shouldn't even think about it. Tonight I took Helen and Anna to a movie—something insipid, about ice-skaters; they both cried when the girl hurt her leg.

I wanted to hit them both. Wonder where my life is, the one I meant to lead? Even fruit tastes like ash.

When I sleep, there is absence. I let go of fear, then. Only I don't sleep well, these days. When I do, too often I dream.

I am dead weight in this house. I sit for hours, wanting to hear something, anything, but there are only the sounds of this small life—nothing beyond. The neighbor calling to her dog. Helen moving quietly through her tooth-brushing routine. Anna laughing at the TV. I am a still, heavy stone in the living room—a lump of a man. Inert.

This afternoon I saw a snake in the yard and I wanted, for a second, to kill it. Then I saw it was just a garter snake, and on a curious impulse, I lifted it in my hands. I looked into its eyes, and I saw there the truth: cold, silent, impersonal.

We try to warm ourselves with small fires of gossip, scandal, sex, but then the fires go out and we find ourselves lost, wandering among the ashes.

I don't want

And here it ends—one last fragment of a sentence, trailing off into dead space. No signature, no nothing. I read the whole thing again and again, whispering it to myself, and each time I come to those final words, I imagine the sentence will heal itself, become whole before my eyes. It never does.

I can hear a man's voice shouting. It's my father. "Why'd you do it?" he's crying. "Why the fuck did you do it?" I'm bewildered—what have I done? But now I'm being pulled back to Smoke Palace. I can feel the hard black couch beneath me, and it is Arlan's voice shouting, and Lucy is answering him with a half moan, half whimper. She sounds more animal than human. I'm suddenly bristling with fear, wide awake, and I can feel my skin going prickly. After a pause, Arlan speaks again, this time with a terrible sadness: "Please, Lucy, Jesus."

"What do you want from me?" Her words are slurred; she sounds loaded.

"I can't take this again."

"I don't belong to you!"

"Oh God," Arlan says, and the pain in his voice makes my stomach churn. "Don't say anything. Just— Please."

"Get me a drink."

"Don't say anything!" Then, screaming, "DON'T SAY—"

"I NEED A DRINK!" she screams back. Her voice is shrill and hoarse but still louder than his, and she drowns him out.

There's a thud, maybe a chair falling over, and now my heart starts beating so fast it feels like wings in my chest. I get up, but my legs are wobbly beneath me. More sounds from the bedroom—not words, just sounds of bodies moving and furniture shifting. I listen carefully as I navigate the dark living room. When I get to the bedroom door, I pause, trying to slow my heart by breathing more deeply. "You guys?"

"What?" Arlan says.

"Everything okay?" No answer. I hear a drawer being dragged open. Everything polite and respectful in me says, *return to couch,* but somehow I can't make myself. I stand there with my ear almost touching the door and one hand on the knob. I hear that sound from Lucy again—that half animal, half human murmur. Without deciding to, I push the door open.

There's one lamp on—I remember it from my first night inside Smoke Palace; it's draped with a red scarf that casts the whole room in a fiery hue. Arlan is standing near the chest of drawers with his long hair draped over his shoulders like Jesus. As I enter, his eyes move to take me in, but the rest of him stays perfectly still. He looks more than ever like those old photos of Indian chiefs—high cheekbones, sepia skin, dark eyes burning.

"Fuck you," Lucy moans from the tangle of sheets. She is half naked but her shoes are on. She stares up at the ceiling. One hand hangs limp over the side of the bed; her pale fingers are dyed red by the light in the room. Slowly, she turns her head toward me, and though most of her face is draped in shadow, her vacant eyes stir a terrible, haunted feeling in the pit of my stomach. "Fuck…" She draws in her breath as if preparing to say more, but then she just sighs, scratches her face and closes her eyes.

"What's wrong with her?" I ask Arlan. He doesn't answer. He turns toward the chest of drawers and slams the top one closed with such force it makes me jump. "Arlan? Talk to me."

"'Arlan, talk to me,'" Lucy mimics, her eyes still closed.

He runs one hand through his hair, grabs his jacket off the bed. Lucy curls into a fetal position. He looks at me. "I got to get out of—" he begins, but his voice falters. "Keep an eye on her."

"I don't need anybody's fucking eye on—"

"Lucinda—" I say sharply. She curls her knees closer to her chin and moans.

"I gotta go." He moves toward the door, but I'm in his way. I touch his arm and the warmth of his skin makes my mouth go dry. His eyes search my face.

Lucy mumbles, "God, this sucks," from the bed, and then he disappears, slamming the door as he goes.

"Anna," Lucy calls out. "Why is this happening?"

I go to her, and hesitate there at the side of the bed, looking down at her half-naked body, her dark mess of hair, before I lie down next to her. She's still curled up, her eyes closed. "Never mind," I say. "Go to sleep, now. It'll be okay."

"God," she moans. "Why do I do it?"

"I don't know. But whatever it is, it's done."

When she falls asleep, I move silently to the foot of the bed; taking infinite care not to wake her, I unlace and remove her shoes. Her feet are incredibly small and delicate. I tuck them under the quilt. Standing above her, watching her eyelids tremble with sleep, I find myself hating her. I wish Arlan had never met her—I wish she was never born. So her mother lives in a trailer, her stepdad has a hollow-eyed, lumpy face and her sister yanks her around by her hair. So what? Does it mean she can do whatever she wants—hurt whoever she feels like hurting—even Arlan, who worships her?

I sit back down on the bed and try to redirect my thoughts. I remember how she seemed that first night downtown: impulsive, colorful, like a bright red kite swooping and diving in the wind. She was someone I'd never imagined I could know; her confidence was palpably magnetic. I thought if I could absorb even a little of her magic, something in me would come alive, and someone like Arlan—who am I kidding? Arlan himself—would want me the way he wants Lucy. But sitting next to her, listening to the sound of her breathing thicken as Arlan drives through the night, I can't get it back—the affection and awe I felt just a few months ago.

For the first time all summer, I seriously consider leaving Bellingham. I threatened to go once, but she and I both knew I was only bluffing. I sit staring at the low, yellow moon glimmering through the branches of the elm outside, and a trace of life beyond the Land of Skin floats within my peripheral vision. I lie down and gaze at the ceiling, preparing for the hours of insomnia that stretch out before me, wondering why loving Lucinda ever seemed like a good idea.

★ ★ ★

The days that follow are torturous. We haven't heard or seen from Arlan for over a week. Lucy is alternately sullen, furious and remorseful, with mood cycles that spin quickly, often within minutes. Grady is so anxious, he's taken to wandering around town until three or four in the morning, searching for Arlan in every bar, motel, pancake house and all-night diner, returning more defeated and overwrought each time.

At twilight, I sit out on the porch, watching the bats hunting as the sky peaks in an unbearable brightness of blue. A huge, crushing loneliness seizes me, making it difficult to move. It's worse in the middle of the night, when I can't sleep and I can't fend off visions. I see Arlan in some sleazy motel room, surrounded by empty bottles of booze. The image is painfully detailed, etched into my brain with photographic clarity: the bad watercolor landscape of some distant desert hanging above the bed; his long, beautiful body, dressed in blue jeans and no shirt, lying facedown on top of a cheap, earth-toned bedspread.

No wonder I've never loved anyone except my father. His death left my heart deformed. Now, at the slightest disturbance, it becomes inflamed—tender and soft. Wanting Arlan makes it swell until it's hideous.

My mother calls again. She's completely transformed. She speaks in a light, airy tone, and I can see her clutching her cell phone in the lobby of some opulent hotel with soft Persian carpets on the floor and brass buttons springing from the employees' uniforms.

"Hi, Anna," she says brusquely. "I just wanted you to know, the conference is almost over. I was wondering if you'd like to get together?"

"What conference?"

"I've been in Seattle for a tech conference. You knew that, didn't you?" There's static on the line, and a sound of laughter in the background.

"No. I mean, I knew you were up here, but—"

"You don't think I came all this way just to check up on you?" She lets out a strained, brittle laugh, and suddenly I feel so sorry for her I can hardly stand it.

"No," I say. "Of course not."

"Well, I'd still like to get together," she says, her voice climbing higher on the last word.

"Yeah, okay. I can come down there, if you like." I close my eyes, hoping she'll settle for this. There's a slight pause.

"Okay, fine." We arrange a date, and she gives me the address of her hotel in downtown Seattle. I jot it down and try not to picture her, but I can't help myself. I see her frosted hair, perfectly coiffed and motionless, her restless hands picking at imaginary lint on her smooth, pressed slacks. "You think you can find that?" she asks doubtfully.

"Sure. I can read a map."

"I'm sorry. I didn't mean—"

"I'll be there," I say. "Don't worry."

I walk into Lucy's bedroom as the sky is fading to black. "Okay," I say. "Just tell me what happened."

"Oh God," she says. "Drama, drama."

"Come on. I'm tired of not asking, and you're obviously not going to volunteer the information."

"He found me at Danny's," she says, and I'm shocked at how easily she confesses.

"And...?"

"And yes, we were fucking. So what? You know I don't believe in monogamy." She pulls her knees close to her, rests her chin between them.

"Danny Dog? I thought you hated—"

"I do."

"So why were you—?"

"He's got good drugs." She sighs. "Don't look at me like that, okay? I refuse to feel guilty."

"Aren't you scared?"

"Of what?"

"Losing him!"

She puts a strand of her hair into her mouth and chews on it thoughtfully. "Yeah," she says. "I guess so."

"You *guess* so?"

"Look, me and Arlan have been together a long time, okay? You've been here a few months—you don't know shit about how we operate, so don't barge into my room and lecture me on—"

"I'm not lecturing you."

"You could have fooled me." She leans over and grabs a pack of cigarettes from the nightstand. As she lights one, she flops over onto her stomach and leans out the window, blowing the smoke into the cold night air. "He'll be back. He always comes back."

"You're so smug, Lucy. God. Sometimes people leave and they *don't* come back." My voice is shaking all of a sudden, and I look away.

"He's okay," Lucy says. "He's not hurt or anything. I would know if he was."

"Of course he's hurt, that's why he—"

"Don't be deliberately dense," she says, enunciating carefully. "I mean he's not dead in a ditch or anything." She lowers her voice, like she's telling me a secret. "You're getting him all mixed up with your dad. Arlan would never do that. He just needs time to cool off."

I look at her. Sometimes she's frighteningly perceptive. I wait a moment before I ask what I need to know. "You do love him, right?"

She turns to me. "If I knew how, I would."

I want to slap her. "I wish you two had never met," I say.

"What the hell does that mean?"

"He deserves someone who loves him."

She lets out a puff of smoke with a throaty, sarcastic sound. "Someone like you, huh?"

I feel myself starting to blush, but then a surge of adrenaline kicks in and I'm too mad to be ashamed. "Why not me?" She's silent a second, and for the first time since I met her, she looks authentically taken aback. "At least I care about people. At least I wouldn't put him through hell, just to show I could. Do you have any idea what he goes through with you?"

"Please! Spare me the 'poor Arlan' shit. What do you think keeps him with me? He's sexier—that's obvious. He stays with me because bitches are addictive, plain and simple. You 'care about him'—that's why he's never looked at you twice."

I know she's trying hard to hurt me, and for some reason that makes it easier not to wince. "It's so sad," I say. "You think you've got to have smoke and mirrors just to keep people interested. You're smart and funny and totally original, Lucy. You don't need all this other shit." I pull on a sweater and head for the door.

"Where are you going?" she calls, and her voice sounds like a little girl's. I know she hates to be alone, but tonight that's not my problem.

"Out," I say, and slam the door behind me.

As I walk, the wind picks up, and I'm sure I can smell the icy mountaintops of Canada. My hair tosses wildly. I think about everything Lucy said: about me mixing up Arlan and my dad. About bitches being addictive, and Arlan never even looking at me twice. More than once, I've fancied myself a threat to their perverse stranglehold of love; it's disloyal and selfish, I know, but I wanted Arlan to be seduced by my silent adoration and give up on Lucy's hot–cold roulette. But she's right. Arlan gets adoration every time he climbs on stage—hell, when he walks down the street he's practically smothered by it. Lucy's got him tangled up in a never-ending net of questions, surprises and betrayals. He'll never be bored with her, even if the excitement kills him.

One big difference between Lucy and me: she doesn't know what it's like to lose. She fends off loneliness with a constant supply of willing substitutes, but real loss—the kind where you can never get the person back—is completely foreign to her. That's what allows her to be reckless with other people's hearts. She doesn't know what it's like to have regrets.

That's part of what makes her irresistible—her magical immunity to what-if. I've got regrets that cling to me everywhere I go. At the center of my doubts is my father, the black hole of what-ifs. For fourteen years, the possibilities have festered in me like cancer. What if my father just wanted to get away from us? My mother and I were a unit when I was young—her resentful eyes and my incessant, childish needs must have blended together seamlessly. I think of that day, sitting on the couch with him, crying, while his eyes probed the window of our living room. I wanted him to hold me, but couldn't I have shut up about that? If only I hadn't cried so much. And why couldn't my mother have concentrated on loving him instead of Bender? Why couldn't she have dedicated herself to him alone? We might have kept him, then.

Or maybe we could have let him go; so many fathers leave, anyway. He could have gotten into his old Volvo and driven far away—to Mexico, maybe, or north to Canada. He would be alive now, swimming through turquoise waters, watching the whales lumber slowly through the ocean depths, or trudging through the Canadian snow to a tiny cabin with a curl of delicate smoke twisting out of the chimney, reaching skyward. It would have been hard to let him go, but at least then he'd be somewhere. I could be searching for him now, instead of reading his cryptic letters and quizzing Bender for clues about who he was.

When I reach the docks, Bender is nowhere in sight. I stand at the gate and call out his name. When nothing happens, I imagine him with startling, grim clarity in a pool of vomit, motionless in the bowels of his boat. I remember the gray of Danny's face the day we drove him to the hospital. Fear clutches at my intestines and I call his name again and again, shouting so loudly into the wind that my throat starts to hurt.

"Whoa whoa whoa!" I hear a gruff voice behind me. I spin around and Bender materializes from the darkness, carrying a six-pack of beer by the plastic rings. "Where's the fire, Medina?"

"Oh God. I thought—I don't know. Something happened to you."

"Just ran to the corner for a little Bud. I've stopped buying by the case. I miscalculated a little." He opens the gate, and we walk together to the boat. "What seems to be the problem?" He tears off a beer and hands me one, takes one for himself.

"Did you ever feel like you were losing it?"

"Daily." He cracks open his beer, takes a sip. I just stand there holding mine.

"I'm a basketcase tonight."

"Love or money?" he asks.

"What?"

"All sorrows spring from one or the other."

"Love, I guess." I feel really stupid saying it, though. Who am I kidding? What do I know about love?

"Aha. The worse kind."

"Bender, I'm totally hopeless. I can't bond with people. I've been sleeping half my life, and now that I've woken up, I'm still twelve years old. Here," I say, shoving the beer at him. "I didn't want to tell you before, but I hate Budweiser."

"No problem," he says. "One more for me."

"I always think everyone's going to shoot themselves in a hotel room—it's a phobia with me. I'm not normal. You know sometimes I could swear he killed himself to get away from us—"

"Hold on, now. Slow down. You think your dad—?"

"Yeah."

"Who's this 'us'?"

"Me and Mom."

"Anna…"

"I know, okay, so it sounds ridiculous, but think about it. His letters are all about his life not panning out. He wanted to be jamming with Dylan instead of taking us to the movies. Maybe if he'd just left us, you know, he could've been happy."

Bender shakes his head, comes and stands so close to me that I can smell the yeasty scent of his beer. "Listen to me, Medina. Your father loved you. More than anything, okay?"

"Well, of course—that's the party line—I mean what else are you going to say? 'You're right. He offed himself because of you'?"

"Hey! I don't bullshit—you know that." He furrows his brow in concentration. "I knew your dad a long time, and he was always restless. He was a little unstable. That was just his way."

"Crazy, you mean?"

"I wouldn't call it that. Some people might. I'm telling you he didn't do it because of you. All right? You were the best thing in his life." His blue eyes pin me motionless, and the wrinkles around his mouth deepen as he frowns. "If you didn't get that from his letters, then read them again." He turns away from me and heads for the cabin.

"Where are you going?"

"Hold on," he says. "I want to show you something."

When he reemerges, he's got an envelope in his hand. "What's that?" I ask.

"I didn't know if I should give you this or not. I thought it might make you too sad."

"What is it?" I can feel a strange little lump forming itself in my throat.

"I figured I'd give you the others first, see how that went."

"Is it a—" I have to will my lips to conform to the words "—suicide note?" I've spent the better part of my adolescence writing other peoples' last words. It was one of my favorite parts of the Suicide Maps—making up the excuses they would leave behind. But my father left nothing but silence.

"I don't know. It's just the last one, is all." He stands there holding it, and even in the dim light of the docks, I can see that his hand is shaking. He hands it to me. I hand it back.

"You read it," I whisper.

"You sure?" I nod.

"'Dear Einstein.'" He clears his throat. I reach into my pocket and take hold of Shiva, trying to slow the racing of my heart. Bender looks at me. "You sure you want me to read this?"

"No," I say. "I mean, yes."

He nods. "'Dear Einstein,'" he reads. "'Once again, I'm sending you my fragmentary thoughts for storage, such as they are. You remember when we tripped in Golden Gate Park? Remember how the grass smelled as sad and alive as the music of Robert Johnson? Those were the Times. We were the People. Please remember.

"'The only thing that's kept me here this long is Anna.

She's a flower, man. She's a total source of amazement, and if I think of her for more than a minute at a time, I'll lose my nerve.'" He clears his throat again.

"'I'm a cynical bastard by now, you know that, even though it's been years. For too long I've been tired and cold. I thought she was plenty reason to stay. Anna, I mean. But I'm a shell of a man. She has the eyes of a newborn still, even though she's eleven years old—can you believe it? Eleven. If I stay, she'll absorb the ashes I'm full of. I want her to taste everything, like we did. The grass of Golden Gate Park. The music. Everything this fucking frightening world has to offer.

"'Call Helen soon. I'm asking you nicely.

"'Stay real, brother. You're in me and you know it. I'm sorry.

"'Chet.'"

By now tears are streaming down my cheeks, and I keep my head down, hide my face with my hair. The wind smells of fish and chips from down the street. His voice is thick and fatherly. "It's tough, Anna. I know that. I just—" His voice cracks, and I let out a breath full of sobs. "You should never think he didn't love you. He did. He really did, I swear." I wrap my arms around his neck and hold on.

For a split second, he hesitates, but then he grips me tightly, and the warmth of his body—so human, so real—undoes me, and I cry until I can't cry anymore.

Thirteen nights after Arlan left, I dream a dream that will be burned into my brain forever. I wake from it chilled and terrified, sitting bolt upright on the couch, electric with adrenaline. Leaves slap restlessly against the windows. The old house creaks in the darkness. The microwave in the kitchen reads 3:22.

I creep into Lucy's room, careful to move in silence. I need to find something of Arlan's. I open the closet; the door creaks quietly and I hold my breath as Lucy rolls over, sighs, tucks one hand under her pillow. I find a flannel shirt crumpled up on the floor, hold it to my face and inhale the smell of him.

Lucy mumbles something and I turn, startled, but her eyes are still closed and I can tell by the gentle rise and fall of her chest that she's still sleeping. Something about the sight of her there stops me. I sit at the foot of the bed very gently, not wanting to wake her. I think of the first day I met her, how she stood there with one hand on her hip, squinting at me suspiciously. *"Who are you supposed to be?"* Her dark hair moved this way and that in the wind, restlessly.

I go back to the couch, clutching Arlan's shirt. In the morning, I will stash it in my backpack. For now, I need it near me. The dream comes back to me when I close my eyes: Arlan's limp body, lying facedown on that polyester earth-toned bedspread, the back of his head a grisly mass of fresh, glistening blood. It's Arlan and yet it's my father, too. I walk toward the bed, and everything is absolutely real: the texture of the cheap, dirty shag carpet under my bare feet, the smell of whiskey and blood in the air. I reach out one hand and touch his exploded skull, feel the wet of brain and blood on the tips of my fingers. I touch my fingers to my lips, tasting salt.

I try to think of other things. I picture Rosie in her pink fur coat. The Golden Gate Bridge with the fog rolling in along the bay. The beautiful guitar Bender and I built—the rich, streaky grain of that koa. When none of this helps, I get up, light a candle and cradle my guitar in my arms. I play a few notes, trying to remember the songs my father taught me. I find the right chords for "Folsom Prison Blues" and, strumming very softly, begin to sing under my breath: *"I hear the train a comin', it's rollin' round the bend. I ain't seen the sunshine since—"*

"Anna?" I jump. There's Lucy in the doorway, looking thin and pale as a corpse.

"Jesus, you scared me."

She comes over and sits next to me on the couch. I put the guitar down. She leans into me and sighs against my neck. "I miss him," she whispers.

"Yeah," I say. "I know."

"When's he coming back?"

"Soon," I tell her, because it seems like the right thing to say. "Soon."

I walk into the lobby of the Hilton and there's my mother, perched with her legs crossed on a dark red leather couch. I wonder if she has picked this couch over the others because it looks so good with the charcoal sharkskin suit she has on, and in particular, the burgundy blouse peeking out from beneath the blazer. I am struck once again by how impeccably stylish she is. Not only that, but she's fifty, and her calves are still as sleek as a Broadway dancer's in her sheer black stockings; her face is smooth and the skin above her eyelids doesn't sag, unlike that of most women her age. The only thing that gives away her half-century of existence is her mouth; there's an intricate system of creases that fall into place when she puckers around her Virginia Slim, and they still linger long after she's exhaled.

"Hello, dear," she says, hugging me quickly as if we got together just last week. "Good to see you. You're looking—" she scans my body with her eyes "—thin."

"Oh," I say. "Well, thanks. I guess." She tosses her nonexistent hair, which tells me she's nervous. I take pity on her and say, "That suit looks really great on you."

"This? Oh, thanks. I got it the last time I was in New York. It travels well." She looks pleased by my compliment.

We stand there a moment, not knowing what to say. Her cell phone rings from somewhere deep in her bag and she digs for a moment, retrieves it, removes her clip-on earring with efficient fingers. "This is Helen." She looks at me with that vacant, faraway stare of people on phones. "Hi, Rosie." I smile. "Yes, she just got here. She's—" she looks at her watch "—only fifteen minutes late." I roll my eyes. "Well, do you want to talk to her?" She frowns as she studies her clip-on earring, a large gold teardrop. "Okay, I'll tell her. *Ciao*." She pushes a button and stashes the phone in her bag again. "Rosie loves you," she says flatly. "Now, where should we go? Are you hungry? Do you want to shop? What do you have in mind?"

"Maybe we could just walk," I suggest.

"Walk?"

"Around the city, you know. Look around a little. Talk."

"Oh. Well. I suppose that sounds nice." She looks down at her four-inch heels. "Maybe I should change, then."

"Okay. I'll wait here."

She hesitates, tilts her head like a little bird. "No, hell. I can walk just fine in these. They're very comfortable, actually. I could probably climb Everest in them."

"You sure?"

"Of course I'm sure. Let's go." We move toward the revolving glass doors, and we each catch our own slot.

"So, what are you doing with yourself these days?" she asks as we march through the bustling financial district, surrounded by a sea of gray suits. I've borrowed an orange sweater from Lucinda, and a pair of army-green pants that fit me like pedal-pushers, so I feel a little out of place. But I don't mind, somehow. I feel strangely confident today. I've worn colors on purpose; I want my mother to know I'm no longer the queen of beige.

"I've been apprenticing."

She raises one eyebrow and says, "Apprenticing?" as if this is a term she's not familiar with.

"Yes."

"What trade are you learning—or do I dare to ask?"

"I'm building guitars."

"Is that right?" She lights a new cigarette off the one in her mouth. "Who's teaching you?"

"Come on, Mom. Didn't Rosie tell you all this?"

"No." She gives me an innocent look. "Really. She wouldn't tell me a thing."

"Elliot Bender's teaching me," I say, watching her face for a reaction. She just stares straight ahead and picks up the pace a bit.

"Is that right?" She's quite amazing in her high heels. She hikes along like she's being timed. "How nice." She stops abruptly and stares at a dress displayed in a shop window. It's worn by a silver headless mannequin with its arms out straight, like some high-tech scarecrow. "Isn't that the smartest dress you ever saw? I'll bet you a hundred dollars it's acetate. Amazing what they can do with synthetics these days." She looks at it wistfully for another second, then turns and strides forward again.

"When was the last time you talked to Bender, anyway?" I ask casually.

"Bender? Oh, I don't know. Ages, I guess."

"He says you've kept in touch."

She glances at me sideways. "Well. A note, I guess, here and there." She fumbles in her bag for her cell phone, pushes a button, studies the screen, stashes it away again. "Anyway, won't you need to get a job soon?"

"Wait a second, Mom—slow down, will you? Can we try strolling? I wasn't thinking we'd power-walk Seattle."

The corner of her mouth turns up smugly. "A little out of shape?"

"I'd just like to have a conversation. Now back up, here. So you and Bender 'exchange notes from time to time'? What does that mean?"

Her face is flustered. A thin sweat has broken out through the makeup on her forehead and cheeks. "It was all such a long time ago…." She looks away. "I don't see that it's your business, anyway."

"Maybe not. I'd just like you to level with me. If it's none of my business, just say that, don't try to change the subject." This feels very strange. I've never talked to my mother like this. Our conversations in the past were such complex rituals of avoidance, to question her openly is like willing a river to run in reverse. Her elusiveness is nothing; it's to be expected. What amazes me is that now I know how to ask.

"Okay," she says finally, taking a tissue from her bag and dabbing lightly at her skin. "So I'm telling you—I don't want to talk about it."

"Good. Fine. Maybe some other time."

We walk in silence for a minute. She's slowed down a little.

"And how do you find Bellingham?"

"I find it rainy," I say.

"Yes, well, rainy it most certainly is!" She smiles, then looks uneasy. "From what I hear, anyway." She squints at me, like she's trying to remember who I am. "You seem different, somehow. You've cut your hair, haven't you?"

"Yeah. Months ago."

"There's something…sharper about you."

Suddenly I feel strangely buoyant—victorious, though I've no idea what I've won. "I am different," I say. "Everything's different." I'm tempted to blurt out a frenetic monologue, to tell her the whole story of my summer at once. I'd like to tell her about the Fourth of July and Lucy's awful family and Arlan—how incredible he is when he touches those perfect brown fingers to the strings and pulls songs from the air. Instead, I just walk next to her, feeling all those days inside me. There'll be time to tell her, if she's ever ready to listen.

★ ★ ★

"Coffee!" Her eyes light up at the sight of Starbucks on the next corner. "Oh, let's go! I love having coffee in Seattle."

"It's Starbucks, Mom. They've got those everywhere."

"Yes, I know. But somehow it tastes better here." She practically sprints the rest of the block.

All the chairs and tables are occupied; the café is teeming with pale professionals fresh from their cubicles. They wear expensive glasses and slick, corporate haircuts. She orders a double espresso and I get a mocha.

We go out onto the sidewalk with our paper cups and sit at a table under a dark green umbrella. The weather is not exactly warm, but it's not raining, either. The steam escapes through the tiny rectangular holes in our plastic lids, and joins with the white trail snaking from my mother's cigarette. I sit there thinking about evaporation and fire, steam and smoke—how a cup of coffee can loose little particles of itself to the air. Or take a cigarette—something solid and distinct—light a match, and it drifts off into these fleeting shapes, then nothing. I think of all the smoke my summer's been filled with—the shapes it makes, graceful and seductive. Soon summer will be gone, too. Even now I can feel the edges of it growing thin, starting to dissipate.

"Do you have a boyfriend?" she asks, catching me off guard.

"No," I say. "Just friends."

"Who was the girl that answered the phone the other night?"

"Lucinda. She's one of the people I live with."

"Someone you knew in college?" She flicks her cigarette against the ashtray stiffly.

"No," I say. "I just met her a couple months ago."

"And you live with her?" she asks, her eyebrows arching in surprise.

"Yeah." I hold her skeptical gaze. "Why not?"

"Just seems kind of…impulsive."

"Didn't know I had it in me, did you?" I say, unable to keep from smirking. "What about you? Are you dating anyone?"

She snorts through her nose. "Oh, you know me. A little something here and there, but nothing to speak of." I picture her in the Fiat, driving a young Scandinavian techy to some expensive hotel in Sausalito, where she can overwhelm him in the dark and then put him on a plane and be done with the whole business by eight the next morning. She must be so lonely.

"Why did you leave like that?" she asks, and three deep lines appear between her eyebrows. "Why didn't you tell me you were going?"

"I just needed to get out." I drink my coffee and look around, feeling that weird, unexpected buoyancy again. "You had a mother once, right?" I look her in the eye. "You know what it's like."

She studies me another beat and then, shrugging lightly, as if she can't be bothered with it anymore, says, "As long as you know what you're doing." She finishes her coffee and smacks her lips. "Mmm! I tell you! Coffee in Seattle is just *better!* It really is!" She smiles at the traffic and touches her hair. "Listen," she says. "I'm leaving in a couple weeks for Amsterdam. I've got to lead a training session there for the month of September. I was thinking…why don't you come?"

"What?"

"Why don't you? You've never been to Europe. I'd be busy during the day, but you could explore. We could—" she searches my face "—get to know each other more. You know?" Her voice is very fragile.

"Mom. Wow. I don't know what to say…."

"You don't have to decide this second."

"I'd have to talk to Bender," I say. "We've sort of got a shop."

"Don't decide now," she repeats, standing up and shouldering her bag. "Just think about it. Let's mosey again, shall we? That's the thing about this town, it's too damn cold!"

I stand up and we begin to walk again. She's limping ever so slightly; I suspect she's developing a blister, but she doesn't complain.

"Are you hungry, yet? Can we get a bite soon?" she asks.

"Sure." I remember how she used to love to cook when I was little; she'd move around the kitchen, and I'd watch her long veil of golden hair swinging as she sizzled shrimp in a gigantic wok, fried tofu, sautéed vegetables. "Here," she'd say, blowing a puff of steam from a shrimp clamped between chopsticks; then she'd lean down and pop it into my mouth, her eyes lit up, waiting for praise.

"It was your aunt Rosie's idea," she says.

"What was?"

"Inviting you to Amsterdam. She's thinking of meeting us there." I picture Rosie traipsing around Amsterdam, and wonder what outlandish costumes she'd come up with for such an occasion—surely only the weirdest would do. "She thinks we ought to..." She trails off, squinting at the sky. "I don't know. She's got all sorts of ideas. She thinks I've—oh—squelched you, or something." She flicks a look at me quickly. "What do you think?"

I pause, composing my answer carefully. "I just felt like I couldn't talk about—well, most things."

"Right," she says. "Oh! Here, what do you think of this? You like sushi, don't you?"

"Sure."

"It's so healthy. And maybe they've got warm sake. I'm sure they must." We stand before the menu in the window and she scans it, lips pursed. "Warm sake is just divine on a cold day. It warms you from the inside."

"Like Dad," I say, continuing my last thought. "You wouldn't let me talk about him."

She sighs, considers me in silence, her head cocked a little to one side.

"I learned a lot this summer," I say.

"About what?" Her voice is barely above a whisper.

"Dad. You. Me." I smile. "A little about making guitars." I take a deep breath; the corner of her eye is twitching, but I press on. "You never wanted to talk about anything from the past, and I had to get away from that. I don't hold it against you, I just wish you hadn't been so severe. We were always silent about things that mattered most."

There's a long pause. I can see her struggling for what to say next, and when she speaks again her words come out all in a rush. "There wasn't any conference, Anna."

"What?"

"I lied. I came up here because I—I was crazy with worry. Okay? I missed you."

"You did?"

"Yes. Anyway, that's that." She lights a fresh cigarette and smiles breezily. I've never seen her look so beautiful. "You know, they have some really fabulous museums in Amsterdam. One of them has an exhibit of Hieronymus Bosch. You know him?" I nod. "Well, you'd be amazed if you saw his work up close. It's very different from the photographs."

"I'd like that," I say.

"So would I." Her eyes are shining. "Now let's get some dinner. I'm ravenous."

As I'm driving back to the freeway, I'm thinking so hard about Amsterdam and the way my mother and I actually laughed over sushi—real laughter, the kind from your belly, not the irritating, throaty sort—that I'm completely caught off guard by the sight of Arlan's station wagon. It's unmistakable. There's the fake wood paneling across the side and the chipping, lima-bean-green paint. There just aren't very many cars like that in Seattle. It's sitting in the parking lot of a sad little rundown L-shaped building with a neon sign rising out of its flat roof: the Shangri-La Hotel. I yank my steering wheel to the right and pull up next to his car. I get out and peer into the driver's side window, just to make sure. There's his brown suede hat and his corduroy jacket sitting in the passenger seat. I'm so shocked I don't know what to feel. I decide not to think before I act.

I walk into the pink, carpeted hush of the lobby as the first drops of rain begin to splash against the dirty windows. An impossibly thin man in a yellow cardigan sits behind the glassed-in counter and mumbles through the metal speaker.

"Can I help you?" He has some kind of accent—Indian, maybe. It gives his mumbling a musical lilt.

"I'm supposed to meet Arlan Green here," I say. "But I've forgotten his room number. Can you tell me which one he's in?"

He furrows his brow at me and consults a large, pink ledger. "No, I'm very sorry, I do not see—"

"Are you sure? Can you check again?"

He runs his finger down the page very slowly. "Ah, Green!" he says, and flashes me a delighted grin. "I'm very sorry—we do have a Mr. Green. Room twenty-two."

"Thank you."

I find his room all the way at the tip of the L-shaped building. I knock on the door for a full five minutes before he finally answers.

There he is, wearing only jeans. He's bleary-eyed and his hair hangs in damp strands about his face. He stares at me blankly for a moment, and then he covers his eyes with one hand, leaning against the doorway, and looks at me again, as if I might be a trick of the light. "Anna. Jesus. What are you doing here?" I just stand there, unsure of what to say, and he chuckles. "My God. Of all people."

"Can I come in?" I ask. "It's raining." And it really is starting now, coming down fast and hard. He hesitates, then opens the door wider; I slip past him and hover awkwardly near the bed. As he closes the door, the smell of the place hits me: smoke, dust, the greasy after-odor of fried foods. There are three empty fifths of Absolut vodka crowding each other on the small Formica table, and another one, half empty, near the bed. Two ashtrays filled with twisted butts are on the nightstand. Several empty, industrial-sized bottles of Coke keep each other company on the floor, along with some Chinese takeout cartons and a bottle of aspirin lying on its side, a wad of cotton discarded nearby. He sees me surveying the room and says a little defensively, "You want a drink? Not much selection, but you can have a martini, minus the olive and the vermouth." He goes to the half-empty bottle by the bed and hands it to me. "There you go. Martini-out-of-the-bottle. It's all the rage." I take it, but I don't drink. He sits on the bed. I take a seat on the pink chair near the table.

"Everyone's been worried," I say.

"Yeah. Well."

"Lucy misses you."

He lies back on the bed and gazes up at the ceiling. "You ever been in love, Anna?" He speaks with the queer, distant tone of someone who's been talking to himself for days.

I hesitate. "I guess."

"No," he says. "You don't guess. That's like saying 'I guess I was buried alive.' You *know*, believe me."

"Maybe it's different for everyone."

He fishes a pack of cigarettes from his pocket and puts one between his lips. "Maybe," he mumbles, and I watch the cigarette bob as he speaks. He lights a match and touches the flame to the tip, sitting up on one elbow. "Anyway, I don't recommend it. It's not good for your health."

"Have you been here all this time?" I ask.

He looks at me. "What's it like for you?" he asks, ignoring my question, slurring his words a little.

"What's what like?"

"Love."

"Um," I say. "It's…" I search the room for the right word. I spot the terrible watercolor painting on the wall and the word springs to my lips: "crushing."

"Now see, that's an interesting choice of words. 'Crushing.'"

"Why?" I ask, offended.

He chuckles. "Maybe it's not love, so much as a *crush*."

"Don't condescend," I say quietly, staring at my hands.

"Listen…" He takes a long drag and exhales a beautiful, streaming plume of smoke into the sad, dim light of the room. "I'm not trying to be an asshole. I just want you to know what it's like—what it's really like, because most people don't. Lucy's the only girl I ever loved, so it's not like I'm an expert. But with her, it's like living with a cannibal. Every day she cuts out a piece of my heart, just for fun. Then she sticks a wad of chewing gum where the hole is so the blood won't get on the carpet."

"Maybe it's not supposed to be like that."

"Maybe not." He lies on his back again. "But that's how it is."

I'd like to leap onto the bed and shake him, cry out that he's got it all wrong, that love should be soothing and gentle, like he is, something to wrap yourself in to keep warm. Instead I sit very still and say in a barely audible voice, "It could be different."

He turns to me again, and his eyes are the color of caramel in this light—I can see more yellow in them than I've ever seen before. The rain patters steadily against the roof and the windows. "Of course I've thought about it."

"Thought about what?"

"You know. You. Me. What we'd be like."

I try to sound calm. "And...?"

He reaches across to the nightstand and crushes the cigarette butt into the crowd of others; a small cloud of smoke rises around his fingers. "You're not like us. Me and Lucy. We're like family—haven't you ever noticed that our eyes are almost identical?" He stares at the ceiling for a moment, then sits up and takes a swig of vodka. "Well? Have you noticed that?"

"Not really," I lie.

"It's like somehow our lives—Lucy's and mine—they're wrapped up together, and there's no way out. We've got a mutual stranglehold on each other—if one of us lets go, the other will..." He pauses, struggling to complete the metaphor.

"But that's just it," I say. "If you both let go, you'll be better off, won't you?"

"I love her," he says flatly. Suddenly I feel very stupid. "No, don't look like that," he says. "I know it seems crazy, and you're right to talk me out of it. But I love her. I don't have any choice."

We listen to the rain and pass the bottle of vodka back and forth a couple of times. "How the hell did you find me?" he asks after a while.

"I was just driving by. I saw your car." We look at each other and laugh at the absurdity of it. "Is that bizarre or what?" I look down at my hands. "I was scared. I had a dream that you killed yourself."

"It occurred to me," he says.

"But you didn't."

"Not yet, anyway." I look at him in alarm, and he gets up from the bed, paces the room. "Don't look at me like that. It makes sense."

"What makes sense?"

"She's in my blood. I can't get rid of her." He fingers the stiff brown curtains. "Unless I get rid of my blood."

"Oh God," I say. "Don't even say that. It's so stupid."

"Never mind, then," he says. "I don't want to talk about it." He stands at the window, and we say nothing. The rain is still falling, but lightly now—just a mist, really—and the soft gray hush that comes sometimes after a hard rain is just beginning to come over us. The aqua bedspread, the floor lamp with its pool of amber, and the watercolor of an exotic beach are even more depressing now that this silence, this grace, has begun.

"Come on," I say to Arlan. "Let's go."

"Where?" he asks, taking another swig of vodka.

"I'm taking you home."

One More Dance Before the Apocalypse

The last week of August, Lucy gets an acceptance letter from UC Santa Cruz for winter quarter. I dance around her wildly as she's reading it aloud; I squeal with excitement and hug her hard. I've pictured this scene in my mind a number of times—her gushing and thanking me with moist, grateful eyes, me modestly accepting her insistence that she couldn't have done it without me. But now that the moment's arrived, she gets quiet and stone-faced. She lights a cigarette.

"What? Aren't you happy?" I ask.

She shrugs. "It's cool that they want me."

I hesitate. "I mean, you're going, right?"

"Anna. Come on. Where am I going to get the money?"

"Loans. Scholarships. Financial aid." She exhales little puffs of smoke through her nose and gives me a skeptical look. "What? We can figure it out. I'll help you."

"Yeah, well I'm not a charity case."

"Lucy." I take a breath, try to clear the hurt from my voice. "This is fantastic! Let's celebrate—"

"I'm not going!" She leaps off the bed and stalks to the closet, pulls a leather jacket on and looks at me. "Come on, let's go. The guys have a gig at Fanny's."

I just stare at her in disbelief. "I thought you wanted this."

"It doesn't matter. Arlan would never move to Santa Cruz."

"Why not? It's a great town—you guys would love it."

"We live here, Anna. He's got the band, his business, and I've got *Pulp*. There's no way. Why should I let those fuckers brainwash me? I know how to think."

"But you told me—"

"I changed my mind!" She pulls a tube of lipstick from her pocket and gazes into a mirror on the wall. I just stare, mute, as she applies a dark stain to the top lip, pauses for a drag from her cigarette, and then goes to work on the bottom one. "Don't look at me like that," she says, catching my reflection over her shoulder.

"Okay," I say. "Fine. I guess I misunderstood."

She tries to laugh, but it sounds forced. "Don't be a jerk," she says.

"Me?"

"Oh, Anna. This is just how it is. Don't make me feel like a shit, okay?" She frees a strand of hair from her eyelashes and turns to me. "I'm not like you," she says.

"What does that have to do with anything?"

"It has everything to do with everything, and you know it." For a few seconds, neither of us says anything, we just stare at one another. She looks away first, pockets her Camels and says, brusquely, "You coming, or what?"

"Maybe later."

She walks to the window and stabs her cigarette out in the coffee cup on the sill. "Okay. Suit yourself." She touches my arm for a moment, but as soon as I turn toward her, she's already walking away, moving quickly out the door, calling over her shoulder, "Later."

I sit near the window, watching the Land of Skin. The strange fever of late August has set in; there's nervous friction in the air, mixed with exhaustion. Goat Kid Hovel is pulsating with the sounds of a desperately loud live band; some guys from the halfway house are out on the porch with a couple of anorexic-looking women draped across their laps. I sit there thinking of my father—how much he wanted to be a star. When he didn't get that gig opening for Dylan, maybe he just started to fold in on himself, like a piece of fruit rotting at its core.

I think of Lucy, and I feel sad for her. She's rotting, too, in a painfully slow flirtation with decay. I know she'd hate my pity more than anything, but I can't deny that's what I feel. I can picture her here forever, smoking the same cigarettes, staring out the same windows with her dark, restless eyes. Of course, she's got Arlan, but what good does he do her, when she claims he's like a pair of socks—all comfort, no thrills? Maybe one day Arlan will leave, or she'll leave, or they'll both just explode in a huge, violent mess of drunken resentment. But if they survive each other's abandonment, won't they go on to make the same mistakes all over again? Isn't that how we do things, being human?

I light a couple of candles left over from the night Grady and I tried to have sex. I take my guitar from its case and let my fingers find their way around the frets. I've never known an instrument the way I know this one. After years of living without the gentle pressure of a guitar resting on my thigh, now I have this—the most intimate fit I could imagine, with curves I created and inlay I set with my own hands. I remember how Bender stressed the necessity of a light top, braced strategically from the inside for strength. I can feel it vibrating lightly against the inside of my arm—strong but resonant.

Though the chords I remember are limited, I manage to string enough together to form a cohesive melody. I play the tune again and again, until my fingertips burn against the strings. After a while I start coming up with words, and I'm surprised at the clear simplicity of my voice. The last time I remember singing I had a pronounced lisp, which always made the adults smile. Once my father recorded me, and I was shocked at how childish I sounded; I guess I always assumed I'd sound like him.

I lose myself for hours, strumming and singing quietly until the candles I've lit are molten pools floating stubby black wicks. I light some more and keep playing, letting my voice get louder in the big, yawning silence of the house. I sing about my father, and love, and ashes. I sing about Arlan and rain and Lucy's dark, unnerving eyes. They're not really songs, I guess; they're more like fragments from an anthropologist's notebook, knit together loosely by the same three or four chords.

Finally, around two in the morning, I sit back and gaze out at the street. The band across the way has long since fallen silent, and the couples at the halfway house have abandoned their porch. There are three Goat Kids sitting on the lawn, drinking from cans and smoking. Their faces are angled upward; occasionally I can see their eyes, lit by the glowing embers of their cigarettes. It takes me a couple of seconds to realize it's me they're looking at.

When I walk down to the marina the next morning there's the faintest hint of wood smoke in the air, and it feels like fall is only days away. Bender and I agreed to take a little break after we finished the guitar. I haven't seen him since then. I find myself craving the sight of his wild hair, and missing his gruff commands. To my surprise, he's sitting on deck with a sketchbook in his lap, completely engrossed. It looks like he's cleaned the boat up a bit. The usual pile of Budweiser cans at the bow has disappeared, and though it's hardly the model of sanitary living, there is a general aura of tidiness I never thought I'd see.

"Hey!" I call.

He looks up, startled. When he sees me a wonderful grin spreads across his face and he gets up, comes over to open the gate. "Well, well, well," he says. "If it isn't the devil herself."

"What you working on?"

"Sketches," he says.

"Yeah. I can see that much."

"I'm thinking about building a twelve-string," he says. "Something I can fool around with, you know. Keep the boredom at bay."

"That's great!" I nod at him enthusiastically, getting nervous. "So you're going to keep the shop?"

"I think so," he says. "It's cheap. I didn't know if you were—"

"Yeah," I say. "I guess we left it up in the air...."

"But maybe you have other plans?"

"Well." I lick my lips. "Something has come up. I mean, I wanted to talk to you before I—"

"Oh." He puts the sketchbook down. "You heading out?"

"It would only be for a month...."

He coughs a loud, rattling cough. "Sure," he says, sitting on the ice chest and looking away. "Whatever you want to do—it's no big deal."

"No, it's my mom," I say.

"She okay?"

"Yeah. Well. She's going to Amsterdam for work. She

wants me—me and Rosie—to go." I find the old foldout chair and take a seat. "Only for a month."

Bender nods, considering this. He stands up and starts to pace. "Hell of an opportunity," he says. "You ever been to Europe?" I shake my head. "You can't stick around here forever. I guess you've got to go."

"But it's with my *mother.*"

"So?"

"She can be so..." I search for the right word. "Stiff."

"Come on," he says. "Helen?"

"She's not like you. She's not fun."

"Oh, give her a chance. She might *get* fun, in Amsterdam." He chuckles, but it doesn't sound natural. Then there's an awkward pause, and he walks over to the stern, grabs a piece of rope coiled into a neat little circle, and sits back on the ice chest, busying his hands with a series of knots. "I wish you could see what your mom was like, thirty years ago."

I look at him. "Did you know she was up here?"

"No, I didn't."

"I guess I should have mentioned it. You'd probably like to see her, huh?"

He scratches his neck and looks away. "Oh, I don't know. We don't have much to talk about, these days."

"I asked her about you—she was pretty cagey. She didn't want to admit you'd been in touch."

"Well, we haven't been, for a year or two." He unties the knot and starts on a new one, his fingers moving deftly. "We had tragedy in common, you know. That can be pretty strong stuff. But after a while, even that loses its glue." He looks up at me; his face is tired as usual, but today there's a quiet calm there too. "You'll have a blast in Europe. It's the perfect time for you to see the world."

"Like I said, it won't be for that long."

"Don't worry. You'll meet some bohemian hunk and wander off into the sunset—I know Amsterdam, and it's no place for a tight schedule." He examines the rope in his hands with acute interest. "Your dad would really dig it—you going there, like he did. Oh, to be young…" he says.

"It's overrated."

"Yeah," he laughs. "I guess that's right. But wait till you get to old age."

"So you're going to keep building guitars, huh?" I ask.

"Maybe."

"I mean—you're working on a sketch, so I figured…"

"Sure. Why not? I forgot how much I liked getting up in the morning." He pulls something from the ice chest, and I'm shocked to see a can of tomato juice in his hand. "What?" he says, peeling back the tab and taking a big swig. "You want some?"

"No thanks." I smile at him. "Looks like you're wearing one of those shirts we got."

He glances down. "Sure am. How does it look?"

"Great," I say. "Except it's— Come here." He shuffles a couple of steps closer, looking self-conscious. "Come *here*," I repeat. "You've got a price tag, or something—" He bends down toward me and I peel the label "X-X-L" off his shoulder. "There," I say, rolling it up and putting it in my pocket. "Much better."

He hikes one of his pant legs up a few inches. "Got the new socks on too."

"Oooh! Those look *really* good."

"Yeah," he says. "They do, don't they?"

We sit in silence together for a few minutes. Stumpy is out on the docks, whistling the theme to *Mission Impossible* as he scrapes around in a toolbox.

"So, Medina?" Bender says. "You still got those letters?"

"Of course. You want them back?"

"No, no." He scratches his head. "Did you read them all?"

"Yeah." I look southeast at the land rising up and out of the bay—the houses tucked into the hills, their windows and roofs glittering in the sun. The scent of the mill is strong today; it's dirty and smoky but somehow it smells good to me.

"I could give you that last one," he says. "I still have it, you know."

"You keep it," I tell him.

He just nods.

"He was really afraid," I say.

"Same as everyone, I guess."

"I don't know. He seemed to think you had it figured out."

"Well," Bender sighs. "He got that wrong."

"It's not like reading them explained everything," I say. "I mean, I've still got plenty of questions."

"Like what?"

"Like why he did it."

He sits there, nodding at me, and closes one eye against the sun. "I wish I knew. Or maybe I don't." He leans forward, resting his elbows on his knees. He picks at his fingernails and shakes his head. "All I know is, the living can't dwell on the dead all the time. It fucks everything up."

"Yeah," I say. "I think you're right about that."

Stumpy takes a hammer from his toolbox and starts pounding nails into a piece of trim on his boat. The sound reverberates across the water and makes conversation nearly impossible for a good three minutes. When he stops, the silence that falls over us is as soft and light as mist.

Bender gets up, shoves his hands into his pockets. "You go to Amsterdam, Medina. Hang out with Rosie. Get your mom to loosen up a little."

"Oh man. You don't know what you're asking!" I laugh.

"You can handle it." He comes closer and swats me on the back. "If you can get me out of bed, you can do anything."

★ ★ ★

After I leave Bender, I walk around town for a while. I follow the streets named after trees until I reach those named after states. I wander past quiet cul-de-sacs lined with faded pastel houses. I pass a garage adorned with a worn basketball hoop, eaten by weather and years. A small boy appears from the side of the house, dribbling a basketball and humming to himself. I come to a tire shop. Its windows are plastered with lurid pink letters and frantic punctuation: DON'T MISS OUR END OF THE SUMMER SALE!!! I walk past a little blue-and-white fish and chips place, with a striped awning out front and huge, fly-infested Dumpsters to one side.

I think about Amsterdam, and the stories people tell of cafés selling chocolate cake baked with hashish, or the red light district where women line up in the windows, combing their hair and flicking their tongues for the people passing by. I figure I won't need binoculars there; I can watch from the streets, if I feel like it. I wonder if it's possible for my mother and me to laugh there like we did over sushi. I don't want to be overly optimistic, but then, this summer was a season of people and smells, colors and tastes that never seemed possible when I was huddled naked in my beige apartment clinging to my binoculars. Maybe Amsterdam will be riddled with impossibilities too.

I loop back toward downtown and make my way past bars and cafés and funky old thrift shops piled high with junk. I pass the Ranch Room, and I remember how we went there when Grady first returned from Argentina—I think of the moose head and the jukebox, the cheap drinks and Arlan's eyes. I walk on, and as I near the corner of Walnut and Garden, my legs feel strong and my lungs seem to take in more air than I'm used to. I look up at the windows of Smoke Palace. There's someone new moving into an apartment downstairs. I can see her standing amidst boxes, her hair tied up in a yellow bandanna.

I realize with a little tremor of surprise that I'm almost done with this place—this corner with its natives and their gleaming white skin. Lucy and her toxic affection, Arlan and his scent of paint, sweat, smoke. I think of how different I was the day I showed up here. When I first got my room at Gottlieb's, there was nothing I liked better than to disappear completely, melting into the shadows. My life was all about windows. I wonder now how I could have settled for so little. Windows are cold and fragile, silent. It's one thing to cultivate the anthropologist's eye for detail, but making myself invisible was one step from death. I don't ever want to live like a ghost again.

Across the street, Raggedy Ann is out in the yard, standing barefoot in the tall grass. She is dancing—at least, I think she's dancing. She's got a boom box balanced on her shoulder; it's pounding out a frenetic bass beat as she thrusts her hips wildly this way and that. The wind is picking up, and it spreads her red hair about in a wild, stormy halo. She keeps flinging her body around the yard, letting the wind make a tent of her trench coat.

That night, we go to The Skins' gig at a new bar downtown. Actually, it's an old bar with a new name; it used to be the Three B, now it's called the Double Wide. This is supposed to be their grand opening, but it looks pretty much the same inside: pool tables at the front, stage at the back, booths along the walls, a couple of filthy bathrooms by the rear exit filled with inane graffiti. I tell myself not to drink too much, since I know I'm liable to get weepy when I bring up Amsterdam with Lucy. I end up downing a couple of gin and tonics within the first hour, though, out of nervousness and a sort of celebratory sadness that alcohol enhances so effortlessly.

I sit across from Lucy in a corner booth, watching her smoke. I study her eyelashes and her lips, try to memorize the crafty expression she's wearing now; she's assessing the night, toying with her options, and it shows in the set of her mouth, the barely veiled calculations in her eyes. Not for the first time this summer, I wonder what it's like to be Lucy. I consider all the hidden corridors I never did shed light on—what her childhood was really like, who taught her that sex is hostile, why she's willing to spend her time in these little dives when there are thousands of other places she could thrive in. There's so much I still don't know.

I watch her stirring her drink with the miniature straw, flicking the red ember of her cigarette into the ashtray. She is a mess of contradictions; it's part of what makes her so electric. She's fearless and yet she's terrified of clinics, boredom, being alone. She's selfish when it comes to her own survival, but she's generous with her laughter and her philosophy; she'll always buy the next round.

We can never really know what people contain. Their hearts are like sealed boxes. We shake them, trying to gauge by the rattling sounds they make what secret treasures or broken pieces might be in there, but guessing is as far as we ever get. We have to live with the uneasiness of our ignorance, knowing only that we're vast and combustible, shifting, mostly hidden, probably fucked up, but alive and mysterious while we last.

"So, Lucy," I say, as we're nursing our third round. "I'm thinking about taking off pretty soon."

"You're not staying for the second set?"

"No, I mean—I'm going to leave town. Next week, actually. I'm going to Amsterdam." Her eyes get wide. "I know—it came up kind of suddenly. My mom's going and she wants me to go, too."

"Oh."

"Well, don't look like that," I say. "It's only for a month."

She stares into her drink. "And then what?"

"And then…I don't know. I guess I'll just wait and see."

She nods. "You're never coming back," she says simply.

"No, I will. I'll visit, at least." But it sounds a little hollow even to me.

"You're mad because I'm not going to school, aren't you." I start to protest, but she holds her hand up. "No, you are. You're pissed. You think I'm stupid and I'll never amount to anything."

"Lucy! It's nothing like that."

She downs half her drink and slumps back in the booth, looking very small and deflated. "Yeah, right," she says. For a moment I see her at forty, sitting in a dark, cheaply furnished room, the shades drawn tight against sunlight. In her hands she cradles a highball glass as if it might explode.

The Skins start in on a slow, mournful ballad—a love song about Rosemary, one of Arlan's countless fictional women. "Lucinda, listen. You're not stupid, okay? It doesn't matter if you go to school or not, you're still brilliant. This summer was—" I stumble, wanting so much to find the right words "—so incredibly important to me. Okay? You know that, don't you?"

"Oh God," she says. "I hate it when you get cheesy."

"I—I just want you to know, you know—?" I stammer, tears stinging my eyes. "Come on—come dance with me."

"To this? No way."

"Please? Suppose the apocalypse comes and we're brutally killed—you want to spend your last minutes slumped in a stupid booth at the Double Wide?"

"No, but I don't want to spend it making a fool of myself, either."

"Come on!" I cry, jumping up and grabbing her hand. "Just one song." I drag her forward until we're right in front of the stage and we wrap our arms around each other like shy fifth graders at a school dance. I can tell she's giggling because her chin is bobbing up and down as it rests on my shoulder. We move in slow, deliberate circles, like two moons in orbit; we're the only ones on the dance floor, and I can see people on the fringes laughing behind their fingers, but we just keep spinning, letting Arlan's music wind us round and round, and I think to myself, if the apocalypse comes, I'm ready.

In Amsterdam, I've discovered an amazing instrument: the harp guitar. The minute I saw it I knew it would suit me perfectly; it's curvaceous and eccentric, sensual and freakish. It took me over a year to make one of my own, but when I finally finished, it was worth it. It looks like a regular acoustic guitar, except on one side this big, sweeping arm reaches up and curves back, ending in a strange mushroom shape. It's got twelve strings, and the sound it makes is so spectacular, like the score to some wild lucid dream. I could never go back to a regular acoustic; I've finally found something that fits me in every way.

I told Mom during her last visit that it's DNA in action—a little bit of her, a little bit of Dad. She didn't say much, but I could tell she was thinking about that. I joked that if I could only play the sax and Rosie's old drum kit at the same time, I'd be channeling the whole family tree. She laughed uneasily.

She's still not exactly free and easy when it comes to the topic of my father, but I will say we've inched our way carefully in that direction. Every time she visits, things get a little bit easier. At least now her mouth doesn't clamp tight and form all those furious wrinkles when I mention him; she'll even tell me stories sometimes, when she's had a bit of wine. Funny how you get what you need as soon as you don't really need it anymore. Of course my father still fascinates me, and I've spent long hours with Rosie soaking up elaborate tales about their wild years when music was everything. As my own musical identity struggles on wobbly knees to stand upright and move about, I love to hear about his past as an artist. But he's no longer my obsession. I've got other things to think about, like harp guitars, and turning my Suicide Maps into a medley of ballads. I figure I spent all those years dreaming up people's deaths; I might as well turn them into something I can use. I'm thinking about calling it "Another Garden of Earthly Delights."

I've been in Amsterdam two years now. Almost immediately I started working nights at a bar in the red light district, where the tips are really good and the education is priceless. Nothing can tear me away from the visual orgy of street life here—I can lose myself, just watching, for hours. These days I talk to the people that interest me, if I feel like it—I don't just imagine them. I figure a good anthropologist has to get right in there and ask questions—you can't live on speculation alone. That's how I met Peter. He was playing slide guitar on the corner outside a bakery when I noticed his moody eyes, and his skin, which was several shades darker than that of the pale, wintry crowd around him. I just walked up to him at the end of a song, threw a couple of coins in his guitar case and said, "You remind me of someone. Can I buy you a cup of coffee?"

Of course, I still think about Arlan. And Lucy—how could I not? They were the beginning of all this, the alchemical elements that began a shift in my chemistry so dramatic, I'm hardly recognizable anymore. I don't know if I'll contact them when I go back to the States. Occasionally I fantasize about showing up on the doorstep of Smoke Palace, savoring that rare moment of surprise, a look Lucy's face seldom wears. But then what? My daydream never takes me past that point, and when I force myself to speculate, I have to admit it would end up just being awkward. Who knows? They might not even be there anymore, though I suspect they probably are. We had our summer; it was crazy, and hard, and just what I needed. I was ripe for their brand of moodiness, for Bellingham's charms and disasters. That's good enough for me.

I won't be caught dead in beige anymore. I shop in secondhand stores and flea markets where my eye is always drawn to explosive colors—indigo stripes, magenta silk, even a shocking orange now and then. Rosie's beside herself; she sends me leopard-print skirts and bloodred sweaters, glittery sunglasses and canary-yellow go-go boots. I wear most of what she sends me; some of the really out-there stuff I give to the prostitutes that hang out at work. I think I slept through most of my adolescence, and now, at twenty-eight, I'm still making up for all those dull, numb years with all the sensory stimulation I can get.

I've discovered that I like to be watched. I started playing a few gigs with Peter—just at small coffee shops and local pubs, no big deal—but I'm gradually learning to crave the sweet high of stage fright and the even sweeter narcotic of getting over it. Rosie's crazy outfits come in handy on those nights; Peter says I'm getting to be a full-blown exhibitionist. I guess we've all got a little rock star in us, aching for a debut. I'm no exception. When my harp guitar is in my arms and I'm finding all the right notes, letting my voice reach into the air like some strange, prehistoric bird taking flight, I feel something extraordinary—sexual, almost—the pleasure of being absorbed by strangers. I can see why my father wanted it so badly, why he would give anything for the baptism of a screaming crowd's applause. I don't need to play Carnegie Hall with Dylan, though. A handful of stoned admirers is plenty luxurious, at this point.

I just got a letter from Bender last week. We share a spotty correspondence—irregular, but nourishing. He's building guitars with gusto these days. He even teaches classes a couple of nights a week at Whatcom Community College. He's not so sure about this harp guitar kick I'm on. He insists it's just a stage, and I'll come back to the good old classic shape before long: "We all have our weird fascinations." His letter is written on a torn-up paper bag, and there are smudges of something—peanut butter, maybe—here and there. "Chet used to mess around with mandolins, when he got bored. Hell, for a couple years I did nothing but sitars. Those head-trips are exotic, for a while—they teach you a lot—but you'll get tired of them. Everyone comes home, eventually."

He's got it half right. It's true that we circle back to what we're made of—isn't that what home is? The place that shares your most intimate ingredients? But he doesn't understand that the harp guitar is more me than anything I've ever known; it's the freakish hybrid I've always been, but never understood.

Tonight it's raining in Amsterdam. I take the garbage out, and then I find myself standing on the sidewalk, closing my eyes, letting the drops cover my face and hair. Peter's leaning out the window, bare-chested and laughing. "Anna!" he yells in his thick Australian accent. "Come inside! You're crazy!" But it's a good night, one of those smooth August evenings, and the rain is a sweet surprise after a long, hot day. The pavement is turning fragrant as it gets wet, and I just want to smell it for a while. A window is open across the street, and there's a hand reaching out of it, holding a cigarette, though the face is lost in shadows. I think of that summer, filled with smoke, gin and tonics, that aromatic rosewood sawdust. It seems like a long time ago, now, but when I smell the rain, it all comes rushing back.

On sale in September

Mean Season

by Heather Cochran

What would you do if you had a Hollywood star living under your roof?

The summer she was twenty-five was anything but normal for Leanne Gitlin. She finds herself playing hostess to Hollywood's next leading man, Joshua Reed, who has to serve out his drunk-driving conviction sentence under house arrest, in *her* home. Yes, the summer is anything but normal, and one the small town of Pinecob, West Virginia, won't soon forget.

Available wherever trade paperbacks are sold.

www.RedDressInk.com

RDI0904TR3

Don't miss the book *People* magazine picked as one of Spring's Best Chick Lit.

Starting from Square Two

by Caren Lissner

With the death of her husband two years earlier, twenty-nine-year-old Gert Healy is forced to face the dating world…again.

It's back to square one on everything. Well, actually, she's done it all before. Square two, then.

"Lissner's sturdy prose and sympathetic detailed evocation of young widowhood makes this a solid entry in the genre."
—*Publishers Weekly* on *Starting from Square Two*

www.RedDressInk.com

RDI03043TRR